FRANKENSTEIN

broadview editions
series editor: L.W. Conolly

Mary Wollstonecraft Shelley
By R. Rothwell, 1841

(Photo courtesy of the National Portrait Gallery)

FRANKENSTEIN;
OR, THE MODERN PROMETHEUS

Mary Wollstonecraft Shelley
the original 1818 text

third edition

edited by D.L. Macdonald and Kathleen Scherf

broadview editions

Library and Archives Canada Cataloguing in Publication

Shelley, Mary Wollstonecraft, 1797-1851
  Frankenstein, or, The modern Prometheus / Mary Wollstonecraft Shelley ; edited by D.L. Macdonald and Kathleen Scherf.—3rd ed.

(Broadview editions)
"The original 1818 text".
Includes bibliographical references.
ISBN 978-1-55481-103-8

  I. Scherf, Kathleen, 1960- II. Macdonald, D. L. (David Lorne), 1955-2010
III. Title. IV. Series: Broadview editions

PR5397.F7 2012   823'.7   C2012-903323-5

Broadview Editions
The Broadview Editions series represents the ever-changing canon of literature in English by bringing together texts long regarded as classics with valuable lesser-known works.

Broadview Press is an independent, international publishing house, incorporated in 1985.

We welcome comments and suggestions regarding any aspect of our publications— please feel free to contact us at the addresses below or at broadview@broadviewpress.com.

North America
Post Office Box 1243, Peterborough, Ontario, Canada K9J 7H5
2215 Kenmore Avenue, Buffalo, NY, USA 14207
Tel: (705) 743-8990; Fax: (705) 743-8353
email: customerservice@broadviewpress.com

UK, Europe, Central Asia, Middle East, Africa, India, and Southeast Asia
Eurospan Group, 3 Henrietta St., London WC2E 8LU, United Kingdom
Tel: 44 (0) 1767 604972; Fax: 44 (0) 1767 601640
email: eurospan@turpin-distribution.com

Australia and New Zealand
NewSouth Books
c/o TL Distribution, 15-23 Helles Ave., Moorebank, NSW, Australia 2170
Tel: (02) 8778 9999; Fax: (02) 8778 9944
email: orders@tldistribution.com.au

www.broadviewpress.com

Broadview Press acknowledges the financial support of the Government of Canada through the Canada Book Fund for our publishing activities.

This book is printed on paper containing 100% post-consumer fibre.

Typesetting and assembly: True to Type Inc., Claremont, Canada.

PRINTED IN CANADA

In Memoriam

IAN FAIRCLOUGH

(1951-1995)

and

DAVID LORNE MACDONALD

(1955-2010)

Contents

Preface

The hunt for sources for *Frankenstein*, as Maurice Hindle has remarked, has become something of a sport (xxxv). One might add that the hunters have bagged some big game. An edition like this one, which tries to give a sense of the whole intertextual network within which Mary Shelley's novel was written and received, must be rigorously selective. In choosing excerpts for our Appendices, therefore, we confined ourselves to those authors who demonstrably shaped Shelley's thinking on politics (Godwin and Wollstonecraft) and science (Darwin and Davy) and to those whom her monster mentions as having shaped his own thinking (Volney, Goethe, Plutarch, and Milton). As well, in order to provide a comprehensive picture of the atmosphere that inspired *Frankenstein* we have included two other ghost stories written at the Villa Diodati in the summer of 1816: Lord Byron's "A Fragment," and John Polidori's adaptation of the fragment, which he called "The Vampyre." Since he starts out as a sort of noble savage, it is interesting, Anne McWhir argues, that Shelley does *not* allow him to read Rousseau (75), but such interests cannot be pursued within the limits of this edition.

Readers may be surprised not to find Shelley's husband more extensively represented in our Appendices. There are two reasons for this omission. First, *Frankenstein* has been extensively studied as a response to the character and works of Percy Shelley, notably in books by Christopher Small and William Veeder. Second, Percy's work does not lend itself well to excerption. Shelley's novel certainly responds to his *Alastor* (1815), but it responds to it as a whole, and we can only urge our readers to read the whole, which is readily available. (Moreover, Percy was an enthusiastic disciple of Godwin and Wollstonecraft, so that much of what *Frankenstein* responds to in him came from them in the first place.)

Similar principles guided our treatment of the authors we were able to include. A great deal has been said about Shelley's use of Milton but very little about her use of Plutarch; accordingly, we have been more generous in our excerpts from the latter. Our notes, of course, identify all Shelley's overt allusions to other authors, whether or not they are represented in our Appendices.

Roberta Jackson was of great help at every stage in the preparation of the text and of Appendix H, from the initial collation to the final proofreading. We are also grateful for the generous assistance of Bill Blackburn, Roswitha Burwick, Gordon Fulton, Bruce Harper, Stephanie Kepros, David Ketterer, Jack Kolb, Anne McWhir, David Oakleaf, Charles E. Robinson, Vivienne Rundle, Lisa Storozynsky, and Jānis Svilpis.

We are grateful to Doubleday and Company, for permission to quote from *The Complete Poetry of John Milton*, ed. John T. Shawcross (rev. ed. 1971); to Ohio University Press, for permission to quote from *Seven Gothic Dramas*, ed. Jeffrey N. Cox (1992); and to Oxford University Press, for permission to quote from the 1831 version of *Frankenstein; or, The Modern Prometheus*, by Mary Wollstonecraft Shelley, ed. M.K. Joseph (1980).

★ ★ ★

Note to the Second Edition: For this edition, we have expanded our annotations to show how Shelley responded to her parents' fiction as well as to their political writings, and to outline the chronology of her novel. We have added appendices including lessons by Wollstonecraft, which may have suggested the monster's education (C.5), and P.B. Shelley's review (D.4). The work of Nora Crook, David Ketterer, E.B. Murray, and Charles E. Robinson has enabled us to improve our account of the evolution of the novel, both in the Introduction and in Appendix H. In Appendix H, we have indicated which revisions were made by Shelley in the copy of the novel that she gave to her friend Mrs. Thomas in 1823, which were made (probably by Godwin) in the second edition (1823), and which were made by Shelley in the third edition (1831). We are grateful to the Pierpont Morgan Library, New York, for permission to quote manuscript material from the Thomas copy of *Frankenstein* (PML 16799).

★ ★ ★

Note to the Third Edition: It has been almost two decades since the publication of the first edition of Broadview's *Frankenstein: The Original 1818 Text* in 1994. A second edition was published in 1999; my co-editor and friend for thirty years, Dr. D. Lorne Macdonald, passed away before he could contribute to this third edition. Our colleagues at Broadview Press and I have kept his memory foremost as we have prepared revisions for this new edition.

The changes for the third edition are relatively modest. Perhaps most important among them is the addition of appendices comprising other narratives arising out of the "ghost story project" that was part of the genesis of *Frankenstein*. There is also a substantial addition to the Introduction, providing more detail on the sometime controversy over the degree of Percy Shelley's involvement in the creation of the work.

Introduction

Frankenstein began, as Mary Shelley recalled, with a waking nightmare in the small hours of 16 June 1816:

> I saw the hideous phantasm of a man stretched out, and then, on the working of some powerful engine, show signs of life, and stir with an uneasy, half vital motion.... His success would terrify the artist; he would rush away from his odious handywork, horror-stricken ... and he might sleep in the belief that the silence of the grave would quench for ever the transient existence of the hideous corpse which he had looked upon as the cradle of life. He sleeps; but he is awakened; he opens his eyes; behold the horrid thing stands at his bedside, opening his curtains, and looking on him with yellow, watery, but speculative eyes.
>
> I opened mine in terror. (351)

Behind this dream of the dead brought to life, Ellen Moers has suggested, lay the memory of another dream. On 6 March 1815, the seventeen-year-old Mary Godwin lost her first child, a daughter, who like Frankenstein's creature had no name: she had not lived long enough to be given one. On 19 March, the bereaved mother wrote in her journal: "Dream that my little baby came to life again—that it had only been cold & that we rubbed it by the fire & it lived—I ... awake & find no baby—I think about the little thing all day—not in good spirits" (1: 70). Behind the nightmare of the disastrous birth of Frankenstein's monster there may also have lain the thought of Mary Godwin's own birth, and her mother's death, eleven days of agony later (Moers 84-85). *Frankenstein* is a book whose roots go deep into the psyche.

They also go deep into the culture. If readers have always got a lot out of *Frankenstein*, it is because Mary Shelley put a lot into it. Chris Baldick has suggested that she made a living book out of pieces of other books, just as her hero made a living body out of pieces of other bodies (30); and while she is actually careful not to specify precisely what Victor made his monster out of, the analogy still seems apt. Her own account of the book corroborates it: "Invention, it must be humbly admitted, does not consist in creating out of void, but out of chaos; the materials must, in the first place, be afforded: it can give form to dark, shapeless substances, but cannot bring into being the substance itself" (350). The "dark, shapeless substances" that she shaped into *Frankenstein* were drawn partly from her personal memories, and partly from her knowledge of the texts that articulated her culture's deepest and most central concerns. Together, they enabled her to create a modern myth.

The Education of Mary Shelley:
Godwin and Wollstonecraft

Perhaps the most important materials Shelley had to hand were personal and political at once. The first thing that she says about herself in her Introduction to the 1831 edition of the book is that she is "the daughter of two persons of distinguished literary celebrity," William Godwin and Mary Wollstonecraft (347). *Frankenstein* is dedicated to her father, the author of *Political Justice* (1793; 3rd ed. 1798) and *Caleb Williams* (1794). Even without this clue, the reviewers would probably have identified the anonymous author as one of his disciples. In the years preceding the publication of her novel, perhaps as a way of keeping in touch with the father who had virtually disowned her for eloping with Percy Bysshe Shelley, she had read not only the two works mentioned in her dedication, but also *The Enquirer* (1797), *St. Leon* (1799), *Life of Geoffrey Chaucer* (1803), *Fleetwood* (1805), *Essay on Sepulchres* (1809), *The Lives of Edward and John Philips, Nephews and Pupils of Milton* (1815), and *Mandeville* (1817), as well as a number of shorter works (*Journals* 2: 649-50). Several of them left their mark on *Frankenstein*. The alchemist-hero of *St. Leon*, for example, anticipates Victor Frankenstein's interest in Cornelius Agrippa, Albertus Magnus, and Paracelsus, and his discovery of the principle of life. The influence of *Caleb Williams* is pervasive, both in Caleb's fatal curiosity, which anticipates Victor's, and in the mutual persecution of Caleb and his patron Falkland, which anticipates the relations between Victor and his monster.

Of all her father's works, however, Mary Shelley engaged most deeply and in most detail with his *Enquiry Concerning Political Justice and Its Influence on Morals and Happiness*. This was the most famous radical text of its time. As the radical William Hazlitt would recall in 1825,

No work in our time gave such a blow to the philosophical mind of the country as the celebrated *Enquiry Concerning Political Justice*. Tom Paine was considered for the time as a Tom Fool to him; Paley an old woman; Edmund Burke a flashy sophist. Truth, moral truth, it was supposed, had here taken up its abode; and these were the oracles of thought. "Throw aside your books of chemistry," said Wordsworth to a young man, a student in the Temple, "and read Godwin on Necessity." (24)

Frankenstein engages with *Political Justice* frequently enough to place it firmly within the radical tradition. On many points (see the notes), this engagement can be described simply as influence. Shelley's deepest and most interesting engagements with *Political Justice*, however, are more like examples of critique than of influence. Like many of her contemporaries, Shelley felt that the relentless rationalism that initially made her father's book so exciting ultimately made it forbidding. Hazlitt seems almost to have had the Arctic frame of her novel in mind when he summed up the achievement of *Political Justice*:

Captain Parry would be thought to have rendered a service to navigation and his country, no less by proving that there is no North-West Passage, than if he had ascertained that there is one: so Mr. Godwin has rendered an essential service to moral science, by attempting (in vain) to pass the Arctic Circle and Frozen Regions, where the understanding is no longer warmed by the affections, nor fanned by the breeze of fancy! (31-32)

Shelley's critique tends to focus on those points in Godwin's arguments where the abstract claims of political justice impinge on the personal—or, in Godwin's own terms, where it influences morals and happiness. The scientific ambitions with which Victor is inspired by M. Waldman, and the way in which they alienate him from his family (76, 82), comment on Godwin's sanguine expectations for technological progress—which, he believes, will make it less and less necessary for human beings to co-operate with each other (see Appendix A.1.a). Godwin ends the passage with references to Benjamin Franklin, whom Immanuel Kant described as "the new Prometheus" (qtd. in Hindle xxxn.), and to Lycurgus, the Spartan lawgiver whose biography the monster reads in *Plutarch's Lives* (see Appendix C.3.d). The same quotation from Franklin introduces Godwin's most startling speculation—one which even Godwin considers "eminently a deviation into the land of conjecture" (A.1.b). If Victor believes that scientific reason has enabled him to discover the principle of life, Godwin believes that reason itself may be the principle of life.

Godwin does not believe in moral evil as it is usually understood. People always, he believes, do what they think is right; vice is always a consequence of misunderstanding (1: 108-9; I.vii). Nevertheless, he shares the Romantic interest in Milton's Satan (A.1.c), and since *Paradise Lost* is one of the three books the monster reads (see Appendix C.4), it is interesting to compare what he and Godwin make of it.

The monster's central complaint is that he is solitary, and his request is that Victor make a companion for him (156-57). These concerns reflect Godwin's conception of humanity as essentially social, a conception that is perhaps expressed most clearly in his condemnation of solitary confinement (A.1.d). Despite the monster's pleas and threats, Victor destroys the unfinished female monster because he believes that his duty to humanity outweighs any other considerations (174, 190). His reasoning recalls one of the most notorious passages in *Political Justice* (A.1.e), which argues that even decisions on matters of life and death should be based on purely impersonal considerations (Pollin 105). The disastrous outcome of Victor's reasoning suggests that Shelley is skeptical about Godwin's. Her treatment of the relations between Victor and the monster also seems to comment on Godwin's brief remarks on the father's motives in begetting a son and the son's consequent duty to the father.

If Godwin was directly responsible for the meeting of Mary and Percy Shelley, since Percy eagerly sought out the author of *Political Justice*, then Mary Wollstonecraft, the author of *A Vindication of the Rights of Woman* (1792) may be said to have presided over their falling in love, since they used to meet surreptitiously at her grave in Old St. Pancras churchyard, and it was there that Mary finally declared her love for him. In the years between their elopement and *Frankenstein*, she read or reread not only the *Vindication* but also Wollstonecraft's *Mary* (1788), *Elements of Morality* (1790), *An Historical and Moral View of the Origin and Progress of the French Revolution* (1794), *Letters Written during a Short Residence in Sweden, Norway, and Denmark* (1796), *The Wrongs of Woman* (1798), and *Posthumous Works* (1798) (*Journals* 2: 684). If reading was the only way that Shelley could keep in touch with her father during these difficult years, it was, of course, the only way she could know her mother at all.

Shelley's novel draws on the *Vindication* almost as often as on *Political Justice*.[1] In his Preface to her novel, Percy suggests that the author's moral concern "has been limited to the avoiding the enervating effects of the novels of the present day, and to the exhibition of the amiableness of domestic affection, and the excellence of universal virtue" (49). If the excellence of universal virtue is a characteristically Godwinian theme, the amiableness of domestic affection is a characteristically Wollstonecraftian one, and Percy significantly places it first. (Wollstonecraft also, as it happens, has quite a lot to say about the enervating effects of novels [XIII.ii].) Wollstonecraft is more conscious than Godwin of the interdependence of the universal, or public, and the domestic; of the rational and the emotional. She is also aware of the way that the first of these spheres has been characterized as masculine and the second as feminine, and of the disastrous effects of their separation. On the one hand, she asserts, "a man can only be prepared to discharge the [masculine] duties of public life, by the habitual practice of those inferiour [because domestic, feminine] ones which form the man" (312; XII); on the other, "make women rational creatures, and free citizens, and they will quickly become good wives, and mothers" (323; XII). Victor's downfall begins when he allows himself to become entirely alienated from the domestic sphere in his masculine quest for scientific glory (82); the monster he creates completes his alienation by virtually wiping out his family (Poovey 123-26).

The portrait of the De Lacey family, Shelley's most fully developed, most emphatic, and most unambiguous celebration of the domestic affections, recalls many passages from the *Vindication* (Appendix A.2.a). Shelley's ideal family, however, is differently configured than Wollstonecraft's, perhaps because the values it embodies are different: more egalitarian and less bourgeois. The monster argues that he has become evil because he has been

---

1 Joyce Zonana has shown, for example, how Wollstonecraft's habitual allusions to the Islamic oppression of women, and the supposed Islamic belief that women have no souls (e.g., 109, 113 [Introd.], 126 [II], 138 [II], 191 [IV], 317 [XIII], 335 [XIII.iii]), inspired the story of Safie, who escapes from her Turkish father to join the De Laceys, who help her to cultivate her mind. (Another Orientalist touch added in the 1831 Introduction—"The Hindoos give the world an elephant to support it, but they make the elephant stand upon a tortoise"—is also recalled from Wollstonecraft [226].)

deprived of such affections. Shelley's account of his disillusionment and degradation draws on a number of passages in the *Vindication* (A.2.b).

The monster is not the only character whose education is mismanaged. Feminist critics have sometimes expressed disappointment with the conventionality of Shelley's female characters (Jacobus 132, Johnson 7). This very conventionality, however, seems to be a comment on the conventions that confine them. Her brief account of the education of Elizabeth Lavenza (65-66), for example, recalls Wollstonecraft's analysis of the miseducation of women (A.2.c).

Wollstonecraft recognizes that domestic affection is grounded on sexual love, and she gives sexuality a much greater importance than Godwin does. But she sees its power as, at best, ambiguous—as only barely redeemed, and only barely controlled, by the domesticity it makes possible (A.2.d). These anxieties enter Shelley's novel in an inverted form: Victor's crime of non-sexual procreation reflects what Wollstonecraft considers the crime of non-procreative sex.

Perhaps because Wollstonecraft is so conscious of the interdependence of the rational and the emotional, her rhetoric is much more flamboyant than Godwin's. She supports her arguments with a rich pattern of metaphors, images, and allusions; and *Frankenstein* engages with the latter as frequently, as deeply, and as critically, as with the former.

Wollstonecraft's most frequent and most important literary allusions, like Shelley's, are to Milton.[1] As the extract that we have chosen shows, she, like Shelley, recognizes and exploits the contradictions in Milton's text (A.2.e; cf. Hatlen 23). And the boldness with which she speaks of co-operating with the supreme Being anticipates the boldness with which Shelley calls a mere man a creator—a boldness that offended one of her reviewers (see Appendix D.2).

Wollstonecraft combines her allusions to *Paradise Lost* with allusions to other creation myths, notably that of Prometheus, which gives Shelley's novel its subtitle. In our first and last extracts in Appendix A.2, she associates the Promethean with the revolutionary, and in the second and third, she couples it with genius, both common Romantic associations. In the third extract, most strik-

---

1 For example, 118 [I], 143, 144 [II], 150 [III], 166, 167, 175, 193 [IV], 211 [V.i], 250 [VI], 252 [VII], 286 [IX], 340 [XIII.vi].

ingly, she associates it with galvanism. Her lightning imagery anticipates not only the imagery with which Victor describes his discovery of the principle of life (78-79), but also the imagery with which Shelley describes, in her 1831 Introduction, the inspiration for her novel (351).

The Education of Victor Frankenstein: Darwin and Davy

In 1974, James Rieger dismissed the science of *Frankenstein* as "switched-on magic, souped-up alchemy, the electrification of Agrippa and Paracelsus.... [T]he technological plausibility that is essential to science fiction is not even pretended at here" (xxvii). It is true that Victor does not reveal the secret of life to Walton, for two excellent reasons: because he has come to realize that it is too dangerous (79-80), and because Mary Shelley herself did not know what it was. She did, however, know more about natural science than Rieger gave her credit for, and she made extensive use of it in her novel. Since it was, of course, the science of her own day, rather than of ours, it is easy to dismiss. She herself, unfortunately, encouraged such errors, by deleting some of the scientific references in the 1831 edition of her novel, and by describing Victor, quite inappropriately, as a sort of sorcerer, a "student of unhallowed arts," not only in her Introduction but even in the text (Vasbinder 53; see Appendix H, note to 109.31-110.3, and Appendix I, 350).

Even among those critics who have recognized the importance of Shelley's science, its precise significance is still controversial. Samuel Holmes Vasbinder demonstrates clearly that the novel contrasts modern science to sorcery and alchemy, rather than identifying it with them, as critics like Rieger had assumed (51-60). He believes that its attitude towards science is largely affirmative (71). As long as Victor adheres to science, he is successful; when he loses his nerve and abandons the monster, he also abandons modern science, reverting to a magical way of thinking characterized by his belief in spirits and his frequent references to the monster as a demon (66). Anne K. Mellor believes that the novel draws a distinction between the aggressive, masculinist science of Sir Humphry Davy and the non-interventionist, ecologically sensitive science of Erasmus Darwin (91-103). Marilyn Butler believes that it draws a different distinction: between the old, vitalist biology which conceived of life as a substance, a "subtle fluid" something like electricity, and the new, mechanist or materialist biology which conceived of life (as it still does) simply as the totality of an organism's functions. Shelley, Butler believes, sides with the materialists (their most notable English representative was Percy's physician, William Lawrence) and presents Victor as a "blundering experimenter, still working with superseded [vitalist] notions" (xvii-xix). Butler considers Shelley's later revision of the novel to be a retreat from the radical implications of materialism (xlvii-xlviii).

All three of these approaches are suggestive, but all of them are problematic. Even if, as Vasbinder contends, Shelley approves of modern science in some general way, she clearly does not approve of the way Victor practises it. Mellor passes over the fact that Darwin, a physician and inventor, was as enthusiastic an interventionist as Davy. Butler is certainly correct in identifying Victor's science as vitalist—he discovers the principle of life first, and then constructs a body to lodge it in—but it is hard to see how he is a blundering one, since he does, after all, succeed.

Mary Shelley attributes the nightmare that inspired her novel to a conversation between her lover and Byron about "the nature of the principle of life, and whether there was any probability of its ever being discovered and communicated" (350). Most critics identify this conversation with the one mentioned in the only contemporary record of the ghost-story project, the diary of Byron's personal physician, John William Polidori: "Shelley and I had a conversation about principles—whether man was to be thought merely an instrument" (123; 15 June 1816). Butler argues that Polidori, a graduate of the conservative University of Edinburgh, "frames the question in a theologically-sensitive way ... by using a word associated pejoratively with materialism," and that Shelley's phrase about "the nature of the principle of life" is "neutral" (xxi). In fact, the terms "instrument" and "principle" were both associated with the vitalism of Georg-Ernst Stahl (1659-1734), best remembered for the phlogiston theory, which conceived of heat as a subtle fluid, much as vitalism conceived of life (King 146).

Admittedly, Polidori's telegraphic diary entry and Shelley's understandably vague fifteen-year-old recollection are not much to go on; but the other external evidence about the novel's science points in the same direction. Percy's Preface refers to Erasmus Darwin, a vitalist, and to "some of the physiological writers of Germany" (49). This admittedly vague phrase could be a reference to Stahl, or perhaps to a more recent group of *Naturphilosophen* including Johann Wilhelm Ritter, Friedrich Wilhelm Joseph von Schelling, and Friedrich von Schlegel, all vitalists (see Wetzels). Shelley's 1831 Introduction repeats the reference to Darwin and adds a reference to galvanism. Luigi Galvani himself had been too cautious a researcher to make any grand claims about electricity as the vital principle, but some of his followers, including his nephew Luigi Aldini and Johann Wilhelm Ritter, were bolder.

There is a certain amount of mechanist terminology in *Frankenstein* (most of it contributed by Percy [Mellor 64]), but on the whole, it seems that Butler's characterization of the novel as essentially mechanist is a well-intentioned but misguided attempt to align Shelley with the most progressive science of her day. Shelley's use of a now-outmoded scientific theory does not, however, mean that her book is not relevant to the science of today. The example of Erasmus Darwin should suffice to remind us that a vitalist could be progressive in other ways. For example, vitalism is consonant with what we now think of as environmentalism, a sense of nature as an organic whole or sacred order—an order that Victor violates (Mellor 122-25).

Erasmus Darwin (1731-1802), the grandfather of Charles, was probably the most popular scientific writer of the Romantic period. He published two encyclopedic technical works, *Zoonomia; or, The Laws of Organic Life* (1794-96; 3rd ed. 1801) and *Phytologia*, a treatise on vegetation and agriculture (1800); and also two long poems, *The Botanic Garden* (1791) (comprising *The Loves of the Plants* [1789] and *The Economy of Vegetation* [1791]) and *The Temple of Nature* (1803). Shelley may have known him since childhood, since he was a friend of her father (St. Clair 222); and Percy was a keen admirer: he first read *The Botanic Garden* in 1811 and bought both *Zoonomia* and *The Temple of Nature* in 1812 (Mellor 99). We have chosen to refer to Darwin's poems rather than to his technical works because it is interesting to compare the way he puts science into literature with the way Shelley does it.

Darwin's vitalism is revealed in a passage from *The Economy of Vegetation* (see Appendix B.1.a) in which the poem's main speaker, the Goddess of Botany, addresses the Nymphs of Fire—who preside, in Darwin's poetic symbolism, not only over fire but also over electricity and the vital principle. The Goddess begins by describing the therapeutic benefits of electricity and then moves on to the principle of life, by way of an allegory in which she compares Benjamin Franklin to Cupid playing the role of Prometheus and stealing lightning from Jove. (Like Kant, Darwin thought of Franklin as the new Prometheus.)[1]

---

1 Robinson suggests that Frankenstein's name recalls Franklin's (I.lx).

A later passage from the same poem (B.1.b), in which the Goddess addresses the spirits of Earth, identifies Franklin's scientific activities with his revolutionary ones. By the end of the passage, a revolutionary monster has been galvanized into consciousness.

Darwin believes that life is actually being created all the time, by spontaneous generation. When Victor speaks of studying decomposition to analyze "the change from life to death, and death to life" (79), he is following the doctrine explained in Darwin's last long poem, *The Temple of Nature* (B.1.c). Darwin defends this doctrine in a long "Additional Note" to the poem (B.1.d); it is clearly the third section of this note that Shelley has in mind when she refers to "the experiments of Dr. Darwin" in her 1831 Introduction (350). Her account of an animated piece of vermicelli, in particular, derives from Darwin's reference to spontaneous generation in "a paste composed of flour and water." Readers who object that the body parts Victor collects would decay before he had a chance to assemble them are unaware that decomposition, and the spontaneous generation that it supposedly causes, may be part of Victor's method.

Although Darwin's vitalism and his belief in spontaneous generation might have led him to suppose that Victor's project was "not of impossible occurrence," as Percy's Preface puts it (49), he would not have thought that it was a very good idea. An early theorist of evolution, he believed that sexual reproduction was the highest, and spontaneous generation the lowest, method of creating life (B.1.e). As Mellor has argued (100), Victor's asexual creation of a "new species" (80) is actually an evolutionary regression.

Darwin, who wrote a two-thousand-line poem about the sexual lives of plants, and who fathered fourteen children, was an enthusiastic advocate of sexual reproduction. In avoiding it, Victor is not simply descending some abstract biological hierarchy, but committing a serious offence. *The Temple of Nature* explains why (B.1.e). Darwin thinks of the organisms that reproduce by "solitary reproduction" as male, not as asexual or bisexual. Their offspring resemble them completely: thus the common interpretation of the monster as a sort of double of Victor is solidly grounded in Darwinian biology. Sexual reproduction, by contrast, allows not only for variation but for the blending of masculine and feminine traits, leading to what William Veeder considers Shelley's psychological ideal, androgyny (16). Victor's resort to solitary reproduction shows how far he is from this ideal.

If the content of the science in *Frankenstein* is drawn from Darwin, its scientific style seems to be based on that of Davy. Like Darwin, Davy was an acquaintance of Godwin's (Sharrock 58); and in late October and early November of 1816, while working on her novel, Shelley described herself as reading "the Introduction to Sir H. Davy's Chemistry" (*Journals* 1: 142-44). This may have been the Introduction to his *Elements of Chemical Philosophy* (1812), which Percy bought in 1812, but internal evidence suggests that it was probably a famous earlier work, *A Discourse, Introductory to a Course of Lectures on Chemistry*, a lecture given at the Royal Institution, and published, in 1802 (Crouch 35-36).

Davy was a poet as well as a scientist, and a friend of Coleridge and Wordsworth as well as of Godwin. He corrected the proofs of the second edition of *Lyrical Ballads* (1800)—whose two most notable poems, Coleridge's "The Rime of the Ancient Mariner" and Wordsworth's "Lines Composed a Few Miles above Tintern Abbey" are both quoted in *Frankenstein*—and the *Discourse* he delivered two years later is in part a response to Wordsworth's famous Preface, claiming for the scientist something of the prestige that Wordsworth had awarded the poet (Sharrock 65-68). When the third edition of *Lyrical Ballads* appeared later in 1802, Wordsworth in turn responded to Davy by incorporating into the Preface a long passage distinguishing between the poet and the scientist (Sharrock 69-72), a passage which uncannily (if ironically) anticipates Shelley's novel:

> If the time should ever come when what is now called science, thus familiarised to men, shall be ready to put on, as it were, a form of flesh and blood, the Poet will lend his divine spirit to aid the transfiguration, and will welcome the Being thus produced, as a dear and genuine inmate of the household of man. (738; qtd. in McWhir 73)

If only there had been a Poet in the De Laceys' cottage!

The young Davy had been a vitalist, and although the author of the *Discourse*, unlike Darwin, would no longer have thought that Victor's project was possible, he still spoke intriguingly of "the conversion of dead matter into living matter" (B.2.a) and of "produc[ing] from combinations of dead matter effects which were formerly occasioned only by animal organs" (B.2.g), and he still used vitalist terms like "principle," "instrument," and even "the spirit of life" (B.2.b). He also dared to call science almost "creative," a word which still had powerful religious connotations in the Romantic period (B.2.f; cf. Appendix D.2). Just as Waldman advises Victor to "apply to every branch of natural philosophy" (76), so Davy urges the scientist to "combine together mechanical, chemical, and physiological knowledge" (B.2.d). He anticipates Victor's domineering attitude toward his research when he urges the scientist "to interrogate nature with power, not simply as a scholar, passive and seeking only to understand her operations, but rather as a master, active with his own instruments," and he even anticipates the sexual imagery that both Waldman and Victor apply to scientific research when he asks rhetorically "who would not be ambitious of becoming acquainted with the most profound secrets of nature; of ascertaining her hidden operations...?" (B.2.f), or speaks of "penetrat[ing] into her bosom" (B.2.e; Mellor 93).

If Victor's ambitions and their consequences constitute a criticism of Davy, however, Shelley also uses the real scientist to criticize Victor, for Davy warns against the presumptions of "speculative philosophers," once again using sexual imagery: "Instead of slowly endeavouring to lift up the veil concealing the wonderful phenomena of living nature; full of ardent imaginations, they have vainly and presumptuously attempted to tear it asunder" (B.2.c). Moreover, his insistence that the study of science should "giv[e] a permanent and placid enjoyment to the mind" and even "destroy diseases of the imagination" constitutes a critique of Victor's obsessiveness (B.2.h-i).

The Education of the Monster:
Volney, Goethe, Plutarch, Milton, Wollstonecraft

The monster's account of his education is a carefully designed philosophical fable, in which the ontogeny of this first member of a new species recapitulates the phylogeny of the human species (cf. Butler xxxvii). The charges of implausibility that are still sometimes laid against it could as plausibly be laid against *Rasselas* or *Candide*.

As Peter Brooks has pointed out, the three books the monster finds in an abandoned satchel make up a "Romantic *cyclopedia universalis*" (210): Goethe teaches him about the domestic, of which he already knows something from observing the De Laceys; Plutarch expands his horizons to the political; and Milton introduces him to the cosmic. Moreover, all three books seem also to have influenced Victor: in addition to teaching the monster about the Romantic world view, they help to make him into the counterpart of his creator.

The monster has already received glimpses of all three spheres from the first book to which he is exposed, *The Ruins, or, Meditation on the Revolutions of Empires* (1791) by Constantin-François de Chasseboeuf, comte de Volney (1757-1820), which Felix De Lacey reads to his beloved Safie in order to teach her French. This was a favourite book of Percy Shelley's: it heavily influenced both *Queen Mab* (1813), which was read and discussed in Geneva in 1816 (Polidori 107), and *The Revolt of Islam* (1818), which he wrote while Shelley was writing *Frankenstein* (see Cameron).

The Ruins, like *Queen Mab*, is a dream vision; it includes both an overview of world history, culminating in the French Revolution, and a survey of the world's major religions, which Volney treats with a remarkably even-handed contempt. The monster says little about the second part of the book, perhaps because, even with the help of Felix's "minute explanations" (134), he cannot understand it; but Volney's hostility towards religion may predispose him to read *Paradise Lost* as "the picture of an omnipotent God warring with his creatures" (143): he may read Milton through Volney.

Some of the things the monster claims to have learned from Volney are dealt with only cursorily in *The Ruins*; presumably Felix's explanations were more ample. The deplorable state of the "Asiatics" and the decline of the Roman empire are both discussed in a long footnote on the development of political despotism out of domestic despotism (Appendix C.1.a). In addition to preparing the monster for his reading of Goethe and Plutarch, Volney's critique of patriarchy may help to shape what he feels when he first learns about his own "father" from Victor's lab notes. He may learn about "the several empires at present existing in the world" and about "the discovery of the American hemisphere, and ... the hapless fate of its original inhabitants" (135) from a passage in the religious section of the book, which accuses Christianity of fostering domestic tyranny and imperialist aggression, among other things (C.1.b). This passage anticipates Victor's account of the conquest of America: his lament for "the empires of Mexico and Peru" borrows the phrasing of Barlow's translation (82). The passage (C.1.c) which perhaps inspires the monster's rhetorical question "Was man, indeed, at once so powerful, so virtuous, and magnificent, yet so vicious and base?" (it ends with a similar rhetorical question: "Ah! how are so many sublime energies allied to so many errors?") may also have given him his first intimations of his own origins. Volney's secular version of the origins of humanity must remind the monster of his own earliest experiences (as well as preparing him for Milton's religious version, which he will soon encounter); and the description of the first human as "an orphan, abandoned by the unknown power which had produced him" must have appealed to his own feelings of abandonment.

The three books that the monster finds and reads for himself are all books that Shelley herself had read in 1815 and 1816 (*Journals* 2: 650, 663, 668). It is not surprising that *The Sorrows of Werter* (to use the title, and the spelling, that Shelley adopts) should be among them. Goethe's epistolary novella had been a *succès de scandale* ever since its original publication in 1774: all over Europe, young men allegedly took to wearing blue coats and blowing their brains out in imitation of its hero. It had a special resonance for Shelley: her father had described her mother as "a female Werter," because of her sensibility, her letters to her first lover, and her suicide attempts after he had abandoned her (*Memoirs* 242; cf. Burwick 47-48).

The monster is attracted, first of all, by Goethe's depiction of "gentle and domestic manners" (142), presumably in the scenes showing Werter's beloved Charlotte with her brothers and sisters, or with her fiancé Albert. Since Werter cannot marry Charlotte, he is excluded from this domesticity, much as the monster is excluded from the De Laceys' cottage; moreover, since Werter's father is dead and his relationship with his mother appears to be bad (Dawson 253-54), he may, like Volney's first human, have struck the monster as a fellow-orphan. In saying that he took Werter's side in the "disquisitions on death and suicide," the monster seems to have in mind Werter's debate with Albert (Appendix C.2.a). As Roswitha Burwick has pointed out (50), the subject was brought home to Shelley by two suicides that occurred while she was at work on her novel: that of her half-sister, Fanny Imlay, and that of Percy's first wife, Harriet, who drowned herself, as Wollstonecraft had tried to, and as the girl in Werter's story does.

Shelley draws on Werter's less attractive side for her portrayal of Victor. P.D. Fleck has suggested that Werter's "inordinate desire," his refusal to compromise, anticipates Victor's overreaching (245); Burwick adds that in spite of this narcissistic trait, both characters manage to inspire affection in others (49). Shelley's most detailed use of *The Sorrows of Werter*, in fact, has to do with Victor: her account of the death of Victor's mother is based on Charlotte's account of her mother, right down to the unsettling hints of incest (C.2.b; cf. Burwick 50).

The "volume of *Plutarch's Lives*" that the monster finds is the first; the five biographies he mentions are traditionally placed first in the collection. It is appropriate that a being in search of his own origins should find himself reading these stories of the origins of society; it is particularly appropriate that the first words he reads, the introduction to the life of Theseus, the founder of Athens, should be a meditation on the difficulty of investigating origins (Appendix C.3.a). No doubt the monster is struck by Plutarch's account of Theseus's search for his father (1: 5), and of the mysterious paternity of Romulus, the founder of Rome (1: 37-40). If he finds Theseus an unsatisfactory hero and prefers the lawgivers— Lycurgus of Sparta, Numa Pompilius of Rome, and Solon of Athens—this may be partly because of Theseus's reputation as a killer of monsters. Leonard Wolf suggests another reason why the daughter of Mary Wollstonecraft would have considered both Theseus and Romulus unsatisfactory (186n. 8): among his other accomplishments, Theseus was a serial rapist and Romulus was a mass rapist, who abducted some eight hundred Sabine women to provide wives for his citizens (C.3.b). Despite the monster's disapproval, however, their acts of filicide, fratricide, and patricide foreshadow his future career.

Plutarch's account of how Numa used "religious terrors" to pacify the Romans (C.3.c) may remind the monster of Volney's analysis of the political uses of religion. It may also make him think of the way that the De Laceys regard his help around the cottage as the work of a good spirit (131). This detail from Plutarch is also relevant to Victor, who repeatedly invokes spirits, only to be answered by the monster (99, 117, 203-04), and who convinces himself that the help the monster gives him during their final chase is the work of a good spirit (204; Victor's belief in spirits may also owe something to the discussion of the afterlife in Goethe, C.2.b).

Since Safie's story has taught the monster about the difference between Turkish marriage customs and French ones (at least, as practised by the De Laceys), he is likely to be interested in Plutarch's comparison of Spartan and Roman marriage laws (C.3.d); the passage would also remind him of Volney's analysis of the Roman patriarchy and its consequences (C.1.a). As an abandoned child, he is probably horrified by the Spartans' custom of exposing "ill-shaped" children (1: 97; cf. Appendix A.2.d), but he probably approves of the care they took of the ones they decided to keep. The results of Lycurgus's educational policy would have been particularly striking to such a lonely reader:

he bred up his citizens in such a way that they neither would nor could live by themselves; they were to make themselves one with the public good, and, clustering like bees around their commander, be by their zeal and public spirit carried all but out of themselves, and devoted wholly to their country. (1: 108)

Lycurgus's policy provides, by contrast, another foreshadowing of the rest of the novel: if his care for the Spartan children produces law-abiding adults, Victor's abandonment of the monster is likely to produce a lawless outcast.

The novel's first allusion to Plutarch is in Victor's narrative, not the monster's: in trying to console Victor for the murder of William (97), Henry Clerval recalls the grief of Cato the Younger at the death of his brother Caepio (C.3.e). This contribution to the parallel between the two characters is lost in the 1831 version, which drops the allusion to Cato.

Of the books in the monster's satchel, *Paradise Lost* has been the most thoroughly studied in connection with *Frankenstein*, but its bearing on the novel is still controversial. The most famous account of the relations between the two works is probably that of Sandra Gilbert and Susan Gubar; their analysis is subtle and detailed, but its thesis is simple and bold: they see Milton as unambiguously misogynistic (214, 218-19), and Shelley as his submissive daughter, clarifying his message for women but not attempting to challenge it (220). As we have already seen, however (cf. Appendix A.2.e), Wollstonecraft knew that Milton's attitude towards women was self-contradictory; since her daughter had read the *Vindication*, and since she alludes in her novel to precisely the passage that Wollstonecraft quotes to illustrate Milton's egalitarian side (*Paradise Lost* VIII.381-91), it seems likely that she knew it too.

Moreover, it is clear from her title page that Shelley intends to challenge Milton. Her epigraph from *Paradise Lost* (X.743-45) is Adam's protest against God:

Did I request thee, Maker, from my clay
To mould me man? Did I solicit thee
From darkness to promote me?—

Burton Hatlen has pointed out that in the original, within ten lines, Adam has begun to argue himself out of his protest and into an admission that God is just. By quoting the lines out of context, Shelley allows the protest to stand in all its original force, without concessions or qualifications (31). Even when she uses Milton's precise words, she can give them a new meaning.

Moreover, the monster, though he is fond of comparing himself to Milton's characters, knows that there are significant differences between his story and either Adam's or Satan's: "God in pity made man beautiful and alluring, after his own image; but my form is a filthy type of your's, more horrid from its very resemblance. Satan had his companions, fellow-devils, to admire and encourage him; but I am solitary and detested" (144).

The crux of Gilbert and Gubar's argument is that the monster is really "a female in disguise," so that his monstrousness represents Shelley's admission of the monstrousness of womanhood (237). The monster, like Victor, certainly has some conventionally feminine characteristics; this would not have surprised Wollstonecraft, who knew that men could be feminized (173-74); in other words, that gender was socially constructed, not biologically predetermined.

The feminization of men should not be confused with what William Veeder calls androgyny, a harmonious balance of masculine and feminine. It has more to do with what he calls bifurcation, the polarization of "masculine and feminine traits ... into wilfulness and weakness" (17). At times Victor is effeminate: weak, passive, and emotional. At other times, he displays a highly masculine aggression, "penetrat[ing] into the recesses of nature," as his teacher M. Waldman puts it (75), and usurping the procreative power of the female. In so doing, he aligns himself with the series of solitary male parents in *Paradise Lost*: God, who creates the angels, begets the Son, and creates Adam; Satan, who gives birth to Sin; and Adam, who gives birth to Eve (Hatlen 27-28). As Darwin would have predicted, Victor's solitary act of procreation produces a being curiously like himself, a monster bifurcated into feminine extremes of shame and emotional dependency and masculine extremes of aggression and violence.

The bifurcated monster identifies himself both with Adam and with Eve. His earliest memories, for example (120-22), are closely based on Adam's account of his awakening, right down to the warbling of birds (Appendix C.4.a). This detailed similarity helps to emphasize the poignant differences between them: unlike the monster, Adam is able to speak, effortlessly, as soon as he wants to and has a creator who watches over him and leads him to his home. The monster identifies most strongly with Adam's loneliness before the creation of Eve. His reference to "Adam's supplication to his Creator" (145) is usually taken to refer to the lines quoted in Shelley's epigraph, but the epigraph is a protest, not a supplication. He is thinking, of course, of Adam's request for an equal mate, the request towards which his whole narrative is tending (cf. Appendix A.2.e).

The monster's identification with Eve is most obvious in his account of his first sight of himself, reflected in a pool (130), which closely parallels Eve's account of her awakening (C.4.b). Here Shelley's ironies are particularly complex. Eve falls in love with her own beauty; the monster is repelled by his own ugliness. Both cases oppose language to vision: Eve is led away from her reflection, and towards Adam, by a voice in the air; the monster, who has already learned a few words, determines to learn how to speak in order to communicate with others despite his ugliness (Brooks 209-10). Within this similarity, however, is a further difference: Eve passively follows the voice; the monster actively sets out to acquire language. As a wholly solitary being, he has to show more initiative than she does. Eve is guilty of narcissism, a weakness that foreshadows her fall; the monster is an ugly image of Victor's narcissism, the pride that leads him to style himself as a creator.

As Anne McWhir has suggested, the monster "can be educated only to know the full extent of his exclusion" from humanity (76-77). As he puts it, "sorrow only increased with knowledge" (136). Here Shelley seems to be alluding not directly to the forbidden fruit of knowledge in *Paradise Lost*, but to the allusion to it in another work begun in Geneva in 1816, Byron's *Manfred*:

> Sorrow is Knowledge: they who know the most
> Must mourn the deepest o'er the fatal truth,
> The Tree of Knowledge is not that of Life. (I.i.10-12)

And so the monster is expelled from his Edenic pig-sty. In fact, he expels himself: in burning down the De Laceys' cottage, he takes on the role of the cherub with the fiery sword who guards the gate of Eden (*Paradise Lost* XII.632-34). He finds himself with the whole world before him (151), just as the expelled Adam and Eve find it before them (*Paradise Lost* XII.646), and he sets out to find his creator.

The monster's sufferings are only beginning, but they are already making the point that Percy Shelley thought was the moral of the novel, and that is certainly the moral of the monster's narrative: "Treat a person ill, and he will become wicked. Requite affection with scorn;—let one being be selected, for whatever cause, as the refuse of his kind—divide him, a social being, from society, and you impose upon him the irresistible obligations—malevolence and selfishness" (7: 13; Appendix D.4). The monster puts it more strongly: "I ought to be thy Adam," he tells Victor; "but I am rather the fallen angel" (118-19). Again, the ironies in Shelley's use of Milton are complex. As the monster decides to destroy the cottage (151), he is at once in the position of Adam and Eve, expelled from Eden, of the cherub who enforces their expulsion, and of Satan, whose attack on Eve leads to their expulsion (C.4.c).

Victor also compares himself first to Adam and then to Satan. If he does not compare himself to Eve, he compares himself to Adam at his most feminine. The night of the monster's animation, he has a nightmare: he meets his fiancée Elizabeth and embraces her, only to have her turn into the corpse of his mother in his arms. He awakes in terror, to find the monster standing beside his bed (84). He has awakened from one dream into another; one might say that his nightmare comes true, since the monster does eventually turn Elizabeth into a corpse. His nightmare, of course, recalls the nightmare that inspired Shelley to write the book. The idea of a creative dream, of a dream that comes true, recalls the creation of Eve (C.4.d), for the Romantics, a symbol for human creativity in general. As Keats famously put it: "The Imagination may be compared to Adam's dream—he woke and found it truth" (1: 185; cf. Homans 114). Part of Shelley's critique of Romanticism is her suggestion that nightmares are the dreams most likely to come true.

In addition to the texts the monster mentions, one unmentioned text may have influenced Shelley's account of his education. His acquisition of language, and his cognitive development, strikingly recall the "Lessons" which Wollstonecraft prepared for her first daughter, Fanny Imlay, and which Godwin included in her *Posthumous Works* (2: 169-96). Both proceed from concrete to abstract, and both place learning in a supportive family context. Wollstonecraft's lessons may even have suggested the De Laceys' cow (Appendix C.5).

The Evolution of the Novel:
Composition, Publication, Reception, Revision

Mary and Percy travelled with Mary's stepsister, Claire Clairmont, to Switzerland in the summer of 1816, staying near Lord Byron and his resident physician, John Polidori. The summer was miserable and wet, so the group spent much time indoors, reading ghost stories aloud. Byron suggested that each of them write a ghost story. Lord Byron's contribution to the stories has come to be known as "A Fragment" or "The Burial: A Fragment," which was eventually printed at the end of his 1819 collection *Mazeppa* by publisher John Murray, albeit without Byron's knowledge or permission. John Polidori's ghost story was eventually published as *Ernestus Berchtold; or, The Modern Oedipus* in 1819. Byron and Polidori parted ways at the end of that wet summer of 1816, and at some point between then and early 1819, Polidori wrote "The Vampyre," based on Byron's fragment. It was published in 1819, without the knowledge or permission of either man. On the evening of 16 June 1816, Mary listened to Shelley and Byron discuss Erasmus Darwin's work, during which they pondered about the possibility of reanimating corpses; that night, she had a nightmare on which her ghost story, *Frankenstein*, is based.

Shelley's immediate reaction to her nightmare was exhilaration:

> Swift as light and as cheering was the idea that broke in upon me. "I have found it! What terrified me will terrify others; and I need only describe the spectre which had haunted my midnight pillow." On the morrow I announced that I had *thought of a story*. (351)

Shelley began her ghost story the morning after her nightmare with an account of the monster's animation.[1] Because Shelley's letters and journals are irregular through June of 1816 (no doubt a result of that period's itinerant lifestyle), no contemporary record of the manuscript's conception exists in Shelley's hand. However, the start date of 16 June 1816 can be corroborated by Polidori's journal entry for 17 June: "the ghost stories are begun by all but me" (125).

Shelley worked steadily at her manuscript through the late summer and fall of 1816. On 24 July, she noted in her journal that she continued to "write my story" (1: 118); on 21 August, she and Percy "talk about my story" (1: 130); on 5 December, back in England since September, she wrote to him from Bath that she had "finished the 4 Chap. of Frankenstein which is a very long one & I think you would like it" (*Letters* 1: 22).

During the winter of 1816-17, however, Shelley's work was disturbed for two months. On 10 December 1816, Harriet Shelley's

---

1 See "*Frankenstein* Chronology," Robinson 1: lxxvi-cx.

body was found in the Serpentine. On 15 December, Percy Shelley received word of this death from Thomas Hookham, and the ensuing circumstances prevented Mary Shelley from returning to her manuscript. Although now free to marry Percy (she did so on 30 December), she still had to endure the custody battle for Percy and Harriet Shelley's two children, which commenced immediately after Hookham's news and raged until 17 March 1817. In her suicide note, Harriet had begged Percy to allow their daughter Ianthe to remain with her sister, Eliza Westbrook, but offered him their son Charles (P.B. Shelley, *Letters* 1: 520n.). On 18 December 1816, Percy wrote to the Westbrooks, asking them to hand both children over to him. They refused, and, on 10 January 1817, Mr. Westbrook petitioned the Chancery court to deny custody to the Shelleys, by now married. The case came to trial on 24 January, and on 17 March was decided against Percy (P.B. Shelley, *Letters* 1: 522-24 and 523n.).

Understandably, Shelley was preoccupied with the Chancery suit, but she must have returned to work early in 1817. Although her letters of January 1817 do not mention anything about *Frankenstein*, we know she finished the first draft by 10 April 1817, when she noted that she began to "[c]orrect" the novel (*Journals* 1: 166). Her journal indicates that she revised steadily until 17 April (1: 166-68), after which she began transcribing the second draft into publisher's fair copy, a task completed on Tuesday 13 May 1817 (*Journals* 1: 169). On 14 May, Percy wrote the Preface. Shelley's journal entry on that day reports: "Finis" (1: 169).

There remained, of course, the problem of finding a publisher for such an unusual tale. By 26 May, John Murray, Byron's publisher, had read the manuscript, for Shelley recorded in her journal that "Murray likes F" (1: 171), but evidently he did not like it enough to act against the recommendation of his literary adviser, William Gifford. Mary predicted Murray's rejection in a letter of 29 May to Percy, who had taken their son William back to their house in Marlow while Shelley remained in London (*Letters* 1: 36). Murray rejected *Frankenstein* on 18 June (*Letters* 1: 37). On 3 August, Percy sent the manuscript to his recent publisher, Charles Ollier, describing *Frankenstein* as a novel "which has been consigned to my care by a friend in whom I feel considerable interest" (*Letters* 1: 549). On 8 August, Percy wrote Ollier on another matter, but appended a hope that "Frankenstein did not give you bad dreams" (1: 552). It is unclear whether or not Ollier had already refused the novel by 8 August, but it is certain that Lackington, Allen & Company had accepted *Frankenstein* by 22 August, as Percy's letter of that date to the company proposes the terms of the contract. The Shelleys received a letter from Lackington on 24 August, presumably responding to Percy's terms (*Journals* 1: 178). According to Shelley's journal, a bargain was finally struck on 19 September 1817 (1: 180).

Percy, acting as agent for the anonymous author, immediately started receiving proofs at Marlow. However, he had to go to London to arrange for the publication of *The Revolt of Islam*. On 24 September, Shelley, still at Marlow, sent to Percy

> another proof—which arrived tonight in looking it over there appeared to me some abruptness which I have endeavoured to supply—but I am tired and not very clear headed so I give you carte blanche to make what alterations you please. (*Letters* 1: 42)

James Rieger, among others, has cited this passage as evidence that Shelley tacitly approved Percy's proof alterations, thus authorizing him as a collaborator, not only at the manuscript stage, but also through the proofing process (Rieger xviii; Murray, "Shelley's Contribution" 67). The reader of the present edition should note that the 1818 text is one which has been heavily influenced by Shelley's husband. As Mellor has shown, this influence was by no means always for the better (58-65), but Shelley did agree to it, and Percy's contributions, no doubt inadvertently, authenticate the portrait of him that she gives in Victor (cf. Veeder 122).

Percy's correspondence reveals that he proofed *Frankenstein* through the fall of 1817 (*Letters* 1: 558, 564-65, 565). His request of 23 December that Lackington send him the *Frankenstein* copies "as soon as they can be put in boards" indicates that by then the proofreading was complete, but the book had not yet been bound: "On what day do you propose to publish it?" (1: 585). It must have been printed by 31 December, as Shelley noted then in her journal that "Fran[kens]tein comes" (1: 189). The novel was published, anonymously, the following day. The Shelleys obviously received their copies by 2 January 1818, because they were able to send a complimentary copy to Walter Scott, accompanied by Percy's covering letter bearing that date (1: 590).

Frankenstein enjoyed enormous success, not only because of its timely scientific theme, but also as a result of its eerie Gothic motif and its unsettling characterization, all three of which are much more pronounced in the 1818 edition than in the revision of 1831. It was favourably reviewed by Scott, the most eminent novelist of the age, in *Blackwood's Edinburgh Magazine* (Appendix D.1). Scott begins by considering the different kinds of fantastic fiction and deciding that *Frankenstein* belongs to the most "philosophical and refined" variety, which does not simply indulge in the fantastic for its own sake but uses it to explore the "workings of the human mind." He concludes by praising Shelley's "uncommon powers of poetic imagination" and her "plain and forcible English." Shelley's most revolutionary idea, however—giving the monster an articulate voice—was too revolutionary for Scott, who felt that it destroyed the monster's "mysterious sublimity."

The reviewer for *The Edinburgh Magazine* draws attention to the political significance of Shelley's novel (D.2). The fantastic plot could be compared to recent events; and Victor's career, in particular, to that of Napoleon. *Frankenstein*'s most negative review was by the aptly named John Wilson Croker, in the *Quarterly Review* (D.3). Croker is best remembered as the author of the review of *Endymion* that allegedly killed Keats, and as a writer for the reactionary *Quarterly Review*, he would be expected to attack any book dedicated to Godwin, but even he had to admit, grudgingly, to the novel's power. Other reviews appeared in *La Belle Assemblée* 2.17 (March 1818): 139-42, the *British Critic* ns 9 (April 1818): 432-38, the *Gentleman's Magazine* 88 (April 1818): 334-35, the *Monthly Review* ns 85 (April 1818): 439, and the *Literary Panorama* ns 8 (June 1818): 411-14. The first review written, and in some ways the most interesting, appeared last. In February 1818, Percy Shelley wrote a review, for his wife's benefit; it finally appeared in the *Athenaeum* (November 1832): 730, over ten years after his death (D.4). As Mellor points out, Percy's identification with Victor (a portrait, after all) leads him to regard "*both* Frankenstein and his creature [as] innocent victims" (69).

The novel's gloomy atmosphere made it a perfect vehicle for the contemporary proliferation of stage melodramas, and it was duly produced as such. The summer of 1823 saw two different productions based on Shelley's novel: Richard Brinsley Peake's *Presumption; or, The Fate of Frankenstein* opened on 28 July; H.M. Milner's *Frankenstein; or, The Demon of Switzerland* opened on 18 August (*Letters* 1: 372n. 8). That same year, Shelley's father, William Godwin, to capitalize on the novel's theatrical popularity, and to cheer up his daughter after Percy's death in 1822, arranged for the publication of a second edition of *Frankenstein* by G. and W.B. Whittaker. Shelley had nothing whatsoever to do with its production, but she retained almost all of the 123 revisions Godwin had seen fit to make when she revised the novel herself in 1831 (Crook xcvi, xcviii; Murray, "Changes" 323-24).

Interestingly, 1823 saw another, though unrelated, event in the history of the text. Shelley began revising the first edition relatively soon after its appearance, and in 1823 she presented a copy of the 1818 text, with holograph annotations for a possible new edition, to her friend Mrs. Thomas. These revisions were never implemented, but the annotations to the Thomas copy, now housed at the J. Pierpont Morgan Library in New York, represent a significant stage in the evolution of the text and the author's relationship with it. In the 1831 edition, Shelley revised many of the same passages she had marked for revision eight years earlier, though not in the same ways (see Appendix H).

On 29 August 1823, after her return to England, Shelley saw Peake's play at the English Opera House. The play is a skilful condensation of the novel, unifying its plot by having Victor in love with Agatha De Lacey (Elizabeth is consigned to Clerval) and by incorporating the incident in which the monster rescues a girl from drowning in the De Lacey subplot (see Appendix E). It does, however, as Jeffrey N. Cox has shown (66-71), simplify and distort the novel, especially by overemphasizing Shelley's praise of the domestic affections—in addition to Victor and Agatha and Elizabeth and Henry, there is a comic, lower-class couple, Fritz and Ninon. And it deprives the monster of a voice, thus depriving the story of much of its subversive power and forcing Thomas P. Cooke, the actor who played the monster, to indulge in some extremely elaborate dumb-show. Nevertheless, Shelley was "much amused" (*Letters* 1: 378), and she was impressed enough by Peake's moralizing interpretation to incorporate a reference to Frankenstein's presumption into the 1831 edition (Baldick 61; see Appendix H, note to 102.18-19).

During the next eight years, Shelley established herself in London, raised her son Percy Florence, earned her living as a writer, and tried hard to live down her youth and become a respectable member of London society. On 16 January 1827 she wrote to Henry Colburn's publishing firm, inquiring about the likelihood of its procuring the copyright to *Frankenstein* (*Letters* 1: 539). Colburn, who had pirated Polidori's *The Vampyre* in 1819, should have seemed like a logical choice for a new edition of *Frankenstein*, but Shelley sounded less than confident about Colburn's ability or desire to publish it. Her fears were unjustified, as the revised novel eventually did reappear, four years later.

The 1831 edition is more than a stage in the text's evolution; it may, in fact, be more accurate to characterize it as a revolution in the text's history. Shelley substantially revised the novel for its 1831 appearance as volume No. 9 in H. Colburn and R. Bentley's Standard Novels series. Anne K. Mellor discusses some of the differences between the 1818 and 1831 editions in Chapter Nine of her *Mary Shelley: Her Life, Her Fiction, Her Monsters*. Maurice Hindle's Note on the Text to his Penguin edition (1984; rpt. 1992), and Marilyn Butler's Introduction and Note on the Text to her Pickering edition (1993), also succinctly summarize the significant differences. It was for the 1831 edition that Shelley wrote her famous Introduction (Appendix H). As an account of the genesis of the novel, it is not entirely reliable, but as an analysis of the psychology of literary creation, it is unsurpassed.

After the appearance of the 1831 edition, Shelley did no further work on *Frankenstein*.

The Contributions of Percy Shelley: Recent Scholarship

The original publication of *Frankenstein* was attended by various rumours attributing the book to Percy rather than to Mary Shelley. That it is fundamentally her book rather than his has long been accepted by scholars, but discussion of the extent of Percy Shelley's involvement has periodically resurfaced over the years. In his 1974 University of Chicago Press edition of the 1818 text, James Rieger gave voice to his uncertainty over this issue:

> Shelley oversaw his wife's manuscript at every stage. Not only did he correct her frequent grammatical solecisms, her spelling, and her awkward phrasing.... His assistance at every point in the book's manufacture was so extensive that one hardly knows whether to regard him as editor or minor collaborator.

Controversy over the degree of Percy's involvement was fanned in 2008, in response to the work of Charles E. Robinson, author of two immaculate archival studies of the *Frankenstein* manuscripts. The first, in 1996, was the two-volume *The Frankenstein Notebooks: A Facsimile Edition of Mary Shelley's Novel 1816-17 (Parts One and Two)*, a full reproduction and transcription of the Mary Shelley manuscripts held at the Bodleian, published by Garland. The second, in 2008, was *The Original Frankenstein; or, The Modern Prometheus*, by Mary Shelley (with Percy Bysshe

Shelley), published by the Bodleian. In this book, Robinson attempts to "take us as far back as possible to the 'original' novel that Mary Shelley first drafted during the famous and rainy summer of 1816 in Geneva" (*OF* 16). In reconstructing that lost version, Robinson presents two new texts of *Frankenstein: 1816-1817*: the first corrected version includes Percy's contributions (thus "with Percy Shelley"), in a separate font to indicate visually to the reader the extent of Percy's involvement; the second is an uncorrected text that removes as far as possible all of Percy's efforts in order to give Shelley's voice free range. Robinson's contribution to the textual work associated with *Frankenstein*, especially the pre-1818 first edition, is immense—the novel's scholars need no longer travel to the Bodleian to access the minutiae of the novel's manuscripts. But if the excellence of Robinson's work is unquestioned, his inclusion of Percy on the title page, albeit duly bracketed and prepositioned, has once again ignited discussion of Percy's role in the construction of the novel.

Few serious scholars debate Robinson's contention that Percy contributed between 4,000 and 5,000 words of the 72,000 word novel. Indeed, given Robinson's superb work, it is a pretty hard case to debate. There has never been much doubt about Percy's important role in the creation of what we believe is still very much Mary Shelley's novel. Even without access to the manuscripts, where Percy's changes are plain to see, letters between the two make clear her willingness to have his help. A look through the list of major Shelley scholars and their publications makes clear that the topic of Percy's contributions is hardly a new enough topic to warrant the sensational headline of Lynda Pratt's 28 October 2008 *TLS* review of *The Original Frankenstein*, "Who Wrote the Original Frankenstein?" Or for Stephen Adams of *The Daily Telegraph* to take on the persona of investigative journalist by reporting before the publication of Robinson's 2008 edition that:

> The academic, who is to publish his research this October in a book, *The Original Frankenstein*, said: "He [Shelley] made very significant changes in words, themes and style. The book should now be credited as 'by Mary Shelley with Percy Shelley.'"

> The professor postulated that the couple may have added their comments to the manuscript while sitting in bed together.

"It seems they were using the same pen and very likely were often writing in bed together," he said. (*Telegraph*, 24 August 2008)

Adams—or his editors—affect a kind of gleefully voyeuristic spin on Robinson's approach. It is interesting that after almost two centuries of discussion, this literary collaboration still packs an emotional punch. Yet Robinson himself—much as his use of Percy's name on the title page has caused so much comment—does not wish to sensationalize, or to be lured into a critical discussion of which version—with Percy or without him—is "better." In conversation with Jennifer Howard of *The Chronicle of Higher Education*, he says,

> Some people are going to argue that Percy is usurping his authority and changing Mary. Other people would argue, at the other extreme, that Mary needs this advice.... I like to give them the benefit of the doubt. Here are two people who love each other. One is giving a manuscript to the other for editorial advice, one suggests changes, the other accepts them, the end. But that makes no drama. (*Chronicle*, 7 November 2008)

Facts are, after all, facts. Robinson does not argue that Percy's emendations always improve the work, although he believes they are "mostly for the better"; nor does he seek to divest Mary Shelley of her authorial status:

> ... we may conclude that he contributed at least 4,000 to 5,000 words to this 72,000-word novel. Despite the number of Percy's words, the novel was conceived and written mainly by Mary Shelley, as attested not only by others in their circle (e.g. Byron, Godwin, Claire and Charles Clairmont, Leigh Hunt) but by the nature of the manuscript evidence in the surviving pages of the Draft. (*OF* 25)

Robinson never really addresses his decision to put Percy on the title-page. He is reasonable in referring to the first text he presents as the "... Draft that the Shelleys prepared" (*OF* 41), as we know in fact that the Shelleys *did* prepare the Draft together. As the first text in *The Original Frankenstein*—the one with Percy Shelley—makes perfectly clear, it would be impossible for any *Frankenstein* scholar to ignore Percy's role in the text. Whether any other scholar would make the bold choice to elevate a collaborator or editor to the title page is another question entirely. We should note, however, that the subtitle of Robinson's book is very clear and in no way misleading; there are two texts, one of which involves Percy: "Two New Versions: Mary Shelley's Earliest Draft, and Percy Shelley's Revised Text." We don't see Robinson claiming authorship for Percy; what we do see is what Lynda Pratt describes in her *TLS* review:

> What emerges from the first draft of *Frankenstein* is a sense of the collaborative energy that helped to forge the novel. The image, vividly evoked in Robinson's introduction, of Mary and Percy passing the manuscript draft between them, each responding to the ideas of the other, is a powerful reminder that the popular myth of the Romantic author as an isolated, creative genius is just that—a myth.

The controversy, such as it is, may perhaps at this point be safely laid to rest. But thanks to Robinson's careful scholarship, readers can better see for themselves in these pre-texts of 1816 and 1817 what Percy contributed—as well as how Mary herself composed the novel.

Mary Wollstonecraft Shelley: A Brief Chronology

1797   Birth of Mary Wollstonecraft Godwin (30 August); death of her mother (10 September)

1801   Marriage of her father to Mary Jane Clairmont (21 December)

1812   Visit to Dundee (June); first meeting with Percy (11 November)

1814   Elopement with Percy and her stepsister, Claire Clairmont (28 July); first trip to the Continent (August-September)

1815   Birth (22 February) and death (6 March) of her first daughter; move to Bishopsgate, Windsor (August)

1816   Birth of her son William (24 January); second trip to the Continent, meeting with Byron and Polidori in Geneva (May); *Frankenstein* begun (16 June); return to England (September); suicide of her half-sister, Fanny Imlay (9 October); suicide of Percy's wife, Harriet Shelley (discovered 10 December); marriage to Percy (30 December)

1817   Move to Marlow (March); *Frankenstein* finished (14 May); birth of her daughter Clara (2 September); publication of *History of a Six Weeks' Tour* (November)

1818   Publication of *Frankenstein* (January); departure for Italy (March); settled in Bagni di Lucca (June); move to Este; death of Clara (24 September); move to Rome (November); to Naples (December)

1819   Move to Rome (March); death of William (7 June); move to Livorno (June); composition of *Mathilda* (August-February 1820); move to Florence (September); birth of her son Percy Florence (12 November)

1820   Move to Pisa (January); composition of *Proserpine* and *Midas* (April-May); move to Livorno (June); to Bagni di San Giuliano (August); to Pisa (October)

1821   Move to Bagni di San Giuliano (April); to Pisa (October)

1822   Move to Lerici (May); miscarriage (16 June); death of Percy (8 July); move to Genoa (September)

1823   Publication of *Valperga* (February); of the second edition of *Frankenstein*; return to London (August)

1824	Death of Byron (19 April); publication of Percy's *Posthumous Poems*, edited by Shelley (June), suppressed by Percy's father
1826	Publication of *The Last Man* (February)
1830	Publication of *Perkin Warbeck* (May)
1831	publication of the revised third edition of *Frankenstein* (November)
1835	Publication of *Lodore* (March)
1836	Death of her father (7 April)
1837	Publication of *Falkner* (February)
1839	Publication of Percy's *Poetical Works* (January-May), and his *Essays and Letters* (December), edited by Shelley
1840	Trip to the Continent with Percy Florence and his friends (June-November)
1842-43	Another Continental trip
1844	Death of Percy's father, succession of Percy Florence to the estate (24 April); publication of *Rambles in Germany and Italy* (August)
1851	Death of Shelley, from a brain tumor (1 February)

A Note on the Text

All told, there are five editorially significant versions of *Franken-stein*: Shelley's manuscript, the fair copy manuscript, the 1818 first edition, the annotated Thomas copy, and the 1831 edition. The 1823 edition, prepared by Godwin without any participation from the author, has no textual authority. The question facing any editor of *Frankenstein*, of course, is which edition to use as copytext. Most modern editors have chosen the 1831 edition. Such editors are on solid Bowersian ground in preferring the author's final intentions for the text. However, we have chosen the 1818 first edition as the copytext for this book.

It is our contention that the 1831 edition is largely a different book from the 1818 edition. Anne K. Mellor argues that Shelley's personal circumstances and tragedies convinced her that "human beings [are] ... mere puppets in the hands of destiny" (Mellor 173), as opposed to being free agents in control of their own destinies, as the young Shelley had believed in 1816-18, and that she accordingly made Frankenstein much less in control of his own actions:

> In 1818 Victor Frankenstein possessed free will or the capacity for meaningful moral choice—he could have abandoned his quest for the "principle of life," he could have cared for his creature, he could have protected Elizabeth. In 1831 such choice is denied to him. He is the pawn of forces beyond his knowledge or control. Again and again, Mary Shelley reassigns human actions to chance or fate. (171)

This fatalistic view of human nature is matched, Mellor argues, by a mechanistic view of non-human nature (172): the 1831 version is more, not less, mechanistic than the original.

Maurice Hindle, in an analysis particularly relevant to an edition like this one, argues that the 1831 version strips the novel of much of its context, removing a number of references to contemporary science (such as the electrical experiments that Victor's father performs for him [70]) and Godwinian philosophy (such as Elizabeth's denunciation of the justice system [108]). It also removes the most obvious pointer to one of the novel's most important intertexts by omitting the epigraph from Milton. Hindle does not discuss this omission, perhaps because, like all other modern editors of the 1831 version, he retains the 1818 epigraph: all modern editions of 1831 are, to this slight extent, composite texts. Hindle also points out that the original three-volume format helps to highlight "the Chinese box structure of the narrative-worlds-within-worlds of the book": he thinks it is so helpful, in fact, that he retains it for his edition of the 1831 text, thus producing a somewhat more composite text than the other editions of 1831 (xliv-xlviii).

These and other arguments have convinced us that the 1818 and 1831 editions of *Frankenstein* are best treated as two separate texts, each interesting and significant, but for different reasons. The 1831 text is the one available in almost all modern paper-back editions. We believe that, given the difference in the texts in this case, the 1818 edition is closer to the imaginative act and atmosphere that spawned this influential novel. We have chosen to use the 1818 version as our copytext, thereby making a clean first edition accessible to students. James Rieger's edition, the first modern edition of the 1818 text, is still in print, but we find it problematical because he has chosen to reprint the 1818 edition almost exactly, including the typographical errors, "in order to show the carelessness with which the novel was proof-read" (xlv). We find this decision very strange, considering that Mary Shelley left the proofreading to Percy; it seems unwise to leave his errors in her book. This method is doubly perplexing as Rieger leaves no stone unturned in his desire to show how much Percy's contributions improved the novel (see Mellor 58). At the same time, Rieger splices Shelley's 1823 revisions into his text; we feel that such a decision violates the integrity of the 1818 edition, making Rieger's version even more of a composite than Hindle's.

Unlike Rieger, we silently correct any typographical errors for the readers of the present edition. We record the variants in the 1831 edition, not only to salute the author's final intentions, but also to encourage discussion about the kinds of changes Shelley made to her novel. We should like to point out, however, that the authorial variants between the 1818 and 1831 editions document only a segment of the text's history and development. We can only amplify Mellor's plea for an edition of Shelley's manuscript (62) into a call for a variorum edition, which would collect in one volume all the authorial versions of the text. Such a book would be an invaluable addition to *Frankenstein* scholarship.

The 1831 variants appear as Appendix H; the headnote explains their format. Our edition of the 1818 text is based on a copy in the Library of Congress, Washington, DC, and the Thomas copy in the Pierpont Morgan Library, New York. We have corrected the misprints in the 1818 text that Shelley corrected in the 1831 edition. They are:

a. page 65, line 33 mistakenly prints "her" for "his";
b. page 91, line 4 (and afterwards) prints "Ingoldstadt" for "Ingolstadt";
c. page 146, line 17 (and afterwards) prints "De Lacy" for "De Lacey";
d. page 169, line 20 prints "Gower", which is a mistake for "Goring";
e. page 172, lines 22-23 omits "of my" from "the scene of my labours";
f. page 215, line 7 prints "September 19th" for "September 9th".

We also wish to note that the reference to "December" on page 167 must be incorrect, as it contradicts what Victor says about the vintage on page 165, as well as the month given on page 168. Shelley did not correct this error in the 1831 edition, however, so we have let it stand. To save space, we have omitted the title pages of the second and third volumes (they are identical to the first, except for reading "VOL. II." and "VOL. III.").

FRANKENSTEIN;

OR,

THE MODERN PROMETHEUS.

IN THREE VOLUMES.

Did I request thee, Maker, from my clay
To mould me man ?   Did I solicit thee
From darkness to promote me ?——
                          PARADISE LOST. [1]

VOL. I.

London :

PRINTED FOR

LACKINGTON, HUGHES, HARDING, MAVOR, & JONES,
FISSBURY SQUARE.

1818.

---

1 Milton, *Paradise Lost* X.743-45.

TO

WILLIAM GODWIN,

AUTHOR OF POLITICAL JUSTICE, CALEB WILLIAMS,

&c.

THESE VOLUMES

Are respectfully inscribed

BY

THE AUTHOR.

PREFACE.[1]

THE event on which this fiction is founded has been supposed, by Dr. Darwin, and some of the physiological writers of Germany, as not of impossible occurrence. I shall not be supposed as according the remotest degree of serious faith to such an imagination; yet, in assuming it as the basis of a work of fancy, I have not considered myself as merely weaving a series of supernatural terrors. The event on which the interest of the story depends is exempt from the disadvantages of a mere tale of spectres or enchantment. It was recommended by the novelty of the situations which it developes; and, however impossible as a physical fact, affords a point of view to the imagination for the delineating of human passions more comprehensive and commanding than any which the ordinary relations of existing events can yield.

I have thus endeavoured to preserve the truth of the elementary principles of human nature, while I have not scrupled to innovate upon their combinations. The *Iliad*, the tragic poetry of Greece,—Shakespeare, in the *Tempest* and *Midsummer Night's Dream*,—and most especially Milton, in *Paradise Lost*, conform to this rule; and the most humble novelist, who seeks to confer or receive amusement from his labours, may, without presumption, apply to prose fiction a licence, or rather a rule, from the adoption of which so many exquisite combinations of human feeling have resulted in the highest specimens of poetry.

The circumstance on which my story rests was suggested in casual conversation. It was commenced, partly as a source of amusement, and partly as an expedient for exercising any untried resources of mind. Other motives were mingled with these, as the work proceeded. I am by no means indifferent to the manner in which whatever moral tendencies exist in the sentiments or characters it contains shall affect the reader; yet my chief concern in this respect has been limited to the avoiding the enervating effects of the novels of the present day, and to the exhibition of the amiableness of domestic affection, and the excellence of universal virtue. The opinions which naturally spring from the character and situation of the hero are by no means to be conceived as existing always in my own conviction; nor is any inference justly to be drawn from the following pages as prejudicing any philosophical doctrine of whatever kind.

---

1 Written for Shelley by her husband.

It is a subject also of additional interest to the author, that this story was begun in the majestic region where the scene is principally laid, and in society which cannot cease to be regretted. I passed the summer of 1816 in the environs of Geneva. The season was cold and rainy, and in the evenings we crowded around a blazing wood fire, and occasionally amused ourselves with some German stories of ghosts, which happened to fall into our hands.[1] These tales excited in us a playful desire of imitation. Two other friends (a tale from the pen of one of whom would be far more acceptable to the public than any thing I can ever hope to produce) and myself agreed to write each a story, founded on some supernatural occurrence.[2]

The weather, however, suddenly became serene; and my two friends left me on a journey among the Alps, and lost, in the magnificent scenes which they present, all memory of their ghostly visions. The following tale is the only one which has been completed.

---

1 *Fantasmagoriana, ou recueil d'histoires d'apparitions de spectres, revenans, fantômes, etc.* (1812), translated anonymously by Jean-Baptiste-Benoît Eyriès (1767-1846), from the first two volumes of the five-volume *Gespensterbuch* (1811-15) edited by Friedrich Schulze and Johann Apel. Eyriès's translation had been translated into English, as *Tales of the Dead* (1813), by Sarah Elizabeth Brown Utterson (1782?-1851).

2 In addition to P.B. Shelley and Byron, the two friends Shelley has in mind, Polidori contributed a novel, *Ernestus Berchtold; or, The Modern Oedipus* (1819). He also completed Byron's abandoned story; it was published as *The Vampyre* (1819). P.B. Shelley's story has been tentatively identified as the verse "Fragment of a Ghost Story" (1816).

FRANKENSTEIN;
OR, THE
MODERN PROMETHEUS.

LETTER I.

To Mrs. SAVILLE, *England.*

St. Petersburgh, Dec. 11th, 17—.[1]

YOU will rejoice to hear that no disaster has accompanied the commencement of an enterprise which you have regarded with such evil forebodings. I arrived here yesterday; and my first task is to assure my dear sister of my welfare, and increasing confidence in the success of my undertaking.

I am already far north of London; and as I walk in the streets of Petersburgh, I feel a cold northern breeze play upon my cheeks, which braces my nerves, and fills me with delight. Do you understand this feeling? This breeze, which has travelled from the regions towards which I am advancing, gives me a foretaste of those icy climes. Inspirited by this wind of promise, my day dreams become more fervent and vivid. I try in vain to be persuaded that the pole is the seat of frost and desolation; it ever presents itself to my imagination as the region of beauty and delight. There, Margaret, the sun is for ever visible; its broad disk just skirting the horizon, and diffusing a perpetual splendour. There—for with your leave, my sister, I will put some trust in preceding navigators—there snow and frost are banished; and, sailing over a calm sea, we may be wafted to a land surpassing in wonders and in beauty every region hitherto discovered on the habitable globe.[2] Its productions and features may be without example, as the phaenomena of the heavenly bodies undoubtedly are in those undiscovered solitudes. What may not be expected in a country of eternal light? I may there discover the wondrous

---

1 As Robinson shows (1: lxv–lxvi), the year is 1796; Walton's story begins at about the date of Shelley's conception and ends thirteen days after her birth (two days after her mother's death).

2 The classical notion of a temperate Hyperborean zone still retained some credibility in Shelley's time. It also appears in P.B. Shelley, *The Revolt of Islam* (1818) I.xlvii–liv, whose composition overlaps with that of *Frankenstein.*

power which attracts the needle;[1] and may regulate a thousand celestial observations, that require only this voyage to render their seeming eccentricities consistent for ever. I shall satiate my ardent curiosity with the sight of a part of the world never before visited, and may tread a land never before imprinted by the foot of man. These are my enticements, and they are sufficient to conquer all fear of danger or death, and to induce me to commence this laborious voyage with the joy a child feels when he embarks in a little boat, with his holiday mates, on an expedition of discovery up his native river. But, supposing all these conjectures to be false, you cannot contest the inestimable benefit which I shall confer on all mankind to the last generation, by discovering a passage near the pole to those countries, to reach which at present so many months are requisite; or by ascertaining the secret of the magnet, which, if at all possible, can only be effected by an undertaking such as mine.

These reflections have dispelled the agitation with which I began my letter, and I feel my heart glow with an enthusiasm which elevates me to heaven; for nothing contributes so much to tranquillize the mind as a steady purpose,—a point on which the soul may fix its intellectual eye. This expedition has been the favourite dream of my early years. I have read with ardour the accounts of the various voyages which have been made in the prospect of arriving at the North Pacific Ocean through the seas which surround the pole. You may remember, that a history of all the voyages made for purposes of discovery composed the whole of our good uncle Thomas's library. My education was neglected, yet I was passionately fond of reading. These volumes were my study day and night, and my familiarity with them increased that regret which I had felt, as a child, on learning that my father's dying injunction had forbidden my uncle to allow me to embark in a sea-faring life.

These visions faded when I perused, for the first time, those poets whose effusions entranced my soul, and lifted it to heaven. I also became a poet, and for one year lived in a Paradise of my own creation; I imagined that I also might obtain a niche in the temple where the names of Homer and Shakespeare are consecrated. You are well acquainted with my failure, and how heavily I bore the disappointment. But just at that time I inherited the

---

1 Cf. Darwin's speculations on electromagnetism, *The Economy of Vegetation* (1791) II.193n.

fortune of my cousin, and my thoughts were turned into the channel of their earlier bent.

Six years have passed since I resolved on my present undertaking. I can, even now, remember the hour from which I dedicated myself to this great enterprise. I commenced by inuring my body to hardship. I accompanied the whale-fishers on several expeditions to the North Sea; I voluntarily endured cold, famine, thirst, and want of sleep; I often worked harder than the common sailors during the day, and devoted my nights to the study of mathematics, the theory of medicine, and those branches of physical science from which a naval adventurer might derive the greatest practical advantage. Twice I actually hired myself as an under-mate in a Greenland whaler, and acquitted myself to admiration. I must own I felt a little proud, when my captain offered me the second dignity in the vessel, and entreated me to remain with the greatest earnestness; so valuable did he consider my services.

And now, dear Margaret, do I not deserve to accomplish some great purpose. My life might have been passed in ease and luxury; but I preferred glory to every enticement that wealth placed in my path. Oh, that some encouraging voice would answer in the affirmative! My courage and my resolution is firm; but my hopes fluctuate, and my spirits are often depressed. I am about to proceed on a long and difficult voyage; the emergencies of which will demand all my fortitude: I am required not only to raise the spirits of others, but sometimes to sustain my own, when their's are failing.

This is the most favourable period for travelling in Russia. They fly quickly over the snow in their sledges; the motion is pleasant, and, in my opinion, far more agreeable than that of an English stage-coach. The cold is not excessive, if you are wrapt in furs, a dress which I have already adopted; for there is a great difference between walking the deck and remaining seated motionless for hours, when no exercise prevents the blood from actually freezing in your veins. I have no ambition to lose my life on the post-road between St. Petersburgh and Archangel.

I shall depart for the latter town in a fortnight or three weeks; and my intention is to hire a ship there, which can easily be done by paying the insurance for the owner, and to engage as many sailors as I think necessary among those who are accustomed to the whale-fishing. I do not intend to sail until the month of June: and when shall I return? Ah, dear sister, how can I answer this question? If I succeed, many, many months, perhaps years, will pass before you and I may meet. If I fail, you will see me again soon, or never.

Farewell, my dear, excellent, Margaret. Heaven shower down blessings on you, and save me, that I may again and again testify my gratitude for all your love and kindness.

Your affectionate brother,
R. WALTON

LETTER II.

To Mrs. SAVILLE, *England.*

Archangel, 28th March, 17—.[1]

HOW slowly the time passes here, encompassed as I am by frost and snow; yet a second step is taken towards my enterprise. I have hired a vessel, and am occupied in collecting my sailors; those whom I have already engaged appear to be men on whom I can depend, and are certainly possessed of dauntless courage.

But I have one want which I have never yet been able to satisfy; and the absence of the object of which I now feel as a most severe evil. I have no friend, Margaret: when I am glowing with the enthusiasm of success, there will be none to participate my joy; if I am assailed by disappointment, no one will endeavour to sustain me in dejection. I shall commit my thoughts to paper, it is true; but that is a poor medium for the communication of feeling. I desire the company of a man who could sympathize with me; whose eyes would reply to mine. You may deem me romantic, my dear sister, but I bitterly feel the want of a friend. I have no one near me, gentle yet courageous, possessed of a cultivated as well as of a capacious mind, whose tastes are like my own, to approve or amend my plans. How would such a friend repair the faults of your poor brother! I am too ardent in execution, and too impatient of difficulties. But it is a still greater evil to me that I am self-educated: for the first fourteen years of my life I ran wild on a common, and read nothing but our uncle Thomas's books of voyages. At that age I became acquainted with the celebrated poets of our own country; but it was only when it

---

1 I.e., 1797 (Wollstonecraft and Godwin were married on 29 March).

had ceased to be in my power to derive its most important benefits from such a conviction, that I perceived the necessity of becoming acquainted with more languages than that of my native country. Now I am twenty-eight, and am in reality more illiterate than many school-boys of fifteen. It is true that I have thought more, and that my day dreams are more extended and magnificent; but they want (as the painters call it) *keeping*;[1] and I greatly need a friend who would have sense enough not to despise me as romantic, and affection enough for me to endeavour to regulate my mind.

Well, these are useless complaints; I shall certainly find no friend on the wide ocean, nor even here in Archangel, among merchants and seamen. Yet some feelings, unallied to the dross of human nature, beat even in these rugged bosoms. My lieutenant, for instance, is a man of wonderful courage and enterprise; he is madly desirous of glory. He is an Englishman, and in the midst of national and professional prejudices, unsoftened by cultivation, retains some of the noblest endowments of humanity. I first became acquainted with him on board a whale vessel: finding that he was unemployed in this city, I easily engaged him to assist in my enterprise.

The master is a person of an excellent disposition, and is remarkable in the ship for his gentleness, and the mildness of his discipline. He is, indeed, of so amiable a nature, that he will not hunt (a favourite, and almost the only amusement here), because he cannot endure to spill blood. He is, moreover, heroically generous. Some years ago he loved a young Russian lady, of moderate fortune; and having amassed a considerable sum in prize-money,[2] the father of the girl consented to the match. He saw his mistress once before the destined ceremony; but she was bathed in tears, and, throwing herself at his feet, entreated him to spare her, confessing at the same time that she loved another, but that he was poor, and that her father would never consent to the union. My generous friend reassured the suppliant, and on being informed of the name of her lover instantly abandoned his pursuit. He had already bought a farm with his money, on which he had designed to pass the remainder of his life; but he bestowed the whole on his rival, together with the remains of his prize-money to purchase stock, and then himself solicited the young

---

1 Perspective.
2 The bounty distributed, according to rank, among the officers and crew of a ship that captured an enemy vessel.

woman's father to consent to her marriage with her lover. But the old man decidedly refused, thinking himself bound in honour to my friend; who, when he found the father inexorable, quitted his country, nor returned until he heard that his former mistress was married according to her inclinations.[1] "What a noble fellow!" you will exclaim. He is so; but then he has passed all his life on board a vessel, and has scarcely an idea beyond the rope and the shroud.[2]

But do not suppose that, because I complain a little, or because I can conceive a consolation for my toils which I may never know, that I am wavering in my resolutions. Those are as fixed as fate; and my voyage is only now delayed until the weather shall permit my embarkation. The winter has been dreadfully severe; but the spring promises well, and it is considered as a remarkably early season; so that, perhaps, I may sail sooner than I expected. I shall do nothing rashly; you know me sufficiently to confide in my prudence and considerateness whenever the safety of others is committed to my care.

I cannot describe to you my sensations on the near prospect of my undertaking. It is impossible to communicate to you a conception of the trembling sensation, half pleasurable and half fearful, with which I am preparing to depart. I am going to unexplored regions, to "the land of mist and snow";[3] but I shall kill no albatross, therefore do not be alarmed for my safety.

Shall I meet you again, after having traversed immense seas, and returned by the most southern cape of Africa or America? I dare not expect such success, yet I cannot bear to look on the reverse of the picture. Continue to write to me by every opportunity: I may receive your letters (though the chance is very doubtful) on some occasions when I need them most to support my spirits. I love you very tenderly. Remember me with affection, should you never hear from me again.

Your affectionate brother,
ROBERT WALTON.

---

1 Cf. Wollstonecraft's account of the generosity of Crown Prince Frederik of Denmark in *Letters Written during a Short Residence in Sweden, Norway, and Denmark* (1796) VII.

2 Cf. the magnanimous jailer in Godwin, *St. Leon* 237; XXII.

3 S.T. Coleridge (1772-1834), "The Rime of the Ancyent Marinere" (1798) 408.

LETTER III.

To Mrs. SAVILLE, England.

July 7th, 17—.

MY DEAR SISTER,

I WRITE a few lines in haste, to say that I am safe, and well advanced on my voyage. This letter will reach England by a merchant-man now on its homeward voyage from Archangel; more fortunate than I, who may not see my native land, perhaps, for many years. I am, however, in good spirits: my men are bold, and apparently firm of purpose; nor do the floating sheets of ice that continually pass us, indicating the dangers of the region towards which we are advancing, appear to dismay them. We have already reached a very high latitude; but it is the height of summer, and although not so warm as in England, the southern gales, which blow us speedily towards those shores which I so ardently desire to attain, breathe a degree of renovating warmth which I had not expected.

No incidents have hitherto befallen us, that would make a figure in a letter. One or two stiff gales, and the breaking of a mast, are accidents which experienced navigators scarcely remember to record; and I shall be well content, if nothing worse happen to us during our voyage.

Adieu, my dear Margaret. Be assured, that for my own sake, as well as your's, I will not rashly encounter danger. I will be cool, persevering, and prudent.

Remember me to all my English friends.

Most affectionately yours,
R.W.

LETTER IV.

To Mrs. SAVILLE, England.

August 5th, 17—.

SO strange an accident has happened to us, that I cannot forbear recording it, although it is very probable that you will see me before these papers can come into your possession.

Last Monday (July 31st), we were nearly surrounded by ice, which closed in the ship on all sides, scarcely leaving her the sea room in which she floated. Our situation was somewhat dangerous, especially as we were compassed round by a very thick fog. We accordingly lay to, hoping that some change would take place in the atmosphere and weather.

About two o'clock the mist cleared away, and we beheld, stretched out in every direction, vast and irregular plains of ice, which seemed to have no end. Some of my comrades groaned, and my own mind began to grow watchful with anxious thoughts, when a strange sight suddenly attracted our attention, and diverted our solicitude from our own situation. We perceived a low carriage, fixed on a sledge and drawn by dogs, pass on towards the north, at the distance of half a mile: a being which had the shape of a man, but apparently of gigantic stature, sat in the sledge, and guided the dogs. We watched the rapid progress of the traveller with our telescopes, until he was lost among the distant inequalities of the ice.

This appearance excited our unqualified wonder. We were, as we believed, many hundred miles from any land; but this apparition seemed to denote that it was not, in reality, so distant as we had supposed. Shut in, however, by ice, it was impossible to follow his track, which we had observed with the greatest attention.

About two hours after this occurrence, we heard the ground sea;[1] and before night the ice broke, and freed our ship. We, however, lay to until the morning, fearing to encounter in the dark those large loose masses which float about after the breaking up of the ice. I profited of this time to rest for a few hours.

In the morning, however, as soon as it was light, I went upon deck, and found all the sailors busy on one side of the vessel, apparently talking to some one in the sea. It was, in fact, a sledge, like that we had seen before, which had drifted towards us in the night, on a large fragment of ice. Only one dog remained alive; but there was a human being within it, whom the sailors were persuading to enter the vessel. He was not, as the other traveller seemed to be, a savage inhabitant of some undiscovered island, but an European. When I appeared on deck, the master said, "Here is our captain, and he will not allow you to perish on the open sea."

---

1 A "heavy sea in which large waves rise and dash upon the coast without apparent cause" (*OED*).

On perceiving me, the stranger addressed me in English, although with a foreign accent. "Before I come on board your vessel," said he, "will you have the kindness to inform me whither you are bound?"

You may conceive my astonishment on hearing such a question addressed to me from a man on the brink of destruction, and to whom I should have supposed that my vessel would have been a resource which he would not have exchanged for the most precious wealth the earth can afford. I replied, however, that we were on a voyage of discovery towards the northern pole.

Upon hearing this he appeared satisfied, and consented to come on board. Good God! Margaret, if you had seen the man who thus capitulated for his safety, your surprise would have been boundless. His limbs were nearly frozen, and his body dreadfully emaciated by fatigue and suffering. I never saw a man in so wretched a condition. We attempted to carry him into the cabin; but as soon as he had quitted the fresh air, he fainted. We accordingly brought him back to the deck, and restored him to animation by rubbing him with brandy, and forcing him to swallow a small quantity. As soon as he shewed signs of life, we wrapped him up in blankets, and placed him near the chimney of the kitchen-stove.[1] By slow degrees he recovered, and ate a little soup, which restored him wonderfully.

Two days passed in this manner before he was able to speak; and I often feared that his sufferings had deprived him of understanding. When he had in some measure recovered, I removed him to my own cabin, and attended on him as much as my duty would permit. I never saw a more interesting creature: his eyes have generally an expression of wildness, and even madness; but there are moments when, if any one performs an act of kindness towards him, or does him any the most trifling service, his whole countenance is lighted up, as it were, with a beam of benevolence and sweetness that I never saw equalled. But he is generally melancholy and despairing; and sometimes he gnashes his teeth, as if impatient of the weight of woes that oppresses him.

When my guest was a little recovered, I had great trouble to keep off the men, who wished to ask him a thousand questions; but I would not allow him to be tormented by their idle curiosity, in a state of body and mind whose restoration evidently depended upon entire repose. Once, however, the lieutenant

---

1 Cf. Shelley's dream of 19 March 1815, *Journals* 1: 70.

asked, Why he had come so far upon the ice in so strange a vehicle?

His countenance instantly assumed an aspect of the deepest gloom; and he replied, "To seek one who fled from me."

"And did the man whom you pursued travel in the same fashion?"

"Yes."

"Then I fancy we have seen him; for, the day before we picked you up, we saw some dogs drawing a sledge, with a man in it, across the ice."

This aroused the stranger's attention; and he asked a multitude of questions concerning the route which the daemon, as he called him, had pursued. Soon after, when he was alone with me, he said, "I have, doubtless, excited your curiosity, as well as that of these good people; but you are too considerate to make inquiries."

"Certainly; it would indeed be very impertinent and inhuman in me to trouble you with any inquisitiveness of mine."

"And yet you rescued me from a strange and perilous situation; you have benevolently restored me to life."

Soon after this he inquired, if I thought that the breaking up of the ice had destroyed the other sledge? I replied, that I could not answer with any degree of certainty; for the ice had not broken until near midnight, and the traveller might have arrived at a place of safety before that time; but of this I could not judge.

From this time the stranger seemed very eager to be upon deck, to watch for the sledge which had before appeared; but I have persuaded him to remain in the cabin, for he is far too weak to sustain the rawness of the atmosphere. But I have promised that some one should watch for him, and give him instant notice if any new object should appear in sight.

Such is my journal of what relates to this strange occurrence up to the present day. The stranger has gradually improved in health, but is very silent, and appears uneasy when any one except myself enters his cabin. Yet his manners are so conciliating and gentle, that the sailors are all interested in him, although they have had very little communication with him. For my own part, I begin to love him as a brother; and his constant and deep grief fills me with sympathy and compassion. He must have been a noble creature in his better days, being even now in wreck so attractive and amiable.

I said in one of my letters, my dear Margaret, that I should find no friend on the wide ocean; yet I have found a man who, before his spirit had been broken by misery, I should have been happy to have possessed as the brother of my heart.

I shall continue my journal concerning the stranger at intervals, should I have any fresh incidents to record.

August 13th, 17—.

My affection for my guest increases every day. He excites at once my admiration and my pity to an astonishing degree. How can I see so noble a creature destroyed by misery without feeling the most poignant grief? He is so gentle, yet so wise; his mind is so cultivated; and when he speaks, although his words are culled with the choicest art, yet they flow with rapidity and unparalleled eloquence.

He is now much recovered from his illness, and is continually on the deck, apparently watching for the sledge that preceded his own. Yet, although unhappy, he is not so utterly occupied by his own misery, but that he interests himself deeply in the employments of others. He has asked me many questions concerning my design; and I have related my little history frankly to him. He appeared pleased with the confidence, and suggested several alterations in my plan, which I shall find exceedingly useful. There is no pedantry in his manner; but all he does appears to spring solely from the interest he instinctively takes in the welfare of those who surround him. He is often overcome by gloom, and then he sits by himself, and tries to overcome all that is sullen or unsocial in his humour. These paroxysms pass from him like a cloud from before the sun, though his dejection never leaves him. I have endeavoured to win his confidence; and I trust that I have succeeded. One day I mentioned to him the desire I had always felt of finding a friend who might sympathize with me, and direct me by his counsel. I said, I did not belong to that class of men who are offended by advice. "I am self-educated, and perhaps I hardly rely sufficiently upon my own powers. I wish therefore that my companion should be wiser and more experienced than myself, to confirm and support me; nor have I believed it impossible to find a true friend."

"I agree with you," replied the stranger, "in believing that friendship is not only a desirable, but a possible acquisition. I once had a friend, the most noble of human creatures, and am entitled, therefore, to judge respecting friendship. You have hope, and the world before you,[1] and have no cause for despair. But I—I have lost every thing, and cannot begin life anew."

---

1 An ironic allusion to Milton, *Paradise Lost* XII.646.

As he said this, his countenance became expressive of a calm settled grief, that touched me to the heart. But he was silent, and presently retired to his cabin.

Even broken in spirit as he is, no one can feel more deeply than he does the beauties of nature. The starry sky, the sea, and every sight afforded by these wonderful regions, seems still to have the power of elevating his soul from earth. Such a man has a double existence: he may suffer misery, and be overwhelmed by disappointments; yet when he has retired into himself, he will be like a celestial spirit, that has a halo around him, within whose circle no grief or folly ventures.

Will you laugh at the enthusiasm I express concerning this divine wanderer? If you do, you must have certainly lost that simplicity which was once your characteristic charm. Yet, if you will, smile at the warmth of my expressions, while I find every day new causes for repeating them.

August 19th, 17—.

Yesterday the stranger said to me, "You may easily perceive, Captain Walton, that I have suffered great and unparalleled misfortunes. I had determined, once, that the memory of these evils should die with me; but you have won me to alter my determination. You seek for knowledge and wisdom, as I once did; and I ardently hope that the gratification of your wishes may not be a serpent to sting you, as mine has been. I do not know that the relation of my misfortunes will be useful to you, yet, if you are inclined, listen to my tale. I believe that the strange incidents connected with it will afford a view of nature, which may enlarge your faculties and understanding. You will hear of powers and occurrences, such as you have been accustomed to believe impossible: but I do not doubt that my tale conveys in its series internal evidence of the truth of the events of which it is composed."

You may easily conceive that I was much gratified by the offered communication; yet I could not endure that he should renew his grief by a recital of his misfortunes. I felt the greatest eagerness to hear the promised narrative, partly from curiosity, and partly from a strong desire to ameliorate his fate, if it were in my power. I expressed these feelings in my answer.

"I thank you," he replied, "for your sympathy, but it is useless; my fate is nearly fulfilled. I wait but for one event, and then I shall repose in peace. I understand your feeling," continued he, perceiving that I wished to interrupt him; "but you are mistaken, my friend, if thus you will allow me to name you; nothing can alter my destiny: listen to my history, and you will perceive how irrevocably it is determined."

He then told me, that he would commence his narrative the next day when I should be at leisure. This promise drew from me the warmest thanks. I have resolved every night, when I am not engaged, to record, as nearly as possible in his own words, what he has related during the day. If I should be engaged, I will at least make notes. This manuscript will doubtless afford you the greatest pleasure: but to me, who know him, and who hear it from his own lips, with what interest and sympathy shall I read it in some future day!

FRANKENSTEIN;
OR,
THE MODERN PROMETHEUS.

CHAPTER I.

I AM by birth a Genevese; and my family is one of the most distinguished of that republic. My ancestors had been for many years counsellors and syndics;[1] and my father had filled several public situations with honour and reputation. He was respected by all who knew him for his integrity and indefatigable attention to public business. He passed his younger days perpetually occupied by the affairs of his country; and it was not until the decline of life that he thought of marrying, and bestowing on the state sons who might carry his virtues and his name down to posterity.

As the circumstances of his marriage illustrate his character, I cannot refrain from relating them. One of his most intimate friends was a merchant, who, from a flourishing state, fell, through numerous mischances, into poverty. This man, whose name was Beaufort, was of a proud and unbending disposition, and could not bear to live in poverty and oblivion in the same country where he had formerly been distinguished for his rank and magnificence. Having paid his debts, therefore, in the most honourable manner, he retreated with his daughter to the town of Lucerne, where he lived unknown and in wretchedness. My father loved Beaufort with the truest friendship, and was deeply grieved by his retreat in these unfortunate circumstances. He grieved also for the loss of his society, and resolved to seek him out and endeavour to persuade him to begin the world again through his credit and assistance.

Beaufort had taken effectual measures to conceal himself; and it was ten months before my father discovered his abode. Overjoyed at this discovery, he hastened to the house, which was situated in a mean street, near the Reuss. But when he entered, misery and despair alone welcomed him. Beaufort had saved but a very small sum of money from the wreck of his fortunes; but it was sufficient to provide him with sustenance for some months, and in the mean time he hoped to procure some respectable employment in a merchant's house. The interval was consequently spent in inaction; his grief only became more deep and

---

1 Genevan legislators.

rankling, when he had leisure for reflection; and at length it took so fast hold of his mind, that at the end of three months he lay on a bed of sickness, incapable of any exertion.

His daughter attended him with the greatest tenderness; but she saw with despair that their little fund was rapidly decreasing, and that there was no other prospect of support. But Caroline Beaufort possessed a mind of an uncommon mould; and her courage rose to support her in her adversity. She procured plain work;[1] she plaited straw; and by various means contrived to earn a pittance scarcely sufficient to support life.

Several months passed in this manner. Her father grew worse; her time was more entirely occupied in attending him; her means of subsistence decreased; and in the tenth month her father died in her arms, leaving her an orphan and a beggar. This last blow overcame her; and she knelt by Beaufort's coffin, weeping bitterly, when my father entered the chamber. He came like a protecting spirit to the poor girl, who committed herself to his care, and after the interment of his friend he conducted her to Geneva, and placed her under the protection of a relation. Two years after this event Caroline became his wife.

When my father became a husband and a parent, he found his time so occupied by the duties of his new situation, that he relinquished many of his public employments, and devoted himself to the education of his children. Of these I was the eldest, and the destined successor to all his labours and utility. No creature could have more tender parents than mine. My improvement and health were their constant care, especially as I remained for several years their only child. But before I continue my narrative, I must record an incident which took place when I was four years of age.

My father had a sister, whom he tenderly loved, and who had married early in life an Italian gentleman. Soon after her marriage, she had accompanied her husband into his native country, and for some years my father had very little communication with her. About the time I mentioned she died; and a few months afterwards he received a letter from her husband, acquainting him with his intention of marrying an Italian lady, and requesting my father to take charge of the infant Elizabeth, the only child of his deceased sister. "It is my wish," he said, "that you should consider her as your own daughter, and educate her thus. Her mother's fortune is secured to her, the documents of which I will

---

1 Plain sewing.

commit to your keeping. Reflect upon this proposition; and decide whether you would prefer educating your niece yourself to her being brought up by a stepmother."

My father did not hesitate, and immediately went to Italy, that he might accompany the little Elizabeth to her future home. I have often heard my mother say, that she was at that time the most beautiful child she had ever seen, and shewed signs even then of a gentle and affectionate disposition. These indications, and a desire to bind as closely as possible the ties of domestic love, determined my mother to consider Elizabeth as my future wife; a design which she never found reason to repent.[1]

From this time Elizabeth Lavenza became my playfellow, and, as we grew older, my friend. She was docile and good tempered, yet gay and playful as a summer insect. Although she was lively and animated, her feelings were strong and deep, and her disposition uncommonly affectionate. No one could better enjoy liberty, yet no one could submit with more grace than she did to constraint and caprice. Her imagination was luxuriant, yet her capability of application was great. Her person was the image of her mind; her hazel eyes, although as lively as a bird's, possessed an attractive softness. Her figure was light and airy; and, though capable of enduring great fatigue, she appeared the most fragile creature in the world. While I admired her understanding and fancy, I loved to tend on her, as I should on a favourite animal; and I never saw so much grace both of person and mind united to so little pretension. Every one adored Elizabeth. If the servants had any request to make, it was always through her intercession. We were strangers to any species of disunion and dispute; for although there was a great dissimilitude in our characters, there was an harmony in that very dissimilitude. I was more calm and philosophical than my companion; yet my temper was not so yielding. My application was of longer endurance; but it was not so severe whilst it endured. I delighted in investigating the facts relative to the actual world; she busied herself in following the aërial creations of the poets. The world was to me a secret, which I desired to discover; to her it was a vacancy, which she sought to people with imaginations of her own.[2]

---

1 Cf. the story of Laura in Godwin, *Caleb Williams* 290-91 (III.xiii).

2 Cf. Wollstonecraft's critique of women's education, *Vindication* 130-31; II (Appendix A.2.c), and Caleb's fatal curiosity in Godwin, *Caleb Williams* 4 (I.i).

My brothers were considerably younger than myself; but I had a friend in one of my schoolfellows, who compensated for this deficiency. Henry Clerval was the son of a merchant of Geneva, an intimate friend of my father. He was a boy of singular talent and fancy. I remember, when he was nine years old, he wrote a fairy tale, which was the delight and amazement of all his companions. His favourite study consisted in books of chivalry and romance; and when very young, I can remember, that we used to act plays composed by him out of these favourite books, the principal characters of which were Orlando,[1] Robin Hood, Amadis,[2] and St. George.

No youth could have passed more happily than mine. My parents were indulgent, and my companions amiable. Our studies were never forced; and by some means we always had an end placed in view, which excited us to ardour in the prosecution of them. It was by this method, and not by emulation, that we were urged to application. Elizabeth was not incited to apply herself to drawing, that her companions might not outstrip her; but through the desire of pleasing her aunt, by the representation of some favourite scene done by her own hand. We learned Latin and English, that we might read the writings in those languages; and so far from study being made odious to us through punishment, we loved application, and our amusements would have been the labours of other children. Perhaps we did not read so many books, or learn languages so quickly, as those who are disciplined according to the ordinary methods; but what we learned was impressed the more deeply on our memories.

In this description of our domestic circle I include Henry Clerval; for he was constantly with us. He went to school with me, and generally passed the afternoon at our house; for being an only child, and destitute of companions at home, his father was well pleased that he should find associates at our house; and we were never completely happy when Clerval was absent.

I feel pleasure in dwelling on the recollections of childhood, before misfortune had tainted my mind, and changed its bright visions of extensive usefulness into gloomy and narrow reflections upon self. But, in drawing the picture of my early days, I

---

1 The hero of *Orlando Furioso* (1532), by Ludovico Ariosto (1474-1533).
2 The hero of *Amadis de Gaula*, a traditional Spanish or Portuguese chivalric romance, written down by Garcia de Montalvo in the later fifteenth century and translated by Robert Southey (1774-1843) in 1803.

must not omit to record those events which led, by insensible steps to my after tale of misery: for when I would account to myself for the birth of that passion, which afterwards ruled my destiny, I find it arise, like a mountain river, from ignoble and almost forgotten sources; but, swelling as it proceeded, it became the torrent which, in its course, has swept away all my hopes and joys.

Natural philosophy[1] is the genius that has regulated my fate; I desire therefore, in this narration, to state those facts which led to my predilection for that science. When I was thirteen years of age, we all went on a party of pleasure to the baths near Thonon: the inclemency of the weather obliged us to remain a day confined to the inn. In this house I chanced to find a volume of the works of Cornelius Agrippa.[2] I opened it with apathy; the theory which he attempts to demonstrate, and the wonderful facts which he relates, soon changed this feeling into enthusiasm. A new light seemed to dawn upon my mind; and, bounding with joy, I communicated my discovery to my father. I cannot help remarking here the many opportunities instructors possess of directing the attention of their pupils to useful knowledge, which they utterly neglect. My father looked carelessly at the title-page of my book, and said, "Ah! Cornelius Agrippa! My dear Victor, do not waste your time upon this; it is sad trash."

If, instead of this remark, my father had taken the pains to explain to me, that the principles of Agrippa had been entirely exploded, and that a modern system of science had been introduced, which possessed much greater powers than the ancient, because the powers of the latter were chimerical, while those of the former were real and practical; under such circumstances, I should certainly have thrown Agrippa aside, and, with my imagination warmed as it was, should probably have applied myself to the more rational theory of chemistry which has resulted from modern discoveries. It is even possible, that the train of my ideas would never have received the fatal impulse that led to my ruin. But the cursory glance my father had taken of my volume by no means assured me that he was acquainted with its contents; and I continued to read with the greatest avidity.

---

1 The common eighteenth-century term for natural science.

2 Henricus Cornelius Agrippa of Nettesheim (1486-1535), author of *De Occulta Philosophia* (1529) and *De Vanitate Scientiarum* (1530). Cf. Godwin, *St. Leon* 307; XXIX.

When I returned home, my first care was to procure the whole works of this author, and afterwards of Paracelsus and Albertus Magnus.[1] I read and studied the wild fancies of these writers with delight; they appeared to me treasures known to few beside myself; and although I often wished to communicate these secret stores of knowledge to my father, yet his indefinite censure of my favourite Agrippa always withheld me. I disclosed my discoveries to Elizabeth, therefore, under a promise of strict secrecy; but she did not interest herself in the subject, and I was left by her to pursue my studies alone.

It may appear very strange, that a disciple of Albertus Magnus should arise in the eighteenth century; but our family was not scientifical, and I had not attended any of the lectures given at the schools of Geneva. My dreams were therefore undisturbed by reality; and I entered with the greatest diligence into the search of the philosopher's stone and the elixir of life.[2] But the latter obtained my most undivided attention: wealth was an inferior object; but what glory would attend the discovery, if I could banish disease from the human frame, and render man invulnerable to any but a violent death!

Nor were these my only visions. The raising of ghosts or devils was a promise liberally accorded by my favourite authors, the fulfilment of which I most eagerly sought; and if my incantations were always unsuccessful, I attributed the failure rather to my own inexperience and mistake, than to a want of skill or fidelity in my instructors.[3]

The natural phaenomena that take place every day before our eyes did not escape my examinations. Distillation, and the wonderful effects of steam,[4] processes of which my favourite authors were utterly ignorant, excited my astonishment; but my utmost wonder was engaged by some experiments on an air-pump, which I saw employed by a gentleman whom we were in the habit of visiting.

The ignorance of the early philosophers on these and several other points served to decrease their credit with me: but I could

---

1 Theophrastus Bombastus von Hohenheim (1493?-1541), known as Paracelsus, Swiss physician, alchemist, and mystic; and Albertus Magnus (1193?-1280), German Dominican monk, philosopher, and teacher of Thomas Aquinas. Both authors were favourites of the young Percy Shelley.

2 The hero of Godwin's *St. Leon* (1799) acquires both secrets.

3 Cf. P.B. Shelley, "Hymn to Intellectual Beauty" (1816) 49-54.

4 Cf. Darwin on steam power, *The Economy of Vegetation* I.289-96.

not entirely throw them aside, before some other system should occupy their place in my mind.

When I was about fifteen years old, we had retired to our house near Belrive, when we witnessed a most violent and terrible thunder-storm. It advanced from behind the mountains of Jura; and the thunder burst at once with frightful loudness from various quarters of the heavens. I remained, while the storm lasted, watching its progress with curiosity and delight. As I stood at the door, on a sudden I beheld a stream of fire issue from an old and beautiful oak, which stood about twenty yards from our house; and so soon as the dazzling light vanished, the oak had disappeared, and nothing remained but a blasted stump. When we visited it the next morning, we found the tree shattered in a singular manner. It was not splintered by the shock, but entirely reduced to thin ribbands of wood. I never beheld any thing so utterly destroyed.

The catastrophe of this tree excited my extreme astonishment; and I eagerly inquired of my father the nature and origin of thunder and lightning. He replied, "Electricity"; describing at the same time the various effects of that power. He constructed a small electrical machine, and exhibited a few experiments; he made also a kite, with a wire and string, which drew down that fluid from the clouds.[1]

This last stroke completed the overthrow of Cornelius Agrippa, Albertus Magnus, and Paracelsus, who had so long reigned the lords of my imagination. But by some fatality I did not feel inclined to commence the study of any modern system; and this disinclination was influenced by the following circumstance.

My father expressed a wish that I should attend a course of lectures upon natural philosophy, to which I cheerfully consented. Some accident prevented my attending these lectures until the course was nearly finished. The lecture, being therefore one of the last, was entirely incomprehensible to me. The professor discoursed with the greatest fluency of potassium and boron, of sulphates and oxyds, terms to which I could affix no idea; and I became disgusted with the science of natural philosophy, although I still read Pliny and Buffon with delight, authors, in my estimation, of nearly equal interest and utility.[2]

---

1 Cf. Darwin, *The Economy of Vegetation* I.362-70, 383-412 (Appendix B.1.a).

2 Caius Plinius Secundus (23-79), author of the encyclopedic *Historia Naturalis*; and Georges-Louis Leclerc, comte de Buffon (1707-88), author of *Histoire naturelle* (44 vols., 1749-1804). Shelley read both in 1817.

My occupations at this age were principally the mathematics, and most of the branches of study appertaining to that science. I was busily employed in learning languages; Latin was already familiar to me, and I began to read some of the easiest Greek authors without the help of a lexicon. I also perfectly understood English and German. This is the list of my accomplishments at the age of seventeen; and you may conceive that my hours were fully employed in acquiring and maintaining a knowledge of this various literature.

Another task also devolved upon me, when I became the instructor of my brothers. Ernest was six years younger than myself, and was my principal pupil. He had been afflicted with ill health from his infancy, through which Elizabeth and I had been his constant nurses: his disposition was gentle, but he was incapable of any severe application. William, the youngest of our family, was yet an infant, and the most beautiful little fellow in the world; his lively blue eyes, dimpled cheeks, and endearing manners, inspired the tenderest affection.

Such was our domestic circle, from which care and pain seemed for ever banished. My father directed our studies, and my mother partook of our enjoyments. Neither of us possessed the slightest pre-eminence over the other; the voice of command was never heard amongst us; but mutual affection engaged us all to comply with and obey the slightest desire of each other.

[handwritten margin note: Father on strict education]

CHAPTER II.

WHEN I had attained the age of seventeen, my parents resolved that I should become a student at the university of Ingolstadt.[1] I had hitherto attended the schools of Geneva; but my father thought it necessary, for the completion of my education, that I should be made acquainted with other customs than those of my native country. My departure was therefore fixed at an early date; but, before the day resolved upon could arrive, the first misfortune of my life occurred—an omen, as it were, of my future misery.

---

1 The University of Ingolstadt (1472-1800), on the Danube in Upper Bavaria, had a medical school, but it was more famous, or infamous, as the headquarters of the Illuminati, a revolutionary secret society founded by Adam Weishaupt in 1776. Victor goes there in 1789.

Elizabeth had caught the scarlet fever; but her illness was not severe, and she quickly recovered. During her confinement, many arguments had been urged to persuade my mother to refrain from attending upon her. She had, at first, yielded to our entreaties; but when she heard that her favourite was recovering, she could no longer debar herself from her society, and entered her chamber long before the danger of infection was past. The consequences of this imprudence were fatal. On the third day my mother sickened; her fever was very malignant, and the looks of her attendants prognosticated the worst event. On her death-bed the fortitude and benignity of this admirable woman did not desert her. She joined the hands of Elizabeth and myself: "My children," she said, "my firmest hopes of future happiness were placed on the prospect of your union. This expectation will now be the consolation of your father. Elizabeth, my love, you must supply my place to your younger cousins. Alas! I regret that I am taken from you; and, happy and beloved as I have been, is it not hard to quit you all? But these are not thoughts befitting me; I will endeavour to resign myself cheerfully to death, and will indulge a hope of meeting you in another world."[1]

She died calmly; and her countenance expressed affection even in death. I need not describe the feelings of those whose dearest ties are rent by that most irreparable evil, the void that presents itself to the soul, and the despair that is exhibited on the countenance. It is so long before the mind can persuade itself that she, whom we saw every day, and whose very existence appeared a part of our own, can have departed for ever—that the brightness of a beloved eye can have been extinguished, and the sound of a voice so familiar, and dear to the ear, can be hushed, never more to be heard. These are the reflections of the first days; but when the lapse of time proves the reality of the evil, then the actual bitterness of grief commences. Yet from whom has not that rude hand rent away some dear connexion; and why should I describe a sorrow which all have felt, and must feel? The time at length arrives, when grief is rather an indulgence than a necessity; and the smile that plays upon the lips, although it may be deemed a sacrilege, is not banished. My mother was dead, but we had still duties which we ought to perform; we must continue our course with the rest, and learn to think ourselves fortunate, whilst one remains whom the spoiler has not seized.

---

1 Cf. Goethe, *The Sorrows of Werter* 102-08; Letter XXXVII (Appendix C.2.b).

My journey to Ingolstadt, which had been deferred by these events, was now again determined upon. I obtained from my father a respite of some weeks. This period was spent sadly; my mother's death, and my speedy departure, depressed our spirits; but Elizabeth endeavoured to renew the spirit of cheerfulness in our little society. Since the death of her aunt, her mind had acquired new firmness and vigour. She determined to fulfil her duties with the greatest exactness; and she felt that that most imperious duty, of rendering her uncle and cousins happy, had devolved upon her. She consoled me, amused her uncle, instructed my brothers; and I never beheld her so enchanting as at this time, when she was continually endeavouring to contribute to the happiness of others, entirely forgetful of herself.

The day of my departure at length arrived. I had taken leave of all my friends, excepting Clerval, who spent the last evening with us. He bitterly lamented that he was unable to accompany me: but his father could not be persuaded to part with him, intending that he should become a partner with him in business, in compliance with his favourite theory, that learning was superfluous in the commerce of ordinary life. Henry had a refined mind; he had no desire to be idle, and was well pleased to become his father's partner, but he believed that a man might be a very good trader, and yet possess a cultivated understanding.

We sat late, listening to his complaints, and making many little arrangements for the future. The next morning early I departed. Tears gushed from the eyes of Elizabeth; they proceeded partly from sorrow at my departure, and partly because she reflected that the same journey was to have taken place three months before, when a mother's blessing would have accompanied me.

I threw myself into the chaise[1] that was to convey me away, and indulged in the most melancholy reflections. I, who had ever been surrounded by amiable companions, continually engaged in endeavouring to bestow mutual pleasure, I was now alone. In the university, whither I was going, I must form my own friends, and be my own protector. My life had hitherto been remarkably secluded and domestic; and this had given me invincible repugnance to new countenances. I loved my brothers, Elizabeth, and Clerval; these were "old familiar faces";[2] but I believed myself totally unfitted for the company of strangers. Such were my

---

1 A small, open carriage.
2 "The Old Familiar Faces" is the title and refrain of a poem (1798) by Charles Lamb (1775-1834).

reflections as I commenced my journey; but as I proceeded, my spirits and hopes rose. I ardently desired the acquisition of knowledge. I had often, when at home, thought it hard to remain during my youth cooped up in one place, and had longed to enter the world, and take my station among other human beings. Now my desires were complied with, and it would, indeed, have been folly to repent.

I had sufficient leisure for these and many other reflections during my journey to Ingolstadt, which was long and fatiguing. At length the high white steeple of the town met my eyes. I alighted, and was conducted to my solitary apartment, to spend the evening as I pleased.

The next morning I delivered my letters of introduction, and paid a visit to some of the principal professors, and among others to M. Krempe, professor of natural philosophy. He received me with politeness, and asked me several questions concerning my progress in the different branches of science appertaining to natural philosophy. I mentioned, it is true, with fear and trembling, the only authors I had ever read upon those subjects. The professor stared: "Have you," he said, "really spent your time in studying such nonsense?"

I replied in the affirmative. "Every minute," continued M. Krempe with warmth, "every instant that you have wasted on those books is utterly and entirely lost. You have burdened your memory with exploded systems, and useless names. Good God! in what desert land have you lived, where no one was kind enough to inform you that these fancies, which you have so greedily imbibed, are a thousand years old, and as musty as they are ancient? I little expected in this enlightened and scientific age to find a disciple of Albertus Magnus and Paracelsus. My dear Sir, you must begin your studies entirely anew."

So saying, he stept aside, and wrote down a list of several books treating of natural philosophy, which he desired me to procure, and dismissed me, after mentioning that in the beginning of the following week he intended to commence a course of lectures upon natural philosophy in its general relations, and that M. Waldman, a fellow-professor, would lecture upon chemistry the alternate days that he missed.

I returned home, not disappointed, for I had long considered those authors useless whom the professor had so strongly reprobated; but I did not feel much inclined to study the books which I procured at his recommendation. M. Krempe was a little squat man, with a gruff voice and repulsive countenance; the teacher, therefore, did not prepossess me in favour of his doctrine. Besides, I had a contempt for the uses of modern natural philosophy. It was very different, when the masters of the science sought immortality and power; such views, although futile, were grand: but now the scene was changed. The ambition of the inquirer seemed to limit itself to the annihilation of those visions on which my interest in science was chiefly founded. I was required to exchange chimeras of boundless grandeur for realities of little worth.

Such were my reflections during the first two or three days spent almost in solitude. But as the ensuing week commenced, I thought of the information which M. Krempe had given me concerning the lectures. And although I could not consent to go and hear that little conceited fellow deliver sentences out of a pulpit, I recollected what he had said of M. Waldman, whom I had never seen, as he had hitherto been out of town.

Partly from curiosity, and partly from idleness, I went into the lecturing room, which M. Waldman entered shortly after. This professor was very unlike his colleague. He appeared about fifty years of age, but with an aspect expressive of the greatest benevolence; a few gray hairs covered his temples, but those at the back of his head were nearly black. His person was short, but remarkably erect; and his voice the sweetest I had ever heard. He began his lecture by a recapitulation of the history of chemistry and the various improvements made by different men of learning, pronouncing with fervour the names of the most distinguished discoverers. He then took a cursory view of the present state of the science, and explained many of its elementary terms. After having made a few preparatory experiments, he concluded with a panegyric upon modern chemistry, the terms of which I shall never forget:—

"The ancient teachers of this science," said he, "promised impossibilities, and performed nothing. The modern masters promise very little; they know that metals cannot be transmuted, and that the elixir of life is a chimera. But these philosophers, whose hands seem only made to dabble in dirt, and their eyes to pour over the microscope or crucible, have indeed performed miracles. They penetrate into the recesses of nature, and shew how she works in her hiding places.[1] They ascend into the heavens; they have discovered how the blood circulates, and the nature of the air we breathe. They have acquired new and almost

---

1 Cf. Davy, *Discourse* 14-15 (Appendix B.2.e).

unlimited powers; they can command the thunders of heaven, mimic the earthquake, and even mock the invisible world with its own shadows."[1]

I departed highly pleased with the professor and his lecture, and paid him a visit the same evening. His manners in private were even more mild and attractive than in public; for there was a certain dignity in his mien during his lecture, which in his own house was replaced by the greatest affability and kindness. He heard with attention my little narration concerning my studies, and smiled at the names of Cornelius Agrippa, and Paracelsus, but without the contempt that M. Krempe had exhibited. He said, that "these were men to whose indefatigable zeal modern philosophers were indebted for most of the foundations of their knowledge. They had left to us, as an easier task, to give new names, and arrange in connected classifications, the facts which they in a great degree had been the instruments of bringing to light. The labours of men of genius, however erroneously directed, scarcely ever fail in ultimately turning to the solid advantage of mankind." I listened to his statement, which was delivered without any presumption or affectation; and then added, that his lecture had removed my prejudices against modern chemists; and I, at the same time, requested his advice concerning the books I ought to procure.

"I am happy," said M. Waldman, "to have gained a disciple; and if your application equals your ability, I have no doubt of your success. Chemistry is that branch of natural philosophy in which the greatest improvements have been and may be made; it is on that account that I have made it my peculiar study; but at the same time I have not neglected the other branches of science. A man would make but a very sorry chemist, if he attended to that department of human knowledge alone. If your wish is to become really a man of science, and not merely a petty experimentalist, I should advise you to apply to every branch of natural philosophy, including mathematics."[2]

He then took me into his laboratory, and explained to me the uses of his various machines; instructing me as to what I ought to procure, and promising me the use of his own, when I should have advanced far enough in the science not to derange their

---

1 Cf. Godwin, *Political Justice* 2: 502-04; VIII.viii.appendix (Appendix A.1.a); and Davy, *Discourse* 15-17 (Appendix B.2.f), and 18-19 (Appendix B.2.g).

2 Cf. Davy, *Discourse* 10-11 (Appendix B.2.d).

mechanism. He also gave me the list of books which I had requested; and I took my leave.

Thus ended a day memorable to me; it decided my future destiny.

CHAPTER III.

FROM this day natural philosophy, and particularly chemistry, in the most comprehensive sense of the term, became nearly my sole occupation. I read with ardour those works, so full of genius and discrimination, which modern inquirers have written on these subjects. I attended the lectures, and cultivated the acquaintance, of the men of science of the university; and I found even in M. Krempe a great deal of sound sense and real information, combined, it is true, with a repulsive physiognomy and manners, but not on that account the less valuable. In M. Waldman I found a true friend. His gentleness was never tinged by dogmatism; and his instructions were given with an air of frankness and good nature, that banished every idea of pedantry. It was, perhaps, the amiable character of this man that inclined me more to that branch of natural philosophy which he professed, than an intrinsic love for the science itself. But this state of mind had place only in the first steps towards knowledge: the more fully I entered into the science, the more exclusively I pursued it for its own sake. That application, which at first had been a matter of duty and resolution, now became so ardent and eager, that the stars often disappeared in the light of morning whilst I was yet engaged in my laboratory.

As I applied so closely, it may be easily conceived that I improved rapidly. My ardour was indeed the astonishment of the students; and my proficiency, that of the masters. Professor Krempe often asked me, with a sly smile, how Cornelius Agrippa went on? whilst M. Waldman expressed the most heartfelt exultation in my progress. Two years passed in this manner, during which I paid no visit to Geneva, but was engaged, heart and soul, in the pursuit of some discoveries, which I hoped to make. None but those who have experienced them can conceive of the enticements of science. In other studies you go as far as others have gone before you, and there is nothing more to know; but in a scientific pursuit there is continual food for discovery and wonder. A mind of moderate capacity, which closely pursues one study, must infallibly arrive at great proficiency in that study; and I, who continually sought the attainment of one object of pursuit, and was solely wrapt up in this, improved so rapidly, that, at the end of two years, I made some discoveries in the improvement of some chemical instruments, which procured me great esteem and admiration at the university. When I had arrived at this point, and had become as well acquainted with the theory and practice of natural philosophy as depended on the lessons of any of the professors at Ingolstadt, my residence there being no longer conducive to my improvements, I thought of returning to my friends and my native town, when an incident happened that protracted my stay.

One of the phaenomena which had peculiarly attracted my attention was the structure of the human frame, and, indeed, any animal endued with life. Whence, I often asked myself, did the principle of life proceed? It was a bold question, and one which has ever been considered as a mystery; yet with how many things are we upon the brink of becoming acquainted, if cowardice or carelessness did not restrain our inquiries. I revolved these circumstances in my mind, and determined thenceforth to apply myself more particularly to those branches of natural philosophy which relate to physiology.[1] Unless I had been animated by an almost supernatural enthusiasm, my application to this study would have been irksome, and almost intolerable. To examine the causes of life, we must first have recourse to death. I became acquainted with the science of anatomy: but this was not sufficient; I must also observe the natural decay and corruption of the human body. In my education my father had taken the greatest precautions that my mind should be impressed with no supernatural horrors. I do not ever remember to have trembled at a tale of superstition, or to have feared the apparition of a spirit. Darkness had no effect upon my fancy; and a church-yard was to me merely the receptacle of bodies deprived of life, which, from being the seat of beauty and strength, had become food for the worm. Now I was led to examine the cause and progress of this decay, and forced to spend days and nights in vaults and charnel houses.[2] My attention was fixed upon every object the most insupportable to the delicacy of the human feelings. I saw how the fine form of man was degraded and wasted; I beheld the corruption of death succeed to the blooming cheek of life; I saw how the worm inherited the wonders of the eye and brain. I paused,

---

1 Cf. Davy, *Discourse* 8 (Appendix B.2.b).

2 Cf. P.B. Shelley, "Alastor" (1815) 23-29.

examining and analysing all the minutiae of causation, as exemplified in the change from life to death, and death to life,[1] until from the midst of this darkness a sudden light broke in upon me—a light so brilliant and wondrous, yet so simple, that while I became dizzy with the immensity of the prospect which it illustrated, I was surprised that among so many men of genius, who had directed their inquiries towards the same science, that I alone should be reserved to discover so astonishing a secret.[2]

Remember, I am not recording the vision of a madman. The sun does not more certainly shine in the heavens, than that which I now affirm is true. Some miracle might have produced it, yet the stages of the discovery were distinct and probable. After days and nights of incredible labour and fatigue, I succeeded in discovering the cause of generation and life; nay, more, I became myself capable of bestowing animation upon lifeless matter.[3]

The astonishment which I had at first experienced on this discovery soon gave place to delight and rapture. After so much time spent in painful labour, to arrive at once at the summit of my desires, was the most gratifying consummation of my toils. But this discovery was so great and overwhelming, that all the steps by which I had been progressively led to it were obliterated, and I beheld only the result. What had been the study and desire of the wisest men since the creation of the world, was now within my grasp. Not that, like a magic scene, it all opened upon me at once: the information I had obtained was of a nature rather to direct my endeavours so soon as I should point them towards the object of my search, than to exhibit that object already accomplished. I was like the Arabian who had been buried with the dead, and found a passage to life aided only by one glimmering, and seemingly ineffectual, light.[4]

I see by your eagerness, and the wonder and hope which your eyes express, my friend, that you expect to be informed of the secret with which I am acquainted; that cannot be: listen patiently until the end of my story, and you will easily perceive

---

1 Cf. Darwin, *The Temple of Nature* IV.383-404 (Appendix B.1.c); and Davy, *Discourse* 5-6 (Appendix B.2.a).

2 Cf. Wollstonecraft, *Vindication* 244-45; VI (Appendix A.2.f).

3 Cf. Godwin's speculations on the indefinite extension of human life, *Political Justice* 2: 519-28; VIII.ix.appendix (Appendix A.1.b); and Davy, *Discourse* 18-19 (Appendix B.2.g).

4 An allusion to the Fourth Voyage of Sinbad in *The Thousand Nights and One Night*.

why I am reserved upon that subject. I will not lead you on, unguarded and ardent as I then was, to your destruction and infallible misery. Learn from me, if not by my precepts, at least by my example, how dangerous is the acquirement of knowledge, and how much happier that man is who believes his native town to be the world, than he who aspires to become greater than his nature will allow.[1]

When I found so astonishing a power placed within my hands, I hesitated a long time concerning the manner in which I should employ it. Although I possessed the capacity of bestowing animation, yet to prepare a frame for the reception of it, with all its intricacies of fibres, muscles, and veins, still remained a work of inconceivable difficulty and labour. I doubted at first whether I should attempt the creation of a being like myself or one of simpler organization; but my imagination was too much exalted by my first success to permit me to doubt of my ability to give life to an animal as complex and wonderful as man. The materials at present within my command hardly appeared adequate to so arduous an undertaking; but I doubted not that I should ultimately succeed. I prepared myself for a multitude of reverses; my operations might be incessantly baffled, and at last my work be imperfect: yet, when I considered the improvement which every day takes place in science and mechanics, I was encouraged to hope my present attempts would at least lay the foundations of future success. Nor could I consider the magnitude and complexity of my plan as any argument of its impracticability. It was with these feelings that I began the creation of a human being. As the minuteness of the parts formed a great hindrance to my speed, I resolved, contrary to my first intention, to make the being of a gigantic stature; that is to say, about eight feet in height, and proportionably large. After having formed this determination, and having spent some months in successfully collecting and arranging my materials, I began.

No one can conceive the variety of feelings which bore me onwards, like a hurricane, in the first enthusiasm of success. Life and death appeared to me ideal bounds, which I should first break through, and pour a torrent of light into our dark world. A new species would bless me as its creator and source; many happy and excellent natures would owe their being to me. No father could claim the gratitude of his child so completely as I

---

1 Cf. Davy, *Discourse* 9 (Appendix B.2.c).

should deserve their's.[1] Pursuing these reflections, I thought, that if I could bestow animation upon lifeless matter, I might in process of time (although I now found it impossible) renew life where death had apparently devoted the body to corruption.

These thoughts supported my spirits, while I pursued my undertaking with unremitting ardour. My cheek had grown pale with study, and my person had become emaciated with confinement. Sometimes, on the very brink of certainty, I failed; yet still I clung to the hope which the next day or the next hour might realize. One secret which I alone possessed was the hope to which I had dedicated myself; and the moon gazed on my midnight labours, while, with unrelaxed and breathless eagerness, I pursued nature to her hiding places. Who shall conceive the horrors of my secret toil, as I dabbled among the unhallowed damps of the grave, or tortured the living animal to animate the lifeless clay? My limbs now tremble, and my eyes swim with the remembrance; but then a resistless, and almost frantic impulse, urged me forward; I seemed to have lost all soul or sensation but for this one pursuit. It was indeed but a passing trance, that only made me feel with renewed acuteness so soon as, the unnatural stimulus ceasing to operate, I had returned to my old habits. I collected bones from charnel houses; and disturbed, with profane fingers, the tremendous secrets of the human frame. In a solitary chamber, or rather cell, at the top of the house, and separated from all the other apartments by a gallery and staircase, I kept my workshop of filthy creation; my eyeballs were starting from their sockets in attending to the details of my employment. The dissecting room and the slaughter-house furnished many of my materials; and often did my human nature turn with loathing from my occupation, whilst, still urged on by an eagerness which perpetually increased, I brought my work near to a conclusion.

The summer months passed while I was thus engaged, heart and soul, in one pursuit. It was a most beautiful season; never did the fields bestow a more plentiful harvest, or the vines yield a more luxuriant vintage: but my eyes were insensible to the charms of nature. And the same feelings which made me neglect the scenes around me caused me also to forget those friends who were so many miles absent, and whom I had not seen for so long a time. I knew my silence disquieted them; and I well remembered the words of my father: "I know that while you are pleased with yourself, you will think of us with affection, and we shall

dedicated

---

1 Cf. Darwin, *The Temple of Nature* II.103-24, 159-66 (Appendix B.1.e).

hear regularly from you. You must pardon me, if I regard any interruption in your correspondence as a proof that your other duties are equally neglected."[1]

I knew well therefore what would be my father's feelings; but I could not tear my thoughts from my employment, loathsome in itself, but which had taken an irresistible hold of my imagination. I wished, as it were, to procrastinate all that related to my feelings of affection until the great object, which swallowed up every habit of my nature, should be completed.[2]

I then thought that my father would be unjust if he ascribed my neglect to vice, or faultiness on my part; but I am now convinced that he was justified in conceiving that I should not be altogether free from blame. A human being in perfection ought always to preserve a calm and peaceful mind, and never to allow passion or a transitory desire to disturb his tranquillity. I do not think that the pursuit of knowledge is an exception to this rule. If the study to which you apply yourself has a tendency to weaken your affections, and to destroy your taste for those simple pleasures in which no alloy can possibly mix, then that study is certainly unlawful, that is to say, not befitting the human mind. If this rule were always observed; if no man allowed any pursuit whatsoever to interfere with the tranquillity of his domestic affections, Greece had not been enslaved; Caesar would have spared his country; America would have been discovered more gradually; and the empires of Mexico and Peru[3] had not been destroyed.

But I forget that I am moralizing in the most interesting part of my tale; and your looks remind me to proceed.

My father made no reproach in his letters; and only took notice of my silence by inquiring into my occupations more particularly than before. Winter, spring, and summer, passed away during my labours; but I did not watch the blossom or the expanding leaves—sights which before always yielded me supreme delight, so deeply was I engrossed in my occupation. The leaves of that year had withered before my work drew near

---

1 Cf. Godwin's analysis of the scientist's need for society, *Political Justice* 1: 311; IV.v; but also of the tendency of technology to reduce humans' reliance on each other, *Political Justice* 2: 502-04; VIII.viii.appendix (Appendix A.1.a).

2 Cf. Davy's warning, *Discourse* 23 (Appendix B.2.h).

3 Quoted from Volney, *The Ruins* 167 (see Appendix C.1.c).

to a close; and now every day shewed me more plainly how well I had succeeded. But my enthusiasm was checked by my anxiety, and I appeared rather like one doomed by slavery to toil in the mines, or any other unwholesome trade, than an artist occupied by his favourite employment. Every night I was oppressed by a slow fever, and I became nervous to a most painful degree; a disease that I regretted the more because I had hitherto enjoyed most excellent health, and had always boasted of the firmness of my nerves. But I believed that exercise and amusement would soon drive away such symptoms; and I promised myself both of these, when my creation should be complete.[1]

Frank.

CHAPTER IV.

IT was on a dreary night of November,[2] that I beheld the accomplishment of my toils. With an anxiety that almost amounted to agony, I collected the instruments of life around me, that I might infuse a spark of being into the lifeless thing that lay at my feet.[3] It was already one in the morning; the rain pattered dismally against the panes, and my candle was nearly burnt out, when, by the glimmer of the half-extinguished light, I saw the dull yellow eye of the creature open; it breathed hard, and a convulsive motion agitated its limbs.

How can I describe my emotions at this catastrophe, or how delineate the wretch whom with such infinite pains and care I had endeavoured to form? His limbs were in proportion, and I had selected his features as beautiful. Beautiful!—Great God! His yellow skin scarcely covered the work of muscles and arteries beneath; his hair was of a lustrous black, and flowing; his teeth of a pearly whiteness; but these luxuriances only formed a more horrid contrast with his watery eyes, that seemed almost of the same colour as the dun white sockets in which they were set, his shrivelled complexion, and straight black lips.

The different accidents of life are not so changeable as the feelings of human nature. I had worked hard for nearly two years, for the sole purpose of infusing life into an inanimate body. For this I had deprived myself of rest and health. I had desired it with an ardour that far exceeded moderation; but now that I had fin-

---

1 Cf. Davy's warning, *Discourse* 24-26 (Appendix B.2.i).
2 In 1793.
3 Cf. Darwin, *The Economy of Vegetation* II.355-94 (Appendix B.1.b).

ished, the beauty of the dream vanished, and breathless horror and disgust filled my heart. Unable to endure the aspect of the being I had created, I rushed out of the room, and continued a long time traversing my bed-chamber, unable to compose my mind to sleep. At length lassitude succeeded to the tumult I had before endured; and I threw myself on the bed in my clothes, endeavouring to seek a few moments of forgetfulness. But it was in vain: I slept indeed, but I was disturbed by the wildest dreams. I thought I saw Elizabeth, in the bloom of health, walking in the streets of Ingolstadt. Delighted and surprised, I embraced her; but as I imprinted the first kiss on her lips, they became livid with the hue of death; her features appeared to change, and I thought that I held the corpse of my dead mother in my arms; a shroud enveloped her form, and I saw the grave-worms crawling in the folds of the flannel. I started from my sleep with horror; a cold dew covered my forehead, my teeth chattered, and every limb became convulsed; when, by the dim and yellow light of the moon, as it forced its way through the window-shutters, I beheld the wretch—the miserable monster whom I had created.[1] He held up the curtain of the bed; and his eyes, if eyes they may be called, were fixed on me. His jaws opened, and he muttered some inarticulate sounds, while a grin wrinkled his cheeks. He might have spoken, but I did not hear; one hand was stretched out, seemingly to detain me, but I escaped, and rushed down stairs. I took refuge in the court-yard belonging to the house which I inhabited; where I remained during the rest of the night, walking up and down in the greatest agitation, listening attentively, catching and fearing each sound as if it were to announce the approach of the demoniacal corpse to which I had so miserably given life.

Oh! no mortal could support the horror of that countenance. A mummy again endued with animation could not be so hideous as that wretch. I had gazed on him while unfinished; he was ugly then; but when those muscles and joints were rendered capable of motion, it became a thing such as even Dante could not have conceived.

I passed the night wretchedly. Sometimes my pulse beat so quickly and hardly, that I felt the palpitation of every artery; at others, I nearly sank to the ground through languor and extreme weakness. Mingled with this horror, I felt the bitterness of disappointment: dreams that had been my food and pleasant rest for

---

1 Cf. Adam's dream and awakening, Milton, *Paradise Lost* VIII.460-89 (Appendix C.4.d); and Osmond's dream in Matthew Gregory Lewis (1775-1818), *The Castle Spectre* (1797) IV.i.

so long a space, were now become a hell to me; and the change was so rapid, the overthrow so complete!

Morning, dismal and wet, at length dawned, and discovered to my sleepless and aching eyes the church of Ingolstadt, its white steeple and clock, which indicated the sixth hour. The porter opened the gates of the court, which had that night been my asylum, and I issued into the streets, pacing them with quick steps, as if I sought to avoid the wretch whom I feared every turning of the street would present to my view. I did not dare return to the apartment which I inhabited, but felt impelled to hurry on, although wetted by the rain, which poured from a black and comfortless sky.

I continued walking in this manner for some time, endeavouring, by bodily exercise, to ease the load that weighed upon my mind. I traversed the streets, without any clear conception of where I was, or what I was doing. My heart palpitated in the sickness of fear; and I hurried on with irregular steps, not daring to look about me:

> Like one who, on a lonely road,
>   Doth walk in fear and dread,
> And, having once turn'd round, walks on,
>   And turns no more his head;
> Because he knows a frightful fiend
>   Doth close behind him tread.[1]

Continuing thus, I came at length opposite to the inn at which the various diligences[2] and carriages usually stopped. Here I paused, I knew not why; but I remained some minutes with my eyes fixed on a coach that was coming towards me from the other end of the street. As it drew nearer, I observed that it was the Swiss diligence: it stopped just where I was standing; and, on the door being opened, I perceived Henry Clerval, who, on seeing me, instantly sprung out. "My dear Frankenstein," exclaimed he, "how glad I am to see you! how fortunate that you should be here at the very moment of my alighting!"

Nothing could equal my delight on seeing Clerval; his presence brought back to my thoughts my father, Elizabeth, and all those scenes of home so dear to my recollection. I grasped his hand, and in a moment forgot my horror and misfortune; I felt suddenly, and

---

1 Coleridge's "Ancient Mariner." [Shelley's note; lines 451-56.]
2 Stage-coaches.

for the first time during many months, calm and serene joy. I welcomed my friend, therefore, in the most cordial manner, and we walked towards my college. Clerval continued talking for some time about our mutual friends, and his own good fortune in being permitted to come to Ingolstadt. "You may easily believe," said he, "how great was the difficulty to persuade my father that it was not absolutely necessary for a merchant not to understand any thing except book-keeping; and, indeed, I believe I left him incredulous to the last, for his constant answer to my unwearied entreaties was the same as that of the Dutch school-master in the Vicar of Wakefield: 'I have ten thousand florins a year without Greek, I eat heartily without Greek.'[1] But his affection for me at length overcame his dislike of learning, and he has permitted me to undertake a voyage of discovery to the land of knowledge."

"It gives me the greatest delight to see you; but tell me how you left my father, brothers, and Elizabeth."

"Very well, and very happy, only a little uneasy that they hear from you so seldom. By the bye, I mean to lecture you a little upon their account myself.—But, my dear Frankenstein," continued he, stopping short, and gazing full in my face, "I did not before remark how very ill you appear; so thin and pale; you look as if you had been watching for several nights."

"You have guessed right; I have lately been so deeply engaged in one occupation, that I have not allowed myself sufficient rest, as you see: but I hope, I sincerely hope, that all these employments are now at an end, and that I am at length free."

I trembled excessively; I could not endure to think of, and far less to allude to the occurrences of the preceding night. I walked with a quick pace, and we soon arrived at my college. I then reflected, and the thought made me shiver, that the creature whom I had left in my apartment might still be there, alive, and walking about. I dreaded to behold this monster; but I feared still more that Henry should see him. Entreating him therefore to remain a few minutes at the bottom of the stairs, I darted up towards my own room. My hand was already on the lock of the door before I recollected myself. I then paused; and a cold shivering came over me. I threw the door forcibly open, as children are accustomed to do when they expect a spectre to stand in waiting for them on the other side; but nothing appeared. I stepped fearfully in: the apartment was empty; and my bedroom was also freed from its hideous guest. I could hardly believe that

---

1 Oliver Goldsmith, *The Vicar of Wakefield* (1766) XX.

so great a good-fortune could have befallen me; but when I became assured that my enemy had indeed fled, I clapped my hands for joy, and ran down to Clerval.

We ascended into my room, and the servant presently brought breakfast; but I was unable to contain myself. It was not joy only that possessed me; I felt my flesh tingle with excess of sensitiveness, and my pulse beat rapidly. I was unable to remain for a single instant in the same place; I jumped over the chairs, clapped my hands, and laughed aloud. Clerval at first attributed my unusual spirits to joy on his arrival; but when he observed me more attentively, he saw a wildness in my eyes for which he could not account; and my loud, unrestrained, heartless laughter, frightened and astonished him.

"My dear Victor," cried he, "what, for God's sake, is the matter? Do not laugh in that manner. How ill you are! What is the cause of all this?"

"Do not ask me," cried I, putting my hands before my eyes, for I thought I saw the dreaded spectre glide into the room; "*he* can tell.—Oh, save me! save me!" I imagined that the monster seized me; I struggled furiously, and fell down in a fit.

Poor Clerval! what must have been his feelings? A meeting, which he anticipated with such joy, so strangely turned to bitterness. But I was not the witness of his grief; for I was lifeless, and did not recover my senses for a long, long time.

This was the commencement of a nervous fever, which confined me for several months. During all that time Henry was my only nurse. I afterwards learned that, knowing my father's advanced age, and unfitness for so long a journey, and how wretched my sickness would make Elizabeth, he spared them this grief by concealing the extent of my disorder. He knew that I could not have a more kind and attentive nurse than himself; and, firm in the hope he felt of my recovery, he did not doubt that, instead of doing harm, he performed the kindest action that he could towards them.

But I was in reality very ill; and surely nothing but the unbounded and unremitting attentions of my friend could have restored me to life. The form of the monster on whom I had bestowed existence was for ever before my eyes, and I raved incessantly concerning him. Doubtless my words surprised Henry: he at first believed them to be the wanderings of my disturbed imagination; but the pertinacity with which I continually recurred to the same subject persuaded him that my disorder indeed owed its origin to some uncommon and terrible event.

By very slow degrees, and with frequent relapses, that alarmed and grieved my friend, I recovered. I remember the first time I became capable of observing outward objects with any kind of pleasure, I perceived that the fallen leaves had disappeared, and that the young buds were shooting forth from the trees that shaded my window. It was a divine spring; and the season contributed greatly to my convalescence. I felt also sentiments of joy and affection revive in my bosom; my gloom disappeared, and in a short time I became as cheerful as before I was attacked by the fatal passion.

"Dearest Clerval," exclaimed I, "how kind, how very good you are to me. This whole winter, instead of being spent in study, as you promised yourself, has been consumed in my sick room. How shall I ever repay you? I feel the greatest remorse for the disappointment of which I have been the occasion; but you will forgive me."

"You will repay me entirely, if you do not discompose yourself, but get well as fast as you can; and since you appear in such good spirits, I may speak to you on one subject, may I not?"

I trembled. One subject! what could it be? Could he allude to an object on whom I dared not even think?

"Compose yourself," said Clerval, who observed my change of colour, "I will not mention it, if it agitates you; but your father and cousin would be very happy if they received a letter from you in your own hand-writing. They hardly know how ill you have been, and are uneasy at your long silence."

"Is that all? my dear Henry. How could you suppose that my first thought would not fly towards those dear, dear friends whom I love, and who are so deserving of my love."

"If this is your present temper, my friend, you will perhaps be glad to see a letter that has been lying here some days for you: it is from your cousin, I believe."

CHAPTER V.

CLERVAL then put the following letter into my hands.

"*To* V. FRANKENSTEIN.

"MY DEAR COUSIN,

"I cannot describe to you the uneasiness we have all felt concerning your health. We cannot help imagining that your friend

Clerval conceals the extent of your disorder: for it is now several months since we have seen your hand-writing; and all this time you have been obliged to dictate your letters to Henry. Surely, Victor, you must have been exceedingly ill; and this makes us all very wretched, as much so nearly as after the death of your dear mother. My uncle was almost persuaded that you were indeed dangerously ill, and could hardly be restrained from undertaking a journey to Ingolstadt. Clerval always writes that you are getting better; I eagerly hope that you will confirm this intelligence soon, in your own hand-writing; for indeed, indeed, Victor, we are all very miserable on this account. Relieve us from this fear, and we shall be the happiest creatures in the world. Your father's health is now so vigorous, that he appears ten years younger since last winter. Ernest also is so much improved, that you would hardly know him: he is now nearly sixteen, and has lost that sickly appearance which he had some years ago; he is grown quite robust and active.

"My uncle and I conversed a long time last night about what profession Ernest should follow. His constant illness when young has deprived him of the habits of application; and now that he enjoys good health, he is continually in the open air, climbing the hills, or rowing on the lake. I therefore proposed that he should be a farmer; which you know, Cousin, is a favourite scheme of mine. A farmer's is a very healthy happy life; and the least hurtful, or rather the most beneficial profession of any. My uncle had an idea of his being educated as an advocate, that through his interest he might become a judge. But, besides that he is not at all fitted for such an occupation, it is certainly more creditable to cultivate the earth for the sustenance of man, than to be the confidant, and sometimes the accomplice, of his vices; which is the profession of a lawyer. I said, that the employments of a prosperous farmer, if they were not a more honourable, they were at least a happier species of occupation than that of a judge, whose misfortune it was always to meddle with the dark side of human nature. My uncle smiled, and said, that I ought to be an advocate myself, which put an end to the conversation on that subject.[1]

"And now I must tell you a little story that will please, and perhaps amuse you. Do you not remember Justine Moritz?[2]

---

1 Cf. Godwin's low opinion of lawyers, *Political Justice* 2: 404-05; VII.viii.
2 Possibly named after the heroine of *Justine; or, The Misfortunes of Virtue* (1791), by Donatien-Alphonse de Sade (1740-1814). Among her many misfortunes, Sade's Justine is repeatedly accused of crimes she did not commit. Both Byron and P.B. Shelley knew the book.

Probably you do not; I will relate her history, therefore, in a few words. Madame Moritz, her mother, was a widow with four children, of whom Justine was the third. This girl had always been the favourite of her father; but, through a strange perversity, her mother could not endure her, and, after the death of M. Moritz, treated her very ill. My aunt observed this; and, when Justine was twelve years of age, prevailed on her mother to allow her to live at her house. The republican institutions of our country have produced simpler and happier manners than those which prevail in the great monarchies that surround it. Hence there is less distinction between the several classes of its inhabitants; and the lower orders being neither so poor nor so despised, their manners are more refined and moral. A servant in Geneva does not mean the same thing as a servant in France and England. Justine, thus received in our family, learned the duties of a servant; a condition which, in our fortunate country, does not include the idea of ignorance, and a sacrifice of the dignity of a human being.

"After what I have said, I dare say you well remember the heroine of my little tale: for Justine was a great favourite of your's; and I recollect you once remarked, that if you were in an ill humour, one glance from Justine could dissipate it, for the same reason that Ariosto gives concerning the beauty of Angelica[1]— she looked so frank-hearted and happy. My aunt conceived a great attachment for her, by which she was induced to give her an education superior to that which she had at first intended. This benefit was fully repaid; Justine was the most grateful little creature in the world: I do not mean that she made any professions, I never heard one pass her lips; but you could see by her eyes that she almost adored her protectress. Although her disposition was gay, and in many respects inconsiderate, yet she paid the greatest attention to every gesture of my aunt. She thought her the model of all excellence, and endeavoured to imitate her phraseology and manners, so that even now she often reminds me of her.

"When my dearest aunt died, every one was too much occupied in their own grief to notice poor Justine, who had attended her during her illness with the most anxious affection. Poor Justine was very ill; but other trials were reserved for her.

"One by one, her brothers and sister died; and her mother, with the exception of her neglected daughter, was left childless. The conscience of the woman was troubled; she began to think

---

1 The heroine of *Orlando Furioso*.

that the deaths of her favourites was a judgment from heaven to chastise her partiality. She was a Roman Catholic; and I believe her confessor confirmed the idea which she had conceived. Accordingly, a few months after your departure for Ingolstadt, Justine was called home by her repentant mother. Poor girl! she wept when she quitted our house: she was much altered since the death of my aunt; grief had given softness and a winning mildness to her manners, which had before been remarkable for vivacity. Nor was her residence at her mother's house of a nature to restore her gaiety. The poor woman was very vacillating in her repentance. She sometimes begged Justine to forgive her unkindness, but much oftener accused her of having caused the deaths of her brothers and sister. Perpetual fretting at length threw Madame Moritz into a decline, which at first increased her irritability, but she is now at peace for ever. She died on the first approach of cold weather, at the beginning of this last winter. Justine has returned to us; and I assure you I love her tenderly. She is very clever and gentle, and extremely pretty; as I mentioned before, her mien and her expressions continually remind me of my dear aunt.

"I must say also a few words to you, my dear cousin, of little darling William. I wish you could see him; he is very tall of his age, with sweet laughing blue eyes, dark eye-lashes, and curling hair. When he smiles, two little dimples appear on each cheek, which are rosy with health. He has already had one or two little *wives*, but Louisa Biron is his favourite, a pretty little girl of five years of age.

"Now, dear Victor, I dare say you wish to be indulged in a little gossip concerning the good people of Geneva. The pretty Miss Mansfield has already received the congratulatory visits on her approaching marriage with a young Englishman, John Melbourne, Esq. Her ugly sister, Manon, married M. Duvillard, the rich banker, last autumn. Your favourite schoolfellow, Louis Manoir, has suffered several misfortunes since the departure of Clerval from Geneva. But he has already recovered his spirits, and is reported to be on the point of marrying a very lively pretty Frenchwoman, Madame Tavernier. She is a widow, and much older than Manoir; but she is very much admired, and a favourite with every body.

"I have written myself into good spirits, dear cousin; yet I cannot conclude without again anxiously inquiring concerning your health. Dear Victor, if you are not very ill, write yourself, and make your father and all of us happy; or—I cannot bear to think of the other side of the question; my tears already flow. Adieu, my dearest cousin.

"ELIZABETH LAVENZA.

"Geneva, March 18th, 17—."

"Dear, dear Elizabeth!" I exclaimed when I had read her letter, "I will write instantly, and relieve them from the anxiety they must feel." I wrote, and this exertion greatly fatigued me; but my convalescence had commenced, and proceeded regularly. In another fortnight I was able to leave my chamber.

One of my first duties on my recovery was to introduce Clerval to the several professors of the university. In doing this, I underwent a kind of rough usage, ill befitting the wounds that my mind had sustained. Ever since the fatal night, the end of my labours, and the beginning of my misfortunes, I had conceived a violent antipathy even to the name of natural philosophy. When I was otherwise quite restored to health, the sight of a chemical instrument would renew all the agony of my nervous symptoms. Henry saw this, and had removed all my apparatus from my view. He had also changed my apartment; for he perceived that I had acquired a dislike for the room which had previously been my laboratory. But these cares of Clerval were made of no avail when I visited the professors. M. Waldman inflicted torture when he praised, with kindness and warmth, the astonishing progress I had made in the sciences. He soon perceived that I disliked the subject; but, not guessing the real cause, he attributed my feelings to modesty, and changed the subject from my improvement to the science itself, with a desire, as I evidently saw, of drawing me out. What could I do? He meant to please, and he tormented me. I felt as if he had placed carefully, one by one, in my view those instruments which were to be afterwards used in putting me to a slow and cruel death. I writhed under his words, yet dared not exhibit the pain I felt. Clerval, whose eyes and feelings were always quick in discerning the sensations of others, declined the subject, alleging, in excuse, his total ignorance; and the conversation took a more general turn. I thanked my friend from my heart, but I did not speak. I saw plainly that he was surprised, but he never attempted to draw my secret from me; and although I loved him with a mixture of affection and reverence that knew no bounds, yet I could never persuade myself to confide to him that event which was so often present to my recollection, but which I feared the detail to another would only impress more deeply.

M. Krempe was not equally docile; and in my condition at that time, of almost insupportable sensitiveness, his harsh blunt encomiums gave me even more pain than the benevolent approbation of M. Waldman. "D—n the fellow!" cried he; "why, M. Clerval, I assure you he has outstript us all. Aye, stare if you please; but it is nevertheless true. A youngster who, but a few years ago, believed Cornelius Agrippa as firmly as the gospel, has now set himself at the head of the university; and if he is not soon pulled down, we shall all be out of countenance.—Aye, aye," continued he, observing my face expressive of suffering, "M. Frankenstein is modest; an excellent quality in a young man. Young men should be diffident of themselves, you know, M. Clerval; I was myself when young: but that wears out in a very short time."

M. Krempe had now commenced an eulogy on himself, which happily turned the conversation from a subject that was so annoying to me.

Clerval was no natural philosopher. His imagination was too vivid for the minutiae of science. Languages were his principal study; and he sought, by acquiring their elements, to open a field for self-instruction on his return to Geneva. Persian, Arabic, and Hebrew, gained his attention, after he had made himself perfectly master of Greek and Latin. For my own part, idleness had ever been irksome to me; and now that I wished to fly from reflection, and hated my former studies, I felt great relief in being the fellow-pupil with my friend, and found not only instruction but consolation in the works of the orientalists. Their melancholy is soothing, and their joy elevating to a degree I never experienced in studying the authors of any other country. When you read their writings, life appears to consist in a warm sun and garden of roses,—in the smiles and frowns of a fair enemy, and the fire that consumes your own heart. How different from the manly and heroical poetry of Greece and Rome.

Summer passed away in these occupations, and my return to Geneva was fixed for the latter end of autumn; but being delayed by several accidents, winter and snow arrived, the roads were deemed impassable, and my journey was retarded until the ensuing spring. I felt this delay very bitterly; for I longed to see my native town, and my beloved friends. My return had only been delayed so long from an unwillingness to leave Clerval in a strange place, before he had become acquainted with any of its inhabitants. The winter, however, was spent cheerfully; and although the spring was uncommonly late, when it came, its beauty compensated for its dilatoriness.

The month of May had already commenced, and I expected the letter daily which was to fix the date of my departure, when Henry proposed a pedestrian tour in the environs of Ingolstadt that I might bid a personal farewell to the country I had so long inhabited. I acceded with pleasure to this proposition: I was fond of exercise, and Clerval had always been my favourite companion in the rambles of this nature that I had taken among the scenes of my native country.

We passed a fortnight in these perambulations: my health and spirits had long been restored, and they gained additional strength from the salubrious air I breathed, the natural incidents of our progress, and the conversation of my friend. Study had before secluded me from the intercourse of my fellow-creatures, and rendered me unsocial; but Clerval called forth the better feelings of my heart; he again taught me to love the aspect of nature, and the cheerful faces of children. Excellent friend! how sincerely did you love me, and endeavour to elevate my mind, until it was on a level with your own. A selfish pursuit had cramped and narrowed me, until your gentleness and affection warmed and opened my senses; I became the same happy creature who, a few years ago, loving and beloved by all, had no sorrow or care. When happy, inanimate nature had the power of bestowing on me the most delightful sensations. A serene sky and verdant fields filled me with ecstacy. The present season was indeed divine; the flowers of spring bloomed in the hedges, while those of summer were already in bud: I was undisturbed by thoughts which during the preceding year had pressed upon me, notwithstanding my endeavours to throw them off, with an invincible burden.

Henry rejoiced in my gaiety, and sincerely sympathized in my feelings: he exerted himself to amuse me, while he expressed the sensations that filled his soul. The resources of his mind on this occasion were truly astonishing: his conversation was full of imagination; and very often, in imitation of the Persian and Arabic writers, he invented tales of wonderful fancy and passion. At other times he repeated my favourite poems, or drew me out into arguments, which he supported with great ingenuity.

We returned to our college on a Sunday afternoon: the peasants were dancing, and every one we met appeared gay and happy. My own spirits were high, and I bounded along with feelings of unbridled joy and hilarity.

CHAPTER VI.

ON my return, I found the following letter from my father:—

"*To* V. FRANKENSTEIN.

"MY DEAR VICTOR,

"You have probably waited impatiently for a letter to fix the date of your return to us; and I was at first tempted to write only a few lines, merely mentioning the day on which I should expect you. But that would be a cruel kindness, and I dare not do it. What would be your surprise, my son, when you expected a happy and gay welcome, to behold, on the contrary, tears and wretchedness? And how, Victor, can I relate our misfortune? Absence cannot have rendered you callous to our joys and griefs; and how shall I inflict pain on an absent child? I wish to prepare you for the woeful news, but I know it is impossible; even now your eye skims over the page, to seek the words which are to convey to you the horrible tidings.

"William is dead!—that sweet child, whose smiles delighted and warmed my heart, who was so gentle, yet so gay! Victor, he is murdered!

"I will not attempt to console you; but will simply relate the circumstances of the transaction.

"Last Thursday (May 7th)[1] I, my niece, and your two brothers, went to walk in Plainpalais. The evening was warm and serene, and we prolonged our walk farther than usual. It was already dusk before we thought of returning; and then we discovered that William and Ernest, who had gone on before, were not to be found. We accordingly rested on a seat until they should return. Presently Ernest came, and inquired if we had seen his brother: he said, that they had been playing together, that William had run away to hide himself, and that he vainly sought for him, and afterwards waited for him a long time, but that he did not return.

"This account rather alarmed us, and we continued to search for him until night fell, when Elizabeth conjectured that he might have returned to the house. He was not there. We returned again, with torches; for I could not rest, when I thought that my sweet boy had lost himself, and was exposed to all the damps and dews of night: Elizabeth also suffered extreme anguish. About five in the morning I discovered my lovely boy, whom the night before I

---

1 The year is 1795.

had seen blooming and active in health, stretched on the grass livid and motionless: the print of the murderer's finger was on his neck.

"He was conveyed home, and the anguish that was visible in my countenance betrayed the secret to Elizabeth. She was very earnest to see the corpse. At first I attempted to prevent her; but she persisted, and entering the room where it lay, hastily examined the neck of the victim, and clasping her hands exclaimed, 'O God! I have murdered my darling infant!'

"She fainted, and was restored with extreme difficulty. When she again lived, it was only to weep and sigh. She told me, that that same evening William had teazed her to let him wear a very valuable miniature that she possessed of your mother. This picture is gone, and was doubtless the temptation which urged the murderer to the deed. We have no trace of him at present, although our exertions to discover him are unremitted; but they will not restore my beloved William.

"Come, dearest Victor; you alone can console Elizabeth. She weeps continually, and accuses herself unjustly as the cause of his death; her words pierce my heart. We are all unhappy; but will not that be an additional motive for you, my son, to return and be our comforter? Your dear mother! Alas, Victor! I now say, Thank God she did not live to witness the cruel, miserable death of her youngest darling!

"Come, Victor; not brooding thoughts of vengeance against the assassin, but with feelings of peace and gentleness, that will heal, instead of festering the wounds of our minds. Enter the house of mourning, my friend, but with kindness and affection for those who love you, and not with hatred for your enemies.

"Your affectionate and afflicted father,

"ALPHONSE FRANKENSTEIN.
"Geneva, May 12th, 17—."

Clerval, who had watched my countenance as I read this letter, was surprised to observe the despair that succeeded to the joy I at first expressed on receiving news from my friends. I threw the letter on the table, and covered my face with my hands.

"My dear Frankenstein," exclaimed Henry, when he perceived me weep with bitterness, "are you always to be unhappy? My dear friend, what has happened?"

I motioned to him to take up the letter, while I walked up and down the room in the extremest agitation. Tears also gushed from the eyes of Clerval, as he read the account of my misfortune.

"I can offer you no consolation, my friend," said he; "your disaster is irreparable. What do you intend to do?"

"To go instantly to Geneva: come with me, Henry, to order the horses."

During our walk, Clerval endeavoured to raise my spirits. He did not do this by common topics of consolation, but by exhibiting the truest sympathy. "Poor William!" said he, "that dear child; he now sleeps with his angel mother. His friends mourn and weep, but he is at rest: he does not now feel the murderer's grasp; a sod covers his gentle form, and he knows no pain. He can no longer be a fit subject for pity; the survivors are the greatest sufferers, and for them time is the only consolation. Those maxims of the Stoics, that death was no evil, and that the mind of man ought to be superior to despair on the eternal absence of a beloved object, ought not to be urged. Even Cato wept over the dead body of his brother."[1]

Clerval spoke thus as we hurried through the streets; the words impressed themselves on my mind, and I remembered them afterwards in solitude. But now, as soon as the horses arrived, I hurried into a cabriole,[2] and bade farewell to my friend.

My journey was very melancholy. At first I wished to hurry on, for I longed to console and sympathize with my loved and sorrowing friends; but when I drew near my native town, I slackened my progress. I could hardly sustain the multitude of feelings that crowded into my mind. I passed through scenes familiar to my youth, but which I had not seen for nearly six years. How altered every thing might be during that time? One sudden and desolating change had taken place; but a thousand little circumstances might have by degrees worked other alterations, which, although they were done more tranquilly, might not be the less decisive. Fear overcame me; I dared not advance, dreading a thousand nameless evils that made me tremble, although I was unable to define them.

I remained two days at Lausanne, in this painful state of mind. I contemplated the lake: the waters were placid; all around was calm, and the snowy mountains, "the palaces of nature,"[3] were not changed. By degrees the calm and heavenly scene restored me, and I continued my journey towards Geneva.

---

1 Cf. *Plutarch's Lives* 4: 195, 201-02; "Cato the Younger" (Appendix C.3.e).

2 A two-wheeled, one-horse carriage.

3 Byron, *Childe Harold's Pilgrimage* III (1816) lxii.2.

The road ran by the side of the lake, which became narrower as I approached my native town. I discovered more distinctly the black sides of Jura, and the bright summit of Mont Blanc; I wept like a child: "Dear mountains! my own beautiful lake! how do you welcome your wanderer? Your summits are clear; the sky and lake are blue and placid. Is this to prognosticate peace, or to mock at my unhappiness?"

I fear, my friend, that I shall render myself tedious by dwelling on these preliminary circumstances; but they were days of comparative happiness, and I think of them with pleasure. My country, my beloved country! who but a native can tell the delight I took in again beholding thy streams, thy mountains, and, more than all, thy lovely lake.

Yet, as I drew nearer home, grief and fear again overcame me. Night also closed around; and when I could hardly see the dark mountains, I felt still more gloomily. The picture appeared a vast and dim scene of evil, and I foresaw obscurely that I was destined to become the most wretched of human beings. Alas! I prophesied truly, and failed only in one single circumstance, that in all the misery I imagined and dreaded, I did not conceive the hundredth part of the anguish I was destined to endure.

It was completely dark when I arrived in the environs of Geneva; the gates of the town were already shut; and I was obliged to pass the night at Secheron, a village half a league to the east of the city. The sky was serene; and, as I was unable to rest, I resolved to visit the spot where my poor William had been murdered. As I could not pass through the town, I was obliged to cross the lake in a boat to arrive at Plainpalais. During this short voyage I saw the lightnings playing on the summit of Mont Blanc in the most beautiful figures. The storm appeared to approach rapidly; and, on landing, I ascended a low hill, that I might observe its progress. It advanced; the heavens were clouded, and I soon felt the rain coming slowly in large drops, but its violence quickly increased.

I quitted my seat, and walked on, although the darkness and storm increased every minute, and the thunder burst with a terrific crash over my head. It was echoed from Salêve, the Juras, and the Alps of Savoy; vivid flashes of lightning dazzled my eyes, illuminating the lake, making it appear like a vast sheet of fire; then for an instant every thing seemed of a pitchy darkness, until the eye recovered itself from the preceding flash. The storm, as is often the case in Switzerland, appeared at once in various parts of the heavens. The most violent storm hung exactly north of the town, over that part of the lake which lies between the promontory of Belrive and the village of Copêt. Another storm enlighted Jura with faint flashes; and another darkened and sometimes disclosed the Môle, a peaked mountain to the east of the lake.[1]

While I watched the storm, so beautiful yet terrific, I wandered on with a hasty step. This noble war in the sky elevated my spirits; I clasped my hands, and exclaimed aloud, "William, dear angel! this is thy funeral, this thy dirge!" As I said these words, I perceived in the gloom a figure which stole from behind a clump of trees near me; I stood fixed, gazing intently: I could not be mistaken. A flash of lightning illuminated the object, and discovered its shape plainly to me; its gigantic stature, and the deformity of its aspect, more hideous than belongs to humanity, instantly informed me that it was the wretch, the filthy daemon to whom I had given life.[2] What did he there? Could he be (I shuddered at the conception) the murderer of my brother? No sooner did that idea cross my imagination, than I became convinced of its truth; my teeth chattered, and I was forced to lean against a tree for support. The figure passed me quickly, and I lost it in the gloom. Nothing in human shape could have destroyed that fair child. *He* was the murderer! I could not doubt it. The mere presence of the idea was an irresistible proof of the fact. I thought of pursuing the devil; but it would have been in vain, for another flash discovered him to me hanging among the rocks of the nearly perpendicular ascent of Mont Salêve, a hill that bounds Plainpalais on the south. He soon reached the summit, and disappeared.

I remained motionless. The thunder ceased; but the rain still continued, and the scene was enveloped in an impenetrable darkness. I revolved in my mind the events which I had until now sought to forget: the whole train of my progress towards the creation; the appearance of the work of my own hands alive at my bed side; its departure. Two years had now nearly elapsed since the night on which he first received life; and was this his first crime? Alas! I had turned loose into the world a depraved wretch, whose delight was in carnage and misery; had he not murdered my brother?

No one can conceive the anguish I suffered during the remainder of the night, which I spent, cold and wet, in the open air. But I did not feel the inconvenience of the weather; my imagination was busy in scenes of evil and despair. I considered the being

---

1 Cf. Byron, *Childe Harold's Pilgrimage* III.xcii-xcvii.
2 Cf. Wollstonecraft, *Vindication* 232-34; V.v (Appendix A.2.b).

whom I had cast among mankind, and endowed with the will and power to effect purposes of horror, such as the deed which he had now done, nearly in the light of my own vampire, my own spirit let loose from the grave, and forced to destroy all that was dear to me.

Day dawned; and I directed my steps towards the town. The gates were open; and I hastened to my father's house. My first thought was to discover what I knew of the murderer, and cause instant pursuit to be made. But I paused when I reflected on the story that I had to tell. A being whom I myself had formed, and endued with life, had met me at midnight among the precipices of an inaccessible mountain. I remembered also the nervous fever with which I had been seized just at the time that I dated my creation, and which would give an air of delirium to a tale otherwise so utterly improbable. I well knew that if any other had communicated such a relation to me, I should have looked upon it as the ravings of insanity. Besides, the strange nature of the animal would elude all pursuit, even if I were so far credited as to persuade my relatives to commence it. Besides, of what use would be pursuit? Who could arrest a creature capable of scaling the overhanging sides of Mont Salêve? These reflections determined me, and I resolved to remain silent.[1]

It was about five in the morning when I entered my father's house. I told the servants not to disturb the family, and went into the library to attend their usual hour of rising.

Six years had elapsed, passed as a dream but for one indelible trace, and I stood in the same place where I had last embraced my father before my departure for Ingolstadt. Beloved and respectable parent! He still remained to me. I gazed on the picture of my mother, which stood over the mantle-piece. It was an historical subject, painted at my father's desire, and represented Caroline Beaufort in an agony of despair, kneeling by the coffin of her dead father. Her garb was rustic, and her cheek pale; but there was an air of dignity and beauty, that hardly permitted the sentiment of pity. Below this picture was a miniature of William; and my tears flowed when I looked upon it. While I was thus engaged, Ernest entered: he had heard me arrive, and hastened to welcome me. He expressed a sorrowful delight to see me: "Welcome, my dearest Victor," said he. "Ah! I wish you had come three months ago, and then you would have found us all

---

1 Cf. Godwin's insistence on the importance of candour and sincerity, *Political Justice* 1: 332-33; IV.vi.

joyous and delighted. But we are now unhappy; and, I am afraid, tears instead of smiles will be your welcome. Our father looks so sorrowful: this dreadful event seems to have revived in his mind his grief on the death of Mamma. Poor Elizabeth also is quite inconsolable." Ernest began to weep as he said these words.

"Do not," said I, "welcome me thus; try to be more calm, that I may not be absolutely miserable the moment I enter my father's house after so long an absence. But, tell me, how does my father support his misfortunes? and how is my poor Elizabeth?"

"She indeed requires consolation; she accused herself of having caused the death of my brother, and that made her very wretched. But since the murderer has been discovered—"

"The murderer discovered! Good God! how can that be? who could attempt to pursue him? It is impossible; one might as well try to overtake the winds, or confine a mountain-stream with a straw."

"I do not know what you mean; but we were all very unhappy when she was discovered. No one would believe it at first; and even now Elizabeth will not be convinced, notwithstanding all the evidence. Indeed, who would credit that Justine Moritz, who was so amiable, and fond of all the family, could all at once become so extremely wicked?"

"Justine Moritz! Poor, poor girl, is she the accused? But it is wrongfully; every one knows that; no one believes it, surely, Ernest?"

"No one did at first; but several circumstances came out, that have almost forced conviction upon us: and her own behaviour has been so confused, as to add to the evidence of facts a weight that, I fear, leaves no hope for doubt. But she will be tried to-day, and you will then hear all."

He related that, the morning on which the murder of poor William had been discovered, Justine had been taken ill, and confined to her bed; and, after several days, one of the servants, happening to examine the apparel she had worn on the night of the murder, had discovered in her pocket the picture of my mother, which had been judged to be the temptation of the murderer. The servant instantly shewed it to one of the others, who, without saying a word to any of the family, went to a magistrate; and, upon their deposition, Justine was apprehended. On being charged with the fact, the poor girl confirmed the suspicion in a great measure by her extreme confusion of manner.

This was a strange tale, but it did not shake my faith; and I replied earnestly, "You are all mistaken; I know the murderer. Justine, poor, good Justine, is innocent."

At that instant my father entered. I saw unhappiness deeply impressed on his countenance, but he endeavoured to welcome me cheerfully; and, after we had exchanged our mournful greeting, would have introduced some other topic than that of our disaster, had not Ernest exclaimed, "Good God, Papa! Victor says that he knows who was the murderer of poor William."

"We do also, unfortunately," replied my father; "for indeed I had rather have been for ever ignorant than have discovered so much depravity and ingratitude in one I valued so highly."

"My dear father, you are mistaken; Justine is innocent."

"If she is, God forbid that she should suffer as guilty. She is to be tried to-day, and I hope, I sincerely hope, that she will be acquitted."

This speech calmed me. I was firmly convinced in my own mind that Justine, and indeed every human being, was guiltless of this murder. I had no fear, therefore, that any circumstantial evidence could be brought forward strong enough to convict her; and, in this assurance, I calmed myself, expecting the trial with eagerness, but without prognosticating an evil result.

We were soon joined by Elizabeth. Time had made great alterations in her form since I had last beheld her. Six years before she had been a pretty, good-humoured girl, whom every one loved and caressed. She was now a woman in stature and expression of countenance, which was uncommonly lovely. An open and capacious forehead gave indications of a good understanding, joined to great frankness of disposition. Her eyes were hazel, and expressive of mildness, now through recent affliction allied to sadness. Her hair was of a rich dark auburn, her complexion fair, and her figure slight and graceful. She welcomed me with the greatest affection. "Your arrival, my dear cousin," said she, "fills me with hope. You perhaps will find some means to justify my poor guiltless Justine. Alas! who is safe, if she be convicted of crime? I rely on her innocence as certainly as I do upon my own. Our misfortune is doubly hard to us; we have not only lost that lovely darling boy, but this poor girl, whom I sincerely love, is to be torn away by even a worse fate. If she is condemned, I never shall know joy more. But she will not, I am sure she will not; and then I shall be happy again, even after the sad death of my little William."

"She is innocent, my Elizabeth," said I, "and that shall be proved; fear nothing, but let your spirits be cheered by the assurance of her acquittal."

"How kind you are! every one else believes in her guilt, and that made me wretched; for I knew that it was impossible: and to see every one else prejudiced in so deadly a manner, rendered me hopeless and despairing." She wept.

"Sweet niece," said my father, "dry your tears. If she is, as you believe, innocent, rely on the justice of our judges, and the activity with which I shall prevent the slightest shadow of partiality."

CHAPTER VII.

WE passed a few sad hours, until eleven o'clock, when the trial was to commence. My father and the rest of the family being obliged to attend as witnesses, I accompanied them to the court. During the whole of this wretched mockery of justice, I suffered living torture. It was to be decided, whether the result of my curiosity and lawless devices would cause the death of two of my fellow-beings: one a smiling babe, full of innocence and joy; the other far more dreadfully murdered, with every aggravation of infamy that could make the murder memorable in horror. Justine also was a girl of merit, and possessed qualities which promised to render her life happy: now all was to be obliterated in an ignominious grave; and I the cause! A thousand times rather would I have confessed myself guilty of the crime ascribed to Justine; but I was absent when it was committed, and such a declaration would have been considered as the ravings of a madman, and would not have exculpated her who suffered through me.

The appearance of Justine was calm. She was dressed in mourning; and her countenance, always engaging, was rendered, by the solemnity of her feelings, exquisitely beautiful. Yet she appeared confident in innocence, and did not tremble, although gazed on and execrated by thousands; for all the kindness which her beauty might otherwise have excited, was obliterated in the minds of the spectators by the imagination of the enormity she was supposed to have committed. She was tranquil, yet her tranquillity was evidently constrained; and as her confusion had before been adduced as a proof of her guilt, she worked up her mind to an appearance of courage. When she entered the court, she threw her eyes round it, and quickly discovered where we were seated. A tear seemed to dim her eye when she saw us; but she quickly recovered herself, and a look of sorrowful affection seemed to attest her utter guiltlessness.

The trial began; and after the advocate against her had stated the charge, several witnesses were called. Several strange facts combined against her, which might have staggered any one who had not such proof of her innocence as I had. She had been out the whole of the night on which the murder had been committed, and towards morning had been perceived by a market-woman not far from the spot where the body of the murdered child had been afterwards found. The woman asked her what she did there; but she looked very strangely, and only returned a confused and unintelligible answer. She returned to the house about eight o'clock; and when one inquired where she had passed the night, she replied, that she had been looking for the child, and demanded earnestly, if any thing had been heard concerning him. When shewn the body, she fell into violent hysterics, and kept her bed for several days. The picture was then produced, which the servant had found in her pocket; and when Elizabeth, in a faltering voice, proved that it was the same which, an hour before the child had been missed, she had placed round his neck, a murmur of horror and indignation filled the court.

Justine was called on for her defence. As the trial had proceeded, her countenance had altered. Surprise, horror, and misery, were strongly expressed. Sometimes she struggled with her tears; but when she was desired to plead, she collected her powers, and spoke in an audible although variable voice:—

"God knows," she said, "how entirely I am innocent. But I do not pretend that my protestations should acquit me: I rest my innocence on a plain and simple explanation of the facts which have been adduced against me; and I hope the character I have always borne will incline my judges to a favourable interpretation, where any circumstance appears doubtful or suspicious."

She then related that, by the permission of Elizabeth, she had passed the evening of the night on which the murder had been committed, at the house of an aunt at Chêne, a village situated at about a league from Geneva. On her return, at about nine o'clock, she met a man, who asked her if she had seen any thing of the child who was lost. She was alarmed by this account, and passed several hours in looking for him, when the gates of Geneva were shut, and she was forced to remain several hours of the night in a barn belonging to a cottage, being unwilling to call up the inhabitants, to whom she was well known. Unable to rest or sleep, she quitted her asylum early, that she might again endeavour to find my brother. If she had gone near the spot where his body lay, it was without her knowledge. That she had been bewildered when questioned by the market-woman, was not surprising, since she had passed a sleepless night, and the fate of poor William was yet uncertain. Concerning the picture she could give no account.

"I know," continued the unhappy victim, "how heavily and fatally this one circumstance weighs against me, but I have no power of explaining it; and when I have expressed my utter ignorance, I am only left to conjecture concerning the probabilities by which it might have been placed in my pocket. But here also I am checked. I believe that I have no enemy on earth, and none surely would have been so wicked as to destroy me wantonly. Did the murderer place it there? I know of no opportunity afforded him for so doing; or if I had, why should he have stolen the jewel, to part with it again so soon?

"I commit my cause to the justice of my judges, yet I see no room for hope. I beg permission to have a few witnesses examined concerning my character; and if their testimony shall not overweigh my supposed guilt, I must be condemned, although I would pledge my salvation on my innocence."

Several witnesses were called, who had known her for many years, and they spoke well of her; but fear, and hatred of the crime of which they supposed her guilty, rendered them timorous, and unwilling to come forward. Elizabeth saw even this last resource, her excellent dispositions and irreproachable conduct, about to fail the accused, when, although violently agitated, she desired permission to address the court.

"I am," said she, "the cousin of the unhappy child who was murdered, or rather his sister, for I was educated by and have lived with his parents ever since and even long before his birth. It may therefore be judged indecent in me to come forward on this occasion; but when I see a fellow-creature about to perish through the cowardice of her pretended friends, I wish to be allowed to speak, that I may say what I know of her character. I am well acquainted with the accused. I have lived in the same house with her, at one time for five, and at another for nearly two years. During all that period she appeared to me the most amiable and benevolent of human creatures. She nursed Madame Frankenstein, my aunt, in her last illness with the greatest affection and care; and afterwards attended her own mother during a tedious illness, in a manner that excited the admiration of all who knew her. After which she again lived in my uncle's house, where she was beloved by all the family. She was warmly attached to the child who is now dead, and acted towards him like a most affectionate mother. For my own part, I do not hesitate to say, that, notwithstanding all the evidence produced against her, I believe and rely on her perfect innocence. She had no temptation for such an action: as to the bauble on which the chief proof rests, if she had earnestly desired it, I should have willingly given it to her; so much do I esteem and value her."[1]

Excellent Elizabeth! A murmur of approbation was heard; but it was excited by her generous interference, and not in favour of poor Justine, on whom the public indignation was turned with renewed violence, charging her with the blackest ingratitude. She herself wept as Elizabeth spoke, but she did not answer. My own agitation and anguish was extreme during the whole trial. I believed in her innocence; I knew it. Could the daemon, who had (I did not for a minute doubt) murdered my brother, also in his hellish sport have betrayed the innocent to death and ignominy. I could not sustain the horror of my situation; and when I perceived that the popular voice, and the countenances of the judges, had already condemned my unhappy victim, I rushed out of the court in agony. The tortures of the accused did not equal mine; she was sustained by innocence, but the fangs of remorse tore my bosom, and would not forego their hold.

I passed a night of unmingled wretchedness. In the morning I went to the court; my lips and throat were parched. I dared not ask the fatal question; but I was known, and the officer guessed the cause of my visit. The ballots had been thrown; they were all black, and Justine was condemned.

I cannot pretend to describe what I then felt. I had before experienced sensations of horror; and I have endeavoured to bestow upon them adequate expressions, but words cannot convey an idea of the heart-sickening despair that I then endured. The person to whom I addressed myself added, that Justine had already confessed her guilt. "That evidence," he observed, "was hardly required in so glaring a case, but I am glad of it; and, indeed, none of our judges like to condemn a criminal upon circumstantial evidence, be it ever so decisive."

When I returned home, Elizabeth eagerly demanded the result.

"My cousin," replied I, "it is decided as you may have expected; all judges had rather that ten innocent should suffer, than that one guilty should escape.[2] But she has confessed."

This was a dire blow to poor Elizabeth, who had relied with firmness upon Justine's innocence. "Alas!" said she, "how shall I ever again believe in human benevolence? Justine, whom I loved

---

1 Cf. the courtroom speeches of Falkland in Godwin, *Caleb Williams* 174 (II.x) and Maria in Wollstonecraft, *The Wrongs of Woman* 195-98 (XVII).

2 A sarcastic inversion of the maxim from Sir William Blackstone, *Commentaries on the Laws of England* (1765-69) IV.27.

and esteemed as my sister, how could she put on those smiles of innocence only to betray; her mild eyes seemed incapable of any severity or ill-humour, and yet she has committed a murder."

Soon after we heard that the poor victim had expressed a wish to see my cousin. My father wished her not to go; but said, that he left it to her own judgment and feelings to decide. "Yes," said Elizabeth, "I will go, although she is guilty; and you, Victor, shall accompany me: I cannot go alone." The idea of this visit was torture to me, yet I could not refuse.

We entered the gloomy prison-chamber, and beheld Justine sitting on some straw at the further end; her hands were manacled, and her head rested on her knees. She rose on seeing us enter; and when we were left alone with her, she threw herself at the feet of Elizabeth, weeping bitterly. My cousin wept also.

"Oh, Justine!" said she, "why did you rob me of my last consolation. I relied on your innocence; and although I was then very wretched, I was not so miserable as I am now."

"And do you also believe that I am so very, very wicked? Do you also join with my enemies to crush me?" Her voice was suffocated with sobs.

"Rise, my poor girl," said Elizabeth, "why do you kneel, if you are innocent? I am not one of your enemies; I believed you guiltless, notwithstanding every evidence, until I heard that you had yourself declared your guilt. That report, you say, is false; and be assured, dear Justine, that nothing can shake my confidence in you for a moment, but your own confession."

"I did confess; but I confessed a lie. I confessed, that I might obtain absolution; but now that falsehood lies heavier at my heart than all my other sins. The God of heaven forgive me! Ever since I was condemned, my confessor has besieged me; he threatened and menaced, until I almost began to think that I was the monster that he said I was. He threatened excommunication and hell fire in my last moments, if I continued obdurate.[1] Dear lady, I had none to support me; all looked on me as a wretch doomed to ignominy and perdition. What could I do? In an evil hour[2] I subscribed to a lie; and now only am I truly miserable."

She paused, weeping, and then continued—"I thought with horror, my sweet lady, that you should believe your Justine, whom your blessed aunt had so highly honoured, and whom you

---

1 Cf. the critique of "blind obedience" in Wollstonecraft, *Vindication* 133 (II).
2 Cf. Milton, *Paradise Lost* IX.780.

loved, was a creature capable of a crime which none but the devil himself could have perpetrated. Dear William! dearest blessed child! I soon shall see you again in heaven, where we shall all be happy; and that consoles me, going as I am to suffer ignominy and death."

"Oh, Justine! forgive me for having for one moment distrusted you. Why did you confess? But do not mourn, my dear girl; I will every where proclaim your innocence, and force belief. Yet you must die; you, my playfellow, my companion, my more than sister. I never can survive so horrible a misfortune."

"Dear, sweet Elizabeth, do not weep. You ought to raise me with thoughts of a better life, and elevate me from the petty cares of this world of injustice and strife. Do not you, excellent friend, drive me to despair."

"I will try to comfort you; but this, I fear, is an evil too deep and poignant to admit of consolation, for there is no hope. Yet heaven bless thee, my dearest Justine, with resignation, and a confidence elevated beyond this world. Oh! how I hate its shews and mockeries! when one creature is murdered, another is immediately deprived of life in a slow torturing manner; then the executioners, their hands yet reeking with the blood of innocence, believe that they have done a great deed. They call this *retribution*. Hateful name! When that word is pronounced, I know greater and more horrid punishments are going to be inflicted than the gloomiest tyrant has ever invented to satiate his utmost revenge.[1] Yet this is not consolation for you, my Justine, unless indeed that you may glory in escaping from so miserable a den. Alas! I would I were in peace with my aunt and my lovely William, escaped from a world which is hateful to me, and the visages of men which I abhor."

Justine smiled languidly. "This, dear lady, is despair, and not resignation. I must not learn the lesson that you would teach me. Talk of something else, something that will bring peace, and not increase of misery."

During this conversation I had retired to a corner of the prison-room, where I could conceal the horrid anguish that possessed me. Despair! Who dared talk of that? The poor victim, who on the morrow was to pass the dreary boundary between life and death, felt not as I did, such deep and bitter agony. I gnashed my teeth, and ground them together, uttering a groan that came

---

1 Cf. Godwin's analysis of the justice system, *Political Justice* 2: 354-59; VII.iv.

from my inmost soul. Justine started. When she saw who it was, she approached me, and said, "Dear Sir, you are very kind to visit me; you, I hope, do not believe that I am guilty."

I could not answer. "No, Justine," said Elizabeth; "he is more convinced of your innocence than I was; for even when he heard that you had confessed, he did not credit it."

"I truly thank him. In these last moments I feel the sincerest gratitude towards those who think of me with kindness. How sweet is the affection of others to such a wretch as I am! It removes more than half my misfortune; and I feel as if I could die in peace, now that my innocence is acknowledged by you, dear lady, and your cousin."

Thus the poor sufferer tried to comfort others and herself. She indeed gained the resignation she desired. But I, the true murderer, felt the never-dying worm alive in my bosom,[1] which allowed of no hope or consolation. Elizabeth also wept, and was unhappy; but her's also was the misery of innocence, which, like a cloud that passes over the fair moon, for a while hides, but cannot tarnish its brightness. Anguish and despair had penetrated into the core of my heart; I bore a hell within me, which nothing could extinguish.[2] We staid several hours with Justine; and it was with great difficulty that Elizabeth could tear herself away. "I wish," cried she, "that I were to die with you; I cannot live in this world of misery."

Justine assumed an air of cheerfulness, while she with difficulty repressed her bitter tears. She embraced Elizabeth, and said, in a voice of half-suppressed emotion, "Farewell, sweet lady, dearest Elizabeth, my beloved and only friend; may heaven in its bounty bless and preserve you; may this be the last misfortune that you will ever suffer. Live, and be happy, and make others so."

As we returned, Elizabeth said, "You know not, my dear Victor, how much I am relieved, now that I trust in the innocence of this unfortunate girl. I never could again have known peace, if I had been deceived in my reliance on her. For the moment that I did believe her guilty, I felt an anguish that I could not have long sustained. Now my heart is lightened. The innocent suffers; but she whom I thought amiable and good has not betrayed the trust I reposed in her, and I am consoled."

---

1 Cf. Mark 9: 44; Milton, *Paradise Lost* VI.739; and Byron, *The Bride of Abydos* (1813) II.646.

2 Cf. Milton, *Paradise Lost* IV.75, IX.467. Falkland suffers the same fate in Godwin, *Caleb Williams* 280, 284 (III.xii).

Amiable cousin! such were your thoughts, mild and gentle as your own dear eyes and voice. But I—I was a wretch, and none ever conceived of the misery that I then endured.

END OF VOL. I.

FRANKENSTEIN;
OR, THE
MODERN PROMETHEUS.

[VOL. II.]

CHAPTER I.

NOTHING is more painful to the human mind, than, after the feelings have been worked up by a quick succession of events, the dead calmness of inaction and certainty which follows, and deprives the soul both of hope and fear. Justine died; she rested; and I was alive. The blood flowed freely in my veins, but a weight of despair and remorse pressed on my heart, which nothing could remove. Sleep fled from my eyes; I wandered like an evil spirit, for I had committed deeds of mischief beyond description horrible, and more, much more, (I persuaded myself) was yet behind. Yet my heart overflowed with kindness, and the love of virtue. I had begun life with benevolent intentions, and thirsted for the moment when I should put them in practice, and make myself useful to my fellow-beings. Now all was blasted: instead of that serenity of conscience, which allowed me to look back upon the past with self-satisfaction, and from thence to gather promise of new hopes, I was seized by remorse and the sense of guilt, which hurried me away to a hell of intense tortures, such as no language can describe.

This state of mind preyed upon my health, which had entirely recovered from the first shock it had sustained. I shunned the face of man; all sound of joy or complacency was torture to me; solitude was my only consolation—deep, dark, death-like solitude.

My father observed with pain the alteration perceptible in my disposition and habits, and endeavoured to reason with me on the folly of giving way to immoderate grief. "Do you think, Victor," said he, "that I do not suffer also? No one could love a child more than I loved your brother"; (tears came into his eyes as he spoke); "but is it not a duty to the survivors, that we should refrain from augmenting their unhappiness by an appearance of immoderate grief? It is also a duty owed to yourself; for excessive sorrow prevents improvement or enjoyment, or even the discharge of daily usefulness, without which no man is fit for society."

This advice, although good, was totally inapplicable to my case; I should have been the first to hide my grief, and console my friends, if remorse had not mingled its bitterness with my other sensations. Now I could only answer my father with a look of despair, and endeavour to hide myself from his view.

About this time we retired to our house at Belrive. This change was particularly agreeable to me. The shutting of the gates regularly at ten o'clock, and the impossibility of remaining on the lake after that hour, had rendered our residence within the walls of Geneva very irksome to me. I was now free. Often, after the rest of the family had retired for the night, I took the boat, and passed many hours upon the water. Sometimes, with my sails set, I was carried by the wind; and sometimes, after rowing into the middle of the lake, I left the boat to pursue its own course, and gave way to my own miserable reflections. I was often tempted, when all was at peace around me, and I the only unquiet thing that wandered restless in a scene so beautiful and heavenly, if I except some bat, or the frogs, whose harsh and interrupted croaking was heard only when I approached the shore—often, I say, I was tempted to plunge into the silent lake, that the waters might close over me and my calamities for ever.[1] But I was restrained, when I thought of the heroic and suffering Elizabeth, whom I tenderly loved, and whose existence was bound up in mine. I thought also of my father, and surviving brother: should I by my base desertion leave them exposed and unprotected to the malice of the fiend whom I had let loose among them?

At these moments I wept bitterly, and wished that peace would revisit my mind only that I might afford them consolation and happiness. But that could not be. Remorse extinguished every hope. I had been the author of unalterable evils; and I lived in daily fear, lest the monster whom I had created should perpetrate some new wickedness. I had an obscure feeling that all was not over, and that he would still commit some signal crime, which by its enormity should almost efface the recollection of the past. There was always scope for fear, so long as any thing I loved remained behind. My abhorrence of this fiend cannot be conceived. When I thought of him, I gnashed my teeth, my eyes became inflamed, and I ardently wished to extinguish that life which I had so thoughtlessly bestowed. When I reflected on his crimes and malice, my hatred and revenge burst all bounds of moderation. I would have made a pilgrimage to the highest peak

---

1 Cf. Goethe, *The Sorrows of Werter* 77-87; Letter XXIX (Appendix C.2.a).

of the Andes, could I, when there, have precipitated him to their base. I wished to see him again, that I might wreak the utmost extent of anger on his head, and avenge the deaths of William and Justine.

Our house was the house of mourning. My father's health was deeply shaken by the horror of the recent events. Elizabeth was sad and desponding; she no longer took delight in her ordinary occupations; all pleasure seemed to her sacrilege toward the dead; eternal woe and tears she then thought was the just tribute she should pay to innocence so blasted and destroyed. She was no longer that happy creature, who in earlier youth wandered with me on the banks of the lake, and talked with ecstacy of our future prospects. She had become grave, and often conversed of the inconstancy of fortune, and the instability of human life.

"When I reflect, my dear cousin," said she, "on the miserable death of Justine Moritz, I no longer see the world and its works as they before appeared to me. Before, I looked upon the accounts of vice and injustice, that I read in books or heard from others, as tales of ancient days, or imaginary evils; at least they were remote, and more familiar to reason than to the imagination; but now misery has come home, and men appear to me as monsters thirsting for each other's blood. Yet I am certainly unjust. Every body believed that poor girl to be guilty; and if she could have committed the crime for which she suffered, assuredly she would have been the most depraved of human creatures. For the sake of a few jewels, to have murdered the son of her benefactor and friend, a child whom she had nursed from its birth, and appeared to love as if it had been her own! I could not consent to the death of any human being; but certainly I should have thought such a creature unfit to remain in the society of men. Yet she was innocent. I know, I feel she was innocent; you are of the same opinion, and that confirms me. Alas! Victor, when falsehood can look so like the truth, who can assure themselves of certain happiness? I feel as if I were walking on the edge of a precipice, towards which thousands are crowding, and endeavouring to plunge me into the abyss. William and Justine were assassinated, and the murderer escapes; he walks about the world free, and perhaps respected. But even if I were condemned to suffer on the scaffold for the same crimes, I would not change places with such a wretch."

I listened to this discourse with the extremest agony. I, not in deed, but in effect, was the true murderer. Elizabeth read my anguish in my countenance, and kindly taking my hand said, "My dearest cousin, you must calm yourself. These events have affected me, God knows how deeply; but I am not so wretched as you are. There is an expression of despair, and sometimes of revenge, in your countenance, that makes me tremble. Be calm, my dear Victor; I would sacrifice my life to your peace. We surely shall be happy: quiet in our native country, and not mingling in the world, what can disturb our tranquillity?"

She shed tears as she said this, distrusting the very solace that she gave; but at the same time she smiled, that she might chase away the fiend that lurked in my heart. My father, who saw in the unhappiness that was painted in my face only an exaggeration of that sorrow which I might naturally feel, thought that an amusement suited to my taste would be the best means of restoring to me my wonted serenity. It was from this cause that he had removed to the country; and, induced by the same motive, he now proposed that we should all make an excursion to the valley of Chamounix. I had been there before, but Elizabeth and Ernest never had; and both had often expressed an earnest desire to see the scenery of this place, which had been described to them as so wonderful and sublime. Accordingly we departed from Geneva on this tour about the middle of the month of August, nearly two months after the death of Justine.

The weather was uncommonly fine; and if mine had been a sorrow to be chased away by any fleeting circumstance, this excursion would certainly have had the effect intended by my father. As it was, I was somewhat interested in the scene; it sometimes lulled, although it could not extinguish my grief. During the first day we travelled in a carriage. In the morning we had seen the mountains at a distance, towards which we gradually advanced. We perceived that the valley through which we wound, and which was formed by the river Arve, whose course we followed, closed in upon us by degrees; and when the sun had set, we beheld immense mountains and precipices overhanging us on every side, and heard the sound of the river raging among rocks, and the dashing of waterfalls around.

The next day we pursued our journey upon mules; and as we ascended still higher, the valley assumed a more magnificent and astonishing character. Ruined castles hanging on the precipices of piny mountains; the impetuous Arve, and cottages every here and there peeping forth from among the trees, formed a scene of singular beauty. But it was augmented and rendered sublime by the mighty Alps, whose white and shining pyramids and domes towered above all, as belonging to another earth, the habitations of another race of beings.

We passed the bridge of Pelissier, where the ravine, which the river forms, opened before us, and we began to ascend the mountain that overhangs it. Soon after we entered the valley of Chamounix. This valley is more wonderful and sublime, but not so beautiful and picturesque as that of Servox, through which we had just passed. The high and snowy mountains were its immediate boundaries; but we saw no more ruined castles and fertile fields. Immense glaciers approached the road; we heard the rumbling thunder of the falling avelânche, and marked the smoke of its passage. Mont Blanc, the supreme and magnificent Mont Blanc, raised itself from the surrounding *aiguilles*,[1] and its tremendous *dome* overlooked the valley.

During this journey, I sometimes joined Elizabeth, and exerted myself to point out to her the various beauties of the scene. I often suffered my mule to lag behind, and indulged in the misery of reflection. At other times I spurred on the animal before my companions, that I might forget them, the world, and, more than all, myself. When at a distance, I alighted, and threw myself on the grass, weighed down by horror and despair. At eight in the evening I arrived at Chamounix. My father and Elizabeth were very much fatigued; Ernest, who accompanied us, was delighted, and in high spirits: the only circumstance that detracted from his pleasure was the south wind, and the rain it seemed to promise for the next day.

We retired early to our apartments, but not to sleep; at least I did not. I remained many hours at the window, watching the pallid lightning that played above Mont Blanc, and listening to the rushing of the Arve, which ran below my window.

CHAPTER II.

THE next day, contrary to the prognostications of our guides, was fine, although clouded. We visited the source of the Arveiron, and rode about the valley until evening. These sublime and magnificent scenes afforded me the greatest consolation that I was capable of receiving. They elevated me from all littleness of feeling; and although they did not remove my grief, they subdued and tranquillized it. In some degree, also, they diverted my mind from the thoughts over which it had brooded for the last month. I returned in the evening, fatigued, but less unhappy, and con-

---

1 Peaks.

versed with my family with more cheerfulness than had been my custom for some time. My father was pleased, and Elizabeth overjoyed. "My dear cousin," said she, "you see what happiness you diffuse when you are happy; do not relapse again!"

The following morning the rain poured down in torrents, and thick mists hid the summits of the mountains. I rose early, but felt unusually melancholy. The rain depressed me; my old feelings recurred, and I was miserable. I knew how disappointed my father would be at this sudden change, and I wished to avoid him until I had recovered myself so far as to be enabled to conceal those feelings that overpowered me. I knew that they would remain that day at the inn; and as I had ever inured myself to rain, moisture, and cold, I resolved to go alone to the summit of Montanvert. I remembered the effect that the view of the tremendous and ever-moving glacier had produced upon my mind when I first saw it. It had then filled me with a sublime ecstacy that gave wings to the soul, and allowed it to soar from the obscure world to light and joy. The sight of the awful and majestic in nature had indeed always the effect of solemnizing my mind, and causing me to forget the passing cares of life. I determined to go alone, for I was well acquainted with the path, and the presence of another would destroy the solitary grandeur of the scene.

The ascent is precipitous, but the path is cut into continual and short windings, which enable you to surmount the perpendicularity of the mountain. It is a scene terrifically desolate. In a thousand spots the traces of the winter avelânche may be perceived, where trees lie broken and strewed on the ground; some entirely destroyed, others bent, leaning upon the jutting rocks of the mountain, or transversely upon other trees. The path, as you ascend higher, is intersected by ravines of snow, down which stones continually roll from above; one of them is particularly dangerous, as the slightest sound, such as even speaking in a loud voice, produces a concussion of air sufficient to draw destruction upon the head of the speaker. The pines are not tall or luxuriant, but they are sombre, and add an air of severity to the scene. I looked on the valley beneath; vast mists were rising from the rivers which ran through it, and curling in thick wreaths around the opposite mountains, whose summits were hid in the uniform clouds, while rain poured from the dark sky, and added to the melancholy impression I received from the objects around me. Alas! why does man boast of sensibilities superior to those apparent in the brute; it only renders them more necessary beings. If our impulses were confined to hunger, thirst, and desire, we might be nearly free; but now we are moved by every wind that blows, and a chance word or scene that that word may convey to us.

We rest; a dream has power to poison sleep.
We rise; one wand'ring thought pollutes the day.
We feel, conceive, or reason; laugh, or weep,
    Embrace fond woe, or cast our cares away;
It is the same: for, be it joy or sorrow,
    The path of its departure still is free.
Man's yesterday may ne'er be like his morrow;
    Nought may endure but mutability![1]

It was nearly noon when I arrived at the top of the ascent. For some time I sat upon the rock that overlooks the sea of ice. A mist covered both that and the surrounding mountains. Presently a breeze dissipated the cloud, and I descended upon the glacier. The surface is very uneven, rising like the waves of a troubled sea, descending low, and interspersed by rifts that sink deep. The field of ice is almost a league in width, but I spent nearly two hours in crossing it. The opposite mountain is a bare perpendicular rock. From the side where I now stood Montanvert was exactly opposite, at the distance of a league; and above it rose Mont Blanc, in awful majesty. I remained in a recess of the rock, gazing on this wonderful and stupendous scene. The sea, or rather the vast river of ice, wound among its dependent mountains, whose aërial summits hung over its recesses. Their icy and glittering peaks shone in the sunlight over the clouds. My heart, which was before sorrowful, now swelled with something like joy; I exclaimed— "Wandering spirits, if indeed ye wander, and do not rest in your narrow beds, allow me this faint happiness, or take me, as your companion, away from the joys of life."

As I said this, I suddenly beheld the figure of a man, at some distance, advancing towards me with superhuman speed. He bounded over the crevices in the ice, among which I had walked with caution; his stature also, as he approached, seemed to exceed that of man. I was troubled: a mist came over my eyes, and I felt a faintness seize me; but I was quickly restored by the cold gale of the mountains. I perceived, as the shape came nearer, (sight tremendous and abhorred!) that it was the wretch whom I had created. I trembled with rage and horror, resolving to wait his

---

1 Victor anachronistically quotes P.B. Shelley, "Mutability" (1816) 9-16.

approach, and then close with him in mortal combat. He approached; his countenance bespoke bitter anguish, combined with disdain and malignity, while its unearthly ugliness rendered it almost too horrible for human eyes. But I scarcely observed this; anger and hatred had at first deprived me of utterance, and I recovered only to overwhelm him with words expressive of furious detestation and contempt.

"Devil!" I exclaimed, "do you dare approach me? and do not you fear the fierce vengeance of my arm wreaked on your miserable head? Begone, vile insect! or rather stay, that I may trample you to dust! and, oh, that I could, with the extinction of your miserable existence, restore those victims whom you have so diabolically murdered!"

"I expected this reception," said the daemon. "All men hate the wretched; how then must I be hated, who am miserable beyond all living things! Yet you, my creator, detest and spurn me, thy creature, to whom thou art bound by ties only dissoluble by the annihilation of one of us. You purpose to kill me. How dare you sport thus with life? Do your duty towards me, and I will do mine towards you and the rest of mankind. If you will comply with my conditions, I will leave them and you at peace; but if you refuse, I will glut the maw of death, until it be satiated with the blood of your remaining friends."

"Abhorred monster! fiend that thou art! the tortures of hell are too mild a vengeance for thy crimes. Wretched devil! you reproach me with your creation; come on then, that I may extinguish the spark which I so negligently bestowed."

My rage was without bounds; I sprang on him, impelled by all the feelings which can arm one being against the existence of another.

He easily eluded me, and said,

"Be calm! I entreat you to hear me, before you give vent to your hatred on my devoted head. Have I not suffered enough, that you seek to increase my misery? Life, although it may only be an accumulation of anguish, is dear to me, and I will defend it. Remember, thou hast made me more powerful than thyself; my height is superior to thine; my joints more supple. But I will not be tempted to set myself in opposition to thee. I am thy creature, and I will be even mild and docile to my natural lord and king, if thou wilt also perform thy part, the which thou owest me. Oh, Frankenstein, be not equitable to every other, and trample upon me alone, to whom thy justice, and even thy clemency and affection, is most due. Remember, that I am thy creature: I ought to be thy Adam; but I am rather the fallen angel, whom thou drivest from joy for no misdeed. Every where I see bliss, from which I alone am irrevocably excluded. I was benevolent and good; misery made me a fiend. Make me happy, and I shall again be virtuous."[1]

"Begone! I will not hear you. There can be no community between you and me; we are enemies. Begone, or let us try our strength in a fight, in which one must fall."

"How can I move thee? Will no entreaties cause thee to turn a favourable eye upon thy creature, who implores thy goodness and compassion. Believe me, Frankenstein: I was benevolent; my soul glowed with love and humanity: but am I not alone, miserably alone? You, my creator, abhor me; what hope can I gather from your fellow-creatures, who owe me nothing? they spurn and hate me. The desert mountains and dreary glaciers are my refuge. I have wandered here many days; the caves of ice, which I only do not fear, are a dwelling to me, and the only one which man does not grudge. These bleak skies I hail, for they are kinder to me than your fellow-beings.[2] If the multitude of mankind knew of my existence, they would do as you do, and arm themselves for my destruction. Shall I not then hate them who abhor me? I will keep no terms with my enemies. I am miserable, and they shall share my wretchedness. Yet it is in your power to recompense me, and deliver them from an evil which it only remains for you to make so great, that not only you and your family, but thousands of others, shall be swallowed up in the whirlwinds of its rage. Let your compassion be moved, and do not disdain me. Listen to my tale: when you have heard that, abandon or commiserate me, as you shall judge that I deserve. But hear me. The guilty are allowed, by human laws, bloody as they may be, to speak in their own defence before they are condemned. Listen to me, Frankenstein. You accuse me of murder; and yet you would, with a satisfied conscience, destroy your own creature. Oh, praise the eternal justice of man! Yet I ask you not to spare me: listen to me; and then, if you can, and if you will, destroy the work of your hands."

"Why do you call to my remembrance circumstances of which I shudder to reflect, that I have been the miserable origin and author? Cursed be the day, abhorred devil, in which you first saw light! Cursed (although I curse myself) be the hands that formed

---

1 Cf. Godwin on Satan, *Political Justice* 1: 323-25; IV.v.appendix (Appendix A.1.c), and the complaint of Bethlem Gabor in *St. Leon* 415; XLI.
2 Cf. Shakespeare, *King Lear* III.ii.16.

you! You have made me wretched beyond expression. You have left me no power to consider whether I am just to you, or not. Begone! relieve me from the sight of your detested form."

"Thus I relieve thee, my creator," he said, and placed his hated hands before my eyes, which I flung from me with violence; "thus I take from thee a sight which you abhor. Still thou canst listen to me, and grant me thy compassion. By the virtues that I once possessed, I demand this from you. Hear my tale; it is long and strange, and the temperature of this place is not fitting to your fine sensations; come to the hut upon the mountain. The sun is yet high in the heavens; before it descends to hide itself behind yon snowy precipices, and illuminate another world, you will have heard my story, and can decide. On you it rests, whether I quit for ever the neighbourhood of man, and lead a harmless life, or become the scourge of your fellow-creatures, and the author of your own speedy ruin."

As he said this, he led the way across the ice: I followed. My heart was full, and I did not answer him; but, as I proceeded, I weighed the various arguments that he had used, and determined at least to listen to his tale. I was partly urged by curiosity, and compassion confirmed my resolution. I had hitherto supposed him to be the murderer of my brother, and I eagerly sought a confirmation or denial of this opinion. For the first time, also, I felt what the duties of a creator towards his creature were, and that I ought to render him happy before I complained of his wickedness.[1] These motives urged me to comply with his demand. We crossed the ice, therefore, and ascended the opposite rock. The air was cold, and the rain again began to descend: we entered the hut, the fiend with an air of exultation, I with a heavy heart, and depressed spirits. But I consented to listen; and, seating myself by the fire which my odious companion had lighted, he thus began his tale.

CHAPTER III.

"IT is with considerable difficulty that I remember the original aera of my being: all the events of that period appear confused and indistinct.[2] A strange multiplicity of sensations seized me,

---

1 Cf. Wollstonecraft's warning against parental neglect, *Vindication* 293; XI (Appendix A.2.b).
2 Cf. *Plutarch's Lives* 1: 1; "Theseus" (Appendix C.3.a).

and I saw, felt, heard, and smelt, at the same time; and it was, indeed, a long time before I learned to distinguish between the operations of my various senses. By degrees, I remember, a stronger light pressed upon my nerves, so that I was obliged to shut my eyes. Darkness then came over me, and troubled me; but hardly had I felt this, when, by opening my eyes, as I now suppose, the light poured in upon me again. I walked, and, I believe, descended; but I presently found a great alteration in my sensations. Before, dark and opaque bodies had surrounded me, impervious to my touch or sight; but I now found that I could wander on at liberty, with no obstacles which I could not either surmount or avoid. The light became more and more oppressive to me; and, the heat wearying me as I walked, I sought a place where I could receive shade. This was the forest near Ingolstadt; and here I lay by the side of a brook resting from my fatigue, until I felt tormented by hunger and thirst. This roused me from my nearly dormant state, and I ate some berries which I found hanging on the trees, or lying on the ground. I slaked my thirst at the brook; and then lying down, was overcome by sleep.

"It was dark when I awoke; I felt cold also, and half-frightened as it were instinctively, finding myself so desolate. Before I had quitted your apartment, on a sensation of cold, I had covered myself with some clothes; but these were insufficient to secure me from the dews of night. I was a poor, helpless, miserable wretch; I knew, and could distinguish, nothing; but, feeling pain invade me on all sides, I sat down and wept.[1]

"Soon a gentle light stole over the heavens, and gave me a sensation of pleasure. I started up, and beheld a radiant form rise from among the trees. I gazed with a kind of wonder. It moved slowly, but it enlightened my path; and I again went out in search of berries. I was still cold, when under one of the trees I found a huge cloak, with which I covered myself, and sat down upon the ground. No distinct ideas occupied my mind; all was confused. I felt light, and hunger, and thirst, and darkness; innumerable sounds rung in my ears, and on all sides various scents saluted me: the only object that I could distinguish was the bright moon, and I fixed my eyes on that with pleasure.

"Several changes of day and night passed, and the orb of night had greatly lessened when I began to distinguish my sensations from each other. I gradually saw plainly the clear stream that supplied me with drink, and the trees that shaded me with their

---

1 Cf. Psalm 137: 1.

foliage. I was delighted when I first discovered that a pleasant sound, which often saluted my ears, proceeded from the throats of the little winged animals who had often intercepted the light from my eyes. I began also to observe, with greater accuracy, the forms that surrounded me, and to perceive the boundaries of the radiant roof of light which canopied me. Sometimes I tried to imitate the pleasant songs of the birds, but was unable. Sometimes I wished to express my sensations in my own mode, but the uncouth and inarticulate sounds which broke from me frightened me into silence again.[1]

"The moon had disappeared from the night, and again, with a lessened form, shewed itself, while I still remained in the forest. My sensations had, by this time, become distinct, and my mind received every day additional ideas. My eyes became accustomed to the light, and to perceive objects in their right forms; I distinguished the insect from the herb, and, by degrees, one herb from another. I found that the sparrow uttered none but harsh notes, whilst those of the blackbird and thrush were sweet and enticing.

"One day, when I was oppressed by cold, I found a fire which had been left by some wandering beggars, and was overcome with delight at the warmth I experienced from it. In my joy I thrust my hand into the live embers, but quickly drew it out again with a cry of pain. How strange, I thought, that the same cause should produce such opposite effects! I examined the materials of the fire, and to my joy found it to be composed of wood. I quickly collected some branches; but they were wet, and would not burn. I was pained at this, and sat still watching the operation of the fire. The wet wood which I had placed near the heat dried, and itself became inflamed. I reflected on this; and, by touching the various branches, I discovered the cause, and busied myself in collecting a great quantity of wood, that I might dry it, and have a plentiful supply of fire. When night came on, and brought sleep with it, I was in the greatest fear lest my fire should be extinguished. I covered it carefully with dry wood and leaves, and placed wet branches upon it; and then, spreading my cloak, I lay on the ground, and sunk into sleep.

---

1 Cf. Davy's philosophical history, *Discourse* 15-17 (Appendix B.2.f); Volney's *The Ruins* 22-23 (Appendix C.1.c); Adam's earliest memories, Milton, *Paradise Lost* VIII.250-99 (Appendix C.4.a); and Godwin's account of the development of the human infant, *Political Justice* 1: 33; I.iv.

"It was morning when I awoke, and my first care was to visit the fire. I uncovered it, and a gentle breeze quickly fanned it into a flame. I observed this also, and contrived a fan of branches, which roused the embers when they were nearly extinguished. When night came again, I found, with pleasure, that the fire gave light as well as heat; and that the discovery of this element was useful to me in my food; for I found some of the offals that the travellers had left had been roasted, and tasted much more savoury than the berries I gathered from the trees. I tried, therefore, to dress my food in the same manner, placing it on the live embers. I found that the berries were spoiled by this operation, and the nuts and roots much improved.

"Food, however, became scarce; and I often spent the whole day searching in vain for a few acorns to assuage the pangs of hunger. When I found this, I resolved to quit the place that I had hitherto inhabited, to seek for one where the few wants I experienced would be more easily satisfied. In this emigration, I exceedingly lamented the loss of the fire which I had obtained through accident, and knew not how to re-produce it. I gave several hours to the serious consideration of this difficulty; but I was obliged to relinquish all attempt to supply it; and, wrapping myself up in my cloak, I struck across the wood towards the setting sun. I passed three days in these rambles, and at length discovered the open country. A great fall of snow had taken place the night before, and the fields were of one uniform white; the appearance was disconsolate, and I found my feet chilled by the cold damp substance that covered the ground.

"It was about seven in the morning, and I longed to obtain food and shelter; at length I perceived a small hut, on a rising ground, which had doubtless been built for the convenience of some shepherd. This was a new sight to me; and I examined the structure with great curiosity. Finding the door open, I entered. An old man sat in it, near a fire, over which he was preparing his breakfast. He turned on hearing a noise; and, perceiving me, shrieked loudly, and, quitting the hut, ran across the fields with a speed of which his debilitated form hardly appeared capable. His appearance, different from any I had ever before seen, and his flight, somewhat surprised me. But I was enchanted by the appearance of the hut: here the snow and rain could not penetrate; the ground was dry; and it presented to me then as exquisite and divine a retreat as Pandaemonium appeared to the daemons of hell after their sufferings in the

lake of fire.[1] I greedily devoured the remnants of the shepherd's breakfast, which consisted of bread, cheese, milk, and
wine; the latter, however, I did not like. Then overcome by
fatigue, I lay down among some straw, and fell asleep.

"It was noon when I awoke; and, allured by the warmth of the
sun, which shone brightly on the white ground, I determined to
recommence my travels; and, depositing the remains of the
peasant's breakfast in a wallet I found, I proceeded across the
fields for several hours, until at sunset I arrived at a village. How
miraculous did this appear! the huts, the neater cottages, and
stately houses, engaged my admiration by turns. The vegetables
in the gardens, the milk and cheese that I saw placed at the
windows of some of the cottages, allured my appetite. One of the
best of these I entered; but I had hardly placed my foot within the
door, before the children shrieked, and one of the women fainted.
The whole village was roused; some fled, some attacked me,
until, grievously bruised by stones and many other kinds of
missile weapons, I escaped to the open country, and fearfully
took refuge in a low hovel, quite bare, and making a wretched
appearance after the palaces I had beheld in the village. This
hovel, however, joined a cottage of a neat and pleasant appearance; but, after my late dearly-bought experience, I dared not
enter it. My place of refuge was constructed of wood, but so low,
that I could with difficulty sit upright in it. No wood, however,
was placed on the earth, which formed the floor, but it was dry;
and although the wind entered it by innumerable chinks, I found
it an agreeable asylum from the snow and rain.

"Here then I retreated, and lay down, happy to have found a
shelter, however miserable, from the inclemency of the season,
and still more from the barbarity of man.

"As soon as morning dawned, I crept from my kennel, that I
might view the adjacent cottage, and discover if I could remain in
the habitation I had found. It was situated against the back of the
cottage, and surrounded on the sides which were exposed by a
pig-stye and a clear pool of water. One part was open, and by that
I had crept in; but now I covered every crevice by which I might
be perceived with stones and wood, yet in such a manner that I
might move them on occasion to pass out: all the light I enjoyed
came through the stye, and that was sufficient for me.

"Having thus arranged my dwelling, and carpeted it with clean
straw, I retired; for I saw the figure of a man at a distance, and I

---

1 An allusion to Milton, *Paradise Lost* I.670-732.

remembered too well my treatment the night before, to trust myself in his power. I had first, however, provided for my sustenance for that day, by a loaf of coarse bread, which I purloined, and a cup with which I could drink, more conveniently than from my hand, of the pure water which flowed by my retreat. The floor was a little raised, so that it was kept perfectly dry, and by its vicinity to the chimney of the cottage it was tolerably warm.

"Being thus provided, I resolved to reside in this hovel, until something should occur which might alter my determination. It was indeed a paradise, compared to the bleak forest, my former residence, the rain-dropping branches, and dank earth. I ate my breakfast with pleasure, and was about to remove a plank to procure myself a little water, when I heard a step, and, looking through a small chink, I beheld a young creature, with a pail on her head, passing before my hovel. The girl was young and of gentle demeanour, unlike what I have since found cottagers and farm-house servants to be. Yet she was meanly dressed, a coarse blue petticoat and a linen jacket being her only garb; her fair hair was plaited, but not adorned; she looked patient, yet sad. I lost sight of her; and in about a quarter of an hour she returned, bearing the pail, which was now partly filled with milk. As she walked along, seemingly incommoded by the burden, a young man met her, whose countenance expressed a deeper despondence. Uttering a few sounds with an air of melancholy, he took the pail from her head, and bore it to the cottage himself. She followed, and they disappeared. Presently I saw the young man again, with some tools in his hand, cross the field behind the cottage; and the girl was also busied, sometimes in the house, and sometimes in the yard.

"On examining my dwelling, I found that one of the windows of the cottage had formerly occupied a part of it, but the panes had been filled up with wood. In one of these was a small and almost imperceptible chink, through which the eye could just penetrate. Through this crevice, a small room was visible, whitewashed and clean, but very bare of furniture. In one corner, near a small fire, sat an old man, leaning his head on his hands in a disconsolate attitude. The young girl was occupied in arranging the cottage; but presently she took something out of a drawer, which employed her hands, and she sat down beside the old man, who, taking up an instrument, began to play, and to produce sounds, sweeter than the voice of the thrush or the nightingale. It was a lovely sight, even to me, poor wretch! who had never beheld aught beautiful before. The silver hair and benevolent countenance of the aged cottager, won my reverence; while the gentle manners of the girl enticed my love. He played a sweet mournful air, which I perceived drew tears from the eyes of his amiable companion, of which the old man took no notice, until she sobbed audibly; he then pronounced a few sounds, and the fair creature, leaving her work, knelt at his feet. He raised her, and smiled with such kindness and affection, that I felt sensations of a peculiar and overpowering nature: they were a mixture of pain and pleasure, such as I had never before experienced, either from hunger or cold, warmth or food; and I withdrew from the window, unable to bear these emotions.

"Soon after this the young man returned, bearing on his shoulders a load of wood. The girl met him at the door, helped to relieve him of his burden, and, taking some of the fuel into the cottage, placed it on the fire; then she and the youth went apart into a nook of the cottage, and he shewed her a large loaf and a piece of cheese. She seemed pleased; and went into the garden for some roots and plants, which she placed in water, and then upon the fire. She afterwards continued her work, whilst the young man went into the garden, and appeared busily employed in digging and pulling up roots. After he had been employed thus about an hour, the young woman joined him, and they entered the cottage together.

"The old man had, in the mean time, been pensive; but, on the appearance of his companions, he assumed a more cheerful air, and they sat down to eat. The meal was quickly dispatched. The young woman was again occupied in arranging the cottage; the old man walked before the cottage in the sun for a few minutes, leaning on the arm of the youth. Nothing could exceed in beauty the contrast between these two excellent creatures. One was old, with silver hairs and a countenance beaming with benevolence and love: the younger was slight and graceful in his figure, and his features were moulded with the finest symmetry; yet his eyes and attitude expressed the utmost sadness and despondency. The old man returned to the cottage; and the youth, with tools different from those he had used in the morning, directed his steps across the fields.

"Night quickly shut in; but, to my extreme wonder, I found that the cottagers had a means of prolonging light, by the use of tapers, and was delighted to find, that the setting of the sun did not put an end to the pleasure I experienced in watching my human neighbours. In the evening, the young girl and her companion were employed in various occupations which I did not understand; and the old man again took up the instrument, which produced the divine sounds that had enchanted me in the morning. So soon as he had finished, the youth began, not to play, but to utter sounds that were monotonous, and neither resembling the harmony of the old man's instrument or the songs of the birds; I since found that he read aloud, but at that time I knew nothing of the science of words or letters.

"The family, after having been thus occupied for a short time, extinguished their lights, and retired, as I conjectured, to rest.[1]

CHAPTER IV.

"I LAY on my straw, but I could not sleep. I thought of the occurrences of the day. What chiefly struck me was the gentle manners of these people; and I longed to join them, but dared not. I remembered too well the treatment I had suffered the night before from the barbarous villagers, and resolved, whatever course of conduct I might hereafter think it right to pursue, that for the present I would remain quietly in my hovel, watching, and endeavouring to discover the motives which influenced their actions.

"The cottagers arose the next morning before the sun. The young woman arranged the cottage, and prepared the food; and the youth departed after the first meal.

"This day was passed in the same routine as that which preceded it. The young man was constantly employed out of doors, and the girl in various laborious occupations within. The old man, whom I soon perceived to be blind, employed his leisure hours on his instrument, or in contemplation. Nothing could exceed the love and respect which the younger cottagers exhibited towards their venerable companion. They performed towards him every little office of affection and duty with gentleness; and he rewarded them by his benevolent smiles.

"They were not entirely happy. The young man and his companion often went apart, and appeared to weep. I saw no cause for their unhappiness; but I was deeply affected by it. If such lovely creatures were miserable, it was less strange that I, an imperfect and solitary being, should be wretched. Yet why were these gentle beings unhappy? They possessed a delightful house

---

1 Cf. Wollstonecraft's portrait of an ideal family, *Vindication* 279-80; IX (Appendix A.2.a).

(for such it was in my eyes), and every luxury; they had a fire to warm them when chill, and delicious viands when hungry; they were dressed in excellent clothes; and, still more, they enjoyed one another's company and speech, interchanging each day looks of affection and kindness. What did their tears imply? Did they really express pain? I was at first unable to solve these questions; but perpetual attention, and time, explained to me many appearances which were at first enigmatic.

"A considerable period elapsed before I discovered one of the causes of the uneasiness of this amiable family; it was poverty: and they suffered that evil in a very distressing degree. Their nourishment consisted entirely of the vegetables of their garden, and the milk of one cow, who gave very little during the winter, when its masters could scarcely procure food to support it. They often, I believe, suffered the pangs of hunger very poignantly, especially the two younger cottagers; for several times they placed food before the old man, when they reserved none for themselves.

"This trait of kindness moved me sensibly. I had been accustomed, during the night, to steal a part of their store for my own consumption; but when I found that in doing this I inflicted pain on the cottagers, I abstained, and satisfied myself with berries, nuts, and roots, which I gathered from a neighbouring wood.

"I discovered also another means through which I was enabled to assist their labours. I found that the youth spent a great part of each day in collecting wood for the family fire; and, during the night, I often took his tools, the use of which I quickly discovered, and brought home firing sufficient for the consumption of several days.

"I remember, the first time that I did this, the young woman, when she opened the door in the morning, appeared greatly astonished on seeing a great pile of wood on the outside. She uttered some words in a loud voice, and the youth joined her, who also expressed surprise. I observed, with pleasure, that he did not go to the forest that day, but spent it in repairing the cottage, and cultivating the garden.[1]

"By degrees I made a discovery of still greater moment. I found that these people possessed a method of communicating their experience and feelings to one another by articulate sounds.[2] I perceived that the words they spoke sometimes pro-

---

1 Cf. the closing words of Voltaire, *Candide* (1759).
2 Cf. Godwin's account of the development of the human species, *Political Justice* 1: 110-18; I.viii.

duced pleasure or pain, smiles or sadness, in the minds and countenances of the hearers. This was indeed a godlike science, and I ardently desired to become acquainted with it. But I was baffled in every attempt I made for this purpose. Their pronunciation was quick; and the words they uttered, not having any apparent connexion with visible objects, I was unable to discover any clue by which I could unravel the mystery of their reference. By great application, however, and after having remained during the space of several revolutions of the moon in my hovel, I discovered the names that were given to some of the most familiar objects of discourse: I learned and applied the words *fire, milk, bread,* and *wood.* I learned also the names of the cottagers themselves. The youth and his companion had each of them several names, but the old man had only one, which was *father.* The girl was called *sister,* or *Agatha*; and the youth *Felix, brother,* or *son.* I cannot describe the delight I felt when I learned the ideas appropriated to each of these sounds, and was able to pronounce them. I distinguished several other words, without being able as yet to understand or apply them; such as *good, dearest, unhappy.*[1]

"I spent the winter in this manner. The gentle manners and beauty of the cottagers greatly endeared them to me: when they were unhappy, I felt depressed; when they rejoiced, I sympathized in their joys. I saw few human beings beside them; and if any other happened to enter the cottage, their harsh manners and rude gait only enhanced to me the superior accomplishments of my friends. The old man, I could perceive, often endeavoured to encourage his children, as sometimes I found that he called them, to cast off their melancholy. He would talk in a cheerful accent, with an expression of goodness that bestowed pleasure even upon me. Agatha listened with respect, her eyes sometimes filled with tears, which she endeavoured to wipe away unperceived; but I generally found that her countenance and tone were more cheerful after having listened to the exhortations of her father. It was not thus with Felix. He was always the saddest of the groupe; and, even to my unpractised senses, he appeared to have suffered more deeply than his friends. But if his countenance was more sorrowful, his voice was more cheerful than that of his sister, especially when he addressed the old man.

"I could mention innumerable instances, which, although slight, marked the dispositions of these amiable cottagers. In the midst of poverty and want, Felix carried with pleasure to his

---

1 Cf. Wollstonecraft, "Lessons" (Appendix C.5).

sister the first little white flower that peeped out from beneath the snowy ground. Early in the morning before she had risen, he cleared away the snow that obstructed her path to the milk-house, drew water from the well, and brought the wood from the out-house, where, to his perpetual astonishment, he found his store always replenished by an invisible hand. In the day, I believe, he worked sometimes for a neighbouring farmer, because he often went forth, and did not return until dinner, yet brought no wood with him. At other times he worked in the garden; but, as there was little to do in the frosty season, he read to the old man and Agatha.

"This reading had puzzled me extremely at first; but, by degrees, I discovered that he uttered many of the same sounds when he read as when he talked. I conjectured, therefore, that he found on the paper signs for speech which he understood, and I ardently longed to comprehend these also; but how was that possible, when I did not even understand the sounds for which they stood as signs? I improved, however, sensibly in this science, but not sufficiently to follow up any kind of conversation, although I applied my whole mind to the endeavour: for I easily perceived that, although I eagerly longed to discover myself to the cottagers, I ought not to make the attempt until I had first become master of their language; which knowledge might enable me to make them overlook the deformity of my figure; for with this also the contrast perpetually presented to my eyes had made me acquainted.

"I had admired the perfect forms of my cottagers—their grace, beauty, and delicate complexions: but how was I terrified, when I viewed myself in a transparent pool! At first I started back, unable to believe that it was indeed I who was reflected in the mirror; and when I became fully convinced that I was in reality the monster that I am, I was filled with the bitterest sensations of despondence and mortification. Alas! I did not yet entirely know the fatal effects of this miserable deformity.[1]

"As the sun became warmer, and the light of day longer, the snow vanished, and I beheld the bare trees and the black earth. From this time Felix was more employed; and the heart-moving indications of impending famine disappeared. Their food, as I afterwards found, was coarse, but it was wholesome; and they procured a sufficiency of it. Several new kinds of plants sprung

---

1 Cf. Eve's first sight of herself, Milton, *Paradise Lost* IV.449-91 (Appendix C.4.b).

up in the garden, which they dressed; and these signs of comfort increased daily as the season advanced.

"The old man, leaning on his son, walked each day at noon, when it did not rain, as I found it was called when the heavens poured forth its waters. This frequently took place; but a high wind quickly dried the earth, and the season became far more pleasant than it had been.

"My mode of life in my hovel was uniform. During the morning I attended the motions of the cottagers; and when they were dispersed in various occupations, I slept: the remainder of the day was spent in observing my friends. When they had retired to rest, if there was any moon, or the night was starlight, I went into the woods, and collected my own food and fuel for the cottage. When I returned, as often as it was necessary, I cleared their path from the snow, and performed those offices that I had seen done by Felix. I afterwards found that these labours, performed by an invisible hand, greatly astonished them; and once or twice I heard them, on these occasions, utter the words *good spirit, wonderful*; but I did not then understand the signification of these terms.

"My thoughts now became more active, and I longed to discover the motives and feelings of these lovely creatures; I was inquisitive to know why Felix appeared so miserable, and Agatha so sad. I thought (foolish wretch!) that it might be in my power to restore happiness to these deserving people. When I slept, or was absent, the forms of the venerable blind father, the gentle Agatha, and the excellent Felix, flitted before me. I looked upon them as superior beings, who would be the arbiters of my future destiny. I formed in my imagination a thousand pictures of presenting myself to them, and their reception of me. I imagined that they would be disgusted, until, by my gentle demeanour and conciliating words, I should first win their favour, and afterwards their love.

"These thoughts exhilarated me, and led me to apply with fresh ardour to the acquiring the art of language. My organs were indeed harsh, but supple; and although my voice was very unlike the soft music of their tones, yet I pronounced such words as I understood with tolerable ease. It was as the ass and the lap-dog; yet surely the gentle ass, whose intentions were affectionate, although his manners were rude, deserved better treatment than blows and execration.[1]

---

1 An allusion to La Fontaine, *Fables* IV.5.

"The pleasant showers and genial warmth of spring greatly altered the aspect of the earth. Men, who before this change seemed to have been hid in caves, dispersed themselves, and were employed in various arts of cultivation. The birds sang in more cheerful notes, and the leaves began to bud forth on the trees. Happy, happy earth! fit habitation for gods,[1] which, so short a time before, was bleak, damp, and unwholesome. My spirits were elevated by the enchanting appearance of nature; the past was blotted from my memory, the present was tranquil, and the future gilded by bright rays of hope, and anticipations of joy.

CHAPTER V.

"I NOW hasten to the more moving part of my story. I shall relate events that impressed me with feelings which, from what I was, have made me what I am.

"Spring advanced rapidly; the weather became fine, and the skies cloudless. It surprised me, that what before was desert and gloomy should now bloom with the most beautiful flowers and verdure. My senses were gratified and refreshed by a thousand scents of delight, and a thousand sights of beauty.

"It was on one of these days, when my cottagers periodically rested from labour—the old man played on his guitar, and the children listened to him—I observed that the countenance of Felix was melancholy beyond expression: he sighed frequently; and once his father paused in his music, and I conjectured by his manner that he inquired the cause of his son's sorrow. Felix replied in a cheerful accent, and the old man was recommencing his music, when some one tapped at the door.

"It was a lady on horseback, accompanied by a countryman as a guide. The lady was dressed in a dark suit, and covered with a thick black veil. Agatha asked a question; to which the stranger only replied by pronouncing, in a sweet accent, the name of Felix. Her voice was musical, but unlike that of either of my friends. On hearing this word, Felix came up hastily to the lady; who, when she saw him, threw up her veil, and I beheld a countenance of angelic beauty and expression. Her hair of a shining raven black, and curiously braided; her eyes were dark, but gentle, although animated; her features of a regular proportion,

---

1 An ironic allusion to Raphael's description of Hell as a fit habitation for devils, Milton, *Paradise Lost* VI.876.

and her complexion wondrously fair, each cheek tinged with a lovely pink.

"Felix seemed ravished with delight when he saw her, every trait of sorrow vanished from his face, and it instantly expressed a degree of ecstatic joy, of which I could hardly have believed it capable; his eyes sparkled, as his cheek flushed with pleasure; and at that moment I thought him as beautiful as the stranger. She appeared affected by different feelings; wiping a few tears from her lovely eyes, she held out her hand to Felix, who kissed it rapturously, and called her, as well as I could distinguish, his sweet Arabian. She did not appear to understand him, but smiled. He assisted her to dismount, and, dismissing her guide, conducted her into the cottage. Some conversation took place between him and his father; and the young stranger knelt at the old man's feet, and would have kissed his hand, but he raised her, and embraced her affectionately.

"I soon perceived, that although the stranger uttered articulate sounds, and appeared to have a language of her own, she was neither understood by, or herself understood, the cottagers. They made many signs which I did not comprehend; but I saw that her presence diffused gladness through the cottage, dispelling their sorrow as the sun dissipates the morning mists. Felix seemed peculiarly happy, and with smiles of delight welcomed his Arabian. Agatha, the ever-gentle Agatha, kissed the hands of the lovely stranger; and, pointing to her brother, made signs which appeared to me to mean that he had been sorrowful until she came. Some hours passed thus, while they, by their countenances, expressed joy, the cause of which I did not comprehend. Presently I found, by the frequent recurrence of one sound which the stranger repeated after them, that she was endeavouring to learn their language; and the idea instantly occurred to me, that I should make use of the same instructions to the same end. The stranger learned about twenty words at the first lesson, most of them indeed were those which I had before understood, but I profited by the others.

"As night came on, Agatha and the Arabian retired early. When they separated, Felix kissed the hand of the stranger, and said, 'Good night, sweet Safie.' He sat up much longer, conversing with his father; and, by the frequent repetition of her name, I conjectured that their lovely guest was the subject of their conversation. I ardently desired to understand them, and bent every faculty towards that purpose, but found it utterly impossible.

"The next morning Felix went out to his work; and, after the usual occupations of Agatha were finished, the Arabian sat at the feet of the old man, and, taking his guitar, played some airs so entrancingly beautiful, that they at once drew tears of sorrow and delight from my eyes. She sang, and her voice flowed in a rich cadence, swelling or dying away, like a nightingale of the woods.

"When she had finished, she gave the guitar to Agatha, who at first declined it. She played a simple air, and her voice accompanied it in sweet accents, but unlike the wondrous strain of the stranger. The old man appeared enraptured, and said some words, which Agatha endeavoured to explain to Safie, and by which he appeared to wish to express that she bestowed on him the greatest delight by her music.

"The days now passed as peaceably as before, with the sole alteration, that joy had taken place of sadness in the countenances of my friends. Safie was always gay and happy; she and I improved rapidly in the knowledge of language, so that in two months I began to comprehend most of the words uttered by my protectors.

"In the meanwhile also the black ground was covered with herbage, and the green banks interspersed with innumerable flowers, sweet to the scent and the eyes, stars of pale radiance among the moonlight woods; the sun became warmer, the nights clear and balmy; and my nocturnal rambles were an extreme pleasure to me, although they were considerably shortened by the late setting and early rising of the sun; for I never ventured abroad during daylight, fearful of meeting with the same treatment as I had formerly endured in the first village which I entered.

"My days were spent in close attention, that I might more speedily master the language; and I may boast that I improved more rapidly than the Arabian, who understood very little, and conversed in broken accents, whilst I comprehended and could imitate almost every word that was spoken.

"While I improved in speech, I also learned the science of letters, as it was taught to the stranger; and this opened before me a wide field for wonder and delight.

"The book from which Felix instructed Safie was Volney's *Ruins of Empires*. I should not have understood the purport of this book, had not Felix, in reading it, given very minute explanations. He had chosen this work, he said, because the declamatory style was framed in imitation of the eastern authors. Through this work

I obtained a cursory knowledge of history, and a view of the several empires at present existing in the world; it gave me an insight into the manners, governments, and religions of the different nations of the earth. I heard of the slothful Asiatics; of the stupendous genius and mental activity of the Grecians; of the wars and wonderful virtue of the early Romans—of their subsequent degeneration—of the decline of that mighty empire;[1] of chivalry, christianity, and kings. I heard of the discovery of the American hemisphere, and wept with Safie over the hapless fate of its original inhabitants.[2]

"These wonderful narrations inspired me with strange feelings. Was man, indeed, at once so powerful, so virtuous, and magnificent, yet so vicious and base?[3] He appeared at one time a mere scion of the evil principle, and at another as all that can be conceived of noble and godlike. To be a great and virtuous man appeared the highest honour that can befall a sensitive being; to be base and vicious, as many on record have been, appeared the lowest degradation, a condition more abject than that of the blind mole or harmless worm. For a long time I could not conceive how one man could go forth to murder his fellow, or even why there were laws and governments; but when I heard details of vice and bloodshed, my wonder ceased, and I turned away with disgust and loathing.[4]

"Every conversation of the cottagers now opened new wonders to me. While I listened to the instructions which Felix bestowed upon the Arabian, the strange system of human society was explained to me. I heard of the division of property, of immense wealth and squalid poverty; of rank, descent, and noble blood.

"The words induced me to turn towards myself. I learned that the possessions most esteemed by your fellow-creatures were, high and unsullied descent united with riches. A man might be respected with only one of these acquisitions; but without either he was considered, except in very rare instances, as a vagabond and a slave, doomed to waste his powers for the profit of the

---

1 Cf. Volney, *The Ruins* 33-34 (Appendix C.1.a).

2 Cf. Volney, *The Ruins* 166-67 (Appendix C.1.b).

3 Cf. Volney, *The Ruins* 23 (Appendix C.1.c).

4 Cf. Wollstonecraft's warning against a premature knowledge of human failings, *Vindication* 232-34; V.v (Appendix A.2.b).

chosen few. And what was I? Of my creation and creator I was absolutely ignorant; but I knew that I possessed no money, no friends, no kind of property.[1] I was, besides, endowed with a figure hideously deformed and loathsome; I was not even of the same nature as man. I was more agile than they, and could subsist upon coarser diet; I bore the extremes of heat and cold with less injury to my frame; my stature far exceeded their's. When I looked around, I saw and heard of none like me. Was I then a monster, a blot upon the earth, from which all men fled, and whom all men disowned?[2]

"I cannot describe to you the agony that these reflections inflicted upon me; I tried to dispel them, but sorrow only increased with knowledge.[3] Oh, that I had for ever remained in my native wood, nor known or felt beyond the sensations of hunger, thirst, and heat!

"Of what a strange nature is knowledge! It clings to the mind, when it has once seized on it, like a lichen on the rock. I wished sometimes to shake off all thought and feeling; but I learned that there was but one means to overcome the sensation of pain, and that was death—a state which I feared yet did not understand. I admired virtue and good feelings, and loved the gentle manners and amiable qualities of my cottagers; but I was shut out from intercourse with them, except through means which I obtained by stealth, when I was unseen and unknown, and which rather increased than satisfied the desire I had of becoming one among my fellows. The gentle words of Agatha, and the animated smiles of the charming Arabian, were not for me. The mild exhortations of the old man, and the lively conversation of the loved Felix, were not for me. Miserable, unhappy wretch!

"Other lessons were impressed upon me even more deeply. I heard of the difference of sexes; of the birth and growth of children; how the father doated on the smiles of the infant, and the lively sallies of the older child; how all the life and cares of the mother were wrapt up in the precious charge; how the mind of youth expanded and gained knowledge; of brother, sister, and all

---

1   Cf. Godwin's many egalitarian passages, e.g., *Political Justice* 1: 15-20 (I.iii), 2: 111-12 (V.xiii), 2: 427 (VIII.i), 2: 445-46 (VIII.ii), 2: 456-57 (VIII.iii); and Wollstonecraft, *Vindication* 119; I (Appendix A.2.f).

2   Cf. Godwin, *St. Leon* 211 (XIX).

3   Cf. Byron, *Manfred* (1817) I.i.10-12.

the various relationships which bind one human being to another in mutual bonds.[1]

"But where were my friends and relations? No father had watched my infant days, no mother had blessed me with smiles and caresses; or if they had, all my past life was now a blot, a blind vacancy in which I distinguished nothing. From my earliest remembrance I had been as I then was in height and proportion. I had never yet seen a being resembling me, or who claimed any intercourse with me. What was I? The question again recurred, to be answered only with groans.

"I will soon explain to what these feelings tended; but allow me now to return to the cottagers, whose story excited in me such various feelings of indignation, delight, and wonder, but which all terminated in additional love and reverence for my protectors (for so I loved, in an innocent, half painful self-deceit, to call them).

CHAPTER VI.

"Some time elapsed before I learned the history of my friends. It was one which could not fail to impress itself deeply on my mind, unfolding as it did a number of circumstances each interesting and wonderful to one so utterly inexperienced as I was.

"The name of the old man was De Lacey. He was descended from a good family in France, where he had lived for many years in affluence, respected by his superiors, and beloved by his equals. His son was bred in the service of his country; and Agatha had ranked with ladies of the highest distinction. A few months before my arrival, they had lived in a large and luxurious city, called Paris, surrounded by friends, and possessed of every enjoyment which virtue, refinement of intellect, or taste, accompanied by a moderate fortune, could afford.

"The father of Safie had been the cause of their ruin. He was a Turkish merchant, and had inhabited Paris for many years, when, for some reason which I could not learn, he became obnoxious to the government. He was seized and cast into prison the very day that Safie arrived from Constantinople to join him.

---

1 Cf. Wollstonecraft on sexual and familial relations, *Vindication* 273-75; VIII (Appendix A.2.d) and "Lessons" (Appendix C.5); and *Plutarch's Lives* 1: 150-52; "Comparison of Numa with Lycurgus" (Appendix C.3.d).

He was tried, and condemned to death. The injustice of his sentence was very flagrant; all Paris was indignant; and it was judged that his religion and wealth, rather than the crime alleged against him, had been the cause of his condemnation.

"Felix had been present at the trial; his horror and indignation were uncontrollable, when he heard the decision of the court. He made, at that moment, a solemn vow to deliver him, and then looked around for the means. After many fruitless attempts to gain admittance to the prison, he found a strongly grated window in an unguarded part of the building, which lighted the dungeon of the unfortunate Mahometan; who, loaded with chains, waited in despair the execution of the barbarous sentence. Felix visited the grate at night, and made known to the prisoner his intentions in his favour. The Turk, amazed and delighted, endeavoured to kindle the zeal of his deliverer by promises of reward and wealth. Felix rejected his offers with contempt; yet when he saw the lovely Safie, who was allowed to visit her father, and who, by her gestures, expressed her lively gratitude, the youth could not help owning to his own mind, that the captive possessed a treasure which would fully reward his toil and hazard.

"The Turk quickly perceived the impression that his daughter had made on the heart of Felix, and endeavoured to secure him more entirely in his interests by the promise of her hand in marriage, so soon as he should be conveyed to a place of safety. Felix was too delicate to accept this offer; yet he looked forward to the probability of that event as to the consummation of his happiness.

"During the ensuing days, while the preparations were going forward for the escape of the merchant, the zeal of Felix was warmed by several letters that he received from this lovely girl, who found means to express her thoughts in the language of her lover by the aid of an old man, a servant of her father's, who understood French. She thanked him in the most ardent terms for his intended services towards her father; and at the same time she gently deplored her own fate.

"I have copies of these letters; for I found means, during my residence in the hovel, to procure the implements of writing; and the letters were often in the hands of Felix or Agatha. Before I depart, I will give them to you, they will prove the truth of my tale; but at present, as the sun is already far declined, I shall only have time to repeat the substance of them to you.

"Safie related, that her mother was a Christian Arab, seized and made a slave by the Turks; recommended by her beauty, she had won the heart of the father of Safie, who married her. The young girl spoke in high and enthusiastic terms of her mother, who, born in freedom spurned the bondage to which she was now reduced. She instructed her daughter in the tenets of her religion, and taught her to aspire to higher powers of intellect, and an independence of spirit, forbidden to the female followers of Mahomet.[1] This lady died; but her lessons were indelibly impressed on the mind of Safie, who sickened at the prospect of again returning to Asia, and the being immured within the walls of a haram, allowed only to occupy herself with puerile amusements, ill suited to the temper of her soul, now accustomed to grand ideas and a noble emulation for virtue. The prospect of marrying a Christian, and remaining in a country where women were allowed to take a rank in society, was enchanting to her.[2]

"The day for the execution of the Turk was fixed; but, on the night previous to it, he had quitted prison, and before morning was distant many leagues from Paris. Felix had procured passports in the name of his father, sister, and himself. He had previously communicated his plan to the former, who aided the deceit by quitting his house, under the pretence of a journey, and concealed himself, with his daughter, in an obscure part of Paris.

"Felix conducted the fugitives through France to Lyons, and across Mont Cenis to Leghorn, where the merchant had decided to wait a favourable opportunity of passing into some part of the Turkish dominions.

"Safie resolved to remain with her father until the moment of his departure, before which time the Turk renewed his promise that she should be united to his deliverer; and Felix remained with them in expectation of that event; and in the mean time he enjoyed the society of the Arabian, who exhibited towards him the simplest and tenderest affection. They conversed with one another through the means of an interpreter, and sometimes with the interpretation of looks; and Safie sang to him the divine airs of her native country.

"The Turk allowed this intimacy to take place, and encouraged the hopes of the youthful lovers, while in his heart he had formed far other plans. He loathed the idea that his daughter should be united to a Christian; but he feared the resentment of Felix if he

---

1 Cf. Wollstonecraft's orientalism, *Vindication* 109, 113 (Introd.), 126 (II), 138 (II), 191 (IV), 317 (XII), 335 (XIII.iii).
2 Cf. *Plutarch's Lives* 1: 150-52; "Comparison of Numa with Lycurgus" (Appendix C.3.d).

should appear lukewarm; for he knew that he was still in the power of his deliverer, if he should choose to betray him to the Italian state which they inhabited. He revolved a thousand plans by which he should be enabled to prolong the deceit until it might be no longer necessary, and secretly to take his daughter with him when he departed. His plans were greatly facilitated by the news which arrived from Paris.

"The government of France were greatly enraged at the escape of their victim, and spared no pains to detect and punish his deliverer. The plot of Felix was quickly discovered, and De Lacey and Agatha were thrown into prison. The news reached Felix, and roused him from his dream of pleasure. His blind and aged father, and his gentle sister, lay in a noisome dungeon, while he enjoyed the free air, and the society of her whom he loved. This idea was torture to him. He quickly arranged with the Turk, that if the latter should find a favourable opportunity for escape before Felix could return to Italy, Safie should remain as a boarder at a convent at Leghorn; and then, quitting the lovely Arabian, he hastened to Paris, and delivered himself up to the vengeance of the law, hoping to free De Lacey and Agatha by this proceeding.

"He did not succeed. They remained confined for five months before the trial took place; the result of which deprived them of their fortune, and condemned them to a perpetual exile from their native country.

"They found a miserable asylum in the cottage in Germany, where I discovered them. Felix soon learned that the treacherous Turk, for whom he and his family endured such unheard-of oppression, on discovering that his deliverer was thus reduced to poverty and impotence, became a traitor to good feeling and honour, and had quitted Italy with his daughter, insultingly sending Felix a pittance of money to aid him, as he said, in some plan of future maintenance.

"Such were the events that preyed on the heart of Felix, and rendered him, when I first saw him, the most miserable of his family. He could have endured poverty, and when this distress had been the meed of his virtue, he would have gloried in it: but the ingratitude of the Turk, and the loss of his beloved Safie, were misfortunes more bitter and irreparable. The arrival of the Arabian now infused new life into his soul.

"When the news reached Leghorn, that Felix was deprived of his wealth and rank, the merchant commanded his daughter to think no more of her lover, but to prepare to return with him to her native country. The generous nature of Safie was outraged by this command; she attempted to expostulate with her father, but he left her angrily, reiterating his tyrannical mandate.

"A few days after, the Turk entered his daughter's apartment, and told her hastily, that he had reason to believe that his residence at Leghorn had been divulged, and that he should speedily be delivered up to the French government; he had, consequently, hired a vessel to convey him to Constantinople, for which city he should sail in a few hours. He intended to leave his daughter under the care of a confidential servant, to follow at her leisure with the greater part of his property, which had not yet arrived at Leghorn.

"When alone, Safie resolved in her own mind the plan of conduct that it would become her to pursue in this emergency. A residence in Turkey was abhorrent to her; her religion and feelings were alike adverse to it. By some papers of her father's, which fell into her hands, she heard of the exile of her lover, and learnt the name of the spot where he then resided. She hesitated some time, but at length she formed her determination. Taking with her some jewels that belonged to her, and a small sum of money, she quitted Italy, with an attendant, a native of Leghorn, but who understood the common language of Turkey, and departed for Germany.

"She arrived in safety at a town about twenty leagues from the cottage of De Lacey, when her attendant fell dangerously ill. Safie nursed her with the most devoted affection; but the poor girl died, and the Arabian was left alone, unacquainted with the language of the country, and utterly ignorant of the customs of the world. She fell, however, into good hands. The Italian had mentioned the name of the spot for which they were bound; and, after her death, the woman of the house in which they had lived took care that Safie should arrive in safety at the cottage of her lover.

CHAPTER VII.

"SUCH was the history of my beloved cottagers. It impressed me deeply. I learned, from the views of social life which it developed, to admire their virtues, and to deprecate the vices of mankind.

"As yet I looked upon crime as a distant evil; benevolence and generosity were ever present before me, inciting within me a desire to become an actor in the busy scene where so many admirable qualities were called forth and displayed. But, in giving an account of the progress of my intellect, I must not omit a circumstance which occurred in the beginning of the month of August of the same year.

"One night, during my accustomed visit to the neighbouring wood, where I collected my own food, and brought home firing for my protectors, I found on the ground a leathern portmanteau, containing several articles of dress and some books. I eagerly seized the prize, and returned with it to my hovel. Fortunately the books were written in the language the elements of which I had acquired at the cottage; they consisted of *Paradise Lost*, a volume of *Plutarch's Lives*, and the *Sorrows of Werter*. The possession of these treasures gave me extreme delight; I now continually studied and exercised my mind upon these histories, whilst my friends were employed in their ordinary occupations.

"I can hardly describe to you the effect of these books. They produced in me an infinity of new images and feelings, that sometimes raised me to ecstacy, but more frequently sunk me into the lowest dejection. In the *Sorrows of Werter*, besides the interest of its simple and affecting story, so many opinions are canvassed, and so many lights thrown upon what had hitherto been to me obscure subjects, that I found in it a never-ending source of speculation and astonishment. The gentle and domestic manners it described, combined with lofty sentiments and feelings, which had for their object something out of self, accorded well with my experience among my protectors, and with the wants which were for ever alive in my own bosom. But I thought Werter himself a more divine being than I had ever beheld or imagined; his character contained no pretension, but it sunk deep. The disquisitions upon death and suicide were calculated to fill me with wonder.[1] I did not pretend to enter into the merits of the case, yet I inclined towards the opinions of the hero, whose extinction I wept, without precisely understanding it.

"As I read, however, I applied much personally to my own feelings and condition. I found myself similar, yet at the same time strangely unlike the beings concerning whom I read, and to whose conversation I was a listener. I sympathized with, and partly understood them, but I was unformed in mind; I was dependent on none, and related to none. 'The path of my departure was free';[2] and there was none to lament my annihilation. My person was hideous, and my stature gigantic: what did this

---

1 Cf. Goethe, *The Sorrows of Werter* 77-87; Letter XXIX (Appendix C.2.a).

2 The monster, like Victor, quotes P.B. Shelley's "Mutability" 14.

mean? Who was I? What was I? Whence did I come? What was my destination? These questions continually recurred, but I was unable to solve them.

"The volume of *Plutarch's Lives* which I possessed, contained the histories of the first founders of the ancient republics. This book had a far different effect upon me from the *Sorrows of Werter*. I learned from Werter's imaginations despondency and gloom: but Plutarch taught me high thoughts; he elevated me above the wretched sphere of my own reflections, to admire and love the heroes of past ages. Many things I read surpassed my understanding and experience. I had a very confused knowledge of kingdoms, wide extents of country, mighty rivers, and boundless seas. But I was perfectly unacquainted with towns, and large assemblages of men. The cottage of my protectors had been the only school in which I had studied human nature; but this book developed new and mightier scenes of action. I read of men concerned in public affairs governing or massacring their species. I felt the greatest ardour for virtue rise within me, and abhorrence for vice, as far as I understood the signification of those terms, relative as they were, as I applied them, to pleasure and pain alone. Induced by these feelings, I was of course led to admire peaceable law-givers, Numa,[1] Solon, and Lycurgus, in preference to Romulus and Theseus.[2] The patriarchal lives of my protectors caused these impressions to take a firm hold on my mind; perhaps, if my first introduction to humanity had been made by a young soldier, burning for glory and slaughter, I should have been imbued with different sensations.

"But *Paradise Lost* excited different and far deeper emotions. I read it, as I had read the other volumes which had fallen into my hands, as a true history. It moved every feeling of wonder and awe, that the picture of an omnipotent God warring with his creatures was capable of exciting. I often referred the several situations, as their similarity struck me, to my own. Like Adam, I was created apparently united by no link to any other being in existence; but his state was far different from mine in every other respect. He had come forth from the hands of God a perfect creature, happy and prosperous, guarded by the especial care of his Creator; he was allowed to converse with, and acquire knowledge

---

1 Cf. *Plutarch's Lives* 1: 126-27, 137-38; "Numa Pompilius" (Appendix C.3.c).
2 Cf. *Plutarch's Lives* 1: 73-75; "Comparison of Romulus with Theseus" (Appendix C.3.b).

from beings of a superior nature: but I was wretched, helpless, and alone. Many times I considered Satan as the fitter emblem of my condition; for often, like him, when I viewed the bliss of my protectors, the bitter gall of envy rose within me.[1]

"Another circumstance strengthened and confirmed these feelings. Soon after my arrival in the hovel, I discovered some papers in the pocket of the dress which I had taken from your laboratory. At first I had neglected them; but now that I was able to decypher the characters in which they were written, I began to study them with diligence. It was your journal of the four months that preceded my creation. You minutely described in these papers every step you took in the progress of your work; this history was mingled with accounts of domestic occurrences. You, doubtless, recollect these papers. Here they are. Every thing is related in them which bears reference to my accursed origin; the whole detail of that series of disgusting circumstances which produced it is set in view; the minutest description of my odious and loathsome person is given, in language which painted your own horrors, and rendered mine ineffaceable. I sickened as I read. 'Hateful day when I received life!' I exclaimed in agony. 'Cursed creator! Why did you form a monster so hideous that even you turned from me in disgust? God in pity made man beautiful and alluring, after his own image; but my form is a filthy type of your's, more horrid from its very resemblance. Satan had his companions, fellow-devils, to admire and encourage him; but I am solitary and detested.'

"These were the reflections of my hours of despondency and solitude; but when I contemplated the virtues of the cottagers, their amiable and benevolent dispositions, I persuaded myself that when they should become acquainted with my admiration of their virtues, they would compassionate me, and overlook my personal deformity. Could they turn from their door one, however monstrous, who solicited their compassion and friendship? I resolved, at least, not to despair, but in every way to fit myself for an interview with them which would decide my fate. I postponed this attempt for some months longer; for the importance attached to its success inspired me with a dread lest I should fail. Besides, I found that my understanding improved so much with every day's experience, that I was unwilling to com-

---

1   Cf. Milton, *Paradise Lost* IV.358-92, 502-11; and Godwin, *St. Leon* 302; XXIX.

mence this undertaking until a few more months should have added to my wisdom.

"Several changes, in the mean time, took place in the cottage. The presence of Safie diffused happiness among its inhabitants; and I also found that a greater degree of plenty reigned there. Felix and Agatha spent more time in amusement and conversation, and were assisted in their labours by servants. They did not appear rich, but they were contented and happy; their feelings were serene and peaceful, while mine became every day more tumultuous. Increase of knowledge only discovered to me more clearly what a wretched outcast I was. I cherished hope, it is true; but it vanished, when I beheld my person reflected in water, or my shadow in the moon-shine, even as that frail image and that inconstant shade.

"I endeavoured to crush these fears, and to fortify myself for the trial which in a few months I resolved to undergo; and sometimes I allowed my thoughts, unchecked by reason, to ramble in the fields of Paradise, and dared to fancy amiable and lovely creatures sympathizing with my feelings and cheering my gloom; their angelic countenances breathed smiles of consolation. But it was all a dream: no Eve soothed my sorrows, or shared my thoughts; I was alone.[1] I remembered Adam's supplication to his Creator;[2] but where was mine? he had abandoned me, and, in the bitterness of my heart, I cursed him.[3]

"Autumn passed thus. I saw, with surprise and grief, the leaves decay and fall, and nature again assume the barren and bleak appearance it had worn when I first beheld the woods and the lovely moon. Yet I did not heed the bleakness of the weather; I was better fitted by my conformation for the endurance of cold than heat. But my chief delights were the sight of the flowers, the birds, and all the gay apparel of summer; when those deserted me, I turned with more attention towards the cottagers. Their happiness was not decreased by the absence of summer. They loved, and sympathized with one another; and their joys, depending on each other, were not interrupted by the casualties that took place around them. The more I saw of them, the greater became my desire to claim their protection and kindness; my heart yearned to be known and loved by these amiable creatures:

---

1 Unlike Adam's dream (or Victor's), the monster's does not come true. Cf. Milton, *Paradise Lost* VIII.460-89 (Appendix C.4.d).

2 Milton, *Paradise Lost* VIII.379-97 (see Appendix A.2.e).

3 Cf. Job 1: 11, 2: 9.

to see their sweet looks turned towards me with affection, was the utmost limit of my ambition. I dared not think that they would turn them from me with disdain and horror. The poor that stopped at their door were never driven away. I asked, it is true, for greater treasures than a little food or rest; I required kindness and sympathy; but I did not believe myself utterly unworthy of it.

"The winter advanced, and an entire revolution of the seasons had taken place since I awoke into life. My attention, at this time, was solely directed towards my plan of introducing myself into the cottage of my protectors. I revolved many projects; but that on which I finally fixed was, to enter the dwelling when the blind old man should be alone. I had sagacity enough to discover, that the unnatural hideousness of my person was the chief object of horror with those who had formerly beheld me. My voice, although harsh, had nothing terrible in it; I thought, therefore, that if, in the absence of his children, I could gain the good-will and mediation of the old De Lacey, I might, by his means, be tolerated by my younger protectors.

"One day, when the sun shone on the red leaves that strewed the ground, and diffused cheerfulness, although it denied warmth, Safie, Agatha, and Felix, departed on a long country walk, and the old man, at his own desire, was left alone in the cottage. When his children had departed, he took up his guitar, and played several mournful, but sweet airs, more sweet and mournful than I had ever heard him play before. At first his countenance was illuminated with pleasure, but, as he continued, thoughtfulness and sadness succeeded; at length, laying aside the instrument, he sat absorbed in reflection.

"My heart beat quick; this was the hour and moment of trial, which would decide my hopes, or realize my fears. The servants were gone to a neighbouring fair. All was silent in and around the cottage: it was an excellent opportunity; yet, when I proceeded to execute my plan, my limbs failed me, and I sunk to the ground. Again I rose; and, exerting all the firmness of which I was master, removed the planks which I had placed before my hovel to conceal my retreat. The fresh air revived me, and, with renewed determination, I approached the door of their cottage.

"I knocked. 'Who is there?' said the old man—'Come in.'

"I entered; 'Pardon this intrusion,' said I, 'I am a traveller in want of a little rest; you would greatly oblige me, if you would allow me to remain a few minutes before the fire.'

"'Enter,' said De Lacey; 'and I will try in what manner I can relieve your wants; but, unfortunately, my children are from home, and, as I am blind, I am afraid I shall find it difficult to procure food for you.'

"'Do not trouble yourself, my kind host, I have food; it is warmth and rest only that I need.'

"I sat down, and a silence ensued. I knew that every minute was precious to me, yet I remained irresolute in what manner to commence the interview; when the old man addressed me—

"'By your language, stranger, I suppose you are my country-man;—are you French?'

"'No; but I was educated by a French family, and understand that language only. I am now going to claim the protection of some friends, whom I sincerely love, and of whose favour I have some hopes.'

"'Are these Germans?'

"'No, they are French. But let us change the subject. I am an unfortunate and deserted creature; I look around, and I have no relation or friend upon earth. These amiable people to whom I go have never seen me, and know little of me. I am full of fears; for if I fail there, I am an outcast in the world for ever.'

"'Do not despair. To be friendless is indeed to be unfortunate; but the hearts of men, when unprejudiced by any obvious self-interest, are full of brotherly love and charity. Rely, therefore, on your hopes; and if these friends are good and amiable, do not despair.'

"'They are kind—they are the most excellent creatures in the world; but, unfortunately, they are prejudiced against me. I have good dispositions; my life has been hitherto harmless, and, in some degree, beneficial; but a fatal prejudice clouds their eyes, and where they ought to see a feeling and kind friend, they behold only a detestable monster.'

"'That is indeed unfortunate; but if you are really blameless, cannot you undeceive them?'

"'I am about to undertake that task; and it is on that account that I feel so many overwhelming terrors. I tenderly love these friends; I have, unknown to them, been for many months in the habits of daily kindness towards them; but they believe that I wish to injure them, and it is that prejudice which I wish to overcome.'

"'Where do these friends reside?'

"'Near this spot.'

"The old man paused, and then continued, 'If you will unre-servedly confide to me the particulars of your tale, I perhaps may be of use in undeceiving them. I am blind, and cannot judge of your countenance, but there is something in your words which persuades me that you are sincere. I am poor, and an exile; but it will afford me true pleasure to be in any way serviceable to a human creature.'

"'Excellent man! I thank you, and accept your generous offer. You raise me from the dust[1] by this kindness; and I trust that, by your aid, I shall not be driven from the society and sympathy of your fellow-creatures.'

"'Heaven forbid! even if you were really criminal; for that can only drive you to desperation, and not instigate you to virtue.[2] I also am unfortunate; I and my family have been condemned, although innocent: judge, therefore, if I do not feel for your misfortunes.'

"'How can I thank you, my best and only benefactor? from your lips first have I heard the voice of kindness directed towards me; I shall be for ever grateful; and your present humanity assures me of success with those friends whom I am on the point of meeting.'

"'May I know the names and residence of those friends?'

"I paused. This, I thought, was the moment of decision, which was to rob me of, or bestow happiness on me for ever. I struggled vainly for firmness sufficient to answer him, but the effort destroyed all my remaining strength; I sank on the chair, and sobbed aloud. At that moment I heard the steps of my younger protectors. I had not a moment to lose; but, seizing the hand of the old man, I cried, 'Now is the time!—save and protect me! You and your family are the friends whom I seek. Do not you desert me in the hour of trial!'

"'Great God!' exclaimed the old man, 'who are you?'

"At that instant the cottage door was opened, and Felix, Safie, and Agatha entered. Who can describe their horror and consternation on beholding me? Agatha fainted; and Safie, unable to attend to her friend, rushed out of the cottage. Felix darted forward, and with supernatural force tore me from his father, to whose knees I clung: in a transport of fury, he dashed me to the ground, and struck me violently with a stick. I could have torn him limb from limb, as the lion rends the antelope. But my heart sunk within me as with bitter sickness, and I refrained. I saw him on the point of repeating his blow, when, overcome by pain and anguish, I quitted the cottage, and in the general tumult escaped unperceived to my hovel.

---

1 Cf. Milton, *Paradise Lost* IV.416.

2 Cf. Godwin on solitary confinement, *Political Justice* 2: 386-88; VII.vi (Appendix A.1.d).

CHAPTER VIII.

"Cursed, cursed creator! Why did I live? Why, in that instant, did I not extinguish the spark of existence which you had so wantonly bestowed? I know not; despair had not yet taken possession of me; my feelings were those of rage and revenge. I could with pleasure have destroyed the cottage and its inhabitants, and have glutted myself with their shrieks and misery.

"When night came, I quitted my retreat, and wandered in the wood; and now, no longer restrained by the fear of discovery, I gave vent to my anguish in fearful howlings. I was like a wild beast that had broken the toils; destroying the objects that obstructed me, and ranging through the wood with a stag-like swiftness. Oh! what a miserable night I passed! the cold stars shone in mockery, and the bare trees waved their branches above me: now and then the sweet voice of a bird burst forth amidst the universal stillness. All, save I, were at rest or in enjoyment: I, like the arch fiend, bore a hell within me;[1] and, finding myself unsympathized with, wished to tear up the trees, spread havoc and destruction around me, and then to have sat down and enjoyed the ruin.

"But this was a luxury of sensation that could not endure; I became fatigued with excess of bodily exertion, and sank on the damp grass in the sick impotence of despair. There was none among the myriads of men that existed who would pity or assist me; and should I feel kindness towards my enemies? No: from that moment I declared everlasting war against the species, and, more than all, against him who had formed me, and sent me forth to this insupportable misery.[2]

"The sun rose; I heard the voices of men, and knew that it was impossible to return to my retreat during that day. Accordingly I hid myself in some thick underwood, determining to devote the ensuing hours to reflection on my situation.

"The pleasant sunshine, and the pure air of day, restored me to some degree of tranquillity; and when I considered what had passed at the cottage, I could not help believing that I had been too hasty in my conclusions. I had certainly acted imprudently. It was apparent that my conversation had interested the father in my behalf, and I was a fool in having exposed my person to the horror of his children. I ought to have familiarized the old De

---

1 Cf. Milton, *Paradise Lost* IX.445-79 (Appendix C.4.c); Victor has already alluded to IX.467.
2 Cf. Milton, *Paradise Lost* II.660-63.

Lacey to me, and by degrees have discovered myself to the rest of his family, when they should have been prepared for my approach. But I did not believe my errors to be irretrievable; and, after much consideration, I resolved to return to the cottage, seek the old man, and by my representations win him to my party.

"These thoughts calmed me, and in the afternoon I sank into a profound sleep; but the fever of my blood did not allow me to be visited by peaceful dreams. The horrible scene of the preceding day was for ever acting before my eyes; the females were flying, and the enraged Felix tearing me from his father's feet. I awoke exhausted; and, finding that it was already night, I crept forth from my hiding-place, and went in search of food.

"When my hunger was appeased, I directed my steps towards the well-known path that conducted to the cottage. All there was at peace. I crept into my hovel, and remained in silent expectation of the accustomed hour when the family arose. That hour past, the sun mounted high in the heavens, but the cottagers did not appear. I trembled violently, apprehending some dreadful misfortune. The inside of the cottage was dark, and I heard no motion; I cannot describe the agony of this suspence.

"Presently two countrymen passed by; but, pausing near the cottage, they entered into conversation, using violent gesticulations; but I did not understand what they said, as they spoke the language of the country, which differed from that of my protectors. Soon after, however, Felix approached with another man: I was surprised, as I knew that he had not quitted the cottage that morning, and waited anxiously to discover, from his discourse, the meaning of these unusual appearances.

"'Do you consider,' said his companion to him, 'that you will be obliged to pay three months' rent, and to lose the produce of your garden? I do not wish to take any unfair advantage, and I beg therefore that you will take some days to consider of your determination.'

"'It is utterly useless,' replied Felix, 'we can never again inhabit your cottage. The life of my father is in the greatest danger, owing to the dreadful circumstance that I have related. My wife and my sister will never recover their horror. I entreat you not to reason with me any more. Take possession of your tenement, and let me fly from this place.'

"Felix trembled violently as he said this. He and his companion entered the cottage, in which they remained for a few minutes, and then departed. I never saw any of the family of De Lacey more.

"I continued for the remainder of the day in my hovel in a state of utter and stupid despair. My protectors had departed, and had broken the only link that held me to the world. For the first time the feelings of revenge and hatred filled my bosom, and I did not strive to controul them; but, allowing myself to be borne away by the stream, I bent my mind towards injury and death. When I thought of my friends, of the mild voice of De Lacey, the gentle eyes of Agatha, and the exquisite beauty of the Arabian, these thoughts vanished, and a gush of tears somewhat soothed me. But again, when I reflected that they had spurned and deserted me, anger returned, a rage of anger; and, unable to injure any thing human, I turned my fury towards inanimate objects. As night advanced, I placed a variety of combustibles around the cottage; and, after having destroyed every vestige of cultivation in the garden, I waited with forced impatience until the moon had sunk to commence my operations.

"As the night advanced, a fierce wind arose from the woods, and quickly dispersed the clouds that had loitered in the heavens: the blast tore along like a mighty avelânche, and produced a kind of insanity in my spirits, that burst all bounds of reason and reflection. I lighted the dry branch of a tree, and danced with fury around the devoted cottage, my eyes still fixed on the western horizon, the edge of which the moon nearly touched.[1] A part of its orb was at length hid, and I waved my brand; it sunk, and, with a loud scream, I fired the straw, and heath, and bushes, which I had collected. The wind fanned the fire, and the cottage was quickly enveloped by the flames, which clung to it, and licked it with their forked and destroying tongues.

"As soon as I was convinced that no assistance could save any part of the habitation, I quitted the scene, and sought for refuge in the woods.

"And now, with the world before me,[2] whither should I bend my steps? I resolved to fly far from the scene of my misfortunes; but to me, hated and despised, every country must be equally horrible. At length the thought of you crossed my mind. I learned from your papers that you were my father, my creator; and to whom could I apply with more fitness than to him who had given me life? Among the lessons that Felix had bestowed upon Safie

---

1 Cf. William Wordsworth (1770-1850), "Strange fits of passion I have known" (1799).
2 An allusion to Milton, *Paradise Lost* XII.646. Victor has made an ironic allusion to the same line.

geography had not been omitted: I had learned from these the relative situations of the different countries of the earth. You had mentioned Geneva as the name of your native town; and towards this place I resolved to proceed.

"But how was I to direct myself? I knew that I must travel in a south-westerly direction to reach my destination; but the sun was my only guide. I did not know the names of the towns that I was to pass through, nor could I ask information from a single human being; but I did not despair. From you only could I hope for succour, although towards you I felt no sentiment but that of hatred. Unfeeling, heartless creator! you had endowed me with perceptions and passions, and then cast me abroad an object for the scorn and horror of mankind. But on you only had I any claim for pity and redress, and from you I determined to seek that justice which I vainly attempted to gain from any other being that wore the human form.

"My travels were long, and the sufferings I endured intense. It was late in autumn when I quitted the district where I had so long resided. I travelled only at night, fearful of encountering the visage of a human being. Nature decayed around me, and the sun became heatless; rain and snow poured around me; mighty rivers were frozen; the surface of the earth was hard, and chill, and bare, and I found no shelter. Oh, earth! how often did I imprecate curses on the cause of my being! The mildness of my nature had fled, and all within me was turned to gall and bitterness. The nearer I approached to your habitation, the more deeply did I feel the spirit of revenge enkindled in my heart. Snow fell, and the waters were hardened, but I rested not. A few incidents now and then directed me, and I possessed a map of the country; but I often wandered wide from my path. The agony of my feelings allowed me no respite: no incident occurred from which my rage and misery could not extract its food; but a circumstance that happened when I arrived on the confines of Switzerland, when the sun had recovered its warmth, and the earth again began to look green, confirmed in an especial manner the bitterness and horror of my feelings.

"I generally rested during the day, and travelled only when I was secured by night from the view of man. One morning, however, finding that my path lay through a deep wood, I ventured to continue my journey after the sun had risen; the day, which was one of the first of spring, cheered even me by the loveliness of its sunshine and the balminess of the air. I felt emotions of gentleness and pleasure, that had long appeared dead, revive within me. Half surprised by the novelty of these sensations, I allowed myself to be borne away by them; and, forgetting my solitude and deformity, dared to be happy. Soft tears again bedewed my cheeks, and I even raised my humid eyes with thankfulness towards the blessed sun which bestowed such joy upon me.

"I continued to wind among the paths of the wood, until I came to its boundary, which was skirted by a deep and rapid river, into which many of the trees bent their branches, now budding with the fresh spring. Here I paused, not exactly knowing what path to pursue, when I heard the sound of voices, that induced me to conceal myself under the shade of a cypress. I was scarcely hid, when a young girl came running towards the spot where I was concealed, laughing as if she ran from some one in sport. She continued her course along the precipitous sides of the river, when suddenly her foot slipt, and she fell into the rapid stream. I rushed from my hiding place, and, with extreme labour from the force of the current, saved her, and dragged her to shore. She was senseless; and I endeavoured, by every means in my power, to restore animation, when I was suddenly interrupted by the approach of a rustic, who was probably the person from whom she had playfully fled. On seeing me, he darted towards me, and, tearing the girl from my arms, hastened towards the deeper parts of the wood. I followed speedily, I hardly knew why; but when the man saw me draw near, he aimed a gun, which he carried, at my body, and fired. I sunk to the ground, and my injurer, with increased swiftness, escaped into the wood.

"This was then the reward of my benevolence! I had saved a human being from destruction, and, as a recompence, I now writhed under the miserable pain of a wound, which shattered the flesh and bone. The feelings of kindness and gentleness, which I had entertained but a few moments before, gave place to hellish rage and gnashing of teeth. Inflamed by pain, I vowed eternal hatred and vengeance to all mankind. But the agony of my wound overcame me; my pulses paused, and I fainted.[1]

"For some weeks I led a miserable life in the woods, endeavouring to cure the wound which I had received. The ball had entered my shoulder, and I knew not whether it had remained there or passed through; at any rate I had no means of extracting it. My sufferings were augmented also by the oppressive sense of the injustice and ingratitude of their infliction. My daily vows rose for revenge—a deep and deadly revenge, such as

---

1 Cf. the death of Charon the dog in Godwin, *St. Leon* 272; XXV.

would alone compensate for the outrages and anguish I had endured.

"After some weeks my wound healed, and I continued my journey. The labours I endured were no longer to be alleviated by the bright sun or gentle breezes of spring; all joy was but a mockery, which insulted my desolate state, and made me feel more painfully that I was not made for the enjoyment of pleasure.

"But my toils now drew near a close; and, two months from this time, I reached the environs of Geneva.

"It was evening when I arrived, and I retired to a hiding-place among the fields that surround it, to meditate in what manner I should apply to you. I was oppressed by fatigue and hunger, and far too unhappy to enjoy the gentle breezes of evening, or the prospect of the sun setting behind the stupendous mountains of Jura.

"At this time a slight sleep relieved me from the pain of reflection, which was disturbed by the approach of a beautiful child, who came running into the recess I had chosen with all the sportiveness of infancy. Suddenly, as I gazed on him, an idea seized me, that this little creature was unprejudiced, and had lived too short a time to have imbibed a horror of deformity. If, therefore, I could seize him, and educate him as my companion and friend, I should not be so desolate in this peopled earth.

"Urged by this impulse, I seized on the boy as he passed, and drew him towards me. As soon as he beheld my form, he placed his hands before his eyes, and uttered a shrill scream: I drew his hand forcibly from his face, and said, 'Child, what is the meaning of this? I do not intend to hurt you; listen to me.'

"He struggled violently; 'Let me go,' he cried; 'monster! ugly wretch! you wish to eat me, and tear me to pieces—You are an ogre—Let me go, or I will tell my papa.'

"'Boy, you will never see your father again; you must come with me.'

"'Hideous monster! let me go; My papa is a Syndic—he is M. Frankenstein—he would punish you. You dare not keep me.'

"'Frankenstein! you belong then to my enemy—to him towards whom I have sworn eternal revenge; you shall be my first victim.'

"The child still struggled, and loaded me with epithets which carried despair to my heart: I grasped his throat to silence him, and in a moment he lay dead at my feet.

"I gazed on my victim, and my heart swelled with exultation and hellish triumph: clapping my hands, I exclaimed, 'I, too, can create desolation; my enemy is not impregnable; this death will carry despair to him, and a thousand other miseries shall torment and destroy him.'

"As I fixed my eyes on the child, I saw something glittering on his breast. I took it; it was a portrait of a most lovely woman. In spite of my malignity, it softened and attracted me. For a few moments I gazed with delight on her dark eyes, fringed by deep lashes, and her lovely lips; but presently my rage returned: I remembered that I was for ever deprived of the delights that such beautiful creatures could bestow; and that she whose resemblance I contemplated would, in regarding me, have changed that air of divine benignity to one expressive of disgust and affright.

"Can you wonder that such thoughts transported me with rage? I only wonder that at that moment, instead of venting my sensations in exclamations and agony, I did not rush among mankind, and perish in the attempt to destroy them.

"While I was overcome by these feelings, I left the spot where I had committed the murder, and was seeking a more secluded hiding-place, when I perceived a woman passing near me. She was young, not indeed so beautiful as her whose portrait I held, but of an agreeable aspect, and blooming in the loveliness of youth and health. Here, I thought, is one of those whose smiles are bestowed on all but me; she shall not escape: thanks to the lessons of Felix, and the sanguinary laws of man, I have learned how to work mischief. I approached her unperceived, and placed the portrait securely in one of the folds of her dress.[1]

"For some days I haunted the spot where these scenes had taken place; sometimes wishing to see you, sometimes resolved to quit the world and its miseries for ever. At length I wandered towards these mountains, and have ranged through their immense recesses, consumed by a burning passion which you alone can gratify. We may not part until you have promised to comply with my requisition. I am alone, and miserable; man will not associate with me; but one as deformed and horrible as myself would not deny herself to me. My companion must be of the same species, and have the same defects. This being you must create."

---

1 Cf. the use of planted evidence in Godwin, *Caleb Williams* 104 (I.xii), 167-68 (II.x).

CHAPTER IX.

THE being finished speaking, and fixed his looks upon me in expectation of a reply. But I was bewildered, perplexed, and unable to arrange my ideas sufficiently to understand the full extent of his proposition. He continued—

"You must create a female for me, with whom I can live in the interchange of those sympathies necessary for my being. This you alone can do; and I demand it of you as a right which you must not refuse."[1]

The latter part of his tale had kindled anew in me the anger that had died away while he narrated his peaceful life among the cottagers, and, as he said this, I could no longer suppress the rage that burned within me.

"I do refuse it," I replied; "and no torture shall ever extort a consent from me. You may render me the most miserable of men, but you shall never make me base in my own eyes. Shall I create another like yourself, whose joint wickedness might desolate the world. Begone! I have answered you; you may torture me, but I will never consent."

"You are in the wrong," replied the fiend; "and, instead of threatening, I am content to reason with you. I am malicious because I am miserable; am I not shunned and hated by all mankind? You, my creator, would tear me to pieces, and triumph; remember that, and tell me why I should pity man more than he pities me? You would not call it murder, if you could precipitate me into one of those ice-rifts, and destroy my frame, the work of your own hands. Shall I respect man, when he contemns me? Let him live with me in the interchange of kindness, and, instead of injury, I would bestow every benefit upon him with tears of gratitude at his acceptance. But that cannot be; the human senses are insurmountable barriers to our union. Yet mine shall not be the submission of abject slavery. I will revenge my injuries: if I cannot inspire love, I will cause fear; and chiefly towards you my arch-enemy, because my creator, do I swear inextinguishable hatred. Have a care: I will work at your destruction, nor finish until I desolate your heart, so that you curse the hour of your birth."[2]

A fiendish rage animated him as he said this; his face was wrinkled into contortions too horrible for human eyes to behold; but presently he calmed himself, and proceeded—

---

1 Cf. Godwin, *Political Justice* 2: 386-88; VII.vi (Appendix A.1.d).
2 An allusion to Job 3: 1-10.

"I intended to reason. This passion is detrimental to me; for you do not reflect that you are the cause of its excess. If any being felt emotions of benevolence towards me, I should return them an hundred and an hundred fold; for that one creature's sake, I would make peace with the whole kind![1] But I now indulge in dreams of bliss that cannot be realized. What I ask of you is reasonable and moderate; I demand a creature of another sex, but as hideous as myself: the gratification is small, but it is all that I can receive, and it shall content me. It is true, we shall be monsters, cut off from all the world; but on that account we shall be more attached to one another. Our lives will not be happy, but they will be harmless, and free from the misery I now feel. Oh! my creator, make me happy; let me feel gratitude towards you for one benefit! Let me see that I excite the sympathy of some existing thing; do not deny me my request!"

I was moved. I shuddered when I thought of the possible consequences of my consent; but I felt that there was some justice in his argument. His tale, and the feelings he now expressed, proved him to be a creature of fine sensations; and did I not, as his maker, owe him all the portion of happiness that it was in my power to bestow? He saw my change of feeling, and continued—

"If you consent, neither you nor any other human being shall ever see us again: I will go to the vast wilds of South America. My food is not that of man; I do not destroy the lamb and the kid, to glut my appetite; acorns and berries afford me sufficient nourishment.[2] My companion will be of the same nature as myself, and will be content with the same fare. We shall make our bed of dried leaves; the sun will shine on us as on man, and will ripen our food. The picture I present to you is peaceful and human, and you must feel that you could deny it only in the wantonness of power and cruelty. Pitiless as you have been towards me, I now see compassion in your eyes; let me seize the favourable moment, and persuade you to promise what I so ardently desire."

"You propose," replied I, "to fly from the habitations of man, to dwell in those wilds where the beasts of the field will be your only companions. How can you, who long for the love and sympathy of man, persevere in this exile? You will return, and again seek their kindness, and you will meet with their detestation; your

---

1 Cf. Genesis 18: 23-33.
2 Cf. P.B. Shelley's defence of vegetarianism in *Queen Mab* (1813) VIII.211-12n. The note includes an attack on Prometheus for giving humanity fire and thus making meat-eating possible.

evil passions will be renewed, and you will then have a companion to aid you in the task of destruction. This may not be; cease to argue the point, for I cannot consent."

"How inconstant are your feelings! but a moment ago you were moved by my representations, and why do you again harden yourself to my complaints? I swear to you, by the earth which I inhabit, and by you that made me, that, with the companion you bestow, I will quit the neighbourhood of man, and dwell, as it may chance, in the most savage of places. My evil passions will have fled, for I shall meet with sympathy; my life will flow quietly away, and, in my dying moments, I shall not curse my maker."

His words had a strange effect upon me. I compassionated him, and sometimes felt a wish to console him; but when I looked upon him, when I saw the filthy mass that moved and talked, my heart sickened, and my feelings were altered to those of horror and hatred. I tried to stifle these sensations; I thought, that as I could not sympathize with him, I had no right to withhold from him the small portion of happiness which was yet in my power to bestow.

"You swear," I said, "to be harmless; but have you not already shewn a degree of malice that should reasonably make me distrust you? May not even this be a feint that will increase your triumph by affording a wider scope for your revenge?"

"How is this? I thought I had moved your compassion, and yet you still refuse to bestow on me the only benefit that can soften my heart, and render me harmless. If I have no ties and no affections, hatred and vice must be my portion; the love of another will destroy the cause of my crimes, and I shall become a thing, of whose existence every one will be ignorant. My vices are the children of a forced solitude that I abhor; and my virtues will necessarily arise when I live in communion with an equal. I shall feel the affections of a sensitive being, and become linked to the chain of existence and events, from which I am now excluded."

I paused some time to reflect on all he had related, and the various arguments which he had employed. I thought of the promise of virtues which he had displayed on the opening of his existence, and the subsequent blight of all kindly feeling by the loathing and scorn which his protectors had manifested towards him. His power and threats were not omitted in my calculations: a creature who could exist in the ice caves of the glaciers, and hide himself from pursuit among the ridges of inaccessible precipices, was a being possessing faculties it would be vain to cope with. After a long pause of reflection, I concluded, that the justice due both to him and my fellow-creatures demanded of me that I should comply with his request. Turning to him, therefore, I said—

"I consent to your demand, on your solemn oath to quit Europe for ever, and every other place in the neighbourhood of man, as soon as I shall deliver into your hands a female who will accompany you in your exile."

"I swear," he cried, "by the sun, and by the blue sky of heaven, that if you grant my prayer, while they exist you shall never behold me again. Depart to your home, and commence your labours: I shall watch their progress with unutterable anxiety; and fear not but that when you are ready I shall appear."

Saying this, he suddenly quitted me, fearful, perhaps, of any change in my sentiments. I saw him descend the mountain with greater speed than the flight of an eagle, and quickly lost him among the undulations of the sea of ice.

His tale had occupied the whole day; and the sun was upon the verge of the horizon when he departed. I knew that I ought to hasten my descent towards the valley, as I should soon be encompassed in darkness; but my heart was heavy, and my steps slow. The labour of winding among the little paths of the mountains, and fixing my feet firmly as I advanced, perplexed me, occupied as I was by the emotions which the occurrences of the day had produced. Night was far advanced, when I came to the half-way resting-place, and seated myself beside the fountain. The stars shone at intervals, as the clouds passed from over them; the dark pines rose before me, and every here and there a broken tree lay on the ground: it was a scene of wonderful solemnity, and stirred strange thoughts within me. I wept bitterly; and, clasping my hands in agony, I exclaimed, "Oh! stars, and clouds, and winds, ye are all about to mock me: if ye really pity me, crush sensation and memory; let me become as nought; but if not, depart, depart and leave me in darkness."

These were wild and miserable thoughts; but I cannot describe to you how the eternal twinkling of the stars weighed upon me, and how I listened to every blast of wind, as if it were a dull ugly siroc[1] on its way to consume me.

Morning dawned before I arrived at the village of Chamounix; but my presence, so haggard and strange, hardly calmed the fears of my family, who had waited the whole night in anxious expectation of my return.

---

1 The sirocco, an oppressive and traditionally destructive wind that blows from Africa across the Mediterranean and southern Europe.

The following day we returned to Geneva. The intention of my father in coming had been to divert my mind, and to restore me to my lost tranquillity; but the medicine had been fatal. And, unable to account for the excess of misery I appeared to suffer, he hastened to return home, hoping the quiet and monotony of a domestic life would by degrees alleviate my sufferings from whatsoever cause they might spring.

For myself, I was passive in all their arrangements; and the gentle affection of my beloved Elizabeth was inadequate to draw me from the depth of my despair. The promise I had made to the daemon weighed upon my mind, like Dante's iron cowl on the heads of the hellish hypocrites.[1] All pleasures of earth and sky passed before me like a dream, and that thought only had to me the reality of life. Can you wonder, that sometimes a kind of insanity possessed me, or that I saw continually about me a multitude of filthy animals inflicting on me incessant torture, that often extorted screams and bitter groans?

By degrees, however, these feelings became calmed. I entered again into the every-day scene of life, if not with interest, at least with some degree of tranquillity.

END OF VOL. II.

---

1 *Inferno* XXIII.58-67. Cf. Godwin's denunciation of promises as fundamentally unjust, *Political Justice* 1: 197; III.iii.

FRANKENSTEIN;
OR, THE
MODERN PROMETHEUS.

[VOL. III.]

CHAPTER I.

DAY after day, week after week, passed away on my return to Geneva; and I could not collect the courage to recommence my work. I feared the vengeance of the disappointed fiend, yet I was unable to overcome my repugnance to the task which was enjoined me. I found that I could not compose a female without again devoting several months to profound study and laborious disquisition. I had heard of some discoveries having been made by an English philosopher, the knowledge of which was material to my success, and I sometimes thought of obtaining my father's consent to visit England for this purpose; but I clung to every pretence of delay, and could not resolve to interrupt my returning tranquillity. My health, which had hitherto declined, was now much restored; and my spirits, when unchecked by the memory of my unhappy promise, rose proportionably. My father saw this change with pleasure, and he turned his thoughts towards the best method of eradicating the remains of my melancholy, which every now and then would return by fits, and with a devouring blackness overcast the approaching sunshine. At these moments I took refuge in the most perfect solitude. I passed whole days on the lake alone in a little boat, watching the clouds, and listening to the rippling of the waves, silent and listless. But the fresh air and bright sun seldom failed to restore me to some degree of composure; and, on my return, I met the salutations of my friends with a readier smile and a more cheerful heart.

It was after my return from one of these rambles that my father, calling me aside, thus addressed me:—

"I am happy to remark, my dear son, that you have resumed your former pleasures, and seem to be returning to yourself. And yet you are still unhappy, and still avoid our society. For some time I was lost in conjecture as to the cause of this; but yesterday an idea struck me, and if it is well founded, I conjure you to avow it. Reserve on such a point would be not only useless, but draw down treble misery on us all."

I trembled violently at this exordium, and my father continued—

"I confess, my son, that I have always looked forward to your marriage with your cousin as the tie of our domestic comfort, and the stay of my declining years. You were attached to each other from your earliest infancy; you studied together, and appeared, in dispositions and tastes, entirely suited to one another. But so blind is the experience of man, that what I conceived to be the best assistants to my plan may have entirely destroyed it. You, perhaps, regard her as your sister, without any wish that she might become your wife. Nay, you may have met with another whom you may love; and, considering yourself as bound in honour to your cousin, this struggle may occasion the poignant misery which you appear to feel."

"My dear father, re-assure yourself. I love my cousin tenderly and sincerely. I never saw any woman who excited, as Elizabeth does, my warmest admiration and affection. My future hopes and prospects are entirely bound up in the expectation of our union."

"The expression of your sentiments on this subject, my dear Victor, gives me more pleasure than I have for some time experienced. If you feel thus, we shall assuredly be happy, however present events may cast a gloom over us. But it is this gloom, which appears to have taken so strong a hold of your mind, that I wish to dissipate. Tell me, therefore, whether you object to an immediate solemnization of the marriage. We have been unfortunate, and recent events have drawn us from that every-day tranquillity befitting my years and infirmities. You are younger; yet I do not suppose, possessed as you are of a competent fortune, that an early marriage would at all interfere with any future plans of honour and utility that you may have formed.[1] Do not suppose, however, that I wish to dictate happiness to you, or that a delay on your part would cause me any serious uneasiness. Interpret my words with candour, and answer me, I conjure you, with confidence and sincerity."

I listened to my father in silence, and remained for some time incapable of offering any reply. I revolved rapidly in my mind a multitude of thoughts, and endeavoured to arrive at some conclusion. Alas! to me the idea of an immediate union with my cousin was one of horror and dismay. I was bound by a solemn promise, which I had not yet fulfilled, and dared not break;[2] or,

---

1 Cf. Wollstonecraft's defense of early marriages, *Vindication* 311-12; XII.
2 Cf. Godwin, *Political Justice* 1: 197; III.iii.

if I did, what manifold miseries might not impend over me and my devoted family! Could I enter into a festival with this deadly weight yet hanging round my neck, and bowing me to the ground.[1] I must perform my engagement, and let the monster depart with his mate, before I allowed myself to enjoy the delight of an union from which I expected peace.

I remembered also the necessity imposed upon me of either journeying to England, or entering into a long correspondence with those philosophers of that country, whose knowledge and discoveries were of indispensable use to me in my present undertaking. The latter method of obtaining the desired intelligence was dilatory and unsatisfactory: besides, any variation was agreeable to me, and I was delighted with the idea of spending a year or two in change of scene and variety of occupation, in absence from my family; during which period some event might happen which would restore me to them in peace and happiness: my promise might be fulfilled, and the monster have departed; or some accident might occur to destroy him, and put an end to my slavery for ever.

These feelings dictated my answer to my father. I expressed a wish to visit England; but, concealing the true reasons of this request, I clothed my desires under the guise of wishing to travel and see the world before I sat down for life within the walls of my native town.

I urged my entreaty with earnestness, and my father was easily induced to comply; for a more indulgent and less dictatorial parent did not exist upon earth. Our plan was soon arranged. I should travel to Strasburgh, where Clerval would join me. Some short time would be spent in the towns of Holland, and our principal stay would be in England. We should return by France; and it was agreed that the tour should occupy the space of two years.

My father pleased himself with the reflection, that my union with Elizabeth should take place immediately on my return to Geneva. "These two years," said he, "will pass swiftly, and it will be the last delay that will oppose itself to your happiness. And, indeed, I earnestly desire that period to arrive, when we shall all be united, and neither hopes or fears arise to disturb our domestic calm."

"I am content," I replied, "with your arrangement. By that time we shall both have become wiser, and I hope happier,[2] than

---

1 Cf. Coleridge, "The Rime of the Ancyent Marinere" 137-38.
2 That is, they will be better off than the wedding-guest in Coleridge, "Rime" 657.

we at present are." I sighed; but my father kindly forbore to question me further concerning the cause of my dejection. He hoped that new scenes, and the amusement of travelling, would restore my tranquillity.

I now made arrangements for my journey; but one feeling haunted me, which filled me with fear and agitation. During my absence I should leave my friends unconscious of the existence of their enemy, and unprotected from his attacks, exasperated as he might be by my departure. But he had promised to follow me wherever I might go; and would he not accompany me to England? This imagination was dreadful in itself, but soothing, inasmuch as it supposed the safety of my friends. I was agonized with the idea of the possibility that the reverse of this might happen. But through the whole period during which I was the slave of my creature, I allowed myself to be governed by the impulses of the moment; and my present sensations strongly intimated that the fiend would follow me, and exempt my family from the danger of his machinations.

It was in the latter end of August that I departed, to pass two years of exile. Elizabeth approved of the reasons of my departure, and only regretted that she had not the same opportunities of enlarging her experience, and cultivating her understanding.[1] She wept, however, as she bade me farewell, and entreated me to return happy and tranquil. "We all," said she, "depend upon you; and if you are miserable, what must be our feelings?"

I threw myself into the carriage that was to convey me away, hardly knowing whither I was going, and careless of what was passing around. I remembered only, and it was with a bitter anguish that I reflected on it, to order that my chemical instruments should be packed to go with me: for I resolved to fulfil my promise while abroad, and return, if possible, a free man. Filled with dreary imaginations, I passed through many beautiful and majestic scenes; but my eyes were fixed and unobserving. I could only think of the bourne of my travels, and the work which was to occupy me whilst they endured.

After some days spent in listless indolence, during which I traversed many leagues, I arrived at Strasburgh, where I waited two days for Clerval. He came. Alas, how great was the contrast between us! He was alive to every new scene; joyful when he saw the beauties of the setting sun, and more happy when he beheld it rise, and recommence a new day. He pointed out to me the

---

1 Cf. Wollstonecraft, *Vindication* 130-31; II (Appendix A.2.c).

shifting colours of the landscape, and the appearances of the sky. "This is what it is to live"; he cried, "now I enjoy existence! But you, my dear Frankenstein, wherefore are you desponding and sorrowful?" In truth, I was occupied by gloomy thoughts, and neither saw the descent of the evening star, nor the golden sunrise reflected in the Rhine.—And you, my friend, would be far more amused with the journal of Clerval, who observed the scenery with an eye of feeling and delight, than to listen to my reflections. I, a miserable wretch, haunted by a curse that shut up every avenue to enjoyment.

We had agreed to descend the Rhine in a boat from Strasburgh to Rotterdam, whence we might take shipping for London. During this voyage, we passed by many willowy islands, and saw several beautiful towns. We staid a day at Manheim, and, on the fifth from our departure from Strasburgh, arrived at Mayence.[1] The course of the Rhine below Mayence becomes much more picturesque. The river descends rapidly, and winds between hills, not high, but steep, and of beautiful forms. We saw many ruined castles standing on the edges of precipices, surrounded by black woods, high and inaccessible. This part of the Rhine, indeed, presents a singularly variegated landscape. In one spot you view rugged hills, ruined castles overlooking tremendous precipices, with the dark Rhine rushing beneath; and, on the sudden turn of a promontory, flourishing vineyards, with green sloping banks, and a meandering river, and populous towns, occupy the scene.

We travelled at the time of the vintage, and heard the song of the labourers, as we glided down the stream. Even I, depressed in mind, and my spirits continually agitated by gloomy feelings, even I was pleased. I lay at the bottom of the boat, and, as I gazed on the cloudless blue sky, I seemed to drink in a tranquillity to which I had long been a stranger. And if these were my sensations, who can describe those of Henry? He felt as if he had been transported to Fairy-land, and enjoyed a happiness seldom tasted by man. "I have seen," he said, "the most beautiful scenes of my own country; I have visited the lakes of Lucerne and Uri, where the snowy mountains descend almost perpendicularly to the water, casting black and impenetrable shades, which would cause a gloomy and mournful appearance, were it not for the most verdant islands that relieve the eye by their gay appearance; I have

---

1 Shelley may have taken the name of her hero from the Castle Frankenstein, which is to the east of the Rhine, between Mannheim and Mainz. See Florescu, *In Search of Frankenstein.*

seen this lake agitated by a tempest, when the wind tore up whirl-winds of water, and gave you an idea of what the water-spout must be on the great ocean, and the waves dash with fury the base of the mountain, where the priest and his mistress were overwhelmed by an avalanche, and where their dying voices are still said to be heard amid the pauses of the nightly wind;[1] I have seen the mountains of La Valais, and the Pays de Vaud: but this country, Victor, pleases me more than all those wonders. The mountains of Switzerland are more majestic and strange; but there is a charm in the banks of this divine river, that I never before saw equalled. Look at that castle which overhangs yon precipice; and that also on the island, almost concealed amongst the foliage of those lovely trees; and now that group of labourers coming from among their vines; and that village half-hid in the recess of the mountain.[2] Oh, surely, the spirit that inhabits and guards this place has a soul more in harmony with man, than those who pile the glacier, or retire to the inaccessible peaks of the mountains of our own country."

Clerval! beloved friend! even now it delights me to record your words, and to dwell on the praise of which you are so eminently deserving. He was a being formed in the "very poetry of nature."[3] His wild and enthusiastic imagination was chastened by the sensibility of his heart. His soul overflowed with ardent affections, and his friendship was of that devoted and wondrous nature that the worldly-minded teach us to look for only in the imagination. But even human sympathies were not sufficient to satisfy his eager mind. The scenery of external nature, which others regard only with admiration, he loved with ardour:

——————————— "The sounding cataract
Haunted *him* like a passion: the tall rock,
The mountain, and the deep and gloomy wood,
Their colours and their forms, were then to him

---

1   In her first prose work, *History of a Six Weeks' Tour* (1817), Shelley writes: "opposite Brunen, they tell the story of a priest and his mistress, who, flying from persecution, inhabited a cottage at the foot of the snows. One winter night an avalanche overwhelmed them, but their plaintive voices are still heard in stormy nights, calling for succour from the peasants" (48-49).

2   Cf. Byron, *Childe Harold's Pilgrimage* III.xlvi.

3   Leigh Hunt's "Rimini." [Shelley's note; Leigh Hunt (1784-1859), *The Story of Rimini* (1816) II.47.]

An appetite; a feeling, and a love,
That had no need of a remoter charm,
By thought supplied, or any interest
Unborrowed from the eye."[1]

And where does he now exist? Is this gentle and lovely being lost for ever? Has this mind so replete with ideas, imaginations fanciful and magnificent, which formed a world, whose existence depended on the life of its creator; has this mind perished? Does it now only exist in my memory? No, it is not thus; your form so divinely wrought, and beaming with beauty, has decayed, but your spirit still visits and consoles your unhappy friend.

Pardon this gush of sorrow; these ineffectual words are but a slight tribute to the unexampled worth of Henry, but they soothe my heart, overflowing with the anguish which his remembrance creates. I will proceed with my tale.

Beyond Cologne we descended to the plains of Holland; and we resolved to post[2] the remainder of our way; for the wind was contrary, and the stream of the river was too gentle to aid us.

Our journey here lost the interest arising from beautiful scenery; but we arrived in a few days at Rotterdam, whence we proceeded by sea to England. It was on a clear morning, in the latter days of December, that I first saw the white cliffs of Britain. The banks of the Thames presented a new scene; they were flat, but fertile, and almost every town was marked by the remembrance of some story. We saw Tilbury Fort, and remembered the Spanish armada; Gravesend, Woolwich, and Greenwich, places which I had heard of even in my country.

At length we saw the numerous steeples of London, St. Paul's towering above all, and the Tower famed in English history.

CHAPTER II.

LONDON was our present point of rest; we determined to remain several months in this wonderful and celebrated city. Clerval desired the intercourse of the men of genius and talent who flourished at this time; but this was with me a secondary object; I was principally occupied with the means of obtaining the information

---

1 Wordsworth's "Tintern Abbey." [Shelley's note; the passage is adapted from "Lines Written a Few Miles above Tintern Abbey" (1798) 77-84.]
2 "To travel with relays of horses" (*OED*).

necessary for the completion of my promise, and quickly availed myself of the letters of introduction that I had brought with me, addressed to the most distinguished natural philosophers.

If this journey had taken place during my days of study and happiness, it would have afforded me inexpressible pleasure. But a blight had come over my existence, and I only visited these people for the sake of the information they might give me on the subject in which my interest was so terribly profound. Company was irksome to me; when alone, I could fill my mind with the sights of heaven and earth; the voice of Henry soothed me, and I could thus cheat myself into a transitory peace. But busy uninteresting joyous faces brought back despair to my heart. I saw an insurmountable barrier placed between me and my fellow-men; this barrier was sealed with the blood of William and Justine; and to reflect on the events connected with those names filled my soul with anguish.

But in Clerval I saw the image of my former self; he was inquisitive, and anxious to gain experience and instruction. The difference of manners which he observed was to him an inexhaustible source of instruction and amusement. He was for ever busy; and the only check to his enjoyments was my sorrowful and dejected mien. I tried to conceal this as much as possible, that I might not debar him from the pleasures natural to one who was entering on a new scene of life, undisturbed by any care or bitter recollection. I often refused to accompany him, alleging another engagement, that I might remain alone. I now also began to collect the materials necessary for my new creation, and this was to me like the torture of single drops of water continually falling on the head. Every thought that was devoted to it was an extreme anguish, and every word that I spoke in allusion to it caused my lips to quiver, and my heart to palpitate.

After passing some months in London, we received a letter from a person in Scotland, who had formerly been our visitor at Geneva. He mentioned the beauties of his native country, and asked us if those were not sufficient allurements to induce us to prolong our journey as far north as Perth, where he resided. Clerval eagerly desired to accept this invitation; and I, although I abhorred society, wished to view again mountains and streams, and all the wondrous works with which Nature adorns her chosen dwelling-places.

We had arrived in England at the beginning of October, and it was now February.[1] We accordingly determined to commence

---

1 I.e., 1796.

our journey towards the north at the expiration of another month. In this expedition we did not intend to follow the great road to Edinburgh, but to visit Windsor, Oxford, Matlock, and the Cumberland lakes, resolving to arrive at the completion of this tour about the end of July. I packed my chemical instruments, and the materials I had collected, resolving to finish my labours in some obscure nook in the northern highlands of Scotland.

We quitted London on the 27th of March, and remained a few days at Windsor, rambling in its beautiful forest. This was a new scene to us mountaineers; the majestic oaks, the quantity of game, and the herds of stately deer, were all novelties to us.

From thence we proceeded to Oxford. As we entered this city, our minds were filled with the remembrance of the events that had been transacted there more than a century and a half before. It was here that Charles I. had collected his forces. This city had remained faithful to him, after the whole nation had forsaken his cause to join the standard of parliament and liberty. The memory of that unfortunate king, and his companions, the amiable Falkland, the insolent Goring, his queen, and son, gave a peculiar interest to every part of the city, which they might be supposed to have inhabited.[1] The spirit of elder days found a dwelling here, and we delighted to trace its footsteps. If these feelings had not found an imaginary gratification, the appearance of the city had yet in itself sufficient beauty to obtain our admiration. The colleges are ancient and picturesque; the streets are almost magnificent; and the lovely Isis, which flows beside it through meadows of exquisite verdure, is spread forth into a placid expanse of waters, which reflects its majestic assemblage of towers, and spires, and domes, embosomed among aged trees.

I enjoyed this scene; and yet my enjoyment was embittered both by the memory of the past, and the anticipation of the future. I was formed for peaceful happiness. During my youthful days discontent never visited my mind; and if I was ever overcome by *ennui*, the sight of what is beautiful in nature, or the study of what is excellent and sublime in the productions of man, could always interest my heart, and communicate elasticity to my spirits. But I am a blasted tree; the bolt has entered my soul; and

---

1 Lucius Cary, second viscount Falkland (1610-43), was the secretary of state for Charles I (1600-49), and, later, the model for the chivalrous Ferdinando Falkland in Godwin's *Caleb Williams*. George, Baron Goring (1608-57) was one of Charles's generals in the Civil War.

I felt then that I should survive to exhibit, what I shall soon cease to be—a miserable spectacle of wrecked humanity, pitiable to others, and abhorrent to myself.

We passed a considerable period at Oxford, rambling among its environs, and endeavouring to identify every spot which might relate to the most animating epoch of English history. Our little voyages of discovery were often prolonged by the successive objects that presented themselves. We visited the tomb of the illustrious Hampden, and the field on which that patriot fell.[1] For a moment my soul was elevated from its debasing and miserable fears to contemplate the divine ideas of liberty and self-sacrifice, of which these sights were the monuments and the remembrancers. For an instant I dared to shake off my chains, and look around me with a free and lofty spirit; but the iron had eaten into my flesh, and I sank again, trembling and hopeless, into my miserable self.

We left Oxford with regret, and proceeded to Matlock, which was our next place of rest. The country in the neighbourhood of this village resembled, to a greater degree, the scenery of Switzerland; but every thing is on a lower scale, and the green hills want the crown of distant white Alps, which always attend on the piny mountains of my native country. We visited the wondrous cave, and the little cabinets of natural history, where the curiosities are disposed in the same manner as in the collections at Servox and Chamounix. The latter name made me tremble, when pronounced by Henry; and I hastened to quit Matlock, with which that terrible scene was thus associated.

From Derby still journeying northward, we passed two months in Cumberland and Westmoreland. I could now almost fancy myself among the Swiss mountains. The little patches of snow which yet lingered on the northern sides of the mountains, the lakes, and the dashing of the rocky streams, were all familiar and dear sights to me. Here also we made some acquaintances, who almost contrived to cheat me into happiness. The delight of Clerval was proportionably greater than mine; his mind expanded in the company of men of talent,[2] and he found in his

---

1 John Hampden (1594-1643), cousin and supporter of Oliver Cromwell, was killed in a skirmish near Oxford.
2 Shelley seems to be thinking anachronistically of the Lake Poets, Wordsworth (who moved to the Lake District in 1799), Coleridge (who moved there in 1800), and Southey (who moved there in 1807). The abolitionist Thomas Clarkson (1760-1846) also lived there from 1794 to 1804.

own nature greater capacities and resources than he could have imagined himself to have possessed while he associated with his inferiors. "I could pass my life here," said he to me; "and among these mountains I should scarcely regret Switzerland and the Rhine."

But he found that a traveller's life is one that includes much pain amidst its enjoyments. His feelings are for ever on the stretch; and when he begins to sink into repose, he finds himself obliged to quit that on which he rests in pleasure for something new, which again engages his attention, and which also he forsakes for other novelties.

We had scarcely visited the various lakes of Cumberland and Westmoreland, and conceived an affection for some of the inhabitants, when the period of our appointment with our Scotch friend approached, and we left them to travel on. For my own part I was not sorry. I had now neglected my promise for some time, and I feared the effects of the daemon's disappointment. He might remain in Switzerland, and wreak his vengeance on my relatives. This idea pursued me, and tormented me at every moment from which I might otherwise have snatched repose and peace. I waited for my letters with feverish impatience: if they were delayed, I was miserable, and overcome by a thousand fears; and when they arrived, and I saw the superscription of Elizabeth or my father, I hardly dared to read and ascertain my fate. Sometimes I thought that the fiend followed me, and might expedite my remissness by murdering my companion. When these thoughts possessed me, I would not quit Henry for a moment, but followed him as his shadow, to protect him from the fancied rage of his destroyer. I felt as if I had committed some great crime, the consciousness of which haunted me. I was guiltless, but I had indeed drawn down a horrible curse upon my head, as mortal as that of crime.

I visited Edinburgh with languid eyes and mind; and yet that city might have interested the most unfortunate being. Clerval did not like it so well as Oxford; for the antiquity of the latter city was more pleasing to him. But the beauty and regularity of the new town of Edinburgh, its romantic castle, and its environs, the most delightful in the world, Arthur's Seat, St. Bernard's Well, and the Pentland Hills, compensated him for the change, and filled him with cheerfulness and admiration. But I was impatient to arrive at the termination of my journey.

We left Edinburgh in a week, passing through Coupar, St. Andrews, and along the banks of the Tay, to Perth, where our friend expected us. But I was in no mood to laugh and talk with strangers, or enter into their feelings or plans with the good humour expected from a guest; and accordingly I told Clerval that I wished to make the tour of Scotland alone. "Do you," said I, "enjoy yourself, and let this be our rendezvous. I may be absent a month or two; but do not interfere with my motions, I entreat you: leave me to peace and solitude for a short time; and when I return, I hope it will be with a lighter heart, more congenial to your own temper."

Henry wished to dissuade me; but, seeing me bent on this plan, ceased to remonstrate. He entreated me to write often. "I had rather be with you," he said, "in your solitary rambles, than with these Scotch people, whom I do not know: hasten then, my dear friend, to return, that I may again feel myself somewhat at home, which I cannot do in your absence."

Having parted from my friend, I determined to visit some remote spot of Scotland, and finish my work in solitude. I did not doubt but that the monster followed me, and would discover himself to me when I should have finished, that he might receive his companion.

With this resolution I traversed the northern highlands, and fixed on one of the remotest of the Orkneys as the scene of my labours. It was a place fitted for such a work, being hardly more than a rock, whose high sides were continually beaten upon by the waves. The soil was barren, scarcely affording pasture for a few miserable cows, and oatmeal for its inhabitants, which consisted of five persons, whose gaunt and scraggy limbs gave tokens of their miserable fare. Vegetables and bread, when they indulged in such luxuries, and even fresh water, was to be procured from the main land, which was about five miles distant.

On the whole island there were but three miserable huts, and one of these was vacant when I arrived. This I hired. It contained but two rooms, and these exhibited all the squalidness of the most miserable penury. The thatch had fallen in, the walls were unplastered, and the door was off its hinges. I ordered it to be repaired, bought some furniture, and took possession; an incident which would, doubtless, have occasioned some surprise, had not all the senses of the cottagers been benumbed by want and squalid poverty. As it was, I lived ungazed at and unmolested, hardly thanked for the pittance of food and clothes which I gave; so much does suffering blunt even the coarsest sensations of men.

In this retreat I devoted the morning to labour; but in the evening, when the weather permitted, I walked on the stony beach of the sea, to listen to the waves as they roared, and dashed at my feet. It was a monotonous, yet ever-changing scene. I thought of Switzerland; it was far different from this desolate and appalling landscape. Its hills are covered with vines, and its cottages are scattered thickly in the plains. Its fair lakes reflect a blue and gentle sky; and, when troubled by the winds, their tumult is but as the play of a lively infant, when compared to the roarings of the giant ocean.

In this manner I distributed my occupations when I first arrived; but, as I proceeded in my labour, it became every day more horrible and irksome to me. Sometimes I could not prevail on myself to enter my laboratory for several days; and at other times I toiled day and night in order to complete my work. It was indeed a filthy process in which I was engaged. During my first experiment, a kind of enthusiastic frenzy had blinded me to the horror of my employment; my mind was intently fixed on the sequel of my labour, and my eyes were shut to the horror of my proceedings. But now I went to it in cold blood, and my heart often sickened at the work of my hands.

Thus situated, employed in the most detestable occupation, immersed in a solitude where nothing could for an instant call my attention from the actual scene in which I was engaged, my spirits became unequal; I grew restless and nervous. Every moment I feared to meet my persecutor. Sometimes I sat with my eyes fixed on the ground, fearing to raise them lest they should encounter the object which I so much dreaded to behold. I feared to wander from the sight of my fellow-creatures, lest when alone he should come to claim his companion.

In the mean time I worked on, and my labour was already considerably advanced. I looked towards its completion with a tremulous and eager hope, which I dared not trust myself to question, but which was intermixed with obscure forebodings of evil, that made my heart sicken in my bosom.

CHAPTER III.

I SAT one evening in my laboratory; the sun had set, and the moon was just rising from the sea; I had not sufficient light for my employment, and I remained idle, in a pause of consideration of whether I should leave my labour for the night, or hasten its conclusion by an unremitting attention to it. As I sat, a train of reflection occurred to me, which led me to consider the effects of what I was now doing. Three years before I was engaged in the same manner, and had created a fiend whose unparalleled barbarity had desolated my heart, and filled it for ever with the bitterest remorse. I was now about to form another being, of whose dispositions I was alike ignorant; she might become ten thousand times more malignant than her mate, and delight, for its own sake, in murder and wretchedness. He had sworn to quit the neighbourhood of man, and hide himself in deserts; but she had not; and she, who in all probability was to become a thinking and reasoning animal, might refuse to comply with a compact made before her creation. They might even hate each other; the creature who already lived loathed his own deformity, and might he not conceive a greater abhorrence for it when it came before his eyes in the female form? She also might turn with disgust from him to the superior beauty of man; she might quit him, and he be again alone, exasperated by the fresh provocation of being deserted by one of his own species.

Even if they were to leave Europe, and inhabit the deserts of the new world, yet one of the first results of those sympathies for which the daemon thirsted would be children, and a race of devils would be propagated upon the earth, who might make the very existence of the species of man a condition precarious and full of terror. Had I a right, for my own benefit, to inflict this curse upon everlasting generations?[1] I had before been moved by the sophisms of the being I had created; I had been struck senseless by his fiendish threats: but now, for the first time, the wickedness of my promise burst upon me; I shuddered to think that future ages might curse me as their pest, whose selfishness had not hesitated to buy its own peace at the price perhaps of the existence of the whole human race.

I trembled, and my heart failed within me; when, on looking up, I saw, by the light of the moon, the daemon at the casement. A ghastly grin wrinkled his lips as he gazed on me, where I sat fulfilling the task which he had allotted to me. Yes, he had followed me in my travels; he had loitered in forests, hid himself in caves, or taken refuge in wide and desert heaths; and he now came to mark my progress, and claim the fulfilment of my promise.

As I looked on him, his countenance expressed the utmost extent of malice and treachery. I thought with a sensation of madness on my promise of creating another like to him, and,

---

1 Cf. Godwin on the impersonality of justice, *Political Justice* 1: 126-29; II.ii (Appendix A.1.e).

trembling with passion, tore to pieces the thing on which I was engaged. The wretch saw me destroy the creature on whose future existence he depended for happiness, and, with a howl of devilish despair and revenge, withdrew.

I left the room, and, locking the door, made a solemn vow in my own heart never to resume my labours; and then, with trembling steps, I sought my own apartment. I was alone; none were near me to dissipate the gloom, and relieve me from the sickening oppression of the most terrible reveries.

Several hours past, and I remained near my window gazing on the sea; it was almost motionless, for the winds were hushed, and all nature reposed under the eye of the quiet moon. A few fishing vessels alone specked the water, and now and then the gentle breeze wafted the sound of voices, as the fishermen called to one another. I felt the silence, although I was hardly conscious of its extreme profundity, until my ear was suddenly arrested by the paddling of oars near the shore, and a person landed close to my house.

In a few minutes after, I heard the creaking of my door, as if some one endeavoured to open it softly. I trembled from head to foot; I felt a presentiment of who it was, and wished to rouse one of the peasants who dwelt in a cottage not far from mine; but I was overcome by the sensation of helplessness, so often felt in frightful dreams, when you in vain endeavour to fly from an impending danger, and was rooted to the spot.[1]

Presently I heard the sound of footsteps along the passage; the door opened, and the wretch whom I dreaded appeared. Shutting the door, he approached me, and said, in a smothered voice—

"You have destroyed the work which you began; what is it that you intend? Do you dare to break your promise? I have endured toil and misery: I left Switzerland with you; I crept along the shores of the Rhine, among its willow islands, and over the summits of its hills. I have dwelt many months in the heaths of England, and among the deserts of Scotland. I have endured incalculable fatigue, and cold, and hunger; do you dare destroy my hopes?"

"Begone! I do break my promise; never will I create another like yourself, equal in deformity and wickedness."

"Slave, I before reasoned with you, but you have proved yourself unworthy of my condescension. Remember that I have power; you believe yourself miserable, but I can make you so

---

1 Cf. Darwin on the nightmare, *The Loves of the Plants* (1789) III.51-78.

wretched that the light of day will be hateful to you. You are my creator, but I am your master;—obey!"

"The hour of my weakness is past, and the period of your power is arrived. Your threats cannot move me to do an act of wickedness; but they confirm me in a resolution of not creating you a companion in vice. Shall I, in cool blood, set loose upon the earth a daemon, whose delight is in death and wretchedness. Begone! I am firm, and your words will only exasperate my rage."[1]

The monster saw my determination in my face, and gnashed his teeth in the impotence of anger. "Shall each man," cried he, "find a wife for his bosom, and each beast have his mate, and I be alone? I had feelings of affection, and they were requited by detestation and scorn. Man, you may hate; but beware! Your hours will pass in dread and misery, and soon the bolt will fall which must ravish from you your happiness for ever. Are you to be happy, while I grovel in the intensity of my wretchedness? You can blast my other passions; but revenge remains—revenge, henceforth dearer than light or food! I may die; but first you, my tyrant and tormentor, shall curse the sun that gazes on your misery. Beware; for I am fearless, and therefore powerful. I will watch with the wiliness of a snake, that I may sting with its venom. Man, you shall repent of the injuries you inflict."

"Devil, cease; and do not poison the air with these sounds of malice. I have declared my resolution to you, and I am no coward to bend beneath words. Leave me; I am inexorable."

"It is well. I go; but remember, I shall be with you on your wedding-night."

I started forward, and exclaimed, "Villain! before you sign my death-warrant, be sure that you are yourself safe."

I would have seized him; but he eluded me, and quitted the house with precipitation: in a few moments I saw him in his boat, which shot across the waters with an arrowy swiftness, and was soon lost amidst the waves.

All was again silent; but his words rung in my ears. I burned with rage to pursue the murderer of my peace, and precipitate him into the ocean. I walked up and down my room hastily and perturbed, while my imagination conjured up a thousand images to torment and sting me. Why had I not followed him, and closed

---

1 Cf. the confrontations between Caleb and Falkland in Godwin, *Caleb Williams* 280-84 (III.xii), and between St. Leon and Bethlem Gabor in *St. Leon* 420 (XLI).

with him in mortal strife? But I had suffered him to depart, and he had directed his course towards the main land. I shuddered to think who might be the next victim sacrificed to his insatiate revenge. And then I thought again of his words—"*I will be with you on your wedding-night.*" That then was the period fixed for the fulfilment of my destiny. In that hour I should die, and at once satisfy and extinguish his malice. The prospect did not move me to fear; yet when I thought of my beloved Elizabeth,—of her tears and endless sorrow, when she should find her lover so barbarously snatched from her,—tears, the first I had shed for many months, streamed from my eyes, and I resolved not to fall before my enemy without a bitter struggle.

The night passed away, and the sun rose from the ocean; my feelings became calmer, if it may be called calmness, when the violence of rage sinks into the depths of despair. I left the house, the horrid scene of the last night's contention, and walked on the beach of the sea, which I almost regarded as an insuperable barrier between me and my fellow-creatures; nay, a wish that such should prove the fact stole across me. I desired that I might pass my life on that barren rock, wearily it is true, but uninterrupted by any sudden shock of misery. If I returned, it was to be sacrificed, or to see those whom I most loved die under the grasp of a daemon whom I had myself created.

I walked about the isle like a restless spectre, separated from all it loved, and miserable in the separation. When it became noon, and the sun rose higher, I lay down on the grass, and was overpowered by a deep sleep. I had been awake the whole of the preceding night, my nerves were agitated, and my eyes inflamed by watching and misery. The sleep into which I now sunk refreshed me; and when I awoke, I again felt as if I belonged to a race of human beings like myself, and I began to reflect upon what had passed with greater composure; yet still the words of the fiend rung in my ears like a death-knell, they appeared like a dream, yet distinct and oppressive as a reality.

The sun had far descended, and I still sat on the shore, satisfying my appetite, which had become ravenous, with an oaten cake, when I saw a fishing-boat land close to me, and one of the men brought me a packet; it contained letters from Geneva, and one from Clerval, entreating me to join him. He said that nearly a year had elapsed since we had quitted Switzerland, and France was yet unvisited. He entreated me, therefore, to leave my solitary isle, and meet him at Perth, in a week from that time, when we might arrange the plan of our future proceedings. This letter in a degree recalled me to life, and I determined to quit my island at the expiration of two days.

Yet, before I departed, there was a task to perform, on which I shuddered to reflect: I must pack my chemical instruments; and for that purpose I must enter the room which had been the scene of my odious work, and I must handle those utensils, the sight of which was sickening to me. The next morning, at daybreak, I summoned sufficient courage, and unlocked the door of my laboratory. The remains of the half-finished creature, whom I had destroyed, lay scattered on the floor, and I almost felt as if I had mangled the living flesh of a human being. I paused to collect myself, and then entered the chamber. With trembling hand I conveyed the instruments out of the room; but I reflected that I ought not to leave the relics of my work to excite the horror and suspicion of the peasants, and I accordingly put them into a basket, with a great quantity of stones, and laying them up, determined to throw them into the sea that very night; and in the mean time I sat upon the beach, employed in cleaning and arranging my chemical apparatus.

Nothing could be more complete than the alteration that had taken place in my feelings since the night of the appearance of the daemon. I had before regarded my promise with a gloomy despair, as a thing that, with whatever consequences, must be fulfilled; but I now felt as if a film had been taken from before my eyes, and that I, for the first time, saw clearly. The idea of renewing my labours did not for one instant occur to me; the threat I had heard weighed on my thoughts, but I did not reflect that a voluntary act of mine could avert it. I had resolved in my own mind, that to create another like the fiend I had first made would be an act of the basest and most atrocious selfishness; and I banished from my mind every thought that could lead to a different conclusion.

Between two and three in the morning the moon rose; and I then, putting my basket aboard a little skiff, sailed out about four miles from the shore. The scene was perfectly solitary: a few boats were returning towards land, but I sailed away from them. I felt as if I was about the commission of a dreadful crime, and avoided with shuddering anxiety any encounter with my fellow-creatures. At one time the moon, which had before been clear, was suddenly overspread by a thick cloud, and I took advantage of the moment of darkness, and cast my basket into the sea; I listened to the gurgling sound as it sunk, and then sailed away from the spot. The sky became clouded; but the air was pure, although chilled by the north-east breeze that was then rising. But it refreshed me, and filled me with such agreeable sensations, that I resolved to prolong my stay on the water, and fixing the rudder in a direct position, stretched myself at the bottom of the boat. Clouds hid the moon, every thing was obscure, and I heard only the sound of the boat, as its keel cut through the waves; the murmur lulled me, and in a short time I slept soundly.

I do not know how long I remained in this situation, but when I awoke I found that the sun had already mounted considerably. The wind was high, and the waves continually threatened the safety of my little skiff. I found that the wind was north-east, and must have driven me far from the coast from which I had embarked. I endeavoured to change my course, but quickly found that if I again made the attempt the boat would be instantly filled with water. Thus situated, my only resource was to drive before the wind. I confess that I felt a few sensations of terror. I had no compass with me, and was so little acquainted with the geography of this part of the world that the sun was of little benefit to me. I might be driven into the wide Atlantic, and feel all the tortures of starvation, or be swallowed up in the immeasurable waters that roared and buffeted around me. I had already been out many hours, and felt the torment of a burning thirst, a prelude to my other sufferings. I looked on the heavens, which were covered by clouds that flew before the wind only to be replaced by others: I looked upon the sea, it was to be my grave. "Fiend," I exclaimed, "your task is already fulfilled!" I thought of Elizabeth, of my father, and of Clerval; and sunk into a reverie, so despairing and frightful, that even now, when the scene is on the point of closing before me for ever, I shudder to reflect on it.

Some hours passed thus; but by degrees, as the sun declined towards the horizon, the wind died away into a gentle breeze, and the sea became free from breakers. But these gave place to a heavy swell; I felt sick, and hardly able to hold the rudder, when suddenly I saw a line of high land towards the south.

Almost spent, as I was, by fatigue, and the dreadful suspense I endured for several hours, this sudden certainty of life rushed like a flood of warm joy to my heart, and tears gushed from my eyes.

How mutable are our feelings, and how strange is that clinging love we have of life even in the excess of misery! I constructed another sail with a part of my dress, and eagerly steered my course towards the land. It had a wild and rocky appearance; but as I approached nearer, I easily perceived the traces of cultivation. I saw vessels near the shore, and found myself suddenly transported back to the neighbourhood of civilized man. I eagerly traced the windings of the land, and hailed a steeple which I at length saw issuing from behind a small promontory. As I was in a state of extreme debility, I resolved to sail directly towards the town as a place where I could most easily procure nourishment. Fortunately I had money with me. As I turned the promontory, I perceived a small neat town and a good harbour, which I entered, my heart bounding with joy at my unexpected escape.

As I was occupied in fixing the boat and arranging the sails, several people crowded towards the spot. They seemed very much surprised at my appearance; but, instead of offering me any assistance, whispered together with gestures that at any other time might have produced in me a slight sensation of alarm. As it was, I merely remarked that they spoke English; and I therefore addressed them in that language: "My good friends," said I, "will you be so kind as to tell me the name of this town, and inform me where I am?"

"You will know that soon enough," replied a man with a gruff voice. "May be you are come to a place that will not prove much to your taste; but you will not be consulted as to your quarters, I promise you."

I was exceedingly surprised on receiving so rude an answer from a stranger; and I was also disconcerted on perceiving the frowning and angry countenances of his companions. "Why do you answer me so roughly?" I replied: "surely it is not the custom of Englishmen to receive strangers so inhospitably."

"I do not know," said the man, "what the custom of the English may be; but it is the custom of the Irish to hate villains."

While this strange dialogue continued, I perceived the crowd rapidly increase. Their faces expressed a mixture of curiosity and anger, which annoyed, and in some degree alarmed me. I inquired the way to the inn; but no one replied. I then moved forward, and a murmuring sound arose from the crowd as they followed and surrounded me; when an ill-looking man approaching, tapped me on the shoulder, and said, "Come, Sir, you must follow me to Mr. Kirwin's, to give an account of yourself."

"Who is Mr. Kirwin? Why am I to give an account of myself? Is not this a free country?"

"Aye, Sir, free enough for honest folks. Mr. Kirwin is a magistrate; and you are to give an account of the death of a gentleman who was found murdered here last night."

This answer startled me; but I presently recovered myself. I was innocent; that could easily be proved: accordingly I followed my conductor in silence, and was led to one of the best houses in the town. I was ready to sink from fatigue and hunger; but, being surrounded by a crowd, I thought it politic to rouse all my strength, that no physical debility might be construed into apprehension or conscious guilt. Little did I then expect the calamity that was in a few moments to overwhelm me, and extinguish in horror and despair all fear of ignominy or death.

I must pause here; for it requires all my fortitude to recall the memory of the frightful events which I am about to relate, in proper detail, to my recollection.

CHAPTER IV.

I WAS soon introduced into the presence of the magistrate, an old benevolent man, with calm and mild manners. He looked upon me, however, with some degree of severity; and then, turning towards my conductors, he asked who appeared as witnesses on this occasion.

About half a dozen men came forward; and one being selected by the magistrate, he deposed, that he had been out fishing the night before with his son and brother-in-law, Daniel Nugent, when, about ten o'clock, they observed a strong northerly blast rising, and they accordingly put in for port. It was a very dark night, as the moon had not yet risen; they did not land at the harbour, but, as they had been accustomed, at a creek about two miles below. He walked on first, carrying a part of the fishing tackle, and his companions followed him at some distance. As he was proceeding along the sands, he struck his foot against something, and fell all his length on the ground. His companions came up to assist him; and, by the light of their lantern, they found that he had fallen on the body of a man, who was to all appearance dead. Their first supposition was, that it was the corpse of some person who had been drowned, and was thrown on shore by the waves; but, upon examination, they found that the clothes were not wet, and even that the body was not then cold. They instantly carried it to the cottage of an old woman near the spot, and endeavoured, but in vain, to restore it to life. He appeared to be a handsome young man, about five and twenty years of age. He had apparently been strangled; for there was no sign of any violence, except the black mark of fingers on his neck.

The first part of this deposition did not in the least interest me; but when the mark of the fingers was mentioned, I remembered the murder of my brother, and felt myself extremely agitated; my limbs trembled, and a mist came over my eyes, which obliged me to lean on a chair for support. The magistrate observed me with a keen eye, and of course drew an unfavourable augury from my manner.

The son confirmed his father's account: but when Daniel Nugent was called, he swore positively that, just before the fall of his companion, he saw a boat, with a single man in it, at a short distance from the shore; and, as far as he could judge by the light of a few stars, it was the same boat in which I had just landed.

A woman deposed, that she lived near the beach, and was standing at the door of her cottage, waiting for the return of the fishermen, about an hour before she heard of the discovery of the body, when she saw a boat, with only one man in it, push off from that part of the shore where the corpse was afterwards found.

Another woman confirmed the account of the fisherman having brought the body into her house; it was not cold. They put it into a bed, and rubbed it; and Daniel went to the town for an apothecary, but life was quite gone.

Several other men were examined concerning my landing; and they agreed, that, with the strong north wind that had arisen during the night, it was very probable that I had beaten about for many hours, and had been obliged to return nearly to the same spot from which I had departed. Besides, they observed that it appeared that I had brought the body from another place, and it was likely, that as I did not appear to know the shore, I might have put into the harbour ignorant of the distance of the town of ——— from the place where I had deposited the corpse.

Mr. Kirwin, on hearing this evidence, desired that I should be taken into the room where the body lay for interment, that it might be observed what effect the sight of it would produce upon me. This idea was probably suggested by the extreme agitation I had exhibited when the mode of the murder had been described. I was accordingly conducted, by the magistrate and several other persons, to the inn. I could not help being struck by the strange coincidences that had taken place during this eventful night; but, knowing that I had been conversing with several persons in the island I had inhabited about the time that the body had been found, I was perfectly tranquil as to the consequences of the affair.

I entered the room where the corpse lay, and was led up to the coffin. How can I describe my sensations on beholding it? I feel yet parched with horror, nor can I reflect on that terrible moment without shuddering and agony, that faintly reminds me of the anguish of the recognition. The trial, the presence of the magistrate and witnesses, passed like a dream from my memory, when I saw the lifeless form of Henry Clerval stretched before me. I gasped for breath; and, throwing myself on the body, I exclaimed, "Have my murderous machinations deprived you also, my dearest Henry, of life? Two I have already destroyed; other victims await their destiny: but you, Clerval, my friend, my benefactor"—

The human frame could no longer support the agonizing suffering that I endured, and I was carried out of the room in strong convulsions.

A fever succeeded to this. I lay for two months on the point of death: my ravings, as I afterwards heard, were frightful; I called myself the murderer of William, of Justine, and of Clerval. Sometimes I entreated my attendants to assist me in the destruction of the fiend by whom I was tormented; and, at others, I felt the fingers of the monster already grasping my neck, and screamed aloud with agony and terror. Fortunately, as I spoke my native language, Mr. Kirwin alone understood me; but my gestures and bitter cries were sufficient to affright the other witnesses.

Why did I not die? More miserable than man ever was before, why did I not sink into forgetfulness and rest? Death snatches away many blooming children, the only hopes of their doating parents: how many brides and youthful lovers have been one day in the bloom of health and hope, and the next a prey for worms and the decay of the tomb! Of what materials was I made, that I could thus resist so many shocks, which, like the turning of the wheel, continually renewed the torture.

But I was doomed to live; and, in two months, found myself as awaking from a dream, in a prison, stretched on a wretched bed, surrounded by gaolers, turnkeys, bolts, and all the miserable apparatus of a dungeon. It was morning, I remember, when I thus awoke to understanding: I had forgotten the particulars of what had happened, and only felt as if some great misfortune had suddenly overwhelmed me; but when I looked around, and saw the barred windows, and the squalidness of the room in which I was, all flashed across my memory, and I groaned bitterly.

This sound disturbed an old woman who was sleeping in a chair beside me. She was a hired nurse, the wife of one of the turnkeys, and her countenance expressed all those bad qualities which often characterize that class. The lines of her face were hard and rude, like that of persons accustomed to see without sympathizing in sights of misery. Her tone expressed her entire indifference; she addressed me in English, and the voice struck me as one that I had heard during my sufferings:

"Are you better now, Sir?" said she.

I replied in the same language, with a feeble voice, "I believe I am; but if it be all true, if indeed I did not dream, I am sorry that I am still alive to feel this misery and horror."

"For that matter," replied the old woman, "if you mean about the gentleman you murdered, I believe that it were better for you if you were dead, for I fancy it will go hard with you; but you will be hung when the next sessions come on. However, that's none of my business, I am sent to nurse you, and get you well; I do my duty with a safe conscience, it were well if every body did the same."

I turned with loathing from the woman who could utter so unfeeling a speech to a person just saved, on the very edge of death; but I felt languid, and unable to reflect on all that had passed. The whole series of my life appeared to me as a dream; I sometimes doubted if indeed it were all true, for it never presented itself to my mind with the force of reality.

As the images that floated before me became more distinct, I grew feverish; a darkness pressed around me; no one was near me who soothed me with the gentle voice of love; no dear hand supported me. The physician came and prescribed medicines, and the old woman prepared them for me; but utter carelessness was visible in the first, and the expression of brutality was strongly marked in the visage of the second. Who could be interested in the fate of a murderer, but the hangman who would gain his fee?

These were my first reflections; but I soon learned that Mr. Kirwin had shewn me extreme kindness. He had caused the best room in the prison to be prepared for me (wretched indeed was the best); and it was he who had provided a physician and a nurse. It is true, he seldom came to see me; for, although he ardently desired to relieve the sufferings of every human creature, he did not wish to be present at the agonies and miserable ravings of a murderer. He came, therefore, sometimes to see that I was not neglected; but his visits were short, and at long intervals.

One day, when I was gradually recovering, I was seated in a chair, my eyes half open, and my cheeks livid like those in death, I was overcome by gloom and misery, and often reflected I had better seek death than remain miserably pent up only to be let loose in a world replete with wretchedness. At one time I considered whether I should not declare myself guilty, and suffer the penalty of the law, less innocent than poor Justine had been. Such were my thoughts, when the door of my apartment was opened, and Mr. Kirwin entered. His countenance expressed sympathy and compassion; he drew a chair close to mine, and addressed me in French—

"I fear that this place is very shocking to you; can I do any thing to make you more comfortable?"

"I thank you; but all that you mention is nothing to me: on the whole earth there is no comfort which I am capable of receiving."

"I know that the sympathy of a stranger can be but of little relief to one borne down as you are by so strange a misfortune. But you will, I hope, soon quit this melancholy abode; for, doubt-less, evidence can easily be brought to free you from the criminal charge."

"That is my least concern: I am, by a course of strange events, become the most miserable of mortals. Persecuted and tortured as I am and have been, can death be any evil to me?"

"Nothing indeed could be more unfortunate and agonizing than the strange chances that have lately occurred. You were thrown, by some surprising accident, on this shore, renowned for its hospitality: seized immediately, and charged with murder. The first sight that was presented to your eyes was the body of your friend, murdered in so unaccountable a manner, and placed, as it were, by some fiend across your path."

As Mr. Kirwin said this, notwithstanding the agitation I endured on this retrospect of my sufferings, I also felt consider-able surprise at the knowledge he seemed to possess concerning me. I suppose some astonishment was exhibited in my counte-nance; for Mr. Kirwin hastened to say—

"It was not until a day or two after your illness that I thought of examining your dress, that I might discover some trace by which I could send to your relations an account of your misfor-tune and illness. I found several letters, and, among others, one which I discovered from its commencement to be from your father. I instantly wrote to Geneva: nearly two months have elapsed since the departure of my letter.—But you are ill; even now you tremble: you are unfit for agitation of any kind."

"This suspense is a thousand times worse than the most hor-rible event: tell me what new scene of death has been acted, and whose murder I am now to lament."

"Your family is perfectly well," said Mr. Kirwin, with gentle-ness; "and some one, a friend, is come to visit you."

I know not by what chain of thought the idea presented itself, but it instantly darted into my mind that the murderer had come to mock at my misery, and taunt me with the death of Clerval, as a new incitement for me to comply with his hellish desires. I put my hand before my eyes, and cried out in agony—

"Oh! take him away! I cannot see him; for God's sake, do not let him enter!"

Mr. Kirwin regarded me with a troubled countenance. He could not help regarding my exclamation as a presumption of my guilt, and said, in rather a severe tone—

"I should have thought, young man, that the presence of your father would have been welcome, instead of inspiring such violent repugnance."

"My father!" cried I, while every feature and every muscle was relaxed from anguish to pleasure. "Is my father, indeed, come? How kind, how very kind. But where is he, why does he not hasten to me?"

My change of manner surprised and pleased the magistrate; perhaps he thought that my former exclamation was a momentary return of delirium, and now he instantly resumed his former benevolence. He rose, and quitted the room with my nurse, and in a moment my father entered it.

Nothing, at this moment, could have given me greater pleasure than the arrival of my father. I stretched out my hand to him, and cried—

"Are you then safe—and Elizabeth—and Ernest?"

My father calmed me with assurances of their welfare, and endeavoured, by dwelling on these subjects so interesting to my heart, to raise my desponding spirits; but he soon felt that a prison cannot be the abode of cheerfulness. "What a place is this that you inhabit, my son!" said he, looking mournfully at the barred windows, and wretched appearance of the room. "You travelled to seek happiness, but a fatality seems to pursue you. And poor Clerval—"

The name of my unfortunate and murdered friend was an agitation too great to be endured in my weak state; I shed tears.

"Alas! yes, my father," replied I; "some destiny of the most horrible kind hangs over me, and I must live to fulfil it, or surely I should have died on the coffin of Henry."

We were not allowed to converse for any length of time, for the precarious state of my health rendered every precaution necessary that could insure tranquillity. Mr. Kirwin came in, and insisted that my strength should not be exhausted by too much exertion. But the appearance of my father was to me like that of my good angel, and I gradually recovered my health.

As my sickness quitted me, I was absorbed by a gloomy and black melancholy, that nothing could dissipate. The image of Clerval was for ever before me, ghastly and murdered. More than once the agitation into which these reflections threw me made my friends dread a dangerous relapse. Alas! why did they preserve so miserable and detested a life? It was surely that I might fulfil my destiny, which is now drawing to a close. Soon, oh, very soon, will death extinguish these throbbings, and relieve me from the mighty weight of anguish that bears me to the dust; and, in executing the award of justice, I shall also sink to rest. Then the appearance of death was distant, although the wish was ever present to my thoughts; and I often sat for hours motionless and speechless, wishing for some mighty revolution that might bury me and my destroyer in its ruins.

The season of the assizes[1] approached. I had already been three months in prison; and although I was still weak, and in continual danger of a relapse, I was obliged to travel nearly a hundred miles to the county-town, where the court was held. Mr. Kirwin charged himself with every care of collecting witnesses, and arranging my defence. I was spared the disgrace of appearing publicly as a criminal, as the case was not brought before the court that decides on life and death. The grand jury rejected the bill, on its being proved that I was on the Orkney Islands at the hour the body of my friend was found, and a fortnight after my removal I was liberated from prison.

My father was enraptured on finding me freed from the vexations of a criminal charge, that I was again allowed to breathe the fresh atmosphere, and allowed to return to my native country. I did not participate in these feelings; for to me the walls of a dungeon or a palace were alike hateful. The cup of life was poisoned for ever; and although the sun shone upon me, as upon the happy and gay of heart, I saw around me nothing but a dense and frightful darkness, penetrated by no light but the glimmer of two eyes that glared upon me.[2] Sometimes they were the expressive eyes of Henry, languishing in death, the dark orbs nearly covered by the lids, and the long black lashes that fringed them; sometimes it was the watery clouded eyes of the monster, as I first saw them in my chamber at Ingolstadt.

My father tried to awaken in me the feelings of affection. He talked of Geneva, which I should soon visit—of Elizabeth, and

---

1 County court sessions.
2 Cf. P.B. Shelley, "Alastor" 489–92.

Ernest; but these words only drew deep groans from me. Sometimes, indeed, I felt a wish for happiness; and thought, with melancholy delight, of my beloved cousin; or longed, with a devouring *maladie du pays*,[1] to see once more the blue lake and rapid Rhone, that had been so dear to me in early childhood: but my general state of feeling was a torpor, in which a prison was as welcome a residence as the divinest scene in nature; and these fits were seldom interrupted, but by paroxysms of anguish and despair. At these moments I often endeavoured to put an end to the existence I loathed; and it required unceasing attendance and vigilance to restrain me from committing some dreadful act of violence.

I remember, as I quitted the prison, I heard one of the men say, "He may be innocent of the murder, but he has certainly a bad conscience." These words struck me. A bad conscience! yes, surely I had one. William, Justine, and Clerval, had died through my infernal machinations; "And whose death," cried I, "is to finish the tragedy? Ah! my father, do not remain in this wretched country; take me where I may forget myself, my existence, and all the world."

My father easily acceded to my desire; and, after having taken leave of Mr. Kirwin, we hastened to Dublin. I felt as if I was relieved from a heavy weight, when the packet sailed with a fair wind from Ireland, and I had quitted for ever the country which had been to me the scene of so much misery.

It was midnight. My father slept in the cabin; and I lay on the deck, looking at the stars, and listening to the dashing of the waves. I hailed the darkness that shut Ireland from my sight, and my pulse beat with a feverish joy, when I reflected that I should soon see Geneva. The past appeared to me in the light of a frightful dream; yet the vessel in which I was, the wind that blew me from the detested shore of Ireland, and the sea which surrounded me, told me too forcibly that I was deceived by no vision, and that Clerval, my friend and dearest companion, had fallen a victim to me and the monster of my creation. I repassed, in my memory, my whole life; my quiet happiness while residing with my family in Geneva, the death of my mother, and my departure for Ingolstadt. I remembered shuddering at the mad enthusiasm that hurried me on to the creation of my hideous enemy, and I called to mind the night during which he first lived. I was unable to pursue the train of thought; a thousand feelings pressed upon me, and I wept bitterly.

---

1 Homesickness.

Ever since my recovery from the fever I had been in the custom of taking every night a small quantity of laudanum;[1] for it was by means of this drug only that I was enabled to gain the rest necessary for the preservation of life. Oppressed by the recollection of my various misfortunes, I now took a double dose, and soon slept profoundly. But sleep did not afford me respite from thought and misery; my dreams presented a thousand objects that scared me. Towards morning I was possessed by a kind of night-mare; I felt the fiend's grasp in my neck, and could not free myself from it; groans and cries rung in my ears. My father, who was watching over me, perceiving my restlessness, awoke me, and pointed to the port of Holyhead, which we were now entering.

CHAPTER V.

WE had resolved not to go to London, but to cross the country to Portsmouth, and thence to embark for Havre. I preferred this plan principally because I dreaded to see again those places in which I had enjoyed a few moments of tranquillity with my beloved Clerval. I thought with horror of seeing again those persons whom we had been accustomed to visit together, and who might make inquiries concerning an event, the very remembrance of which made me again feel the pang I endured when I gazed on his lifeless form in the inn at ———.

As for my father, his desires and exertions were bounded to the again seeing me restored to health and peace of mind. His tenderness and attentions were unremitting; my grief and gloom was obstinate, but he would not despair. Sometimes he thought that I felt deeply the degradation of being obliged to answer a charge of murder, and he endeavoured to prove to me the futility of pride.

"Alas! my father," said I, "how little do you know me. Human beings, their feelings and passions, would indeed be degraded, if such a wretch as I felt pride. Justine, poor unhappy Justine, was as innocent as I, and she suffered the same charge; she died for it; and I am the cause of this—I murdered her. William, Justine, and Henry—they all died by my hands."

---

1 A tincture of opium in alcohol, the form in which the drug was taken by Coleridge and Thomas De Quincey (1785-1859), author of *Confessions of an English Opium-Eater* (1821).

My father had often, during my imprisonment, heard me make the same assertion; when I thus accused myself, he sometimes seemed to desire an explanation, and at others he appeared to consider it as caused by delirium, and that, during my illness, some idea of this kind had presented itself to my imagination, the remembrance of which I preserved in my convalescence. I avoided explanation, and maintained a continual silence concerning the wretch I had created. I had a feeling that I should be supposed mad, and this for ever chained my tongue, when I would have given the whole world to have confided the fatal secret.

Upon this occasion my father said, with an expression of unbounded wonder, "What do you mean, Victor? are you mad? My dear son, I entreat you never to make such an assertion again."

"I am not mad," I cried energetically; "the sun and the heavens, who have viewed my operations, can bear witness of my truth. I am the assassin of those most innocent victims; they died by my machinations. A thousand times would I have shed my own blood, drop by drop, to have saved their lives; but I could not, my father, indeed I could not sacrifice the whole human race."

The conclusion of this speech convinced my father that my ideas were deranged, and he instantly changed the subject of our conversation, and endeavoured to alter the course of my thoughts. He wished as much as possible to obliterate the memory of the scenes that had taken place in Ireland, and never alluded to them, or suffered me to speak of my misfortunes.

As time passed away I became more calm: misery had her dwelling in my heart, but I no longer talked in the same incoherent manner of my own crimes; sufficient for me was the consciousness of them. By the utmost self-violence, I curbed the imperious voice of wretchedness, which sometimes desired to declare itself to the whole world; and my manners were calmer and more composed than they had ever been since my journey to the sea of ice.[1]

We arrived at Havre on the 8th of May, and instantly proceeded to Paris, where my father had some business which detained us a few weeks. In this city, I received the following letter from Elizabeth:—

---

1 The Mer de Glace, at Chamounix, the setting of Victor's long conversation with the monster.

"MY DEAREST FRIEND,

"It gave me the greatest pleasure to receive a letter from my uncle dated at Paris; you are no longer at a formidable distance, and I may hope to see you in less than a fortnight. My poor cousin, how much you must have suffered! I expect to see you looking even more ill than when you quitted Geneva. This winter has been passed most miserably, tortured as I have been by anxious suspense; yet I hope to see peace in your countenance, and to find that your heart is not totally devoid of comfort and tranquillity.

"Yet I fear that the same feelings now exist that made you so miserable a year ago, even perhaps augmented by time. I would not disturb you at this period, when so many misfortunes weigh upon you; but a conversation that I had with my uncle previous to his departure renders some explanation necessary before we meet.

"Explanation! you may possibly say; what can Elizabeth have to explain? If you really say this, my questions are answered, and I have no more to do than to sign myself your affectionate cousin. But you are distant from me, and it is possible that you may dread, and yet be pleased with this explanation; and, in a probability of this being the case, I dare not any longer postpone writing what, during your absence, I have often wished to express to you, but have never had the courage to begin.

"You well know, Victor, that our union had been the favourite plan of your parents ever since our infancy. We were told this when young, and taught to look forward to it as an event that would certainly take place. We were affectionate playfellows during childhood, and, I believe, dear and valued friends to one another as we grew older. But as brother and sister often entertain a lively affection towards each other, without desiring a more intimate union, may not such also be our case? Tell me, dearest Victor. Answer me, I conjure you, by our mutual happiness, with simple truth—Do you not love another?

"You have travelled; you have spent several years of your life at Ingolstadt; and I confess to you, my friend, that when I saw you last autumn so unhappy, flying to solitude, from the society of every creature, I could not help supposing that you might regret our connexion, and believe yourself bound in honour to fulfil the wishes of your parents, although they opposed themselves to your inclinations. But this is false reasoning. I confess to you, my cousin, that I love you, and that in my airy dreams of futurity you have been my constant friend and companion. But it is your happiness I desire as well as my own, when I declare to you, that our marriage would render me eternally miserable, unless it were the dictate of your own free choice. Even now I weep to think, that, borne down as you are by the cruelest misfortunes, you may stifle, by the word *honour*, all hope of that love and happiness which would alone restore you to yourself. I, who have so interested an affection for you, may increase your miseries ten-fold, by being an obstacle to your wishes. Ah, Victor, be assured that your cousin and playmate has too sincere a love for you not to be made miserable by this supposition. Be happy, my friend; and if you obey me in this one request, remain satisfied that nothing on earth will have the power to interrupt my tranquillity.

"Do not let this letter disturb you; do not answer it to-morrow, or the next day, or even until you come, if it will give you pain. My uncle will send me news of your health; and if I see but one smile on your lips when we meet, occasioned by this or any other exertion of mine, I shall need no other happiness.

"ELIZABETH LAVENZA.
"Geneva, May 18th, 17—."

This letter revived in my memory what I had before forgotten, the threat of the fiend—"*I will be with you on your wedding-night!*" Such was my sentence, and on that night would the daemon employ every art to destroy me, and tear me from the glimpse of happiness which promised partly to console my sufferings. On that night he had determined to consummate his crimes by my death. Well, be it so; a deadly struggle would then assuredly take place, in which if he was victorious, I should be at peace, and his power over me be at an end. If he were vanquished, I should be a free man. Alas! what freedom? such as the peasant enjoys when his family have been massacred before his eyes, his cottage burnt, his lands laid waste, and he is turned adrift, homeless, pennyless, and alone, but free. Such would be my liberty, except that in my Elizabeth I possessed a treasure; alas! balanced by those horrors of remorse and guilt, which would pursue me until death.

Sweet and beloved Elizabeth! I read and re-read her letter, and some softened feelings stole into my heart, and dared to whisper paradisaical dreams of love and joy; but the apple was already eaten, and the angel's arm bared to drive me from all hope.[1] Yet I would die to make her happy. If the monster executed his threat, death was inevitable; yet, again, I considered whether my marriage would hasten my fate. My destruction might indeed arrive a few months sooner; but if my torturer should suspect that I postponed it, influenced by his menaces, he would surely find other, and perhaps more dreadful means of revenge. He had vowed *to be with me on my wedding-night*, yet he did not consider that threat as binding him to peace in the mean time; for, as if to shew me that he was not yet satiated with blood, he had murdered Clerval immediately after the enunciation of his threats. I resolved, therefore, that if my immediate union with my cousin would conduce either to her's or my father's happiness, my adversary's designs against my life should not retard it a single hour.

In this state of mind I wrote to Elizabeth. My letter was calm and affectionate. "I fear, my beloved girl," I said, "little happiness remains for us on earth; yet all that I may one day enjoy is concentered in you. Chase away your idle fears; to you alone do I consecrate my life, and my endeavours for contentment. I have one secret, Elizabeth, a dreadful one; when revealed to you, it will chill your frame with horror, and then, far from being surprised at my misery, you will only wonder that I survive what I have endured. I will confide this tale of misery and terror to you the day after our marriage shall take place; for, my sweet cousin, there must be perfect confidence between us. But until then, I conjure you, do not mention or allude to it. This I most earnestly entreat, and I know you will comply."

In about a week after the arrival of Elizabeth's letter, we returned to Geneva. My cousin welcomed me with warm affection; yet tears were in her eyes, as she beheld my emaciated frame and feverish cheeks. I saw a change in her also. She was thinner, and had lost much of that heavenly vivacity that had before charmed me; but her gentleness, and soft looks of compassion, made her a more fit companion for one blasted and miserable as I was.

The tranquillity which I now enjoyed did not endure. Memory brought madness with it; and when I thought on what had passed, a real insanity possessed me; sometimes I was furious, and burnt with rage, sometimes low and despondent. I neither spoke or looked, but sat motionless, bewildered by the multitude of miseries that overcame me.

---

1 Cf. Genesis 3: 24 and Milton, *Paradise Lost* XII.632-40.

Elizabeth alone had the power to draw me from these fits; her gentle voice would soothe me when transported by passion, and inspire me with human feelings when sunk in torpor. She wept with me, and for me. When reason returned, she would remonstrate, and endeavour to inspire me with resignation. Ah! it is well for the unfortunate to be resigned, but for the guilty there is no peace. The agonies of remorse poison the luxury there is otherwise sometimes found in indulging the excess of grief.

Soon after my arrival my father spoke of my immediate marriage with my cousin. I remained silent.

"Have you, then, some other attachment?"

"None on earth. I love Elizabeth, and look forward to our union with delight. Let the day therefore be fixed; and on it I will consecrate myself, in life or death, to the happiness of my cousin."

"My dear Victor, do not speak thus. Heavy misfortunes have befallen us; but let us only cling closer to what remains, and transfer our love for those whom we have lost to those who yet live. Our circle will be small, but bound close by the ties of affection and mutual misfortune. And when time shall have softened your despair, new and dear objects of care will be born to replace those of whom we have been so cruelly deprived."

Such were the lessons of my father. But to me the remembrance of the threat returned: nor can you wonder, that, omnipotent as the fiend had yet been in his deeds of blood, I should almost regard him as invincible; and that when he had pronounced the words, "*I shall be with you on your wedding-night,*" I should regard the threatened fate as unavoidable. But death was no evil to me, if the loss of Elizabeth were balanced with it; and I therefore, with a contented and even cheerful countenance, agreed with my father, that if my cousin would consent, the ceremony should take place in ten days, and thus put, as I imagined, the seal to my fate.

Great God! if for one instant I had thought what might be the hellish intention of my fiendish adversary, I would rather have banished myself for ever from my native country, and wandered a friendless outcast over the earth, than have consented to this miserable marriage. But, as if possessed of magic powers, the monster had blinded me to his real intentions; and when I thought that I prepared only my own death, I hastened that of a far dearer victim.

As the period fixed for our marriage drew nearer, whether from cowardice or a prophetic feeling, I felt my heart sink within me. But I concealed my feelings by an appearance of hilarity, that brought smiles and joy to the countenance of my father, but hardly deceived the ever-watchful and nicer eye of Elizabeth. She looked forward to our union with placid contentment, not unmingled with a little fear, which past misfortunes had impressed, that what now appeared certain and tangible happiness, might soon dissipate into an airy dream, and leave no trace but deep and everlasting regret.

Preparations were made for the event; congratulatory visits were received; and all wore a smiling appearance. I shut up, as well as I could, in my own heart the anxiety that preyed there, and entered with seeming earnestness into the plans of my father, although they might only serve as the decorations of my tragedy. A house was purchased for us near Cologny, by which we should enjoy the pleasures of the country, and yet be so near Geneva as to see my father every day; who would still reside within the walls, for the benefit of Ernest, that he might follow his studies at the schools.

In the mean time I took every precaution to defend my person, in case the fiend should openly attack me. I carried pistols and a dagger constantly about me, and was ever on the watch to prevent artifice; and by these means gained a greater degree of tranquillity. Indeed, as the period approached, the threat appeared more as a delusion, not to be regarded as worthy to disturb my peace, while the happiness I hoped for in my marriage wore a greater appearance of certainty, as the day fixed for its solemnization drew nearer, and I heard it continually spoken of as an occurrence which no accident could possibly prevent.

Elizabeth seemed happy; my tranquil demeanour contributed greatly to calm her mind. But on the day that was to fulfil my wishes and my destiny, she was melancholy, and a presentiment of evil pervaded her; and perhaps also she thought of the dreadful secret, which I had promised to reveal to her the following day. My father was in the mean time overjoyed, and, in the bustle of preparation, only observed in the melancholy of his niece the diffidence of a bride.

After the ceremony was performed, a large party assembled at my father's; but it was agreed that Elizabeth and I should pass the afternoon and night at Evian, and return to Cologny the next morning. As the day was fair, and the wind favourable, we resolved to go by water.

Those were the last moments of my life during which I enjoyed the feeling of happiness. We passed rapidly along: the sun was hot, but we were sheltered from its rays by a kind of canopy, while we enjoyed the beauty of the scene, sometimes on one side of the lake, where we saw Mont Salêve, the pleasant banks of Montalêgre, and at a distance, surmounting all, the beautiful Mont Blanc, and the assemblage of snowy mountains that in vain endeavour to emulate her; sometimes coasting the opposite banks, we saw the mighty Jura opposing its dark side to the ambition that would quit its native country, and an almost insurmountable barrier to the invader who should wish to enslave it.[1]

I took the hand of Elizabeth: "You are sorrowful, my love. Ah! if you knew what I have suffered, and what I may yet endure, you would endeavour to let me taste the quiet, and freedom from despair, that this one day at least permits me to enjoy."

"Be happy, my dear Victor," replied Elizabeth; "there is, I hope, nothing to distress you; and be assured that if a lively joy is not painted in my face, my heart is contented. Something whispers to me not to depend too much on the prospect that is opened before us; but I will not listen to such a sinister voice. Observe how fast we move along, and how the clouds which sometimes obscure, and sometimes rise above the dome of Mont Blanc, render this scene of beauty still more interesting. Look also at the innumerable fish that are swimming in the clear waters, where we can distinguish every pebble that lies at the bottom. What a divine day! how happy and serene all nature appears!"

Thus Elizabeth endeavoured to divert her thoughts and mine from all reflection upon melancholy subjects. But her temper was fluctuating; joy for a few instants shone in her eyes, but it continually gave place to distraction and reverie.

The sun sunk lower in the heavens; we passed the river Drance, and observed its path through the chasms of the higher, and the glens of the lower hills. The Alps here come closer to the lake, and we approached the amphitheatre of mountains which forms its eastern boundary. The spire of Evian shone under the woods that surrounded it, and the range of mountain above mountain by which it was overhung.

The wind, which had hitherto carried us along with amazing rapidity, sunk at sunset to a light breeze; the soft air just ruffled the water, and caused a pleasant motion among the trees as we

---

1 The French invasion of Switzerland in 1798, a disillusionment for
   British sympathizers with the Revolution, provides the historical setting
   for the first part of Polidori's *Ernestus Berchtold*.

approached the shore, from which it wafted the most delightful scent of flowers and hay. The sun sunk beneath the horizon as we landed; and as I touched the shore, I felt those cares and fears revive, which soon were to clasp me, and cling to me for ever.

CHAPTER VI.

IT was eight o'clock when we landed; we walked for a short time on the shore, enjoying the transitory light, and then retired to the inn, and contemplated the lovely scene of waters, woods, and mountains, obscured in darkness, yet still displaying their black outlines.

The wind, which had fallen in the south, now rose with great violence in the west. The moon had reached her summit in the heavens, and was beginning to descend; the clouds swept across it swifter than the flight of the vulture, and dimmed her rays, while the lake reflected the scene of the busy heavens, rendered still busier by the restless waves that were beginning to rise.[1] Suddenly a heavy storm of rain descended.

I had been calm during the day; but so soon as night obscured the shapes of objects, a thousand fears arose in my mind. I was anxious and watchful, while my right hand grasped a pistol which was hidden in my bosom; every sound terrified me; but I resolved that I would sell my life dearly, and not relax the impending conflict until my own life, or that of my adversary, were extinguished.

Elizabeth observed my agitation for some time in timid and fearful silence; at length she said, "What is it that agitates you, my dear Victor? What is it you fear?"

"Oh! peace, peace, my love," replied I, "this night, and all will be safe: but this night is dreadful, very dreadful."

I passed an hour in this state of mind, when suddenly I reflected how dreadful the combat which I momentarily expected would be to my wife, and I earnestly entreated her to retire, resolving not to join her until I had obtained some knowledge as to the situation of my enemy.

She left me, and I continued some time walking up and down the passages of the house, and inspecting every corner that might afford a retreat to my adversary. But I discovered no trace of him, and was beginning to conjecture that some fortunate chance had intervened to prevent the execution of his menaces; when sud-

---

1 Cf. Wordsworth, "There was a Boy" (1798) 24-25.

denly I heard a shrill and dreadful scream. It came from the room into which Elizabeth had retired. As I heard it, the whole truth rushed into my mind, my arms dropped, the motion of every muscle and fibre was suspended; I could feel the blood trickling in my veins, and tingling in the extremities of my limbs. This state lasted but for an instant; the scream was repeated, and I rushed into the room.

Great God! why did I not then expire! Why am I here to relate the destruction of the best hope, and the purest creature of earth. She was there, lifeless and inanimate, thrown across the bed, her head hanging down, and her pale and distorted features half covered by her hair. Every where I turn I see the same figure—her bloodless arms and relaxed form flung by the murderer on its bridal bier. Could I behold this, and live? Alas! life is obstinate, and clings closest where it is most hated. For a moment only did I lose recollection; I fainted.

When I recovered, I found myself surrounded by the people of the inn; their countenances expressed a breathless terror: but the horror of others appeared only as a mockery, a shadow of the feelings that oppressed me. I escaped from them to the room where lay the body of Elizabeth, my love, my wife, so lately living, so dear, so worthy. She had been moved from the posture in which I had first beheld her; and now, as she lay, her head upon her arm, and a handkerchief thrown across her face and neck, I might have supposed her asleep. I rushed towards her, and embraced her with ardour; but the deathly languor and coldness of the limbs told me, that what I now held in my arms had ceased to be the Elizabeth whom I had loved and cherished. The murderous mark of the fiend's grasp was on her neck, and the breath had ceased to issue from her lips.

While I still hung over her in the agony of despair, I happened to look up. The windows of the room had before been darkened; and I felt a kind of panic on seeing the pale yellow light of the moon illuminate the chamber. The shutters had been thrown back; and, with a sensation of horror not to be described, I saw at the open window a figure the most hideous and abhorred. A grin was on the face of the monster; he seemed to jeer, as with his fiendish finger he pointed towards the corpse of my wife. I rushed towards the window, and drawing a pistol from my bosom, shot; but he eluded me, leaped from his station, and, running with the swiftness of lightning, plunged into the lake.

The report of the pistol brought a crowd into the room. I pointed to the spot where he had disappeared, and we followed the track with boats; nets were cast, but in vain. After passing several hours, we returned hopeless, most of my companions believing it to have been a form conjured by my fancy. After having landed, they proceeded to search the country, parties going in different directions among the woods and vines.

I did not accompany them; I was exhausted: a film covered my eyes, and my skin was parched with the heat of fever. In this state I lay on a bed, hardly conscious of what had happened; my eyes wandered round the room, as if to seek something that I had lost.

At length I remembered that my father would anxiously expect the return of Elizabeth and myself, and that I must return alone. This reflection brought tears into my eyes, and I wept for a long time; but my thoughts rambled to various subjects, reflecting on my misfortunes, and their cause. I was bewildered in a cloud of wonder and horror. The death of William, the execution of Justine, the murder of Clerval, and lastly of my wife; even at that moment I knew not that my only remaining friends were safe from the malignity of the fiend; my father even now might be writhing under his grasp, and Ernest might be dead at his feet. This idea made me shudder, and recalled me to action. I started up, and resolved to return to Geneva with all possible speed.

There were no horses to be procured, and I must return by the lake; but the wind was unfavourable, and the rain fell in torrents. However, it was hardly morning, and I might reasonably hope to arrive by night. I hired men to row, and took an oar myself, for I had always experienced relief from mental torment in bodily exercise. But the overflowing misery I now felt, and the excess of agitation that I endured, rendered me incapable of any exertion. I threw down the oar; and, leaning my head upon my hands, gave way to every gloomy idea that arose. If I looked up, I saw the scenes which were familiar to me in my happier time, and which I had contemplated but the day before in the company of her who was now but a shadow and a recollection. Tears streamed from my eyes. The rain had ceased for a moment, and I saw the fish play in the waters as they had done a few hours before; they had then been observed by Elizabeth. Nothing is so painful to the human mind as a great and sudden change. The sun might shine, or the clouds might lour; but nothing could appear to me as it had done the day before. A fiend had snatched from me every hope of future happiness: no creature had ever been so miserable as I was; so frightful an event is single in the history of man.

But why should I dwell upon the incidents that followed this last overwhelming event. Mine has been a tale of horrors; I have reached their *acme*, and what I must now relate can but be tedious to you. Know that, one by one, my friends were snatched away; I was left desolate. My own strength is exhausted; and I must tell, in a few words, what remains of my hideous narration.

I arrived at Geneva. My father and Ernest yet lived; but the former sunk under the tidings that I bore. I see him now, excellent and venerable old man! his eyes wandered in vacancy, for they had lost their charm and their delight—his niece, his more than daughter, whom he doated on with all that affection which a man feels, who, in the decline of life, having few affections, clings more earnestly to those that remain. Cursed, cursed be the fiend that brought misery on his gray hairs, and doomed him to waste in wretchedness! He could not live under the horrors that were accumulated around him; an apoplectic fit was brought on, and in a few days he died in my arms.

What then became of me? I know not; I lost sensation, and chains and darkness were the only objects that pressed upon me. Sometimes, indeed, I dreamt that I wandered in flowery meadows and pleasant vales with the friends of my youth; but awoke, and found myself in a dungeon. Melancholy followed, but by degrees I gained a clear conception of my miseries and situation, and was then released from my prison. For they had called me mad; and during many months, as I understood, a solitary cell had been my habitation.

But liberty had been a useless gift to me had I not, as I awakened to reason, at the same time awakened to revenge. As the memory of past misfortunes pressed upon me, I began to reflect on their cause—the monster whom I had created, the miserable daemon whom I had sent abroad into the world for my destruction. I was possessed by a maddening rage when I thought of him, and desired and ardently prayed that I might have him within my grasp to wreak a great and signal revenge on his cursed head.

Nor did my hate long confine itself to useless wishes; I began to reflect on the best means of securing him; and for this purpose, about a month after my release, I repaired to a criminal judge in the town, and told him that I had an accusation to make; that I knew the destroyer of my family; and that I required him to exert his whole authority for the apprehension of the murderer.

The magistrate listened to me with attention and kindness: "Be assured, sir," said he, "no pains or exertions on my part shall be spared to discover the villain."

"I thank you," replied I; "listen, therefore, to the deposition that I have to make. It is indeed a tale so strange, that I should fear you would not credit it, were there not something in truth which, however wonderful, forces conviction. The story is too connected to be mistaken for a dream, and I have no motive for falsehood." My manner, as I thus addressed him, was impressive, but calm; I had formed in my own heart a resolution to pursue my destroyer to death; and this purpose quieted my agony, and provisionally reconciled me to life. I now related my history briefly, but with firmness and precision, marking the dates with accuracy, and never deviating into invective or exclamation.

The magistrate appeared at first perfectly incredulous, but as I continued he became more attentive and interested; I saw him sometimes shudder with horror, at others a lively surprise, unmingled with disbelief, was painted on his countenance.

When I had concluded my narration, I said, "This is the being whom I accuse, and for whose detection and punishment I call upon you to exert your whole power. It is your duty as a magistrate, and I believe and hope that your feelings as a man will not revolt from the execution of those functions on this occasion."

This address caused a considerable change in the physiognomy of my auditor. He had heard my story with that half kind of belief that is given to a tale of spirits and supernatural events;[1] but when he was called upon to act officially in consequence, the whole tide of his incredulity returned. He, however, answered mildly, "I would willingly afford you every aid in your pursuit; but the creature of whom you speak appears to have powers which would put all my exertions to defiance. Who can follow an animal which can traverse the sea of ice, and inhabit caves and dens, where no man would venture to intrude? Besides, some months have elapsed since the commission of his crimes, and no one can conjecture to what place he has wandered, or what region he may now inhabit."

"I do not doubt that he hovers near the spot which I inhabit; and if he has indeed taken refuge in the Alps, he may be hunted like the chamois, and destroyed as a beast of prey. But I perceive your thoughts: you do not credit my narrative, and do not intend to pursue my enemy with the punishment which is his desert."

As I spoke, rage sparkled in my eyes; the magistrate was intimidated; "You are mistaken," said he, "I will exert myself; and if it is in my power to seize the monster, be assured that he shall suffer punishment proportionate to his crimes. But I fear, from what

---

1 Cf. Coleridge on the "willing suspension of disbelief," *Biographia Literaria* (1817) XIV.

you have yourself described to be his properties, that this will prove impracticable, and that, while every proper measure is pursued, you should endeavour to make up your mind to disappointment."

"That cannot be; but all that I can say will be of little avail. My revenge is of no moment to you; yet, while I allow it to be a vice, I confess that it is the devouring and only passion of my soul. My rage is unspeakable, when I reflect that the murderer, whom I have turned loose upon society, still exists. You refuse my just demand: I have but one resource; and I devote myself, either in my life or death, to his destruction."

I trembled with excess of agitation as I said this; there was a phrenzy in my manner, and something, I doubt not, of that haughty fierceness, which the martyrs of old are said to have possessed. But to a Genevan magistrate, whose mind was occupied by far other ideas than those of devotion and heroism, this elevation of mind had much the appearance of madness. He endeavoured to soothe me as a nurse does a child, and reverted to my tale as the effects of delirium.

"Man," I cried, "how ignorant art thou in thy pride of wisdom! Cease; you know not what it is you say."

I broke from the house angry and disturbed, and retired to meditate on some other mode of action.

CHAPTER VII.

MY present situation was one in which all voluntary thought was swallowed up and lost. I was hurried away by fury; revenge alone endowed me with strength and composure; it modelled my feelings, and allowed me to be calculating and calm, at periods when otherwise delirium or death would have been my portion.

My first resolution was to quit Geneva for ever; my country, which, when I was happy and beloved, was dear to me, now, in my adversity, became hateful. I provided myself with a sum of money, together with a few jewels which had belonged to my mother, and departed.

And now my wanderings began, which are to cease but with life.[1] I have traversed a vast portion of the earth, and have endured all the hardships which travellers, in deserts and barbarous countries, are wont to meet. How I have lived I hardly

---

1 Cf. P.B. Shelley, "Alastor" 224-671.

know; many times have I stretched my failing limbs upon the sandy plain, and prayed for death. But revenge kept me alive; I dared not die, and leave my adversary in being.

When I quitted Geneva, my first labour was to gain some clue by which I might trace the steps of my fiendish enemy. But my plan was unsettled; and I wandered many hours around the confines of the town, uncertain what path I should pursue. As night approached, I found myself at the entrance of the cemetery where William, Elizabeth, and my father, reposed. I entered it, and approached the tomb which marked their graves. Every thing was silent, except the leaves of the trees, which were gently agitated by the wind; the night was nearly dark; and the scene would have been solemn and affecting even to an uninterested observer. The spirits of the departed seemed to flit around, and to cast a shadow, which was felt but seen not, around the head of the mourner.

The deep grief which this scene had at first excited quickly gave way to rage and despair. They were dead, and I lived; their murderer also lived, and to destroy him I must drag out my weary existence. I knelt on the grass, and kissed the earth, and with quivering lips exclaimed, "By the sacred earth on which I kneel, by the shades that wander near me, by the deep and eternal grief that I feel, I swear; and by thee, O Night, and by the spirits that preside over thee, I swear to pursue the daemon, who caused this misery, until he or I shall perish in mortal conflict. For this purpose I will preserve my life: to execute this dear revenge, will I again behold the sun, and tread the green herbage of earth, which otherwise should vanish from my eyes for ever. And I call on you, spirits of the dead; and on you, wandering ministers of vengeance, to aid and conduct me in my work. Let the cursed and hellish monster drink deep of agony; let him feel the despair that now torments me."

I had begun my adjuration with solemnity, and an awe which almost assured me that the shades of my murdered friends heard and approved my devotion; but the furies[1] possessed me as I concluded, and rage choked my utterance.

I was answered through the stillness of night by a loud and fiendish laugh. It rung on my ears long and heavily; the mountains re-echoed it, and I felt as if all hell surrounded me with mockery and laughter. Surely in that moment I should have been possessed by phrenzy, and have destroyed my miserable exis-

---

1 The Eumenides, Greek spirits of vengeance.

tence, but that my vow was heard, and that I was reserved for vengeance. The laughter died away; when a well-known and abhorred voice, apparently close to my ear, addressed me in an audible whisper—"I am satisfied: miserable wretch! you have determined to live, and I am satisfied."

I darted towards the spot from which the sound proceeded; but the devil eluded my grasp. Suddenly the broad disk of the moon arose, and shone full upon his ghastly and distorted shape, as he fled with more than mortal speed.

I pursued him; and for many months this has been my task. Guided by a slight clue, I followed the windings of the Rhone, but vainly. The blue Mediterranean appeared; and, by a strange chance, I saw the fiend enter by night, and hide himself in a vessel bound for the Black Sea. I took my passage in the same ship; but he escaped, I know not how.

Amidst the wilds of Tartary and Russia, although he still evaded me, I have ever followed in his track. Sometimes the peasants, scared by this horrid apparition, informed me of his path; sometimes he himself, who feared that if I lost all trace I should despair and die, often left some mark to guide me. The snows descended on my head, and I saw the print of his huge step on the white plain. To you first entering on life, to whom care is new, and agony unknown, how can you understand what I have felt, and still feel? Cold, want, and fatigue, were the least pains which I was destined to endure; I was cursed by some devil, and carried about with me my eternal hell;[1] yet still a spirit of good followed and directed my steps, and, when I most murmured, would suddenly extricate me from seemingly insurmountable difficulties. Sometimes, when nature, overcome by hunger, sunk under the exhaustion, a repast was prepared for me in the desert, that restored and inspirited me. The fare was indeed coarse, such as the peasants of the country ate; but I may not doubt that it was set there by the spirits that I had invoked to aid me. Often, when all was dry, the heavens cloudless, and I was parched by thirst, a slight cloud would bedim the sky, shed the few drops that revived me, and vanish.

I followed, when I could, the courses of the rivers; but the daemon generally avoided these, as it was here that the population of the country chiefly collected. In other places human beings were seldom seen; and I generally subsisted on the wild animals that crossed my path. I had money with me, and gained

---

1 Another allusion to Milton, *Paradise Lost* IV.75 and IX.467.

the friendship of the villagers by distributing it, or bringing with me some food that I had killed, which, after taking a small part, I always presented to those who had provided me with fire and utensils for cooking.

My life, as it passed thus, was indeed hateful to me, and it was during sleep alone that I could taste joy. O blessed sleep! often, when most miserable, I sank to repose, and my dreams lulled me even to rapture. The spirits that guarded me had provided these moments, or rather hours, of happiness, that I might retain strength to fulfil my pilgrimage. Deprived of this respite, I should have sunk under my hardships. During the day I was sustained and inspirited by the hope of night: for in sleep I saw my friends, my wife, and my beloved country; again I saw the benevolent countenance of my father, heard the silver tones of my Elizabeth's voice, and beheld Clerval enjoying health and youth. Often, when wearied by a toilsome march, I persuaded myself that I was dreaming until night should come, and that I should then enjoy reality in the arms of my dearest friends. What agonizing fondness did I feel for them! how did I cling to their dear forms, as sometimes they haunted even my waking hours, and persuade myself that they still lived! At such moments vengeance, that burned within me, died in my heart, and I pursued my path towards the destruction of the daemon, more as a task enjoined by heaven, as the mechanical impulse of some power of which I was unconscious, than as the ardent desire of my soul.

What his feelings were whom I pursued, I cannot know. Sometimes, indeed, he left marks in writing on the barks of the trees, or cut in stone, that guided me, and instigated my fury. "My reign is not yet over," (these words were legible in one of these inscriptions); "you live, and my power is complete. Follow me; I seek the everlasting ices of the north, where you will feel the misery of cold and frost, to which I am impassive. You will find near this place, if you follow not too tardily, a dead hare; eat, and be refreshed. Come on, my enemy; we have yet to wrestle for our lives; but many hard and miserable hours must you endure, until that period shall arrive."

Scoffing devil! Again do I vow vengeance; again do I devote thee, miserable fiend, to torture and death. Never will I omit my search, until he or I perish; and then with what ecstacy shall I join my Elizabeth, and those who even now prepare for me the reward of my tedious toil and horrible pilgrimage.

As I still pursued my journey to the northward, the snows thickened, and the cold increased in a degree almost too severe to support. The peasants were shut up in their hovels, and only a few of the most hardy ventured forth to seize the animals whom starvation had forced from their hiding-places to seek for prey. The rivers were covered with ice, and no fish could be procured; and thus I was cut off from my chief article of maintenance.

The triumph of my enemy increased with the difficulty of my labours. One inscription that he left was in these words: "Prepare! your toils only begin: wrap yourself in furs, and provide food, for we shall soon enter upon a journey where your sufferings will satisfy my everlasting hatred."

My courage and perseverance were invigorated by these scoffing words; I resolved not to fail in my purpose; and, calling on heaven to support me, I continued with unabated fervour to traverse immense deserts, until the ocean appeared at a distance, and formed the utmost boundary of the horizon. Oh! how unlike it was to the blue seas of the south! Covered with ice, it was only to be distinguished from land by its superior wildness and ruggedness. The Greeks wept for joy when they beheld the Mediterranean from the hills of Asia, and hailed with rapture the boundary of their toils.[1] I did not weep; but I knelt down, and, with a full heart, thanked my guiding spirit for conducting me in safety to the place where I hoped, notwithstanding my adversary's gibe, to meet and grapple with him.

Some weeks before this period I had procured a sledge and dogs, and thus traversed the snows with inconceivable speed. I know not whether the fiend possessed the same advantages; but I found that, as before I had daily lost ground in the pursuit, I now gained on him; so much so, that when I first saw the ocean, he was but one day's journey in advance, and I hoped to intercept him before he should reach the beach. With new courage, therefore, I pressed on, and in two days arrived at a wretched hamlet on the sea-shore. I inquired of the inhabitants concerning the fiend, and gained accurate information. A gigantic monster, they said, had arrived the night before, armed with a gun and many pistols; putting to flight the inhabitants of a solitary cottage, through fear of his terrific appearance. He had carried off their store of winter food, and, placing it in a sledge, to draw which he had seized on a numerous drove of trained dogs, he had harnessed them, and the same night, to the joy of the horror-struck

---

1 An allusion to the famous incident in Xenophon's *Anabasis* IV.iv.24, an account of the retreat of an army of Greek mercenaries through Armenia to the sea at Trebizond.

villagers, had pursued his journey across the sea in a direction that led to no land; and they conjectured that he must speedily be destroyed by the breaking of the ice, or frozen by the eternal frosts.

On hearing this information, I suffered a temporary access of despair. He had escaped me; and I must commence a destructive and almost endless journey across the mountainous ices of the ocean,—amidst cold that few of the inhabitants could long endure, and which I, the native of a genial and sunny climate, could not hope to survive. Yet at the idea that the fiend should live and be triumphant, my rage and vengeance returned, and, like a mighty tide, overwhelmed every other feeling. After a slight repose, during which the spirits of the dead hovered round, and instigated me to toil and revenge, I prepared for my journey.

I exchanged my land sledge for one fashioned for the inequalities of the frozen ocean; and, purchasing a plentiful stock of provisions, I departed from land.

I cannot guess how many days have passed since then; but I have endured misery, which nothing but the eternal sentiment of a just retribution burning within my heart could have enabled me to support. Immense and rugged mountains of ice often barred up my passage, and I often heard the thunder of the ground sea, which threatened my destruction. But again the frost came, and made the paths of the sea secure.

By the quantity of provision which I had consumed I should guess that I had passed three weeks in this journey; and the continual protraction of hope, returning back upon the heart, often wrung bitter drops of despondency and grief from my eyes. Despair had indeed almost secured her prey, and I should soon have sunk beneath this misery; when once, after the poor animals that carried me had with incredible toil gained the summit of a sloping ice mountain, and one sinking under his fatigue died, I viewed the expanse before me with anguish, when suddenly my eye caught a dark speck upon the dusky plain. I strained my sight to discover what it could be, and uttered a wild cry of ecstacy when I distinguished a sledge, and the distorted proportions of a well-known form within. Oh! with what a burning gush did hope revisit my heart! warm tears filled my eyes, which I hastily wiped away, that they might not intercept the view I had of the daemon; but still my sight was dimmed by the burning drops, until, giving way to the emotions that oppressed me, I wept aloud.

But this was not the time for delay; I disencumbered the dogs of their dead companion, gave them a plentiful portion of food;

and, after an hour's rest, which was absolutely necessary, and yet which was bitterly irksome to me, I continued my route. The sledge was still visible; nor did I again lose sight of it, except at the moments when for a short time some ice rock concealed it with its intervening crags. I indeed perceptibly gained on it; and when, after nearly two days' journey, I beheld my enemy at no more than a mile distant, my heart bounded within me.

But now, when I appeared almost within grasp of my enemy, my hopes were suddenly extinguished, and I lost all trace of him more utterly than I had ever done before. A ground sea was heard; the thunder of its progress, as the waters rolled and swelled beneath me, became every moment more ominous and terrific. I pressed on, but in vain. The wind arose; the sea roared; and, as with the mighty shock of an earthquake, it split, and cracked with a tremendous and overwhelming sound. The work was soon finished: in a few minutes a tumultuous sea rolled between me and my enemy, and I was left drifting on a scattered piece of ice, that was continually lessening, and thus preparing for me a hideous death.

In this manner many appalling hours passed; several of my dogs died; and I myself was about to sink under the accumulation of distress, when I saw your vessel riding at anchor, and holding forth to me hopes of succour and life. I had no conception that vessels ever came so far north, and was astounded at the sight. I quickly destroyed part of my sledge to construct oars; and by these means was enabled, with infinite fatigue, to move my ice-raft in the direction of your ship. I had determined, if you were going southward, still to trust myself to the mercy of the seas, rather than abandon my purpose. I hoped to induce you to grant me a boat with which I could still pursue my enemy. But your direction was northward. You took me on board when my vigour was exhausted, and I should soon have sunk under my multiplied hardships into a death, which I still dread,—for my task is unfulfilled.

Oh! when will my guiding spirit, in conducting me to the daemon, allow me the rest I so much desire; or must I die, and he yet live? If I do, swear to me, Walton, that he shall not escape; that you will seek him, and satisfy my vengeance in his death. Yet, do I dare ask you to undertake my pilgrimage, to endure the hardships that I have undergone? No; I am not so selfish. Yet, when I am dead, if he should appear; if the ministers of vengeance should conduct him to you, swear that he shall not live—swear that he shall not triumph over my accumulated woes, and live to make another such a wretch as I am. He is eloquent and persuasive; and once his words had even power over my heart: but trust him not. His soul is as hellish as his form, full of treachery and fiend-like malice. Hear him not; call on the manes[1] of William, Justine, Clerval, Elizabeth, my father, and of the wretched Victor, and thrust your sword into his heart. I will hover near, and direct the steel aright.

WALTON, *in continuation.*

August 26th, 17—.

YOU have read this strange and terrific story, Margaret; and do you not feel your blood congealed with horror, like that which even now curdles mine? Sometimes, seized with sudden agony, he could not continue his tale; at others, his voice broken, yet piercing, uttered with difficulty the words so replete with agony. His fine and lovely eyes were now lighted up with indignation, now subdued to downcast sorrow, and quenched in infinite wretchedness. Sometimes he commanded his countenance and tones, and related the most horrible incidents with a tranquil voice, suppressing every mark of agitation; then, like a volcano bursting forth, his face would suddenly change to an expression of the wildest rage, as he shrieked out imprecations on his persecutor.

His tale is connected, and told with an appearance of the simplest truth; yet I own to you that the letters of Felix and Safie, which he shewed me, and the apparition of the monster, seen from our ship, brought to me a greater conviction of the truth of his narrative than his asseverations, however earnest and connected. Such a monster has then really existence; I cannot doubt it; yet I am lost in surprise and admiration. Sometimes I endeavoured to gain from Frankenstein the particulars of his creature's formation; but on this point he was impenetrable.

"Are you mad, my friend?" said he, "or whither does your senseless curiosity lead you? Would you also create for yourself and the world a demoniacal enemy? Or to what do your questions tend? Peace, peace! learn my miseries, and do not seek to increase your own."[2]

---

1 Ghosts (Latin).
2 Cf. St. Leon's refusal to "furnish the remotest hint respecting the science of which I am the depository" in Godwin, *St. Leon* 214; XIX.

Frankenstein discovered that I made notes concerning his history: he asked to see them, and then himself corrected and augmented them in many places; but principally in giving the life and spirit to the conversations he held with his enemy. "Since you have preserved my narration," said he, "I would not that a mutilated one should go down to posterity."

Thus has a week passed away, while I have listened to the strangest tale that ever imagination formed. My thoughts, and every feeling of my soul, have been drunk up by the interest for my guest, which this tale, and his own elevated and gentle manners have created. I wish to soothe him; yet can I counsel one so infinitely miserable, so destitute of every hope of consolation, to live? Oh, no! the only joy that he can now know will be when he composes his shattered feelings to peace and death. Yet he enjoys one comfort, the offspring of solitude and delirium: he believes, that, when in dreams he holds converse with his friends, and derives from that communion consolation for his miseries, or excitements to his vengeance, that they are not the creations of his fancy, but the real beings who visit him from the regions of a remote world. This faith gives a solemnity to his reveries that render them to me almost as imposing and interesting as truth.

Our conversations are not always confined to his own history and misfortunes. On every point of general literature he displays unbounded knowledge, and a quick and piercing apprehension. His eloquence is forcible and touching; nor can I hear him, when he relates a pathetic incident, or endeavours to move the passions of pity or love, without tears. What a glorious creature must he have been in the days of his prosperity, when he is thus noble and godlike in ruin. He seems to feel his own worth, and the greatness of his fall.

"When younger," said he, "I felt as if I were destined for some great enterprise. My feelings are profound; but I possessed a coolness of judgment that fitted me for illustrious achievements. This sentiment of the worth of my nature supported me, when others would have been oppressed; for I deemed it criminal to throw away in useless grief those talents that might be useful to my fellow-creatures. When I reflected on the work I had completed, no less a one than the creation of a sensitive and rational animal, I could not rank myself with the herd of common projectors.[1] But this feeling, which supported me in the commence-

---

1 The *OED* defines a projector as "One who forms a project, who plans or designs some enterprise or undertaking."

ment of my career, now serves only to plunge me lower in the dust. All my speculations and hopes are as nothing; and, like the archangel who aspired to omnipotence, I am chained in an eternal hell.[1] My imagination was vivid, yet my powers of analysis and application were intense; by the union of these qualities I conceived the idea, and executed the creation of a man. Even now I cannot recollect, without passion, my reveries while the work was incomplete. I trod heaven in my thoughts, now exulting in my powers, now burning with the idea of their effects. From my infancy I was imbued with high hopes and a lofty ambition; but how am I sunk! Oh! my friend, if you had known me as I once was, you would not recognize me in this state of degradation. Despondency rarely visited my heart; a high destiny seemed to bear me on, until I fell, never, never again to rise."

Must I then lose this admirable being? I have longed for a friend; I have sought one who would sympathize with and love me. Behold, on these desert seas I have found such a one; but, I fear, I have gained him only to know his value, and lose him. I would reconcile him to life, but he repulses the idea.

"I thank you, Walton," he said, "for your kind intentions towards so miserable a wretch; but when you speak of new ties, and fresh affections, think you that any can replace those who are gone? Can any man be to me as Clerval was; or any woman another Elizabeth? Even where the affections are not strongly moved by any superior excellence, the companions of our childhood always possess a certain power over our minds, which hardly any later friend can obtain. They know our infantine dispositions, which, however they may be afterwards modified, are never eradicated; and they can judge of our actions with more certain conclusions as to the integrity of our motives. A sister or a brother can never, unless indeed such symptoms have been shewn early, suspect the other of fraud or false dealing, when another friend, however strongly he may be attached, may, in spite of himself, be invaded with suspicion. But I enjoyed friends, dear not only through habit and association, but from their own merits; and, wherever I am, the soothing voice of my Elizabeth, and the conversation of Clerval, will be ever whispered in my ear. They are dead; and but one feeling in such a solitude can persuade me to preserve my life. If I were engaged in any high undertaking or design, fraught with extensive utility to my fellow-creatures, then could I live to fulfil it. But such is not my destiny; I

---

1 Cf. Milton, *Paradise Lost* I.40-49.

must pursue and destroy the being to whom I gave existence; then my lot on earth will be fulfilled, and I may die."

September 2d.

MY BELOVED SISTER,

I write to you, encompassed by peril, and ignorant whether I am ever doomed to see again dear England, and the dearer friends that inhabit it. I am surrounded by mountains of ice, which admit of no escape, and threaten every moment to crush my vessel. The brave fellows, whom I have persuaded to be my companions, look towards me for aid; but I have none to bestow. There is something terribly appalling in our situation, yet my courage and hopes do not desert me. We may survive; and if we do not, I will repeat the lessons of my Seneca,[1] and die with a good heart.

Yet what, Margaret, will be the state of your mind? You will not hear of my destruction, and you will anxiously await my return. Years will pass, and you will have visitings of despair, and yet be tortured by hope. Oh! my beloved sister, the sickening failings of your heart-felt expectations are, in prospect, more terrible to me than my own death. But you have a husband, and lovely children; you may be happy: heaven bless you, and make you so!

My unfortunate guest regards me with the tenderest compassion. He endeavours to fill me with hope; and talks as if life were a possession which he valued. He reminds me how often the same accidents have happened to other navigators, who have attempted this sea, and, in spite of myself, he fills me with cheerful auguries. Even the sailors feel the power of his eloquence: when he speaks, they no longer despair; he rouses their energies, and, while they hear his voice, they believe these vast mountains of ice are mole-hills, which will vanish before the resolutions of man. These feelings are transitory; each day's expectation delayed fills them with fear, and I almost dread a mutiny caused by this despair.

---

1 Lucius Annaeus Seneca (3? BCE-65 CE), Roman tragedian, Stoic philosopher, and tutor of the Emperor Nero, who eventually ordered him to commit suicide.

September 5th.

A scene has just passed of such uncommon interest, that although it is highly probable that these papers may never reach you, yet I cannot forbear recording it.

We are still surrounded by mountains of ice, still in imminent danger of being crushed in their conflict. The cold is excessive, and many of my unfortunate comrades have already found a grave amidst this scene of desolation. Frankenstein has daily declined in health: a feverish fire still glimmers in his eyes; but he is exhausted, and, when suddenly roused to any exertion, he speedily sinks again into apparent lifelessness.

I mentioned in my last letter the fears I entertained of a mutiny. This morning, as I sat watching the wan countenance of my friend—his eyes half closed, and his limbs hanging list-lessly,—I was roused by half a dozen of the sailors, who desired admission into the cabin. They entered; and their leader addressed me. He told me that he and his companions had been chosen by the other sailors to come in deputation to me, to make me a demand, which, in justice, I could not refuse. We were immured in ice, and should probably never escape; but they feared that if, as was possible, the ice should dissipate, and a free passage be opened, I should be rash enough to continue my voyage, and lead them into fresh dangers, after they might happily have surmounted this. They desired, therefore, that I should engage with a solemn promise, that if the vessel should be freed, I would instantly direct my course southward.

This speech troubled me. I had not despaired; nor had I yet conceived the idea of returning, if set free. Yet could I, in justice, or even in possibility, refuse this demand? I hesitated before I answered; when Frankenstein, who had at first been silent, and, indeed, appeared hardly to have force enough to attend, now roused himself; his eyes sparkled, and his cheeks flushed with momentary vigour. Turning towards the men, he said—

"What do you mean? What do you demand of your captain? Are you then so easily turned from your design? Did you not call this a glorious expedition? and wherefore was it glorious? Not because the way was smooth and placid as a southern sea, but because it was full of dangers and terror; because, at every new incident, your fortitude was to be called forth, and your courage exhibited; because danger and death surrounded, and these dangers you were to brave and overcome. For this was it a glori-ous, for this was it an honourable undertaking. You were hereafter to be hailed as the benefactors of your species; your name adored, as belonging to brave men who encountered death for honour and the benefit of mankind. And now, behold, with the first imagination of danger, or, if you will, the first mighty and terrific trial of your courage, you shrink away, and are content to be handed down as men who had not strength enough to endure cold and peril; and so, poor souls, they were chilly, and returned to their warm fire-sides. Why, that requires not this preparation; ye need not have come thus far, and dragged your captain to the shame of a defeat, merely to prove yourselves cowards. Oh! be men, or be more than men. Be steady to your purposes, and firm as a rock. This ice is not made of such stuff as your hearts might be; it is mutable, cannot withstand you, if you say that it shall not. Do not return to your families with the stigma of disgrace marked on your brows. Return as heroes who have fought and conquered, and who know not what it is to turn their backs on the foe."[1]

He spoke this with a voice so modulated to the different feelings expressed in his speech, with an eye so full of lofty design and heroism, that can you wonder that these men were moved. They looked at one another, and were unable to reply. I spoke; I told them to retire, and consider of what had been said: that I would not lead them further north, if they strenuously desired the contrary; but that I hoped that, with reflection, their courage would return.

They retired, and I turned towards my friend; but he was sunk in languor, and almost deprived of life.

How all this will terminate, I know not; but I had rather die, than return shamefully,—my purpose unfulfilled. Yet I fear such will be my fate; the men, unsupported by ideas of glory and honour, can never willingly continue to endure their present hardships.

September 7th.

The die is cast;[2] I have consented to return, if we are not destroyed. Thus are my hopes blasted by cowardice and indecision; I come back ignorant and disappointed. It requires more philosophy than I possess, to bear this injustice with patience.

---

1 An echo of the speech of Ulysses in Dante, *Inferno* XXVI.112-20, on which Alfred, Lord Tennyson (1809-92) later based his famous poem "Ulysses" (1833).

2 An ironic allusion to the famous remark of Julius Caesar on crossing the Rubicon; see Suetonius, *Life of Caesar* I.xxxi.

September 12th.

It is past; I am returning to England. I have lost my hopes of utility and glory;—I have lost my friend. But I will endeavour to detail these bitter circumstances to you, my dear sister; and, while I am wafted towards England, and towards you, I will not despond.

September 9th,[1] the ice began to move, and roarings like thunder were heard at a distance, as the islands split and cracked in every direction. We were in the most imminent peril; but, as we could only remain passive, my chief attention was occupied by my unfortunate guest, whose illness increased in such a degree, that he was entirely confined to his bed. The ice cracked behind us, and was driven with force towards the north; a breeze sprung from the west, and on the 11th the passage towards the south became perfectly free. When the sailors saw this, and that their return to their native country was apparently assured, a shout of tumultuous joy broke from them, loud and long-continued. Frankenstein, who was dozing, awoke, and asked the cause of the tumult. "They shout," I said, "because they will soon return to England."

"Do you then really return?"

"Alas! yes; I cannot withstand their demands. I cannot lead them unwillingly to danger, and I must return."

"Do so, if you will; but I will not. You may give up your purpose; but mine is assigned to me by heaven, and I dare not. I am weak; but surely the spirits who assist my vengeance will endow me with sufficient strength." Saying this, he endeavoured to spring from the bed, but the exertion was too great for him; he fell back, and fainted.

It was long before he was restored; and I often thought that life was entirely extinct. At length he opened his eyes, but he breathed with difficulty, and was unable to speak. The surgeon gave him a composing draught, and ordered us to leave him undisturbed. In the mean time he told me, that my friend had certainly not many hours to live.

His sentence was pronounced; and I could only grieve, and be patient. I sat by his bed watching him; his eyes were closed, and I thought he slept; but presently he called to me in a feeble voice, and, bidding me come near, said—"Alas! the strength I relied on is gone; I feel that I shall soon die, and he, my enemy and perse-cutor, may still be in being. Think not, Walton, that in the last

---

1 Wollstonecraft died on 10 September 1797.

moments of my existence I feel that burning hatred, and ardent desire of revenge, I once expressed, but I feel myself justified in desiring the death of my adversary. During these last days I have been occupied in examining my past conduct; nor do I find it blameable. In a fit of enthusiastic madness I created a rational creature, and was bound towards him, to assure, as far as was in my power, his happiness and well-being. This was my duty; but there was another still paramount to that. My duties towards my fellow-creatures had greater claims to my attention, because they included a greater proportion of happiness or misery.[1] Urged by this view, I refused, and I did right in refusing, to create a companion for the first creature. He shewed unparalleled malignity and selfishness, in evil: he destroyed my friends; he devoted to destruction beings who possessed exquisite sensations, happiness, and wisdom; nor do I know where this thirst for vengeance may end. Miserable himself, that he may render no other wretched, he ought to die. The task of his destruction was mine, but I have failed. When actuated by selfish and vicious motives, I asked you to undertake my unfinished work; and I renew this request now, when I am only induced by reason and virtue.

"Yet I cannot ask you to renounce your country and friends, to fulfil this task; and now, that you are returning to England, you will have little chance of meeting with him. But the consideration of these points, and the well-balancing of what you may esteem your duties, I leave to you; my judgment and ideas are already disturbed by the near approach of death. I dare not ask you to do what I think right, for I may still be misled by passion.

"That he should live to be an instrument of mischief disturbs me; in other respects this hour, when I momentarily expect my release, is the only happy one which I have enjoyed for several years. The forms of the beloved dead flit before me, and I hasten to their arms. Farewell, Walton! Seek happiness in tranquillity, and avoid ambition, even if it be only the apparently innocent one of distinguishing yourself in science and discoveries. Yet why do I say this? I have myself been blasted in these hopes, yet another may succeed."

His voice became fainter as he spoke; and at length, exhausted by his effort, he sunk into silence. About half an hour afterwards he attempted again to speak, but was unable; he pressed my hand feebly, and his eyes closed for ever, while the irradiation of a gentle smile passed away from his lips.

---

1 Cf. Godwin, *Political Justice* 1: 126-29; II.ii (Appendix A.1.e).

Margaret, what comment can I make on the untimely extinction of this glorious spirit? What can I say, that will enable you to understand the depth of my sorrow? All that I should express would be inadequate and feeble. My tears flow; my mind is overshadowed by a cloud of disappointment. But I journey towards England, and I may there find consolation.

I am interrupted. What do these sounds portend? It is midnight; the breeze blows fairly, and the watch on deck scarcely stir. Again; there is a sound as of a human voice, but hoarser; it comes from the cabin where the remains of Frankenstein still lie. I must arise, and examine. Good night, my sister.

Great God! what a scene has just taken place! I am yet dizzy with the remembrance of it. I hardly know whether I shall have the power to detail it; yet the tale which I have recorded would be incomplete without this final and wonderful catastrophe.

I entered the cabin, where lay the remains of my ill-fated and admirable friend. Over him hung a form which I cannot find words to describe; gigantic in stature, yet uncouth and distorted in its proportions. As he hung over the coffin, his face was concealed by long locks of ragged hair; but one vast hand was extended, in colour and apparent texture like that of a mummy. When he heard the sound of my approach, he ceased to utter exclamations of grief and horror, and sprung towards the window. Never did I behold a vision so horrible as his face, of such loathsome, yet appalling hideousness. I shut my eyes involuntarily, and endeavoured to recollect what were my duties with regard to this destroyer. I called on him to stay.

He paused, looking on me with wonder; and, again turning towards the lifeless form of his creator, he seemed to forget my presence, and every feature and gesture seemed instigated by the wildest rage of some uncontrollable passion.

"That is also my victim!" he exclaimed; "in his murder my crimes are consummated; the miserable series of my being is wound to its close! Oh, Frankenstein! generous and self-devoted being! what does it avail that I now ask thee to pardon me? I, who irretrievably destroyed thee by destroying all thou lovedst. Alas! he is cold; he may not answer me."

His voice seemed suffocated; and my first impulses, which had suggested to me the duty of obeying the dying request of my friend, in destroying his enemy, were now suspended by a mixture of curiosity and compassion. I approached this tremendous being; I dared not again raise my looks upon his face, there was something so scaring and unearthly in his ugliness. I attempted to speak, but the words died away on my lips. The monster continued to utter wild and incoherent self-reproaches. At length I gathered resolution to address him, in a pause of the tempest of his passion: "Your repentance," I said, "is now super-fluous. If you had listened to the voice of conscience, and heeded the stings of remorse, before you had urged your diabolical vengeance to this extremity, Frankenstein would yet have lived."

"And do you dream?" said the daemon; "do you think that I was then dead to agony and remorse?—He," he continued, point-ing to the corpse, "he suffered not more in the consummation of the deed;—oh! not the ten-thousandth portion of the anguish that was mine during the lingering detail of its execution. A frightful selfishness hurried me on, while my heart was poisoned with remorse. Think ye that the groans of Clerval were music to my ears? My heart was fashioned to be susceptible of love and sympathy; and, when wrenched by misery to vice and hatred, it did not endure the violence of the change without torture, such as you cannot even imagine.

"After the murder of Clerval, I returned to Switzerland, heart-broken and overcome. I pitied Frankenstein; my pity amounted to horror: I abhorred myself. But when I discovered that he, the author at once of my existence and of its unspeakable torments, dared to hope for happiness; that while he accumulated wretchedness and despair upon me, he sought his own enjoyment in feelings and passions from the indulgence of which I was for ever barred, then impotent envy and bitter indignation filled me with an insatiable thirst for vengeance. I recollected my threat, and resolved that it should be accomplished. I knew that I was preparing for myself a deadly torture; but I was the slave, not the master of an impulse, which I detested, yet could not disobey. Yet when she died!—nay, then I was not miserable. I had cast off all feeling, subdued all anguish to riot in the excess of my despair. Evil thenceforth became my good.[1] Urged thus far, I had no choice but to adapt my nature to an element which I had willingly chosen. The completion of my demoniacal design became an insatiable passion. And now it is ended; there is my last victim!"

I was at first touched by the expressions of his misery; yet when I called to mind what Frankenstein had said of his powers of eloquence and persuasion, and when I again cast my eyes on the lifeless form of my friend, indignation was rekindled within me. "Wretch!" I said, "it is well that you come here to whine over

---

1 Adapted from Milton, *Paradise Lost* IV.110.

the desolation that you have made. You throw a torch into a pile of buildings, and when they are consumed you sit among the ruins, and lament the fall. Hypocritical fiend! if he whom you mourn still lived, still would he be the object, again would he become the prey of your accursed vengeance. It is not pity that you feel; you lament only because the victim of your malignity is withdrawn from your power."

"Oh, it is not thus—not thus," interrupted the being; "yet such must be the impression conveyed to you by what appears to be the purport of my actions. Yet I seek not a fellow-feeling in my misery. No sympathy may I ever find. When I first sought it, it was the love of virtue, the feelings of happiness and affection with which my whole being overflowed, that I wished to be participated. But now, that virtue has become to me a shadow, and that happiness and affection are turned into bitter and loathing despair, in what should I seek for sympathy? I am content to suffer alone, while my sufferings shall endure: when I die, I am well satisfied that abhorrence and opprobrium should load my memory. Once my fancy was soothed with dreams of virtue, of fame, and of enjoyment. Once I falsely hoped to meet with beings, who, pardoning my outward form, would love me for the excellent qualities which I was capable of bringing forth. I was nourished with high thoughts of honour and devotion. But now vice has degraded me beneath the meanest animal. No crime, no mischief, no malignity, no misery, can be found comparable to mine. When I call over the frightful catalogue of my deeds, I cannot believe that I am he whose thoughts were once filled with sublime and transcendent visions of the beauty and the majesty of goodness. But it is even so; the fallen angel becomes a malignant devil. Yet even that enemy of God and man had friends and associates in his desolation; I am quite alone.

"You, who call Frankenstein your friend, seem to have a knowledge of my crimes and his misfortunes. But, in the detail which he gave you of them, he could not sum up the hours and months of misery which I endured, wasting in impotent passions. For whilst I destroyed his hopes, I did not satisfy my own desires. They were for ever ardent and craving; still I desired love and fellowship, and I was still spurned. Was there no injustice in this? Am I to be thought the only criminal, when all human kind sinned against me?[1] Why do you not hate Felix, who drove his friend from his door with contumely? Why do you not execrate

---

1 Cf. Shakespeare, *King Lear* III.ii.60.

the rustic who sought to destroy the saviour of his child? Nay, these are virtuous and immaculate beings! I, the miserable and the abandoned, am an abortion, to be spurned at, and kicked, and trampled on. Even now my blood boils at the recollection of this injustice.

"But it is true that I am a wretch. I have murdered the lovely and the helpless; I have strangled the innocent as they slept, and grasped to death his throat who never injured me or any other living thing. I have devoted my creator, the select specimen of all that is worthy of love and admiration among men, to misery; I have pursued him even to that irremediable ruin. There he lies, white and cold in death. You hate me; but your abhorrence cannot equal that with which I regard myself. I look on the hands which executed the deed; I think on the heart in which the imagination of it was conceived, and long for the moment when they will meet my eyes, when it will haunt my thoughts, no more.

"Fear not that I shall be the instrument of future mischief. My work is nearly complete. Neither your's nor any man's death is needed to consummate the series of my being, and accomplish that which must be done; but it requires my own. Do not think that I shall be slow to perform this sacrifice. I shall quit your vessel on the ice-raft which brought me hither, and shall seek the most northern extremity of the globe; I shall collect my funeral pile, and consume to ashes this miserable frame, that its remains may afford no light to any curious and unhallowed wretch, who would create such another as I have been.[1] I shall die. I shall no longer feel the agonies which now consume me, or be the prey of feelings unsatisfied, yet unquenched. He is dead who called me into being; and when I shall be no more, the very remembrance of us both will speedily vanish. I shall no longer see the sun or stars, or feel the winds play on my cheeks. Light, feeling, and sense, will pass away; and in this condition must I find my happiness. Some years ago, when the images which this world affords first opened upon me, when I felt the cheering warmth of summer, and heard the rustling of the leaves and the chirping of the birds, and these were all to me, I should have wept to die; now it is my only consolation. Polluted by crimes, and torn by the bitterest remorse, where can I find rest but in death?

"Farewell! I leave you, and in you the last of human kind whom these eyes will ever behold. Farewell, Frankenstein! If thou

---

1 Cf. the immolation of Laon and Cythna in P.B. Shelley, *The Revolt of Islam* XII.i-xvi.

wert yet alive, and yet cherished a desire of revenge against me, it would be better satiated in my life than in my destruction. But it was not so; thou didst seek my extinction, that I might not cause greater wretchedness; and if yet, in some mode unknown to me, thou hast not yet ceased to think and feel, thou desirest not my life for my own misery. Blasted as thou wert, my agony was still superior to thine; for the bitter sting of remorse may not cease to rankle in my wounds until death shall close them for ever.

"But soon," he cried, with sad and solemn enthusiasm, "I shall die, and what I now feel be no longer felt. Soon these burning miseries will be extinct. I shall ascend my funeral pile triumphantly, and exult in the agony of the torturing flames. The light of that conflagration will fade away; my ashes will be swept into the sea by the winds. My spirit will sleep in peace; or if it thinks, it will not surely think thus. Farewell."

He sprung from the cabin-window, as he said this, upon the ice-raft which lay close to the vessel. He was soon borne away by the waves, and lost in darkness and distance.

THE END.

Appendix A: The Education of Mary Shelley: Godwin and Wollstonecraft

[William Godwin (1756-1836) and Mary Wollstonecraft (1759-97) were the parents of Mary Shelley (1797-1851). They were, as Mary comments in her introduction to the 1831 edition of *Frankenstein*, "two persons of distinguished literary celebrity." Mary never knew her mother, who died from complications related to Mary's birth, but she certainly knew her mother's works, most notably *A Vindication of the Rights of Woman* (1792), whose celebration of a balanced domesticity is echoed in Mary's depiction of the De Lacey family, viewed through the lonely lens of the monster. William Godwin's *Enquiry Concerning Political Justice and Its Influence on Morals and Happiness* (1793; 3rd ed. 1798) was the most famous radical text of its time. It provided a critique of political institutions, taking the view that an anarchist state could be guided by "the adoption of any principle of morality and truth into the practice of a community." Like her father, Mary's literary approach is that of critique—that social conventions impinge on personal lives.]

1. Godwin

a. *Political Justice* 2: 502-04; VIII.viii.appendix

At present, to pull down a tree, to cut a canal, to navigate a vessel, require the labour of many. Will they always require the labour of many? When we recollect the complicated machines of human contrivance, various sorts of mills, of weaving engines, steam engines, are we not astonished at the compendium of labour they produce? Who shall say where this species of improvement must stop? At present, such inventions alarm the labouring part of the community; and they may be productive of temporary distress, though they conduce, in the sequel, to the most important interests of the multitude. But, in a state of equal labour, their utility will be liable to no dispute. Hereafter it is by no means clear, that the most extensive operations will not be within the reach of one man; or, to make use of a familiar instance, that a plough may not be turned into a field, and perform its office without the need of superintendence. It was in this sense that the celebrated Franklin conjectured, that "mind would one day become omnipotent over matter."

The conclusion of the progress which has here been sketched, is something like a final close to the necessity of manual labour. It may be instructive in such cases, to observe, how the sublime geniuses of former times, anticipated what seems likely to be the future improvement of mankind. It was one of the laws of Lycurgus, that no Spartan should be employed in manual labour. For this purpose, under his system, it was necessary, that they should be plentifully supplied with slaves devoted to drudgery. Matter, or, to speak more accurately, the certain and unintermitting laws of the universe, will be the Helots of the period we are contemplating. We shall end in this respect, oh immortal legislator! at the point from which you began.

b. *Political Justice* 2: 519-28; VIII.ix.appendix

Let us then, in this place, return to the sublime conjecture of Franklin, a man habitually conversant with the system of the external universe, and by no means propense to extravagant speculations, that "mind will one day become omnipotent over matter." The sense which he annexed to this expression, seems to have related to the improvements of human invention, in relation to machines and the compendium of labour. But, if the power of intellect can be established over all other matter, are we not inevitably led to ask, why not over the matter of our own bodies? If over matter at however great a distance, why not over matter which, ignorant as we may be of the tie that connects it with the thinking principle, we seem always to carry about with us, and which is our medium of communication with the external universe?

The different cases in which thought modifies the structure and members of the human body, are obvious to all. First, they are modified by our voluntary thoughts or design. We desire to stretch out our hand, and it is stretched out. We perform a thousand operations of the same species every day, and their familiarity annihilates the wonder. They are not in themselves less wonderful, than any of those modifications we are least accustomed to conceive. Secondly, mind modifies body involuntarily. To omit, for the present, what has been offered upon this subject by way of hypothesis and inference, there are many instances in which this fact presents itself in the most unequivocal manner. Has not a sudden piece of good news been frequently found to dissipate a corporal indisposition? Is it not still more usual for mental impressions to produce indisposition, and even what is called a broken heart? And shall we believe that that which is so powerful in mischief, can be altogether impotent for happiness? ... There is nothing of which the physician is more frequently aware, than of the power of the mind in assisting or retarding convalescence.

Why is it that a mature man loses that elasticity of limb, which characterises the heedless gaiety of youth? The origin of this appears to be, that he desists from youthful habits. He assumes an air of dignity, incompatible with the lightness of childish sallies. He is visited and vexed with the cares that rise out of our mistaken institutions, and his heart is no longer satisfied and gay. His limbs become stiff, unwieldy and aukward. This is the forerunner of old age and of death.

A habit peculiarly favourable to corporeal vigour, is chearfulness. Every time that our mind becomes morbid, vacant and melancholy, our external frame falls into disorder. Listlessness of thought is the brother of death. But chearfulness gives new elasticity to our limbs, and circulation to our juices. Nothing can long be stagnant in the frame of him, whose heart is tranquil, and his imagination active.

A further requisite in the case of which we treat, is clear and distinct apprehension. Disease seems perhaps in all instances to be the concomitant of confusion. When reason resigns the helm, and our ideas fluctuate without order or direction, we sleep. Delirium and insanity are of the same nature. Fainting appears principally to consist in a relaxation of intellect, so that the ideas seem to mix in painful disorder, and nothing is distinguished. He that continues to act, or is led to a renewal of action with perspicuity and decision, is almost inevitably a man in health....

Thus far we have discoursed of a negative power which, if sufficiently exercised, would, it is to be presumed, eminently tend to the prolongation of human life. But there is a power of another description, which seems entitled to our attention in this respect. We have frequently had occasion to point out the distinction between our voluntary and involuntary motions. We have seen that they are continually running into each other; our involuntary motions gradually becoming subject to the power of volition, and our voluntary motions degenerating into involuntary. We concluded in an early part of this work, and that, as it should seem, with sufficient reason, that the true perfection of man was to attain, as nearly as possible, to the perfectly voluntary state; that we ought to be, upon all occasions, prepared to render a reason of our actions; and should remove ourselves to the furthest distance, from the state of mere inanimate machines, acted upon by causes of which they have no understanding.

Our involuntary motions are frequently found gradually to become subject to the power of volition. It seems impossible to set limits to this species of metamorphosis. Its reality cannot be questioned, when we consider that every motion of the human frame was originally involuntary. Is it not then highly probable, in the process of human improvement, that we may finally obtain an empire over every articulation of our frame? The circulation of the blood is a motion, in our present state, eminently involuntary. Yet nothing is more obvious, than that certain thoughts, and states of the thinking faculty, are calculated to affect this process. Reasons have been adduced which seem to lead to an opinion, that thought and animal motion are, in all cases, to be considered as antecedent and consequent. We can now perhaps by an effort of the mind correct certain commencing irregularities of the system, and forbid, in circumstances where those phenomena would otherwise appear, the heart to palpitate, and the limbs to tremble. The voluntary power of some men over their animal frame, is found to extend to various articles, in which other men are impotent....

Nothing can be more irreconcileable to analogy, than to conclude, because a certain species of power is beyond the train of our present observations, that it is beyond the limits of the human mind. We talk familiarly indeed of the extent of our faculties; and our vanity prompts us to suppose that we have reached the goal of human capacity. But there is little plausibility in so arrogant an assumption. If it could have been told to the savage inhabitants of Europe in the times of Theseus and Achilles, that man was capable of predicting eclipses and weighing the air, of reducing to settled rules the phenomena of nature so that no prodigies should remain, and of measuring the distance and size of the heavenly bodies, this would not have appeared to them less incredible, than if we had told them of the possibility of maintaining the human body in perpetual youth and vigour. But we have not only this analogy, showing that the discovery in question forms, as it were, a regular branch of the acquisitions that belong to an intellectual nature; but, in addition to this, we seem to have a glimpse of the manner in which the acquisition will be secured.

One remark may be proper in this place. If the remedies here proposed tend to a total extirpation of the infirmities of our nature, then, though we should not be able to promise them an early or complete success, we may probably find them of some utility. They may contribute to prolong our vigour, if not to immortalise it, and, which is of more consequence, to make us live while we live. Every time the mind is invaded with anguish and gloom, the frame becomes disordered. Every time languor and indifference creep upon us, our functions fall into decay. In proportion as we cultivate fortitude and equanimity, our circulations will be chearful. In proportion as we cultivate a kind and benevolent propensity, we may be secure of finding something to interest and engage us....

The sum of the arguments which have been here offered, amounts to a species of presumption, that the term of human life may be prolonged, and that by the immediate operation of intellect, beyond any limits which we are able to assign. It would be idle to talk of the absolute immortality of man. Eternity and immortality are phrases to which it is impossible for us to annex any distinct ideas, and the more we attempt to explain them, the more we shall find ourselves involved in contradiction.

To apply these remarks to the subject of population. One tendency of a cultivated and virtuous mind is to diminish our eagerness for the gratifications of the senses. They please at present by their novelty, that is, because we know not how to estimate them. They decay in the decline of life, indirectly because the system refuses them, but directly and principally because they no longer excite the ardour of the mind. The gratifications of sense please at present by their imposture. We soon learn to despise the mere animal function, which, apart from the delusions of intellect, would be nearly the same in all cases; and to value it only as it happens to be relieved by personal charms or mental excellence.

The men therefore whom we are supposing to exist, when the earth shall refuse itself to a more extended population, will probably cease to propagate. The whole will be a people of men, and not of children. Generation will not succeed generation, nor truth have, in a certain degree, to recommence her career every thirty years.

c. *Political Justice* 1: 323-25; IV.v.appendix

But justice measures by one unalterable standard the claims of all, weighs their opposite pretensions, and seeks to diffuse happiness, because happiness is the fit and proper condition of a conscious being. Wherever therefore a strong sense of justice exists, it is common and reasonable to say, that in that mind exists considerable virtue, though the individual, from an unfortunate concurrence of circumstances, may, with all his great qualities, be the instrument of a very small portion of benefit. Can great intellectual power exist, without a strong sense of justice?

It has no doubt resulted from a train of speculation similar to this, that poetical readers have commonly remarked Milton's devil to be a being of considerable virtue. It must be admitted that his energies centered too much in personal regards. But why did he rebel against his maker? It was, as he himself informs us, because he saw no sufficient reason, for that extreme inequality of rank and power, which the creator assumed. It was because prescription and precedent form no adequate ground for implicit faith. After his fall, why did he still cherish the spirit of opposition? From a persuasion that he was hardly and injuriously treated. He was not discouraged by the apparent inequality of the contest: because a sense of reason and justice was stronger in his mind, than a sense of brute force; because he had much of the feelings of an Epictetus or a Cato, and little of those of a slave. He bore his torments with fortitude, because he disdained to be subdued by despotic power. He sought revenge, because he could not think with tameness of the unexpostulating authority that assumed to dispose of him. How beneficial and illustrious might the temper from which these qualities flowed, have been found, with a small diversity of situation! ...

Upon the whole it appears, that great talents are great energies, and that great energies cannot flow but from a powerful sense of fitness and justice. A man of uncommon genius, is a man of high passions and lofty design; and our passions will be found, in the last analysis, to have their surest foundation in a sentiment of justice. If a man be of an aspiring and ambitious temper, it is because at present he finds himself out of his place, and wishes to be in it. Even the lover imagines, that his qualities, or his passion, give him a title superior to that of other men. If I accumulate wealth, it is because I think that the most rational plan of life cannot be secured without it; and, if I dedicate my energies to sensual pleasures, it is that I regard other pursuits as irrational and visionary. All our passions would die in the moment they were conceived were it not for this reinforcement. A man of quick resentment, of strong feelings, and who pertinaciously resists every thing that he regards as an unjust assumption, may be considered as having in him the seeds of eminence. Nor is it easily to be conceived, that such a man should not proceed, from a sense of justice, to some degree of benevolence; as Milton's hero felt real compassion and sympathy for his partners in misfortune.

d. *Political Justice* 2: 386-88; VII.vi

Man is a social animal. How far he is necessarily so, will appear, if we consider the sum of advantages resulting from the social, and of which he would be deprived in the solitary state. But, independently of his original structure, he is eminently social by his habits.... The soul yearns, with inexpressible longings, for the society of its like. Because the public safety unwillingly commands the confinement of an offender, must he for that reason never light up his countenance with a smile? Who can tell the sufferings of him who is condemned to uninterrupted solitude? Who can tell that this is not, to the majority of mankind, the bitterest torment that human ingenuity can inflict? A mind sufficiently sublime might perhaps conquer this inconvenience: but the powers of such a mind do not enter into the present question.

From the examination of solitary imprisonment, in itself considered, we are naturally led to enquire into its real tendency, as to the article of reformation. To be virtuous, it is requisite that we should consider men, and their relation to each other. As a preliminary to this study, is it necessary that we should be shut out from the society of men? Shall we be most effectually formed to justice, benevolence and prudence in our intercourse with each other, in a state of solitude? Will not our selfish and unsocial dispositions be perpetually increased? What temptation has he to think of benevolence or justice, who has no opportunity to exercise it? The true soil in which atrocious crimes are found to germinate, is a gloomy and morose disposition.... Solitude, absolutely considered, may instigate us to serve ourselves, but not to serve our neighbours. Solitude, imposed under too few limitations, may be a nursery for madmen and idiots, but not for useful members of society.

e. *Political Justice* 1: 126-29; II.ii

Considerable light will pro[b]ably be thrown upon our investigation, if, quitting for the present the political view, we examine justice merely as it exists among individuals. Justice is a rule of conduct originating in the connection of one percipient being with another. A comprehensive maxim which has been laid down upon the subject is, "that we should love our neighbour as ourselves." But this maxim, though possessing considerable merit as a popular principle, is not modelled with the strictness of philosophical accuracy.

In a loose and general view I and my neighbour are both of us men; and of consequence entitled to equal attention. But, in reality, it is probable that one of us is a being of more worth and importance than the other. A man is of more worth than a beast; because, being possessed of higher faculties, he is capable of a more refined and genuine happiness. In the same manner the illustrious archbishop of Cambray[1] was of more worth than his valet, and there are few of us that would hesitate to pronounce, if his palace were in flames, and the life of only one of them could be preserved, which of the two ought to be preferred.

But there is another ground of preference, beside the private consideration of one of them being further removed from the state of a mere animal. We are not connected with one or two percipient beings, but with a society, a nation, and in some sense with the whole family of mankind. Of consequence that life ought to be preferred which will be most conducive to the general good. In saving the life of Fenelon, suppose at the moment he conceived the project of his immortal

---

1 François de Salignac de la Motte Fénelon (1651-1715), Archbishop of Cambray, author of *Télémaque* (1699), and opponent of the absolutism of Louis XIV.

Telemachus, I should have been promoting the benefit of thousands, who have been cured by the perusal of that work, of some error, vice and consequent unhappiness. Nay, my benefit would extend further than this; for every individual, thus cured, has become a better member of society, and has contributed in his turn to the happiness, information and improvement of others.

Suppose I had been myself the valet; I ought to have chosen to die, rather than Fenelon should have died. The life of Fenelon was really preferable to that of the valet. But understanding is the faculty that perceives the truth of this and similar propositions; and justice is the principle that regulates my conduct accordingly. It would have been just in the valet to have preferred the archbishop to himself. To have done otherwise would have been a breach of justice.

Suppose the valet had been my brother, my father or my benefactor. This would not alter the truth of the proposition. The life of Fenelon would still be more valuable than that of the valet; and justice, pure, unadulterated justice, would still have preferred that which was most valuable. Justice would have taught me to save the life of Fenelon at the expence of the other. What magic is there in the pronoun "my," that should justify us in overturning the decisions of impartial truth? My brother or my father may be a fool or a profligate, malicious, lying or dishonest. If they be, of what consequence is it that they are mine?

"But to my father I am indebted for existence; he supported me in the helplessness of infancy." When he first subjected himself to the necessity of these cares, he was probably influenced by no particular motives of benevolence to his future offspring. Every voluntary benefit however entitles the bestower to some kindness and retribution. Why? Because a voluntary benefit is an evidence of benevolent intention, that is, in a certain degree, of virtue. It is the disposition of the mind, not the external action separately taken, that entitles to respect. But the merit of this disposition is equal, whether the benefit were conferred upon me or upon another. I and another man cannot both be right in preferring our respective benefactors, for my benefactor cannot be at the same time both better and worse than his neighbour. My benefactor ought to be esteemed, not because he bestowed a benefit upon me, but because he bestowed it upon a human being. His desert will be in exact proportion to the degree, in which that human being was worthy of the distinction conferred.

Thus every view of the subject brings us back to the consideration of my neighbour's moral worth, and his importance to the general weal, as the only standard to determine the treatment to which he is entitled.

2. Wollstonecraft

a. *Vindication* 279-80; IX

Cold would be the heart of a husband, were he not rendered unnatural by early debauchery, who did not feel more delight at seeing his child suckled by its mother, than the most artful wanton tricks could ever raise; yet this natural way of cementing the matrimonial tie, and twisting esteem with fonder recollections, wealth leads women to spurn. To preserve their beauty, and wear the flowery crown of the day, which gives them a kind of right to reign for a short time over the sex, they neglect to stamp impressions on their husbands' hearts, that would be remembered with more tenderness when the snow on the head began to chill the bosom, than even their virgin charms. The maternal solicitude of a reasonable affectionate woman is very interesting, and the chastened dignity with which a mother returns the caresses that she and her child receive from a father who has been fulfilling the serious duties of his station, is not only a respectable, but a beautiful sight. So singular, indeed, are my feelings, and I have endeavoured not to catch factitious ones, that after having been fatigued with the sight of insipid grandeur and the slavish ceremonies that with cumberous pomp supplied the place of domestic affections, I have turned to some other scene to relieve my eye by resting it on the refreshing green every where scattered by nature. I have then viewed with pleasure a woman nursing her children, and discharging the duties of her station with, perhaps, merely a servant maid to take off her hands the servile part of the household business. I have seen her prepare herself and children, with only the luxury of cleanliness, to receive her husband, who returning weary home in the evening found smiling babes and a clean hearth. My heart has loitered in the midst of the group, and has even throbbed with sympathetic emotion, when the scraping of the well known foot has raised a pleasing tumult.

Whilst my benevolence has been gratified by contemplating this artless picture, I have thought that a couple of this description, equally necessary and independent of each other, because each fulfilled the respective duties of their station, possessed all that life could give.— Raised sufficiently above abject poverty not to be obliged to weigh the consequence of every farthing they spend, and having sufficient to prevent their attending to a frigid system of oeconomy, which narrows both heart and mind. I declare, so vulgar are my conceptions, that I know not what is wanted to render this the happiest as well as the most respectable situation in the world, but a taste for literature, to throw a little variety and interest into social converse, and some superfluous money to give to the needy and to buy books. For it is not pleasant when the heart is opened by compassion and the head active in arranging plans of usefulness, to have a prim urchin continually twitching back the elbow to prevent the hand from drawing out an almost empty purse, whispering at the same time some prudential maxim about the priority of justice.

b. *Vindication* 232-34; V.v

An early acquaintance with human infirmities; or, what is termed knowledge of the world, is the surest way, in my opinion, to contract the heart and damp the natural youthful ardour which produces not only great talents, but great virtues....

A young man who has been bred up with domestic friends, and led to store his mind with as much speculative knowledge as can be acquired by reading and the natural reflections which youthful ebullitions of animal spirits and instinctive feelings inspire, will enter the world with warm and erroneous expectations. But this appears to be the course of nature; and in morals, as well as in works of taste, we should be observant of her sacred indications, and not presume to lead when we ought obsequiously to follow.

In the world few people act from principle; present feelings, and early habits, are the grand springs: but how would the former be deadened, and the latter rendered iron corroding fetters, if the world were shewn to young people just as it is; when no knowledge of mankind or their own hearts, slowly obtained by experience, rendered them forbearing? Their fellow creatures would not then be viewed as frail beings; like themselves, condemned to struggle with human infirmities, and sometimes displaying the light, and sometimes the dark side of their character; extorting alternate feelings of love and disgust; but guarded against as beasts of prey, till every enlarged social feeling, in a word,—humanity, was eradicated.

In life, on the contrary, as we gradually discover the imperfections of our nature, we discover virtues, and various circumstances attach us to our fellow creatures, when we mix with them, and view the same objects, that are never thought of in acquiring a hasty unnatural knowledge of the world. We see a folly swell into a vice, by almost imperceptible degrees, and pity while we blame; but, if the hideous monster burst suddenly on our sight, fear and disgust rendering us more severe than man ought to be, might lead us with blind zeal to usurp the character of omnipotence, and denounce damnation on our fellow mortals, forgetting that we cannot read the heart, and that we have seeds of the same vices lurking in our own.

c. *Vindication* 293; XI

A great proportion of the misery that wanders, in hideous forms, around the world, is allowed to rise from the negligence of parents....

d. *Vindication* 130-31; II

This contempt of the understanding in early life has more baneful consequences than is commonly supposed; for the little knowledge which women of strong minds attain, is, from various circumstances, of a more desultory kind than the knowledge of men, and it is acquired more by sheer observations on real life, than from comparing what has been individually observed with the results of experience generalized by speculation. Led by their dependent situation and domestic employments more into society, what they learn is rather by snatches; and as learning is with them, in general, only a secondary thing, they do not pursue any one branch with that persevering ardour necessary to give vigour to the faculties, and clearness to the judgment. In the present state of society, a little learning is required to support the character of a gentleman; and boys are obliged to submit to a few years of discipline. But in the education of women, the cultivation of the understanding is always subordinate to the acquirement of some corporeal accomplishment; even while enervated by confinement and false notions of modesty, the body is prevented from attaining that grace and beauty which relaxed half-formed limbs never exhibit. Besides, in youth their faculties are not brought forward by emulation; and having no serious scientific study, if they have natural sagacity it is turned too soon on life and manners. They dwell on effects, and modifications, without tracing them back to causes; and complicated rules to adjust behaviour are a weak substitute for simple principles.

e. *Vindication* 273-75; VIII

The depravity of the appetite which brings the sexes together, has had a still more fatal effect. Nature must ever be the standard of taste, the gauge of appetite—yet how grossly is nature insulted by the voluptuary. Leaving the refinements of love out of the question; nature, by making the gratification of an appetite, in this respect, as well as every other, a natural and imperious law to preserve the species, exalts the appetite, and mixes a little mind and affection with a sensual gust. The feelings of a parent mingling with an instinct merely animal, give it dignity; and the man and woman often meeting on account of the child, a mutual interest and affection is excited by the exercise of a common sympathy. Women then having necessarily some duty to fulfil, more noble than to adorn their persons, would not contentedly be the slaves of casual lust; which is now the situation of a very considerable number who are, literally speaking, standing dishes to which every glutton may have access.

I may be told that great as this enormity is, it only affects a devoted part of the sex—devoted for the salvation of the rest. But, false as every assertion might easily be proved, that recommends the sanctioning a small evil to produce a greater good; the mischief does not stop here, for the moral character, and peace of mind, of the chaster part of the sex, is undermined by the conduct of the very women to whom they allow no refuge from guilt: whom they inexorably consign to the exercise of arts that lure their husbands from them, debauch their sons, and force them, let not modest women start, to assume, in some degree, the same character themselves. For I will venture to assert, that all the causes of female weakness, as well as depravity, which I have already enlarged on, branch out of one grand cause—want of chastity in men.

This intemperance, so prevalent, depraves the appetite to such a degree, that a wanton stimulus is necessary to rouse it; but the parental design of nature is forgotten, and the mere person, and that for a moment, alone engrosses the thoughts. So voluptuous, indeed, often grows the lustful prowler, that he refines on female softness. Something more soft than woman is then sought for; till, in Italy and Portugal, men attend the levees of equivocal beings, to sigh for more than female languor.

To satisfy this genus of men, women are made systematically voluptuous, and though they may not all carry their libertinism to the same height, yet this heartless intercourse with the sex, which they allow themselves, depraves both sexes, because the taste of men is vitiated; and women, of all classes, naturally square their behaviour to gratify the taste by which they obtain pleasure and power. Women becoming, consequently, weaker, in mind and body, than they ought to be, were one of the grand ends of their being taken into the account, that of bearing and nursing children, have not sufficient strength to discharge the first duty of a mother; and sacrificing to lasciviousness the parental affection, that ennobles instinct, either destroy the embryo in the womb, or cast it off when born. Nature in every thing demands respect, and those who violate her laws seldom violate them with impunity. The weak enervated women who particularly catch the attention of libertines, are unfit to be mothers, though they may conceive; so that the rich sensualist, who has rioted among women, spreading depravity and misery, when he wishes to perpetuate his name, receives from his wife only an half-formed being that inherits both its father's and mother's weakness.

Contrasting the humanity of the present age with the barbarism of antiquity, great stress has been laid on the savage custom of exposing the children whom their parents could not maintain; whilst the man of sensibility, who thus, perhaps, complains, by his promiscuous amours produces a most destructive barrenness and contagious flatigiousness of manners. Surely nature never intended that women, by satisfying an appetite, should frustrate the very purpose for which it was implanted?

f. *Vindication* 126-28; II

Women are told from their infancy, and taught by the example of their mothers, that a little knowledge of human weakness, justly termed cunning, softness of temper, *outward* obedience, and a scrupulous attention to a puerile kind of propriety, will obtain for them the protection of man; and should they be beautiful, every thing else is needless, for, at least, twenty years of their lives.

Thus Milton describes our first frail mother; though when he tells us that women are formed for softness and sweet attractive grace,[1] I cannot comprehend his meaning, unless, in the true Mahometan strain, he meant to deprive us of souls, and insinuate that we were beings only designed by sweet attractive grace, and docile blind obedience, to gratify the senses of man when he can no longer soar on the wing of contemplation.

How grossly do they insult us who thus advise us only to render ourselves gentle, domestic brutes! For instance, the winning softness so warmly, and frequently, recommended, that governs by obeying. What childish expressions, and how insignificant is the being—can it be an immortal one? who will condescend to govern by such sinister methods! ... Men, indeed, appear to me to act in a very unphilosophical manner when they try to secure the good conduct of women by attempting to keep them always in a state of childhood. Rousseau was more consistent when he wished to stop the progress of reason in both sexes, for if men eat of the tree of knowledge, women will come in for a taste; but, from the imperfect cultivation which their understandings now receive, they only attain a knowledge of evil.

Children, I grant, should be innocent; but when the epithet is applied to men, or women, it is but a civil term for weakness. For if it be allowed that women were destined by Providence to acquire human virtues, and by the exercise of their understandings, that stability of character which is the firmest ground to rest our future hopes upon, they must be permitted to turn to the fountain of light, and not forced to shape their course by the twinkling of a mere satellite. Milton, I

---

1 Milton, *Paradise Lost* IV.297-98.

grant, was of a very different opinion; for he only bends to the inde-
feasible right of beauty, though it would be difficult to render two passages which I now mean to contrast, consistent. But into similar
inconsistencies are great men often led by their senses.

> To whom thus Eve with *perfect beauty* adorn'd.
> My Author and Disposer, what thou bidst
> *Unargued* I obey; So God ordains;
> God is *thy law, thou mine*: to know no more
> Is Woman's *happiest* knowledge and her *praise*[1]

These are exactly the arguments that I have used to children; but I
have added, your reason is now gaining strength, and, till it arrives at
some degree of maturity, you must look up to me for advice—then you
ought to *think*, and only rely on God.

Yet in the following lines Milton seems to coincide with me; when
he makes Adam thus expostulate with his Maker.

> Hast thou not made me here thy substitute,
> And these inferior far beneath me set?
> Among *unequals* what society
> Can sort, what harmony or true delight?
> Which must be mutual, in proportion due
> Giv'n and receiv'd; but in *disparity*
> The one intense, the other still remiss
> Cannot well suit with either, but soon prove
> Tedious alike: of *fellowship* I speak
> Such as I seek, fit to participate
> All rational delight—[2]

In treating, therefore, of the manners of women, let us, disregard-
ing sensual arguments, trace what we should endeavour to make them
in order to co-operate, if the expression be not too bold, with the
supreme Being.

g. *Vindication* 119; I

Such, indeed, has been the wretchedness that has flowed from hereditary honours, riches, and monarchy, that men of lively sensibility have
almost uttered blasphemy in order to justify the dispensations of prov-

---

1 Milton, *Paradise Lost* IV.634-38.
2 Milton, *Paradise Lost* VIII.381-91.

idence.[1] Man has been held out as independent of his power who made him, or as a lawless planet darting from its orbit to steal the celestial fire of reason; and the vengeance of heaven, lurking in the subtile flame, like Pandora's pent up mischiefs, sufficiently punished his temerity, by introducing evil into the world.[2]

h. *Vindication* 145; II

Do passive indolent women make the best wives? ... And have women, who have early imbibed notions of passive obedience, sufficient character to manage a family or educate children? So far from it, that, after surveying the history of woman, I cannot help, agreeing with the severest satirist, considering the sex as the weakest as well as the most oppressed half of the species. What does history disclose but marks of inferiority, and how few women have emancipated themselves from the galling yoke of sovereign man?—So few, that the exceptions remind me of an ingenious conjecture respecting Newton: that he was probably a being of a superior order, accidentally caged in a human body. Following the same train of thinking, I have been led to imagine that the few extraordinary women who have rushed in eccentrical directions out of the orbit prescribed to their sex, were *male* spirits, confined by mistake in female frames. But if it be not philosophical to think of sex when the soul is mentioned, the inferiority must depend on the organs; or the heavenly fire, which is to ferment the clay, is not given in equal portions.

i. *Vindication* 244-45; VI

The great advantages which naturally result from storing the mind with knowledge, are obvious from the following considerations. The association of our ideas is either habitual or instantaneous; and the latter mode seems rather to depend on the original temperature of the mind than on the will. When the ideas, and matters of fact, are once taken in, they lie by for use, till some fortuitous circumstance makes the information dart into the mind with illustrative force, that has been received at very different periods of our lives. Like the lightning's flash are many recollections; one idea assimilating and explaining another, with astonishing rapidity. I do not now allude to that quick

---

1 Milton, *Paradise Lost* I.26.
2 Pandora, the first woman, was Prometheus's sister-in-law; the fatal curiosity that led her to open the box of evils not only parallels the curiosity that leads Eve to the apple, but also anticipates the fatal curiosity of Victor Frankenstein.

perception of truth, which is so intuitive that it baffles research, and makes us at a loss to determine whether it is reminiscence or ratiocination, lost sight of in its celerity, that opens the dark cloud. Over those instantaneous associations we have little power; for when the mind is once enlarged by excursive flights, or profound reflection, the raw materials will, in some degree, arrange themselves. The understanding, it is true, may keep us from going out of drawing when we group our thoughts, or transcribe from the imagination the warm sketches of fancy; but the animal spirits, the indiv[i]dual character, give the colouring. Over this subtile electric fluid,[1] how little power do we possess, and over it how little power can reason obtain! These fine intractable spirits appear to be the essence of genius, and beaming in its eagle eye, produce in the most eminent degree the happy energy of associating thoughts that surprise, delight, and instruct. These are the glowing minds that concentrate pictures for their fellow-creatures; forcing them to view with interest the objects reflected from the impassioned imagination, which they passed over in nature.

j. *Vindication* 290; X

If the power of reflecting on the past, and darting the keen eye of contemplation into futurity,[2] be the grand privilege of man, it must be granted that some people enjoy this prerogative in a very limited degree. Every thing new appears to them wrong; and not able to distinguish the possible from the monstrous, they fear where no fear should find a place, running from the light of reason, as if it were a firebrand; yet the limits of the possible have never been defined to stop the sturdy innovator's hand.

---

1 I have sometimes, when inclined to laugh at materialists, asked whether, as the most powerful effects in nature are apparently produced by fluids, the magnetic, &c. the passions might not be fine volatile fluids that embraced humanity, keeping the more refractory elementary parts together—or whether they were simply a liquid fire that pervaded the more sluggish materials, giving them life and heat? [Wollstonecraft's note.]

2 An allusion to Prometheus, whose name means "Forethought" and to his brother, Pandora's husband Epimetheus, whose name means "Afterthought."

Appendix B: The Education of Victor Frankenstein: Darwin and Davy

[Erasmus Darwin (1731-1802) was the grandfather of Charles Darwin, an acquaintance of William Godwin, and the most popular scientific writer of the Romantic period. Writing both prose and poetry about science, he believed that all life started from a single "filament," or spark of life, and it was his experiment with vermicelli that Mary refers to in her introduction to the 1831 edition. However, an early theorist of evolution, Darwin believed that sexual reproduction was the highest method of creating life, and spontaneous reproduction the lowest. Victor clearly violates this sacred principle. Sir Humphry Davy (1778-1829) was a well-known doctor and chemist, celebrated for his lectures and experiments. He was a poet as well, and knew Coleridge, Wordsworth, and Godwin. He argued that scientists must be as creative as poets, and "combine together mechanical, chemical, and physiological knowledge," just as Waldman advises Victor.]

1. Darwin

a. *The Economy of Vegetation* I.363-70, 383-412

—Starts the quick Ether[1] through the fibre-trains
Of dancing arteries, and of tingling veins,
Goads each fine nerve, with new sensation thrill'd,
Bends the reluctant limbs with power unwill'd;
Palsy's cold hands the fierce concussion own,
And Life clings trembling on her tottering throne.—
So from dark clouds the playful lightning springs,
Rives the firm oak, or prints the Fairy-rings....[2]

3. "YOU led your FRANKLIN to your glazed retreats,
Your air-built castles, and your silken seats;
Bade his bold arm invade the lowering sky,
And seize the tiptoe lightnings, ere they fly;
O'er the young Sage your mystic mantle spread,
And wreath'd the crown electric round his head.—

---

1 Darwin uses the term "ether," in the sense of "subtle fluid," to refer both to electricity and to air.
2 Darwin thinks that the fairy-rings on grass are caused by lightning, not by a fungus.

Thus when on wanton wing intrepid LOVE
Snatch'd the raised lightning from the arm of JOVE;
Quick o'er his knee the triple bolt He bent,
The cluster'd darts and forky arrows rent,
Snapp'd with illumin'd hands each flaming shaft,[1]
His tingling fingers shook, and stamp'd, and laugh'd;
Bright o'er the floor the scatter'd fragments blaz'd,
And Gods retreating trembled as they gaz'd;
The immortal Sire, indulgent to his child,
Bow'd his ambrosial locks, and Heaven relenting smiled.
VIII. "When Air's pure essence joins the vital flood,
And with phosphoric Acid dyes the blood,
YOUR VIRGIN TRAINS the transient HEAT dispart,[2]
And lead the soft combustion round the heart;
Life's holy lamp with fires successive feed,
From the crown'd forehead to the prostrate weed,
From Earth's proud realms to all that swim or sweep
The yielding ether or tumultuous deep.
YOU swell the bulb beneath the heaving lawn,
Brood the live seed, unfold the bursting spawn;
Nurse with soft lap, and warm with fragrant breath
The embryon panting in the arms of Death;
Youth's vivid eye with living light adorn,
And fire the rising blush of Beauty's golden morn.["]

b. *The Economy of Vegetation* II.355-94

["]—Led by the phosphor-light, with daring tread
Immortal FRANKLIN sought the fiery bed;
Where, nursed in night, incumbent Tempest shrouds
The seeds of Thunder in circumfluent clouds,
Besieged with iron points his airy cell,

---

1 Franklin/Cupid breaks the lightning after stealing it because, by inventing the
   lightning rod, he has made it harmless.
2 [Darwin's footnote to "transient HEAT dispart" discusses respiration, and then
   continues:] BESIDES THIS there would seem to be another material received
   from the air by respiration; which is so necessary to life, that the embryon must
   learn to breath almost within a minute after its birth, or it dies. The perpetual
   necessity of breathing shews, that the material thus acquired is perpetually con-
   suming or escaping, and on that account requires perpetual renovation. Perhaps
   the spirit of animation itself is thus acquired from the atmosphere, which if it be
   supposed to be finer or more subtle than the electric matter, could not long be
   retained in our bodies, and must therefore require perpetual renovation.

And pierced the monster slumbering in the shell.
"So, born on sounding pinions to the WEST,
When Tyrant-Power had built his eagle nest;
While from his eyry shriek'd the famish'd brood,
Clenched their sharp claws, and champ'd their beaks for blood,
Immortal FRANKLIN watch'd the callow crew,
And stabb'd the struggling Vampires, ere they flew.
—The patriot-flame with quick contagion ran,
Hill lighted hill, and man electrised man;
Her heroes slain awhile COLUMBIA mourn'd,
And crown'd with laurels LIBERTY return'd.

    "The Warrior, LIBERTY, with bending sails
Helm'd his bold course to fair HIBERNIA'S vales;—
Firm as he steps, along the shouting lands,
Lo! Truth and Virtue range their radiant bands;
Sad Superstition wails her empire torn,
Art plies his oar, and Commerce pours her horn.

    "Long had the Giant-form on GALLIA'S plains
Inglorious slept, unconscious of his chains;
Round his large limbs were wound a thousand strings
By the weak hands of Confessors and Kings;
O'er his closed eyes a triple veil was bound,
And steely rivets lock'd him to the ground;
While stern Bastile with iron cage inthralls
His folded limbs, and hems in marble walls.
—Touch'd by the patriot-flame, he rent amazed
The flimsy bonds, and round and round him gazed;
Starts up from earth, above the admiring throng
Lifts his Colossal form, and towers along;
High o'er his foes his hundred arms He rears,
Plowshares his swords, and pruning hooks his spears;[1]
Calls to the Good and Brave with voice, that rolls
Like Heaven's own thunder round the echoing poles;
Gives to the winds his banner broad unfurl'd,
And gathers in its shade the living world!["]

c. *The Temple of Nature* IV.383-404

"HENCE when a Monarch or a mushroom dies,
Awhile extinct the organic matter lies;
But, as a few short hours or years revolve,

---

1   A reference to the famous prophecy of peace in Isaiah 2: 4, and its reversal in
    Joel 3: 10.

Alchemic powers the changing mass dissolve;
Born to new life unnumber'd insects pant,
New buds surround the microscopic plant;
Whose embryon senses, and unwearied frames,
Feel finer goads, and blush with purer flames;
Renascent joys from irritation[1] spring,
Stretch the long root, or wave the aurelian wing.

"When thus a squadron or an army yields,
And festering carnage loads the waves or fields;
When few from famines or from plagues survive,
Or earthquakes swallow half a realm alive;—
While Nature sinks in Time's destructive storms,
The wrecks of Death are but a change of forms;
Emerging matter from the grave returns,
Feels new desires, with new sensations burns;
With youth's first bloom a finer sense acquires,
And Loves and Pleasures fan the rising fires.—
Thus sainted PAUL, 'O Death!' exulting cries,
'Where is thy sting? O Grave! thy victories?'["]2

d. *The Temple of Nature*, Additional Note I, 1-3

Prejudices against this doctrine.

I. FROM the misconception of the ignorant or superstitious, it has been thought somewhat profane to speak in favour of spontaneous vital production, as if it contradicted holy writ; which says, that God created animals and vegetables. They do not recollect that God created all things which exist, and that these have been from the beginning in a perpetual state of improvement; which appears from the globe itself, as well as from the animals and vegetables, which possess it. And lastly, that there is more dignity in our idea of the supreme author of all things, when we conceive him to be the cause of causes, than the cause simply of the events, which we see; if there can be any difference in infinity of power! ...

Preliminary observations.

II. Concerning the spontaneous production of the smallest microscopic animals it should be first observed, that the power of reproduction distinguishes organic being, whether vegetable or animal,

---

1 A technical term referring to any stimulation of the senses.
2 1 Corinthians 15: 55.

from inanimate nature. The circulation of fluids in vessels may exist in hydraulic machines, but the power of reproduction belongs alone to life. This reproduction of plants and of animals is of two kinds, which may be termed solitary and sexual. The former of these, as in the reproduction of the buds of trees, and of the bulbs of tulips, and of the polypus, and aphis, appears to be the first or most simple mode of generation, as many of these organic beings afterwards acquire sexual organs, as the flowers of seedling trees, and of seedling tulips, and the autumnal progeny of the aphis....

Secondly, it should be observed, that by reproduction organic beings are gradually enlarged and improved; which may perhaps more rapidly and uniformly occur in the simplest modes of animated being; but occasionally also in the more complicated and perfect kinds. Thus the buds of a seedling tree, or the bulbs of seedling tulips, become larger and stronger in the second year than the first, and thus improve till they acquire flowers or sexes; and the aphis, I believe, increases in bulk to the eighth or ninth generation, and then produces a sexual progeny. Hence the existence of spontaneous vitality is only to be expected to be found in the simplest modes of animation, as the complex ones have been formed by many successive reproductions.

Experimental facts.

III. By the experiments of Buffon, Reaumur, Ellis, Ingenhouz, and others, microscopic animals are produced in three or four days, according to the warmth of the season, in the infusions of all vegetable or animal matter. One or more of these gentlemen put some boiling veal broth into a phial previously heated in the fire, and sealing it up hermetically or with melted wax, observed it to be replete with animalcules in three or four days.

These microscopic animals are believed to possess a power of generating others like themselves by solitary reproduction without sex; and these gradually enlarging and improving for innumerable successive generations. Mr. Ellis ... gives drawings of six kinds of animalcula infusoria, which increase by dividing across the middle into two distinct animals. Thus in paste composed of flour and water, which has been suffered to become acescent, the animalcules called eels, vibrio anguillula, are seen in great abundance; their motions are rapid and strong; they are viviparous, and produce at intervals a numerous progeny: animals similar to these are also found in vinegar.... These eels were probably at first as minute as other microscopic animalcules; but by frequent, perhaps hourly reproduction, have gradually become the large animals above described, possessing wonderful strength and activity.

To suppose the eggs of the former microscopic animals to float in the atmosphere, and pass through the sealed glass phial, is so contrary to apparent nature, as to be totally incredible! and as the latter are viviparous, it is equally absurd to suppose, that their parents float universally in the atmosphere to lay their young in paste or vinegar!

e. *The Temple of Nature* II.103-24, 159-66

"IN these lone births no tender mothers blend
Their genial powers to nourish or defend;
No nutrient streams from Beauty's orbs improve
These orphan babes of solitary love;
Birth after birth the line unchanging runs,
And fathers live transmitted in their sons;
Each passing year beholds the unvarying kinds,
The same their manners, and the same their minds.
Till, as erelong successive buds decay,
And insect-shoals successive pass away,
Increasing wants the pregnant parents vex
With the fond wish to form a softer sex;
Whose milky rills with pure ambrosial food
Might charm and cherish their expected brood.
The potent wish in the productive hour
Calls to its aid Imagination's power,[1]
O'er embryon throngs with mystic charm presides,
And sex from sex the nascent world divides,
With soft affections warms the callow trains,
And gives to laughing Love his nymphs and swains;
Whose mingling virtues interweave at length
The mother's beauty with the father's strength....
IV. "WHERE no new Sex with glands nutritious feeds,
Nurs'd in her womb, the solitary breeds;
No Mother's care their early steps directs,
Warms in her bosom, with her wings protects;
The clime unkind, or noxious food instills

---

1 Darwin believes that the imagination of the male can influence the embryo at the moment of conception. In the context of *The Temple of Nature*, this means that the solitary males dimly sensed the desirability of females and so begot them. In the context of *Frankenstein*, as Mellor (98-99) and Alan Bewell (117-18) have pointed out, it may suggest that Victor's unhealthy mental state is responsible for the monstrosity of his offspring.

To embryon nerves hereditary ills;
The feeble births acquired diseases chase,
Till Death extinguish the degenerate race.["]

2. Davy

a. *Discourse* 5-6

The phenomena of combustion, of the solution of different substances in water, of the agencies of fire; the production of rain, hail, and snow, and the conversion of dead matter into living matter by vegetable organs, all belong to chemistry: and, in their various and apparently capricious appearances, can be accurately explained only by an acquaintance with the fundamental and general chemical principles.

b. *Discourse* 8

Even Botany and Zoology, as branches of natural history, though independent of chemistry as to their primary classifications, yet are related to it, so far as they treat of the constitution and functions of vegetables and animals. How dependent, in fact, upon chemical processes are the nourishment and growth of organized beings: their various alterations of form, their constant production of new substances; and, finally, their death and decomposition, in which nature seems to take unto herself those elements and constituent principles which, for a while, she had lent to a superior agent as the organs and instruments of the spirit of life!

c. *Discourse* 9

Indeed the want of an acquaintance with scientific principles in the processes of pharmacy has often been productive of dangerous consequences; and the study of the simple and unvarying agencies of dead matter ought surely to precede investigations concerning the mysterious and complicated powers of life.... And if the connexion of chemistry with physiology has given rise to some visionary and seductive theories; yet even this circumstance has been useful to the public mind in exciting it by doubt, and in leading it to new investigations. A reproach, to a certain degree just, has been thrown upon those doctrines known by the name of the chemical physiology; for in the applications of them speculative philosophers have been guided rather by the analogies of words than of facts. Instead of slowly endeavouring to lift up the veil concealing the wonderful phenomena of living nature;

full of ardent imaginations, they have vainly and presumptuously attempted to tear it asunder.

d. *Discourse* 10-11

Fortunately for man all the different parts of the human mind are possessed of certain harmonious relations; and it is even difficult to draw the line of distinction between the sciences; for, as they have for their objects only dead and living nature, and as they consist of expressions of facts more or less analogous, they must all be possessed of certain ties of connexion, and of certain dependencies on each other. The man of true genius, who studies science in consequence of its applications, pointing out to himself a definite end, will make use of all the instruments of investigation which are necessary for his purposes: and in the search of discovery, he will rather pursue the plans of his own mind than be limited by the artificial divisions of language. Following extensive views, he will combine together mechanical, chemical, and physiological knowledge, whenever this combination may be essential: in consequence, his facts will be connected together by simple and obvious analogies; and, in studying one class of phenomena more particularly, he will not neglect its relations to other classes.

e. *Discourse* 14-15

By means of this science man has employed almost all the substances in nature either for the satisfaction of his wants, or the gratification of his luxuries. Not contented with what is found upon the surface of the earth, he has penetrated into her bosom, and has even searched the bottom of the ocean, for the purpose of allaying the restlessness of his desires, or of extending and increasing his power. He is to a certain extent ruler of all the elements that surround him; and he is capable of using not only common matter according to his will and inclinations, but likewise of subjecting to his purposes the ethereal principles of heat and light. By his inventions they are elicited from the atmosphere; and under his control they become, according to circumstances, instruments of comfort and enjoyment, or of terror and destruction.

f. *Discourse* 15-17

Man, in what is called a state of nature, is a creature of almost pure sensation. Called into activity only by positive wants, his life is passed either in satisfying the cravings of the common appetites, or in apathy, or in slumber. Living only in moments, he calculates but little on futurity. He has no vivid feelings of hope, or thoughts of permanent and powerful action. And, unable to discover causes, he is either harrassed by superstitious dreams, or quietly and passively submitted to the mercy of nature and the elements. How different is man informed through the beneficence of the Deity, by science, and the arts! Knowing his wants, and being able to provide for them, he is capable of anticipating future enjoyments, and of connecting hope with an infinite variety of ideas. He is in some measure independent of chance or accident for his pleasures. Science has given to him an acquaintance with the different relations of the parts of the external world; and more than that, it has bestowed upon him powers which may be almost called creative; which have enabled him to change and modify the beings surrounding him, and by his experiments to interrogate nature with power, not simply as a scholar, passive and seeking only to understand her operations, but rather as a master, active with his own instruments.

But, though improved and instructed by the sciences, we must not rest contented with what has been done; it is necessary that we should likewise do. Our enjoyment of the fruits of the labours of former times should be rather an enjoyment of activity than of indolence; and, instead of passively admiring, we ought to admire with that feeling which leads to emulation.

Science has done much for man, but it is capable of doing still more; its sources of improvement are not yet exhausted; the benefits that it has conferred ought to excite our hopes of its capability of conferring new benefits; and, in considering the progressiveness of our nature, we may reasonably look forwards to a state of greater cultivation and happiness than that which we at present enjoy.

As a branch of sublime philosophy, chemistry is far from being perfect. It consists of a number of collections of facts, connected together by different relations; but as yet it is not furnished with a precise and beautiful theory. Though we can perceive, develop, and even produce, by means of our instruments of experiment, an almost infinite variety of minute phenomena, yet we are incapable of determining the general laws by which they are governed; and, in attempting to define them, we are lost in obscure, though sublime imaginations concerning unknown agencies. That they may be discovered, however, there is every reason to believe. And who would not be ambitious of becoming acquainted with the most profound secrets of nature; of ascertaining her hidden operations; and of exhibiting to men that system of knowledge which relates so intimately to their own physical and moral constitution?

g. *Discourse* 18-19

At the beginning of the seventeenth century, very little was known concerning the philosophy of the intimate actions of bodies on each other: and before this time vague ideas, superstitious notions, and inaccurate practices, were the only effects of the first efforts of the mind to establish the foundations of chemistry.... Hence arose the dreams of Alchemy concerning the philosophers stone and the elixir of life. Hence for a long while the other metals were destroyed, or rendered useless, by experiments designed to transmute them into gold; and for a long while the means of obtaining earthly immortality were sought for amidst the unhealthy vapours of the laboratory. These views of things have passed away, and a new science has gradually arisen. The dim and uncertain twilight of discovery, which gave to objects false or indefinite appearances, has been succeeded by the steady light of truth, which has shown the external world in its distinct forms, and in its true relations to human powers. The composition of the atmosphere, and the properties of the gases, have been ascertained; the phenomena of electricity have been developed; the lightnings have been taken from the clouds; and, lastly, a new influence has been discovered, which has enabled man to produce from combinations of dead matter effects which were formerly occasioned only by animal organs.

h. *Discourse* 23

The quantity of pleasure which we are capable of experiencing in life, appears to be in a great measure connected with the number of independent sources of enjoyment in our possession. And, though one great object of desire, connected with great exertions, must more or less employ the most powerful faculties of the soul; yet a certain variety of trains of feeling, and of ideas, is essential to its health and permanent activity. In considering the relations of the pursuit of chemistry to this part of our nature, we cannot but perceive, that the contemplation of the various phenomena in the external world is eminently fitted for giving a permanent and placid enjoyment to the mind. For the relations of these phenomena are perpetually changing; and, consequently, they are uniformly obliging us to alter our habits of thinking.

i. *Discourse* 24-26

The study of nature, therefore, in her various operations must be always more or less connected with the love of the beautiful and sublime: and, in consequence of the extent and indefiniteness of the views it presents to us, it is eminently calculated to gratify and to keep alive the more powerful passions and ambitions of the soul; which, delighting in the anticipation of enjoyment is never satisfied with knowledge; and which is, as it were, nourished by futurity, and rendered strong by hope.... it may become a source of consolation and of happiness, in those moments of solitude when the common actions and passions of the world are considered with indifference. It may destroy diseases of the imagination, owing to too deep a sensibility; and it may attach the affections to objects, permanent, important, and intimately related to the interests of the human species.

Appendix C: The Education of the Monster: Volney, Goethe, Plutarch, Milton, and Wollstonecraft

[Constantin-Francois de Chasseboeuf, comte de Volney (1757-1820) is the author of the first book to which the monster is exposed, hearing Felix De Lacey reading it to Safie in order to teach her French. The book was *The Ruins, or, Meditation on the Revolutions of Empires* (1791), which presents an overview of world history, plus a very critical treatment of major world religions. The monster finds three books in a satchel that he reads for himself. *The Sorrows of Werter* (1774; revised 1787) is an epistolary and autobiographical novel by Johann Wolfgang von Goethe (1749-1832). Werter, a hero of Romanticism, feels, like the monster, as though he were abandoned from gentle domesticity. The second book is *Plutarch's Lives* (actually *Lives of the Noble Greeks and Romans*), composed in the late first century. Plutarch (46-120 CE) was interested in depicting how character influenced the actions and lives of famous men. [In the third book of his epic, blank verse poem *Paradise Lost* (1667), John Milton (1608-74)] envisions the awakening of Adam and Eve, and their expulsion from Paradise. The monster sees many parallels, some ironic, between his narrative and Milton's. In addition to the texts mentioned by the monster, his acquisition of language and his cognitive development echo Wollstonecraft's "Lessons," which she prepared for her daughter Fanny Imlay (1794-1816), and which Godwin included in her *Posthumous Works* (1798).]

1. Volney

a. *The Ruins* 33-34

Because the head of a family could be absolute in his house, he made his own affections and desires the rule of his conduct; he gave or resumed his goods without equality, without justice; and paternal despotism laid the foundation of despotism in government.[1]

---

1 Upon this single expression it would be easy to write a long and important chapter. We might prove in it, beyond contradiction, that all the abuses of national governments, have sprung from those of domestic government, from that government called patriarchal, which superficial minds have extolled without having analyzed it. Numberless facts demonstrate, that *(continued)*

b. *The Ruins* 166-67

["]Your gospels in their precepts and their parables, never represent God but as a despot without any rules of equity; a partial father treating a debauched and prodigal son with more favor than his respectful and virtuous children;[1] a capricious master, who gives the same wages to workmen who had wrought but one hour, as to those who had labored through the whole day; one who prefers the last comers to the first.[2] The moral is everywhere misanthropic and antisocial; it disgusts men with life and with society; and tends only to encourage hermitism and celibacy.

"As to the manner in which you have practiced these morals, we appeal in our turn to the testimony of facts. We ask whether it is this evangelical meekness which has excited your interminable wars between your sects, your atrocious persecutions of pretended heretics, your crusades against Arianism, Manicheism, Protestantism, without speaking of your crusades against us,[3] and of those sacrilegious associations, still subsisting, of men who take an oath to continue them?[4]

---

with every infant people, in every savage and barbarous state, the father, the chief of the family, is a despot, and a cruel and insolent despot. The wife is his slave, the children his servants. This king sleeps or smokes his pipe, while his wife and daughters perform all the drudgery of the house, and even that of tillage and cultivation, as far as occupations of this nature are practised in such societies; and no sooner have the boys acquired strength th[a]n they are allowed to beat the females, and make them serve and wait upon them as they do upon their fathers. Similar to this is the state of our own uncivilized peasants. In proportion as civilization spreads, the manners become milder, and the condition of the women improves, till, by a contrary excess, they arrive at dominion, and then a nation becomes effeminate and corrupt. It is remarkable that parental authority is great in proportion as the government is despotic. China, India, and Turkey are striking examples of this. One would suppose that tyrants gave themselve[s] accomplices and interested subaltern despots to maintain their authority. In opposition to this the Romans will be cited, but it remains to be proved that the Romans were men truly free; and their quick passage from their republican despotism to their abject servility under the emperors, gives room at least for considerable doubt as to that freedom. [Volney's note.]

1 Luke 15: 11-32.
2 Matthew 20: 1-16.
3 The speaker is a Muslim.
4 The oath taken by the Knights of the Order of Malta, is to kill, or to make the Mahometans prisoners, for the glory of God. [Volney's note.]

We ask you whether it be gospel charity which has made you extermi-nate whole nations in America, to annihilate the empires of Mexico and Peru; which makes you continue to dispeople Africa and sell its inhabitants like cattle, notwithstanding your abolition of slavery; which makes you ravage India and usurp its dominions; and whether it be the same charity which, for three centuries past, has led you to harass the habitations of the people of three continents, of whom the most prudent, the Chinese and Japanese, were constrained to drive you off, that they might escape your chains and recover their internal peace?"

c. *The Ruins* 22-23

Formed naked in body and in mind, man at first found himself thrown, as it were by chance, on a rough and savage land: an orphan, abandoned by the unknown power which had produced him, he saw not by his side beings descended from heaven to warn him of those wants which arise only from his senses, nor to instruct him in those duties which spring only from his wants. Like to other animals, without experience of the past, without foresight of the future,[1] he wandered in the bosom of the forest, guided only and governed by the affections of his nature. By the pain of hunger, he was led to seek food and provide for his subsistence; by the inclemency of the air, he was urged to cover his body, and he made him clothes; by the attraction of a powerful pleasure, he approached a being like himself, and he per-petuated his kind.

Thus the impressions which he received from every object, awak-ening his faculties, developed by degrees his understanding, and began to instruct his profound ignorance: his wants excited industry, dangers formed his courage; he learned to distinguish useful from noxious plants, to combat the elements, to seize his prey, to defend his life; and thus he alleviated its miseries.

Thus self-love, aversion to pain, the desire of happiness, were the simple and powerful excitements which drew man from the savage and barbarous condition in which nature had placed him. And now, when his life is replete with enjoyments, when he may count each day by the comforts it brings, he may applaud himself and say:

"It is I who have produced the comforts which surround me; it is I who am the author of my own happiness; a safe dwelling, convenient clothing, abundant and wholesome nourishment, smiling fields, fertile hills, populous empires, all is my work; without me this earth, given up

---

1 Volney's primitive human lacks not only a God but also a Prometheus and an Epimetheus.

to disorder, would have been but a filthy fen, a wild wood, a dreary desert."

Yes, creative man, receive my homage! Thou hast measured the span of the heavens, calculated the volume of the stars, arrested the lighting in its clouds,[1] subdued seas and storms, subjected all the elements. Ah! how are so many sublime energies allied to so many errors?

2. Goethe

a. *The Sorrows of Werter* 77-87; Letter XXIX (12 August)

In these reveries, I put the mouth of the pistol to my forehead. "What do you mean," cried Albert, turning back the pistol. "It is not charged," said I. "And if it is not," he answered with impatience, "what do you mean by it? I cannot comprehend how a man should be so mad as to blow out his brains; and the bare idea of it shocks me." "What right has any man," said I, "in speaking of an action, immediately to pronounce that it is mad, or wise, or good, or bad? What is meant by all this? Have you carefully examined the interior motives for the action? Have you fairly unfolded all the reasons which gave rise to it, and which made it necessary? If you did all this, you would not be so quick with your decision." "However," said Albert, "you will allow that some actions are criminal, whatever were the motives for committing them."—I granted it, and shrugged up my shoulders.

"But still, my good friend," I said, "there are more exceptions to make. Theft is a crime: but the man who is driven to it by extreme poverty, with no design but to save himself and his family from perishing for want, must he too be punished? and is he not rather an object of our compassion? Who shall throw the first stone at a husband that, in the first heat of just resentment, sacrifices a faithless wife, and her perfidious seducer? or at a young girl whom love only has led astray? Even our laws, our pedantic laws, our cold, cruel laws, relent and withdraw their punishment."

"These examples are very different," said Albert; "because a man, under the influence of violent passion, is incapable of reflection, and is looked upon as drunk, or out of his senses." "Oh! you people of sound understandings," I replied, smiling, "are very ready to pronounce sentence, and talk of extravagance, and madness, and intoxication; you are quiet, and care for nothing; you avoid the drunken man, and detest the extravagant; you pass on the other side like the Priest, and like the Pharisee you thank God that you are not like one of them. I have more than once experienced the effects of drinking; my

---

1 A Promethean accomplishment.

passions have always bordered upon extravagance, and I am not ashamed to own it. Do I not find that those superior men, who have done any great or extraordinary action, have in all times been treated as if they were intoxicated or mad?

"And in private life too, is it not insufferable, that if a young man does any thing uncommonly noble or generous, the world immediately says he is out of his senses? Take shame to yourselves, ye people of discretion; take shame to yourselves, ye sages of the earth."—"This now is one of your extravagant flights," said Albert; "you always go beyond the mark: and here you are most undoubtedly wrong, to compare suicide, which is in question, with great actions; for it can only be looked upon as a weakness. It is much easier to die than to bear a life of misery with fortitude."

I was upon the point of breaking off the conversation immediately; for nothing puts me out of all patience, like a common-place opinion, which means nothing, whilst I am talking from my inmost heart. However, I got the better of myself; for having often heard this pitiful argument, I now begin to be used to it. But I answered with some warmth, "You call this a weakness; beware of being carried away by sounds! Suppose a people groaning under the yoke of tyranny; do you call them weak, when at length they throw it off and break their chains? The man who, to rescue his house from the flames, exerts all his powers, lifts burthens with ease that he could scarcely move when his mind was at peace; he who attacks and puts to flight half a score of his enemies; are these weak people? My good friend, if resistance is a mark of strength, can the highest degree of resistance be called a weakness?["] Albert looked stedfastly at me, and said, "Begging your pardon, I don't think the examples you have brought have any relation to the subject in question." "That may very likely be," I answered, "for I have been often told, that my way of combining things appeared extravagant. But let us try to set the matter in another light; let us examine what is the situation of a man who resolves to free himself from the burthen of life—a burthen that is in general so much desired—and let us enter into his feelings; for we cannot otherwise reason fairly on the subject.

"Human nature," I continued, "has certain limits; there is a degree of joy, grief, pain, which it is able to endure, and beyond that degree it is annihilated.

"We are not, therefore, to enquire whether a man is weak or strong, but whether he can pass the bounds of nature, and the measure of his sufferings, either of mind or body; and I think it is as absurd to say that a man who destroys himself is a coward, as to call a man a coward who dies of a malignant fever." "Paradox, all paradox!" exclaimed Albert. "Not so paradoxical as you imagine," I replied; "you will allow that we call a disease mortal, in which nature is so severely attacked, and her strength so far exhausted, that what remains is not sufficient to raise her up, and set her going again.

"Let us apply this to the mind; let us see how ideas work, and how impressions fix upon it, till at length a violent passion takes entire possession, destroys all the powers it possessed when at ease, and entirely subdues it.

"It is in vain that a man of sound understanding and cool temper sees the miserable situation of a wretch in such circumstances; it is in vain that he counsels him: 'tis like the man in health, who sits by the bed of his dying friend, but is unable to communicate to him the smallest portion of his strength."

Albert thought this too general. I quoted the girl who lately drowned herself, and made him recollect her story—"A good young creature, so accustomed to the narrow sphere of domestic labour, and the business of the week, that she knew of no pleasure but taking a walk in the fields on a Sunday, dancing once perhaps in the holidays, and the rest of her time only talking with her next neighbour of the news and little quarrels of the village. At length her heart feels new and unknown wishes; all that used to please her, now by degrees becomes tasteless, till she meets with a man to whom a new affection invisibly attaches her; from that time, her hopes are all centered in him; the whole surrounding world is forgotten by her; she sees, hears, desires nothing but him; he alone occupies all her thoughts. Her heart having never felt the baneful pleasure arising from light vanity, her wishes tend immediately to the object of them; she hopes to belong to him, and in eternal bonds expects to enjoy all the desires of her heart, and to realize the ideas of happiness which she has formed. His repeated promises confirm her hopes; his fondness encreases her passion; her whole soul is lost and drowned in pleasure; her heart is all rapture: At length she stretches out her arms to embrace the object of her vows— All is vanished away; her lover forsakes her.—Amazed! petrified! she stands senseless before the abyss of misery she sees encompass her; all around is darkness; for her there is no prospect, nor hope, nor consolation: she is forsaken by him in whom her life was bound up; and in the wide universe which is before her,[1] and among so many who might repair her loss, she feels alone, and abandoned by the whole world. Thus blinded, thus impelled, by the piercing grief which wrings her heart, she plunges into the deep to put an end to her torments. Such, Albert, is the history of many men: And is it not a parallel case with illness? Nature has no way to escape: her powers exhausted, and con-

---

1 Goethe may not have intended the allusion to *Paradise Lost* (XII.646), but his translator probably did.

tending powers to struggle with, death must be the consequence. Woe unto the man who could hear this situation described, and who could say, A foolish girl! why did not she wait till time had worn off the impression? her despair would have been softened, and she would have found another lover to comfort her. One might as well say, A fool! he died of a fever: why did not he wait till he had recovered his strength, till his blood was calm? then all would have been well, and he would have been alive now."

Albert, who did not allow the comparison to be just, made many objections: amongst the rest, that I had only brought the example of a simple and ignorant girl;—but he could not comprehend how a man of sense, whose views are more enlarged, and who sees such various consolations, should ever suffer himself to fall into such a state of despair. "My good friend," said I, "whatever is the education of a man, whatever is his understanding, still he is a man, and the little reason that he possesses, either does not act at all, or acts very feebly, when the passions are let loose, or rather when the boundaries of human nature close in upon him.—But we will talk of this another time," I said, and took up my hat—Alas! my heart was full—and we parted without conviction on either side.—How rarely do men understand one another!

b. *The Sorrows of Werter* 102-08; Letter XXXVII (3 September)

Charlotte made us observe a fine effect of moon-light at the end of the wood, which appeared the more striking and brilliant from the darkness which surrounded the spot where we were. We remained for some time silent; and then Charlotte said, "Whenever I walk by moon-light, it brings to my remembrance all those who were dear to me, and who are no more; and I think of death and a future state.—Yes," continues she, with a firm but touching voice, "we shall still exist; but, Werter, shall we find one another out? Shall we know one another again? What presages have you? What is your opinion?"

"Charlotte," I said, holding out my hand to her, and my eyes full of tears, "we shall again see one another here and hereafter." I could say no more.—My dear friend, should she have put the question to me, just when the thoughts of a cruel separation filled my heart?

"And those persons who have been dear to us," said she, "and who are now no more, do they know that when we are happy, we recall them to our memory with tenderness?—The shade of my mother hovers round me, when in a still evening I sit in the midst of her children—when I see them assembled about me, as they used to be assembled about her! I then raise my swimming eyes to Heaven, and wish she could look down upon us, and see that I fulfil the promise which

I made to her in her last moments, to be a mother to her children! A hundred times I have exclaimed, Pardon, dearest of mothers, pardon me, if I am not to them all that you were!—Alas! I do all that I can; they are properly cloathed and fed, and still more, they are well educated and beloved! If you could behold our mutual attachment, the harmony that subsists amongst us, you would give thanks to that Being to whom, dying, you addressed such fervent prayers for our happiness." This she said, my dear friend; but who could repeat all her words? how should cold unfeeling characters catch the expressions of sentiment and genius? Albert gently interrupted her—"My charming Charlotte, you are too much affected: I know these recollections are dear to you, but I beg—" "Oh! Albert," said she, "you do not forget, I know you do not, the evenings when we three, during the absence of my father, used to sit at our little round table, after the children were gone to bed. You often had a book in your hand, but you seldom read any of it—and who would not have preferred the conversation of that delightful woman to every thing in the world? She was beautiful, mild, chearful, and always active. God knows how often I have knelt before him, and prayed that I might be like her."

I threw myself at her feet; I took her hands, and wetting them with my tears, said, "Charlotte! Charlotte! the benediction of Heaven is upon you, and the spirit of your mother."—"If you had but known her," she said, and pressed my hand—"she was worthy of being known to you."—I was motionless; never had I received praise so flattering. "And this woman was to die in the flower of her age; the youngest of her children was but six months old. Her illness was short; she was resigned and calm: nothing gave her any anxiety but her children, and more particularly the youngest. When she found her end approaching, she bade me go and fetch them; and when they were all around her bed, the little ones who did not know their misfortune, and the great ones who were quite overcome with sorrow, she raised her feeble hands to Heaven, hung over them, and prayed for them, then kissed them one after the other, sent them back, and said to me, Be you their mother. I held out my hand to her. You promise much, my child; a mother's fondness and a mother's care. Your tears of affection and gratitude have often shewn me that you felt what was a mother's tenderness—shew such tenderness to your brothers and sisters: and to your father be dutiful and faithful as a wife; you will be his comfort. She asked for him. He was gone out to hide the bitterness of his grief. He felt all that he was to lose, and his heart was in agonies.

"You, Albert, were in the room. She heard somebody move; asked who it was, and desired you to come to her. She looked at us both with great composure and satisfaction in her countenance, and said, They will be happy, they will be happy with one another!"—Albert, taking her in his arms, cried out, "Yes, Charlotte, we are and shall be happy."—Even the calm Albert was moved;—I was quite out of my senses.

"And such a woman," she continued, "was to leave us, Werter!—Great God! must we thus part with every thing we hold dear in the world! Nobody feels this more keenly than children; they cried and lamented for a long time afterwards, that black men had carried away their dear mamma!"

3. Plutarch

a. *Plutarch's Lives* 1: 1; "Theseus"

As geographers ... crowd into the edges of their maps parts of the world which they do not know about, adding notes in the margin to the effect, that beyond this lies nothing but sandy deserts full of wild beasts, unapproachable bogs, Scythian ice, or a frozen sea, so, in this work of mine, in which I have compared the lives of the greatest men with one another, after passing through those periods which probable reasoning can reach to and real history find a footing in, I might very well say of those that are farther off: Beyond this there is nothing but prodigies and fictions, the only inhabitants are the poets and inventors of fables; there is no credit, or certainty any farther.

b. *Plutarch's Lives* 1: 73-75; "Comparison of Romulus with Theseus"

If men's calamities ... are not to be wholly imputed to fortune, but refer themselves to differences of character, who will acquit either Theseus of rash and unreasonable anger against his son[1] or Romulus against his brother?[2] ...

But Romulus has, first of all, one great plea, that his performances proceeded from very small beginnings; for both the brothers being thought servants and the sons of swine-herds before becoming freemen themselves, gave liberty to almost all the Latins, obtaining at once all the most honorable titles, as destroyers of their country's enemies, preservers of their friends and kindred, princes of the people, founders of cities, not removers, like Theseus, who raised and compiled only one house out of many, demolishing many cities bearing the names of ancient kings and heroes. Romulus, indeed, did the same afterwards, forcing his enemies to deface and ruin their own dwellings,

---

1 Theseus unjustly cursed his son Hippolytus, causing his death.
2 Romulus killed his twin brother Remus for mocking his plans for the fortification of Rome.

and to sojourn with their conquerors; but at first, not by removal, or increase of an existing city, but by foundation of a new one, he obtained himself lands, a country, a kingdom, wives, children, and relations. And, in so doing, he killed or destroyed nobody, but benefited those that wanted houses and homes and were willing to be of a society and become citizens. Robbers and malefactors he slew not; but he subdued nations, he overthrew cities, he triumphed over kings and commanders. As to Remus, it is doubtful by whose hand he fell; it is generally imputed to others. His mother he clearly retrieved from death, and placed his grandfather, who was brought under base and dishonorable vassalage, on the ancient throne of Aeneas, to whom he did voluntarily many good offices, but never did him harm even inadvertently. But Theseus, in his forgetfulness and neglect of the command concerning the flag, can scarcely, methinks, by any excuses, or before the most indulgent judges, avoid the imputation of parricide. And, indeed, one of the Attic writers, perceiving it to be very hard to make an excuse for this, feigns that Aegeus, at the approach of the ship, running hastily to the Acropolis to see what news, slipped and fell down, as if he had no servants, or none would attend him on his way to the shore.[1]

And, indeed, the faults committed in the rapes of women admit of no plausible excuse in Theseus. First, because of the often repetition of the crime; for he stole Ariadne, Antiope, Anaxo the Troezenian, at last Helen, when he was an old man, and she not marriageable; she a child, and he at an age past even lawful wedlock. Then, on account of the cause; for the Troezenian, Lacedaemonian, and Amazonian virgins, beside that they were not betrothed to him, were not worthier to raise children by than the Athenian women, derived from Erechtheus and Cecrops; but it is to be suspected these things were done out of wantonness and lust. Romulus, when he had taken near eight hundred women, chose not all, but only Hersillia, as they say, for himself; the rest he divided among the chief of the city; and afterwards, by the respect and tenderness and justice shown towards them, he made it clear that this violence and injury was a commendable and politic exploit to establish a society; by which he intermixed and united both nations, and made it the fountain of after friendship and public stability.

---

1 On his departure for Crete to kill the Minotaur, Theseus told his father that the returning ship would have white sails if he were successful, black ones if he were not. On his return, he forgot to have the sails changed, and Aegeus, believing that his son was dead, threw himself into the sea.

c. *Plutarch's Lives* 1: 126-27, 137-38; "Numa Pompilius"

... Numa, judging it no slight undertaking to mollify and bend to peace the presumptuous and stubborn spirits of this people, began to operate upon them with the sanctions of religion. He sacrificed often and used processions and religious dances, in which most commonly he officiated in person; by such combinations of solemnity with refined and humanizing pleasures, seeking to win over and mitigate their fiery and warlike tempers. At times, also, he filled their imaginations with religious terrors, professing that strange apparitions had been seen, and dreadful voices heard; thus subduing and humbling their minds by a sense of supernatural fears.... Numa spoke of a certain goddess or mountain nymph [Egeria] that was in love with him, and met him in secret, ... and professed that he entertained familiar conversation with the Muses, to whose teaching he ascribed the greatest part of his revelations; and amongst them, above all, he recommended to the veneration of the Romans one in particular, whom he named Tacita, the silent....

There goes a story that he once invited a great number of citizens to an entertainment, at which the dishes in which the meat was served were very homely and plain, and the repast itself poor and ordinary fare; the guests seated, he began to tell them that the goddess that consulted with him was then at that time come to him; when on a sudden the room was furnished with all sorts of costly drinking-vessels, and the tables loaded with rich meats, and a most sumptuous entertainment. But the dialogue which is reported to have passed between him and Jupiter surpasses all the fabulous legends that were ever invented. They say that before Mount Aventine was inhabited or enclosed within the walls of the city, two demigods, Picus and Faunus, frequented the springs and thick shades of that place; which might be two satyrs, or Pans, except that they went about Italy playing the same sorts of tricks, by skill in drugs and magic, as are ascribed by the Greeks to the Dactyli of Mount Ida. Numa contrived one day to surprise these demigods, by mixing wine and honey in the waters of the spring of which they usually drank. On finding themselves ensnared, they changed themselves into various shapes, dropping their own form and assuming every kind of unusual and hideous appearance; but when they saw they were safely entrapped, and in no possibility of getting free, they revealed to him many secrets and future events; and particularly a charm for thunder and lightning,[1] still in use, performed with onions and hair and pilchards. Some say they did not tell him the charm, but by their magic brought down Jupiter out of heaven; and

---

1 Numa is another Promethean figure.

that he then, in an angry manner answering the inquiries, told Numa, that, if he would charm the thunder and lightning, he must do it with heads. "How," said Numa, "with the heads of onions?" "No," replied Jupiter, "of men." But Numa, willing to elude the cruelty of this receipt, turned it another way, saying, "Your meaning is, the hairs of men's heads." "No," replied Jupiter, "with living"—"pilchards," said Numa, interrupting him. These answers he had learnt from Egeria. Jupiter returned again to heaven, pacified....

These stories, laughable as they are, show us the feelings which people then, by force of habit, entertained towards the deity. And Numa's own thoughts are said to have been fixed to that degree on divine objects, that he once, when a message was brought to him that "Enemies are approaching," answered with a smile, "And I am sacrificing."

d. *Plutarch's Lives* 1: 150-52; "Comparison of Numa with Lycurgus"

Numa's directions ... for the care of young women are better adapted to the female sex and to propriety; Lycurgus's are altogether unreserved and unfeminine.... And so [the Spartan] women, it is said, were bold and masculine, overbearing to their husbands in the first place, absolute mistresses in their houses, giving their opinions about public matters freely, and speaking openly even on the most important subjects. But the matrons, under the government of Numa, still indeed received from their husbands all that high respect and honor which had been paid them under Romulus as a sort of atonement for the violence done to them; nevertheless, great modesty was enjoined upon them; all busy intermeddling forbidden, sobriety insisted on, and silence made habitual. Wine they were not to touch at all, nor to speak, except in their husband's company, even on the most ordinary subjects. So that once when a woman had the confidence to plead her own cause in a court of judicature, the senate, it is said, sent to inquire of the oracle what the prodigy did portend; and, indeed, their general good behavior and submissiveness is justly proved by the record of those that were otherwise; for as the Greek historians record in their annals the names of those who first unsheathed the sword of civil war, or murdered their brothers, or were parricides, or killed their mothers, so the Roman writers report it as the first example, that Spurius Carvilius divorced his wife, being a case that never before happened, in the space of two hundred and thirty years from the foundation of the city; and that one Thalaea, the wife of Pinarius, had a quarrel (the first instance of the kind) with her mother-in-law, Gegania, in the reign of Tarquinius Superbus; so successful was the legislator in securing order and good conduct in the marriage relation. Their respective regulations for marrying the young women are in accordance with those for their education. Lycurgus made them brides when they were of full age and inclination for it. Intercourse, where nature was thus consulted, would produce, he thought, love and tenderness, instead of the dislike and fear attending an unnatural compulsion; and their bodies, also, would be better able to bear the trials of breeding and of bearing children, in his judgment the one end of marriage.

The Romans, on the other hand, gave their daughters in marriage as early as twelve years old, or even under; thus they thought their bodies alike and minds would be delivered to the future husband pure and undefiled. The way of Lycurgus seems the more natural with a view to the birth of children; the other, looking to a life to be spent together, is more moral. However, the rules which Lycurgus drew up for superintendence of children, their collection into companies, their discipline and association, as also his exact regulations for their meals, exercises, and sports, argue Numa no more than an ordinary lawgiver. Numa left the whole matter simply to be decided by the parent's wishes or necessities; he might, if he pleased, make his son a husbandman or carpenter, coppersmith or musician; as if it were of no importance for them to be directed and trained up from the beginning to one and the same common end, or as though it would do for them to be like passengers on shipboard, brought thither each for his own ends and by his own choice, uniting to act for the common good only in time of danger upon occasion of their private fears, in general looking simply to their own interest.

We may forbear, indeed, to blame common legislators, who may be deficient in power or knowledge. But when a wise man like Numa had received the sovereignty over a new and docile people, was there anything that would better deserve his attention than the education of children, and the training up of the young, not to contrariety and discordance of character, but to the unity of the common model of virtue, to which from their cradle they should have been formed and moulded? One benefit among many that Lycurgus obtained by his course was the permanence which it secured to his laws. The obligation of oaths to preserve them would have availed but little, if he had not, by discipline and education, infused them into the children's characters, and imbued their whole early life with a love of his government.

e. *Plutarch's Lives* 4: 195, 201-02; "Cato the Younger"

While he was yet very young, to some that asked him, whom he loved best, he answered, his brother. And being asked, whom next, he replied, his brother, again. So likewise the third time, and still the same, till they left off to ask any further. As he grew in age, this love to his brother grew yet the stronger. When he was about twenty years old, he never supped, never went out of town, nor into the forum, without Caepio....

While Cato was yet in the service, his brother, on a journey towards Asia, fell sick at Aenus in Thrace, letters with intelligence of which were immediately despatched to him. The sea was very rough, and no convenient ship of any size to be had; so Cato getting into a small trading-vessel, with only two of his friends, and three servants, set sail from Thessalonica, and having very narrowly escaped drowning, he arrived at Aenus just as Caepio expired. Upon this occasion, he was thought to have showed himself more a fond brother than a philosopher, not only in the excess of his grief, bewailing, and embracing the dead body, but also in the extravagant expenses of the funeral, the vast quantity of rich perfumes and costly garments which were burnt with the corpse, and the monument of Thasian marble, which he erected, at the cost of eight talents, in the public place of the town of Aenus. For there were some who took upon them to cavil at all this, as not consistent with his usual calmness and moderation, not discerning that though he were steadfast, firm, and inflexible to pleasure, fear or foolish entreaties, yet he was full of natural tenderness and brotherly affection. Divers of the cities and princes of the country sent him many presents, to honor the funeral of his brother; but he took none of their money, only the perfumes and ornaments he received, and paid for them also. And afterwards, when the inheritance was divided between him and Caepio's daughter, he did not require any portion of the funeral expenses to be discharged out of it. Notwithstanding this, it has been affirmed that he made his brother's ashes be passed through a sieve, to find the gold that was melted down when burnt with the body. But he who made this statement appears to have anticipated an exemption for his pen, as much as for his sword, from all question and criticism.

4. Milton

a. *Paradise Lost* VIII.250-99

For Man to tell how human Life began
Is hard; for who himself beginning knew?
Desire with thee still longer to converse
Induc'd me. As new wak't from soundest sleep
Soft on the flowrie herb I found me laid
In Balmie Sweat, which with his Beames the Sun
Soon dri'd, and on the reaking moisture fed.

Strait toward Heav'n my wondring Eyes I turnd,
And gaz'd a while the ample Skie, till rais'd
By quick instinctive motion up I sprung,
As thitherward endevoring, and upright
Stood on my feet; about me round I saw
Hill, Dale, and shadie Woods, and sunnie Plains,
And liquid Lapse of murmuring Streams; by these,
Creatures that liv'd, and mov'd, and walk'd, or flew
Birds on the branches warbling; all things smil'd,
With fragrance and with joy my heart oreflow'd.
My self I then perus'd, and Limb by Limb
Survey'd, and sometimes went, and sometimes ran
With supple joints, as lively vigour led:
But who I was, or where, or from what cause,
Knew not; to speak I tri'd, and forthwith spake,
My Tongue obey'd and readily could name
What e're I saw. Thou Sun, said I, fair Light,
And thou enlight'n'd Earth, so fresh and gay,
Ye Hills and Dales, ye Rivers, Woods, and Plains,
And ye that live and move, fair Creatures, tell,
Tell, if ye saw, how came I thus, how here?
Not of my self, by some great Maker then,
In goodness and in power praeeminent;
Tell me, how may I know him, how adore,
From whom I have that thus I move and live,
And feel that I am happier then I know.
While thus I call'd, and stray'd I knew not whither,
From where I first drew Air, and first beheld
This happie Light, when answer none return'd,
On a green shadie Bank profuse of Flowrs
Pensive I sate me down; there gentle sleep
First found me, and with soft oppression seis'd
My droused sense, untroubl'd, though I thought
I then was passing to my former state
Insensible, and forthwith to dissolve:
When suddenly stood at my Head a dream,
Whose inward apparition gently mov'd
My fancy to believe I yet had being,
And liv'd: One came, methought, of shape Divine,
And said, thy Mansion wants thee, *Adam*, rise,
First Man, of Men innumerable ordain'd
First Father, call'd by thee I come thy Guide
To the Garden of bliss, thy seat prepar'd.

b. *Paradise Lost* IV.449-91

That day I oft remember, when from sleep
I first awak't, and found my self repos'd
Under a shade on flowrs, much wondring where
And what I was, whence thither brought, and how.
Not distant far from thence a murmuring sound
Of waters issu'd from a Cave and spread
Into a liquid Plain, then stood unmov'd
Pure as th' expanse of Heav'n; I thither went
With unexperienc't thought, and laid me down
On the green bank, to look into the cleer
Smooth Lake, that to me seemd another Skie.
As I bent down to look, just opposite,
A Shape within the watry gleam appeerd
Bending to look on me, I started back,
It started back, but pleas'd I soon returnd,
Pleas'd it returnd as soon with answering looks
Of sympathie and love; there I had fixt
Mine eyes till now, and pin'd with vain desire,
Had not a voice thus warnd me, What thou seest,
What there thou seest fair Creature is thy self,
With thee it came and goes: but follow me,
And I will bring thee where no shadow staies
Thy coming, and thy soft imbraces, hee
Whose image thou art, him thou shall enjoy
Inseparablie thine, to him shalt bear
Multitudes like thy self, and thence be call'd
Mother of human Race: what could I doe,
But follow strait, invisibly thus led?
Till I espi'd thee, fair indeed and tall,
Under a Platan, yet methought less fair,
Less winning soft, less amiablie mild,
Then that smooth watry image; back I turnd,
Thou following cryd'st aloud, Return fair *Eve*,
Whom fli'st thou? whom thou fli'st, of him thou art,
His flesh, his bone; to give thee being I lent
Out of my side to thee, neerest my heart
Substantial Life, to have thee by my side
Henceforth an individual solace dear;
Part of my Soul I seek thee, and thee claim
My other half with that thy gentle hand
Seis'd mine, I yeilded, and from that time see
How beauty is excelld by manly grace
And wisdom, which alone is truly fair.

c. *Paradise Lost* IX.445-79

As one who long in populous City pent,
Where Houses thick and Sewers annoy the Air,
Forth issuing on a Summers Morn to breathe
Among the pleasant Villages and Farmes
Adjoynd, from each thing met conceaves delight,
The smell of Grain, or tedded Grass, or Kine,
Or Dairie, each rural sight, each rural sound;
If chance with Nymphlike step fair Virgin pass,
What pleasing seemd, for her now pleases more,
She most, and in her look summs all Delight.
Such Pleasure took the Serpent to behold
This Flowrie Plat, the sweet recess of *Eve*
Thus earlie, thus alone; her Heav'nly form
Angelic, but more soft, and Feminine,
Her graceful Innocence, her every Air
Of gesture or lest action overawd
His Malice, and with rapine sweet bereav'd
His fierceness of the fierce intent it brought:
That space the Evil one abstracted stood
From his own evil, and for the time remaind
Stupidly good, of enmitie disarm'd,
Of guile, of hate, of envie, of revenge;
But the hot Hell that alwayes in him burns,
Though in mid Heav'n, soon ended his delight,
And tortures him now more, the more he sees
Of pleasure not for him ordain'd: then soon
Fierce hate he recollects, and all his thoughts
Of mischief, gratulating, thus excites.
    Thoughts, whither have ye led me, with what sweet
Compulsion thus transported to forget
What hither brought us, hate, not love, nor hope
Of Paradise for Hell, hope here to taste
Of pleasure, but all pleasure to destroy,
Save what is in destroying, other joy
To me is lost.

d. *Paradise Lost* VIII.460-89

Mine eyes he clos'd, but op'n left the Cell
Of Fancie my internal sight, by which
Abstract as in a transe methought I saw,
Though sleeping, where I lay, and saw the shape

Still glorious before whom awake I stood;
Who stooping op'n'd my left side, and took
From thence a Rib, with cordial spirits warm,
And Life-blood streaming fresh; wide was the wound,
But suddenly with flesh fill'd up and heal'd:
The Rib he formd and fashiond with his hands;
Under his forming hands a Creature grew,
Manlike, but different sex, so lovely fair,
That what seemd fair in all the World, seemd now
Mean, or in her summ'd up, in her contain
And in her looks, which from that time infus'd
Sweetness into my heart, unfelt before,
And into all things from her Air inspir'd
The spirit of love and amorous delight.
Shee disappeerd, and left me dark, I wak'd
To find her, or for ever to deplore
Her loss, and other pleasures all abjure:
When out of hope, behold her, not farr off,
Such as I saw her in my dream, adornd
With what all Earth or Heaven could bestow
To make her amiable: On she came,
Led by her Heav'nly Maker, though unseen,
And guided by his voice, nor uninformd
Of nuptial Sanctitie and marriage Rites:
Grace was in all her steps, Heav'n in her Eye,
In every gesture dignitie and love.

5. Wollstonecraft

From *Posthumous Works* 2: 175-82

LESSONS.

The first book of a series which I intended to have written for my unfortunate girl.[1]

LESSON I.

CAT. Dog. Cow. Horse. Sheep. Pig. Bird. Fly.
Man. Boy. Girl. Child.
Head. Hair. Face. Nose. Mouth. Chin. Neck. Arms.
Hand. Leg. Foot. Back. Breast.
House. Wall. Field. Street. Stone. Grass.
Bed. Chair. Door. Pot. Spoon. Knife. Fork. Plate.
Cup. Box. Boy. Bell.
Tree. Leaf. Stick. Whip. Cart. Coach.
Frock. Hat. Coat. Shoes. Shift. Cap.
Bread. Milk. Tea. Meat. Drink. Cake.

LESSON II.

COME. Walk. Run. Go. Jump. Dance. Ride. Sit.
Stand. Play. Hold. Shake. Speak. Sing. Cry. Laugh. Call.
Fall.
Day. Night. Sun. Moon. Light. Dark. Sleep. Wake.
Wash. Dress. Kiss. Comb.
Fire. Hot. Burn. Wind. Rain. Cold.
Hurt. Tear. Break. Spill.
Book. See. Look.
Sweet. Good. Clean.
Gone. Lost. Hide. Keep. Give. Take.
One. Two. Three. Four. Five. Six. Seven. Eight.
Nine. Ten.
White. Black. Red. Blue. Green. Brown.

---

1 This title which is indorsed on the back of the manuscript, I conclude to have been written in a period of desperation, in the month of October, 1795. EDITOR. [Godwin's note; Wollstonecraft attempted suicide in October 1795. Her "unfortunate girl" is her first daughter, Fanny Imlay (1794-1816), Shelley's half-sister.]

LESSON III.

STROKE the cat. Play with the Dog. Eat the bread. Drink the milk. Hold the cup. Lay down the knife.

Look at the fly. See the horse. Shut the door. Bring the chair. Ring the bell. Get your book.

Hide your face. Wipe your nose. Wash your hands. Dirty hands. Why do you cry? A clean mouth. Shake hands. I love you. Kiss me now. Good girl.

The bird sings. The fire burns. The cat jumps. The dog runs. The bird flies. The cow lies down. The man laughs. The child cries.

LESSON IV.

LET me comb your head. Ask Betty to wash your face. Go and see for some bread. Drink milk, if you are dry. Play on the floor with the ball. Do not touch the ink; you will black your hands.

What do you want to say to me? Speak slow, not so fast. Did you fall? You will not cry, not you; the baby cries. Will you walk in the fields?

LESSON V.

COME to me, my little girl. Are you tired of playing? Yes. Sit down and rest yourself, while I talk to you.

Have you seen the baby? Poor little thing. O here it comes. Look at him. How helpless he is. Four years ago you were as feeble as this very little boy.

See, he cannot hold up his head. He is forced to lie on his back, if his mamma do not turn him to the right or left side, he will soon begin to cry. He cries to tell her, that he is tired with lying on his back.

LESSON VI.

PERHAPS he is hungry. What shall we give him to eat? Poor fellow, he cannot eat. Look in his mouth, he has no teeth.

How did you do when you were a baby like him? You cannot tell. Do you want to know? Look then at the dog, with her pretty puppy. You could not help yourself as well as the puppy. You could only open your mouth, when you were lying, like William, on my knee. So I put you to my breast, and you sucked, as the puppy sucks now, for there was milk enough for you.

WHEN you were hungry, you began to cry, because you could not speak. You were seven months without teeth, always sucking. But after you got one, you began to gnaw a crust of bread. It was not long before another came pop. At ten months you had four pretty white teeth, and you used to bite me. Poor mamma! Still I did not cry, because I am not a child, but you hurt me very much. So I said to papa, it is time the little girl should eat. She is not naughty, yet she hurts me. I have given her a crust of bread, and I must look for some other milk.

The cow has got plenty, and her jumping calf eats grass very well. He has got more teeth than my little girl. Yes, says papa, and he tapped you on the cheek, you are old enough to learn to eat? Come to me, and I will teach you, my little dear, for you must not hurt poor mamma, who has given you her milk, when you could not take any thing else.

Appendix D: Reviews of Frankenstein

[*Frankenstein* enjoyed enormous success and was reviewed in all the major literary magazines of the day. Of the many favourable reviews, we provide two of the more noteworthy (*Blackwood's Edinburgh Magazine* and *The Edinburgh Magazine*), one of the most scathing (*Quarterly Review*), and one by Shelley in support of his wife (*Athenaeum*), written in 1818 but not published until 1832, ten years after his death.]

1. "Remarks on Frankenstein, or the Modern Prometheus; a Novel" [by Walter Scott], *Blackwood's Edinburgh Magazine* 2 (1818): 613-20

> Did I request thee, Maker, from my clay
> To mould me man? Did I solicit thee
> From darkness to promote me? ———
>
> *Paradise Lost.*

THIS is a novel, or more properly a romantic fiction, of a nature so peculiar, that we ought to describe the species before attempting any account of the individual production.

The first general division of works of fiction, into such as bound the events they narrate by the actual laws of nature, and such as, passing these limits, are managed by marvellous and supernatural machinery, is sufficiently obvious and decided. But the class of marvellous romances admits of several subdivisions. In the earlier productions of imagination, the poet or tale-teller does not, in his own opinion, transgress the laws of credibility, when he introduces into his narration the witches, goblins, and magicians, in the existence of which he himself, as well as his hearers, is a firm believer. This good faith, however, passes away, and works turning upon the marvellous are written and read merely on account of the exercise which they afford to the imagination of those who, like the poet Collins, love to riot in the luxuriance of oriental fiction, to rove through the meanders of enchantment, to gaze on the magnificence of golden palaces, and to repose by the waterfalls of Elysian gardens. In this species of composition, the marvellous is itself the principal and most important object both to the author and reader. To describe its effect upon the mind of the human personages engaged in its wonders, and dragged along by its machinery, is comparatively an inferior object. The hero and heroine, partakers of the supernatural character which belongs to their adventures, walk the maze of enchantment with a firm and undaunted step, and appear as much at their ease, amid the wonders around them, as the young fellow described by the Spectator, who was discovered taking a snuff with great composure in the midst of a stormy ocean, represented on the stage of the Opera.[1]

A more philosophical and refined use of the supernatural in works of fiction, is proper to that class in which the laws of nature are represented as altered, not for the purpose of pampering the imagination with wonders, but in order to shew the probable effect which the supposed miracles would produce on those who witnessed them. In this case, the pleasure ordinarily derived from the marvellous incidents is secondary to that which we extract from observing how mortals like ourselves would be affected,

> By scenes like these which, daring to depart
> From sober truth, are still to nature true.[2]

Even in the description of his marvels, however, the author, who manages this style of composition with address, gives them an indirect importance with the reader, when he is able to describe, with nature and with truth, the effects which they are calculated to produce upon his dramatis personae. It will be remembered, that the sapient Partridge was too wise to be terrified at the mere appearance of the ghost of Hamlet, whom he knew to be a man dressed up in pasteboard armour for the nonce: it was when he saw the "little man," as he called Garrick, so frightened, that a sympathetic horror took hold of him.[3] Of this we shall presently produce some examples from the narrative before us. But success in this point is still subordinate to the author's principal object, which is less to produce an effect by means of the marvels of the narrations, than to open new trains and channels of thought, by placing men in supposed situations of an extraordinary and preternatural character, and then describing the mode of feeling and conduct which they are most likely to adopt.

To make more clear the distinction we have endeavoured to draw between the marvellous and the effects of the marvellous, considered as separate objects, we may briefly invite our readers to compare the common tale of Tom Thumb with Gulliver's Voyage to Brobdingnag; one of the most childish fictions, with one which is pregnant with wit and satire, yet both turning upon the same assumed possibility of the

---

1 Richard Steele, *The Spectator* 14; 16 March 1711.
2 William Collins (1721-59), "An Ode on the Popular Superstitions of the Highlands of Scotland, Considered as the Subject of Poetry" 188-89.
3 Henry Fielding, *Tom Jones* XVI.5.

existence of a pigmy among a race of giants. In the former case, when the imagination of the story-teller has exhausted itself in every species of hyperbole, in order to describe the diminutive size of his hero, the interest of the tale is at an end; but in the romance of the Dean of St Patrick's, the exquisite humour with which the natural consequences of so strange and unusual a situation is detailed, has a canvass on which to expand itself, as broad as the luxuriance even of the author's talents could desire. Gulliver stuck into a marrow bone, and Master Thomas Thumb's disastrous fall into the bowl of hasty-pudding, are, in the general outline, kindred incidents; but the jest is exhausted in the latter case, when the accident is told; whereas in the former, it lies not so much in the comparatively pigmy size which subjected Gulliver to such a ludicrous misfortune, as in the tone of grave and dignified feeling with which he resents the disgrace of the incident.[1]

In the class of fictitious narrations to which we allude, the author opens a sort of account-current with the reader; drawing upon him, in the first place, for credit to that degree of the marvellous which he proposes to employ; and becoming virtually bound, in consequence of this indulgence, that his personages shall conduct themselves, in the extraordinary circumstances in which they are placed, according to the rules of probability, and the nature of the human heart. In this view, the *probable* is far from being laid out of sight even amid the wildest freaks of imagination; on the contrary, we grant the extraordinary postulates which the author demands as the foundation of his narrative, only on condition of his deducing the consequences with logical precision.

We have only to add, that this class of fiction has been sometimes applied to the purposes of political satire, and sometimes to the general illustration of the powers and workings of the human mind. Swift, Bergerac, and others, have employed it for the former purpose, and a good illustration of the latter is the well known Saint Leon of William Godwin. In this latter work, assuming the possibility of the transmutation of metals and of the *elixir vitae*, the author has deduced, in the course of his narrative, the probable consequences of the possession of such secrets upon the fortunes and mind of him who might enjoy them. Frankenstein is a novel upon the same plan with Saint Leon; it is said to be written by Mr Percy Bysshe Shelley, who, if we are rightly informed, is son-in-law to Mr Godwin; and it is inscribed to that ingenious author.

---

1 Jonathan Swift, *Gulliver's Travels* II.iii. In *The History of Tom Thumbe* (1621), by Richard Johnson, the earliest surviving version of the story, Tom falls into the bowl where his mother is making black puddings (Chapter 4). The version Scott has in mind has not been identified. It is probably Scottish, since "hasty-pudding" is porridge.

[Scott proceeds to summarize the plot of the novel. He takes exception to the monster's account of his education:]

The most material part of his education was acquired in a ruinous pig-stye—a Lyceum which this strange student occupied, he assures us, for a good many months undiscovered, and in constant observance of the motions of an amiable family, from imitating whom, he learns the use of language, and other accomplishments, much more successfully than Caliban, though the latter had a conjuror to his tutor.[1] This detail is not only highly improbable, but it is injudicious, as its unnecessary minuteness tends rather too much to familiarize us with the being whom it regards, and who loses, by this *lengthy* oration, some part of the mysterious sublimity annexed to his first appearance.

[Scott then continues his summary, up to the monster's final suicide threat.]

Whether this singular being executed his purpose or not must necessarily remain an uncertainty, unless the voyage of discovery to the north pole should throw any light on the subject.

So concludes this extraordinary tale, in which the author seems to us to disclose uncommon powers of poetic imagination. The feeling with which we perused the unexpected and fearful, yet, allowing the possibility of the event, very natural conclusion of Frankenstein's experiment, shook a little even our firm nerves; although such, and so numerous have been the expedients for exciting terror employed by the romantic writers of the age, that the reader may adopt Macbeth's words, with a slight alteration:

> "We have supp'd full with horrors:
> Direness, familiar to our 'callous' thoughts,
> Cannot once startle us."[2]

It is no slight merit in our eyes, that the tale, though wild in incident, is written in plain and forcible English, without exhibiting that mixture of hyperbolical Germanisms with which tales of wonder are usually told, as if it were necessary that the language should be as extravagant as the fiction. The ideas of the author are always clearly as well as forcibly expressed; and his descriptions of landscape have in them the choice requisites of truth, freshness, precision, and beauty. The self-education of the monster, considering the slender opportunities of acquiring knowledge that he possessed, we have already noticed as improbable and overstrained. That he should have not only learned to speak, but to

---

1 In fact, the tutor was the conjuror's daughter, Miranda: *The Tempest* I.ii.355-65.

2 Adapted from *Macbeth* V.v.13-15.

read, and, for aught we know, to write—that he should have become acquainted with Werter, with Plutarch's Lives, and with Paradise Lost, by listening through a hole in a wall, seems as unlikely as that he should have acquired, in the same way, the problems of Euclid, or the art of book-keeping by single and double entry. The author has however two apologies—the first, the necessity that his monster should acquire those endowments, and the other, that his neighbours were engaged in teaching the language of the country to a young foreigner. His progress in self-knowledge, and the acquisition of information, is, after all, more wonderful than that of Hai Eben Yokhdan, or Automathes, or the hero of the little romance called the Child of Nature, one of which works might perhaps suggest the train of ideas followed by the author of Frankenstein.[1] We should also be disposed, in support of the principles with which we set out, to question whether the monster, how tall, agile, and strong however, could have perpetrated so much mischief undiscovered; or passed through so many countries without being secured, either on account of his crimes, or for the benefit of some such speculator as Mr Polito, who would have been happy to have added to his museum so curious a specimen of natural history.[2] But as we have consented to admit the leading incident of the work, perhaps some of our readers may be of opinion, that to stickle upon lesser improbabilities, is to incur the censure bestowed by the Scottish proverb on those who start at straws after swallowing *windlings*.[3]

The following lines, which occur in the second volume, mark, we think, that the author possesses the same facility in expressing himself in verse as in prose.

[Quotes the lines from P.B. Shelley's "Mutability."]

Upon the whole, the work impresses us with a high idea of the author's original genius and happy power of expression. We shall be delighted to hear that he has aspired to the *paullo majora*;[4] and, in the

---

1 Scott is thinking of three novels about autodidacts. The hero of Abu Jafar Abu Bakr Ibn Al-Tufail's *An Account of the Oriental Philosophy, Shewing the Profound Wisdom of Hai Ebn Yokdan*, trans. G. Keith (1674), grows up on a desert island. John Kirkby's *The Capacity and Extent of Human Understanding Exemplified in the Extraordinary Case of Automathes* (1745) is an imitation of *Hai Ebn Yokdan*: "Automathes" means "self-taught." *The Child of Nature*, by the Encyclopedist Claude Helvétius, was translated in 1774. There is no evidence that Shelley knew any of these works.

2 S. Polito (d. 1814) claimed to have the largest travelling menagerie in all of Europe.

3 Whole bundles of straw. The *OED* gives a more plausible version of the proverb: "He stumbles at a strae and lowps o'er a wonlyne."

4 From Vergil's *Eclogues*: "paulo maiora canamus [let us sing of somewhat higher things]" (IV.1).

meantime, congratulate our readers upon a novel which excites new reflections and untried sources of emotion. If Gray's definition of Paradise, to lie on a couch, namely, and read new novels, come any thing near truth, no small praise is due to him, who, like the author of Frankenstein, has enlarged the sphere of that fascinating enjoyment.

2. *The Edinburgh Magazine, and Literary Miscellany* 2 (1818): 249-53

HERE is one of the productions of the modern school in its highest style of caricature and exaggeration. It is formed on the Godwinian manner, and has all the faults, but many likewise of the beauties of that model. In dark and gloomy views of nature and of man, bordering too closely on impiety,—in the most outrageous improbability,—in sacrificing every thing to effect,—it even goes beyond its great prototype; but in return, it possesses a similar power of fascination, something of the same mastery in harsh and savage delineations of passion, relieved in like manner by the gentler features of domestic and simple feelings. There never was a wilder story imagined, yet, like most of the fictions of this age, it has an air of reality attached to it, by being connected with the favourite projects and passions of the times. The real events of the world have, in our day, too, been of so wondrous and gigantic a kind,— the shiftings of the scenes in our stupendous drama have been so rapid and various, that Shakespeare himself, in his wildest flights, has been completely distanced by the eccentricities of actual existence. Even he would scarcely have dared to have raised, in one act, a private adventurer to the greatest of European thrones,—to have conducted him, in the next, victorious over the necks of emperors and kings, and then, in a third, to have shewn him an exile, in a remote speck of an island, some thousands of miles from the scene of his triumphs; and the chariot which bore him along covered with glory, quietly exhibited to a gaping mechanical rabble under the roof of one of the beautiful buildings on the North Bridge of Edinburgh.... Our appetite, we say, for every sort of wonder and vehement interest, has in this way become so desperately inflamed, that especially as the world around us has again settled into its old dull state of happiness and legitimacy, we can be satisfied with nothing in fiction that is not highly coloured and exaggerated; we even like a story the better that it is disjointed and irregular, and our greatest inventors, accordingly, have been obliged to accommodate themselves to the taste of the age, more, we believe, than their own judgment can, at all times, have approved of. The very extravagance of the present production will now, therefore, be, perhaps, in its favour, since the events which have actually passed before our eyes have made the atmosphere of miracles that in which we most readily breathe.

[The reviewer summarizes the plot.]

Such is a sketch of this singular performance, in which there is much power and beauty, both of thought and expression, though, in many parts, the execution is imperfect, and bearing the marks of an unpractised hand. It is one of those works, however, which, when we have read, we do not well see why it should have been written;—for a *jeu d'esprit* it is somewhat too long, grave, and laborious,—and some of our highest and most reverential feelings receive a shock from the conception on which it turns, so as to produce a painful and bewildered state of mind while we peruse it. We are accustomed, happily, to look upon the creation of a living and intelligent being as a work that is fitted only to inspire a religious emotion, and there is an impropriety, to say no worse, in placing it in any other light. It might, indeed, be the author's view to shew that the powers of man have been wisely limited, and that misery would follow their extension,—but still the expression "Creator," applied to a mere human being, gives us the same sort of shock with the phrase, "the Man Almighty," and others of the same kind, in Mr Southey's "Curse of Kehama."[1] All these monstrous conceptions are the consequences of the wild and irregular theories of the age; though we do not at all mean to infer that the authors who give into such freedoms have done so with any bad intentions. This incongruity, however, with our established and most sacred notions, is the chief fault in such fictions, regarding them merely in a critical point of view. Shakespeare's Caliban (though his simplicity and suitableness to the place where he is found are very delightful) is, perhaps, a more *hateful* being than our good friend in this book. But Caliban comes into existence in the received way which common superstition had pointed out; we should not have endured him if Prospero had created him. Getting over this original absurdity, the character of our monster is in good keeping;—there is a grandeur, too, in the scenery in which he makes his appearances,—the ice-mountains of the Pole, or the glaciers of the Alps;—his natural tendency to kind feelings, and the manner in which they were blighted,—and all the

---

1   The villain of Robert Southey's Orientalist epic *The Curse of Kehama* (1810) is repeatedly described as "Almighty" (II.26, 136, IV.70, 129, VI.71-73, 121, VII.113, 304, VIII.154, XI.270, XII.116, XVIII.50, XX.17, 38, XXII.71, XXIII.140, XXIV.18, 76, 119, 138, 164, 177), as "Omnipotent" (VII.278, XXIV.209), as "the King of Men" (XVIII.59), and even as "the Man-God" (XXIV.69, 119). The point of Southey's blasphemy is that Kehama, like Victor, is a man of overwhelming ambition: he literally wants to be a god. Like Victor, he finds that his ambition is his undoing. Shelley read the poem in 1814 and 1815 (*Journals* 2: 677).

domestic picture of the cottage, are very interesting and beautiful. We hope yet to have more productions, both from this author and his great model, Mr Godwin; but they would make a great improvement in their writings, if they would rather study the established order of nature as it appears, both in the world of matter and of mind, than continue to revolt our feelings by hazardous innovations in either of these departments.

3. [John Wilson Croker], *Quarterly Review* 18 (1817-18): 379-85

[Croker begins his review with a summary and then comments:]
OUR readers will guess from this summary, what a tissue of horrible and disgusting absurdity this work presents.—It is piously dedicated to Mr. Godwin, and is written in the spirit of his school. The dreams of insanity are embodied in the strong and striking language of the insane, and the author, notwithstanding the rationality of his preface, often leaves us in doubt whether he is not as mad as his hero. Mr. Godwin is the patriarch of a literary family, whose chief skill is in delineating the wanderings of the intellect, and which strangely delights in the most afflicting and humiliating of human miseries. His disciples are a kind of *out-pensioners of Bedlam*, and, like 'Mad Bess' or 'Mad Tom,' are occasionally visited with paroxysms of genius and fits of expression, which make sober-minded people wonder and shudder.

We shall give our readers a very favourable specimen of the vigour of fancy and language with which this work is written, by extracting from it the three passages which struck us the most on our perusal of it.

[Croker quotes Victor's account of the animation of the monster and his nightmare, his account of meeting the monster on the Mer de Glace, and Walton's description of the monster in his cabin.]

It cannot be denied that this is nonsense—but it is nonsense decked out with circumstances and clothed in language highly terrific: it is, indeed,

> ——————————— 'a tale
> Told by an ideot, full of sound and fury,
> Signifying nothing—'[1]

but still there is something tremendous in the unmeaning hollowness of its sound, and the vague obscurity of its images.

---

1 *Macbeth* V.v.26-28.

But when we have thus admitted that Frankenstein has passages which appal the mind and make the flesh creep, we have given it all the praise (if praise it can be called) which we dare to bestow. Our taste and our judgment alike revolt at this kind of writing, and the greater the ability with which it may be executed the worse it is—it inculcates no lesson of conduct, manners, or morality; it cannot mend, and will not even amuse its readers, unless their taste have been deplorably vitiated—it fatigues the feelings without interesting the understanding; it gratuitously harasses the heart, and wantonly adds to the store, already too great, of painful sensations. The author has powers, both of conception and language, which employed in a happier direction might, perhaps, (we speak dubiously,) give him a name among those whose writings amuse or amend their fellow-creatures; but we take the liberty of assuring him, and hope that he may be in a temper to listen to us, that the style which he has adopted in the present publication merely tends to defeat his own purpose, if he really had any other object in view than that of leaving the wearied reader, after a struggle between laughter and loathing, in doubt whether the head or the heart of the author be the most diseased.

4. P.B. Shelley, "On 'Frankenstein,'" *Athenaeum* (10 November 1832): 730

THE novel of "Frankenstein, or The Modern Prometheus," is undoubtedly, as a mere story, one of the most original and complete productions of the day. We debate with ourselves in wonder, as we read it, what could have been the series of thoughts—what could have been the peculiar experiences that awakened them—which conduced, in the author's mind, to the astonishing combinations of motives and incidents, and the startling catastrophe, which compose this tale. There are, perhaps, some points of subordinate importance, which prove that it is the author's first attempt. But in this judgment, which requires a very nice discrimination, we may be mistaken; for it is conducted throughout with a firm and steady hand. The interest gradually accumulates and advances towards the conclusion with the accelerated rapidity of a rock rolled down a mountain. We are led breathless with suspense and sympathy, and the heaping up of incident on incident, and the working of passion out of passion. We cry "hold, hold! enough!"[1]—but there is yet something to come; and, like the victim whose history it relates, we think we can bear no more, and yet more is to be borne. Pelion is heaped on Ossa, and Ossa on Olympus.[2] We

1 Shakespeare, *Macbeth* V.viii.34.
2 Virgil, *Georgics* I.281-82.

climb Alp after Alp, until the horizon is seen blank, vacant, and limitless; and the head turns giddy, and the ground seems to fail under our feet.

This novel rests its claim on being a source of powerful and profound emotion. The elementary feelings of the human mind are exposed to view; and those who are accustomed to reason deeply on their origin and tendency will, perhaps, be the only persons who can sympathize, to the full extent, in the interest of the actions which are their result. But, founded on nature as they are, there is perhaps no reader, who can endure anything beside a new love-story, who will not feel a responsive string touched in his inmost soul. The sentiments are so affectionate and so innocent—the characters of the subordinate agents in this strange drama are clothed in the light of such a mild and gentle mind—the pictures of domestic manners are of the most simple and attaching character: the [pathos][1] is irresistible and deep. Nor are the crimes and malevolence of the single Being, though indeed withering and tremendous, the offspring of any unaccountable propensity to evil, but flow irresistibly from certain causes fully adequate to their production. They are the children, as it were, of Necessity and Human Nature. In this the direct moral of the book consists; and it is perhaps the most important, and of the most universal application, of any moral that can be enforced by example. Treat a person ill, and he will become wicked. Requite affection with scorn;—let one being be selected, for whatever cause, as the refuse of his kind—divide him, a social being, from society, and you impose upon him the irresistible obligations—malevolence and selfishness. It is thus that, too often in society, those who are best qualified to be its benefactors and its ornaments, are branded by some accident with scorn, and changed, by neglect and solitude of heart, into a scourge and a curse.

The Being in "Frankenstein" is, no doubt, a tremendous creature. It was impossible that he should not have received among men that treatment which led to the consequences of his being a social nature. He was an abortion and an anomaly; and though his mind was such as its first impressions framed it, affectionate and full of moral sensibility, yet the circumstances of his existence are so monstrous and uncommon, that, when the consequences of them became developed in action, his original goodness was gradually turned into inextinguishable misanthropy and revenge. The scene between the Being and the blind De Lacey in the cottage, is one of the most profound and extraordinary instances of pathos that we ever recollect. It is impossible to read this dialogue,—and indeed many others of a somewhat similar character,—without feeling the heart suspend its pulsations

---

1 The *Athenaeum* reads "father's," an obvious error.

with wonder, and the "tears stream down the cheeks." The encounter and argument between Frankenstein and the Being on the sea of ice, almost approaches, in effect, to the expostulation of Caleb Williams with Falkland. It reminds us, indeed, somewhat of the style and character of that admirable writer, to whom the author has dedicated his work, and whose productions he seems to have studied.

There is only one instance, however, in which we detect the least approach to imitation; and that is the conduct of the incident of Frankenstein's landing in Ireland. The general character of the tale, indeed, resembles nothing that ever preceded it. After the death of Elizabeth, the story, like a stream which grows at once more rapid and profound as it proceeds, assumes an irresistible solemnity, and the magnificent energy and swiftness of a tempest.

The churchyard scene, in which Frankenstein visits the tombs of his family, his quitting Geneva, and his journey through Tartary to the shores of the Frozen Ocean, resemble at once the terrible reanimation of a corpse and the supernatural career of a spirit. The scene in the cabin of Walton's ship—the more than mortal enthusiasm and grandeur of the Being's speech over the dead body of his victim—is an exhibition of intellectual and imaginative power, which we think the reader will acknowledge has seldom been surpassed.

Appendix E: *Richard Brinsley Peake,* Presumption; or, The Fate of Frankenstein *(1823)*

[Gothic melodrama, with its exaggerated plot, character, and emotional appeal, first appeared on the English stage in 1802, with *A Tale of Mystery* by Thomas Holcroft (1745-1809). *Frankenstein* provided rich melodramatic material for the stage; the summer of 1823 saw two different theatrical adaptations. Peake's production, which Mary saw on 29 August 1823, summarized the plot but added melodramatic effects.]

ACT II, SCENE V

Evening.—Interior of the cottage of De Lacey.—The thatched roof in sight. A wood fire.—Through an open rustic porch are visible a rivulet, and small wooden bridge—a wooden couch—Music.—De Lacey discovered seated thereon, with Agatha next him in attendance. The Monster appears through the portico, watching them, and regards Agatha with rapture.—Agatha kisses her father's hand, takes a small pail or hand bucket, and trips through the portico on to the bridge to procure water. The Monster having retreated on Agatha's approach, pursues her on the bridge. Agatha, turning suddenly perceives the Monster, screams loudly, and swoons, falling into the rivulet. The Monster leaps from the bridge, and rescues her.

DEL. (*Speaks during the melo-music.*) Gracious Heaven! (*Starting forward from the couch.*) That cry of horror! Agatha!—Despair!—My sweet child where art you? Agatha! Agatha!

The Monster appears at the portico entrance, with Agatha insensible in his arms. The Monster comes forward, gently places Agatha in her father's arms, tenderly guiding the hand of old De Lacey to support his daughter. Agatha recovers, and perceiving the Monster, with a shriek, faints—the Monster hovering over them with fondness.—Felix, with his gun (loaded), suddenly enters through the open portico, and speaks whilst entering.

FELIX. Agatha! Victor Frankenstein is here! What horrid monster is this! Agatha! My father in danger!

Music.—The Monster retreats, Felix following him—discharges his gun— wounds the Monster in the shoulder—who writhes under the agony of the wound from which the blood flows—would rush on Felix, who keeps the gun presented—he is deterred by fear of a repetition of the wound. Felix remaining on the defensive.—Safie, alarmed at the firing of the gun by Felix, rushes on to Agatha and De Lacey.—Enter Frankenstein through the portico. The Monster rushes up to Frankenstein, and casts himself at his feet, imploring protection.

FRANK. Misery! The Fiend! Hence, avoid me! Do not approach me—thy horrid contact would spread a pestilence throughout my veins!—hence—no, no! You shall not quit this spot—but thus—thus I destroy the wretch I have created!

Music.—Frankenstein endeavours to stab him with his dagger, which the Monster strikes from his hand—and expresses that his kindly feeling[s] towards the human race, have been met by abhorrence and violence; that they are all now converted into hate and vengeance.—In desperation, the Monster pulls a flaming brand from the fire, and in agony of feeling, dashes through the portico, setting fire to the whole of the portico, and the entire back of the cottage—the thatched roof and rafters.

FELIX. Ha! Frankenstein! 'tis no time to parley—the cottage is on fire! That fierce gigantic figure of terrific aspect waves aloft his torch, as if in triumph of the deed.

The large doors in the centre are suddenly closed from without, as if to prevent escape. A coarse yelling laugh is heard.

FRANK. Ha! 'Tis that hideous voice! Quick, quick, let us fly! His hellish malice pursues me, and but with his death or mine, will this persecution cease. Could I but place you beyond his power.

Felix and Frankenstein (as soon as the Monster disappears, having climbed outside of the portico) force open the doors, when flaming faggots are thrown down at the portico entrance, and falling trees on fire block up the entrance. Felix and Frankenstein place the couch longways over the fallen trees, and fiery pile of faggots at the portico entrance, and Felix forces his way through the flames with old De Lacey, and then Safie—and, lastly, Frankenstein rushes out, bearing Agatha in his arms over the couch, in the midst of which parts of the building fall. The Monster brandishing the burning brand on the bridge, laughs exultingly, on which the drop falls.—Continue the 'Presto music' until

END OF ACT II

Appendix F: Lord Byron, "A Fragment" (1819)

[George Gordon, Lord Byron's (1788-1824) untitled contribution to the ghost stories was composed in an old account book of his wife's; the manuscript now resides in the Brotherton Collection of the Leeds University Library. When Polidori's "The Vampyre" was published in Henry Colburn's *New Monthly Magazine* on 1 April 1819, it was attributed to Lord Byron. Byron then sent his publisher, John Murray, the "Fragment" manuscript in order to prove that he was not responsible for Polidori's tale. Byron gave Murray permission to publish the "Fragment" in *The Edinburgh Magazine* with an explanation of its origin and how it differs from "The Vampyre," but instead, Murray appended it to Byron's *Mazeppa* (1819), without any prefatory remarks.]

June 17, 1816.

IN the year 17—, having for some time determined on a journey through countries not hitherto much frequented by travellers, I set out, accompanied by a friend, whom I shall designate by the name of Augustus Darvell. He was a few years my elder, and a man of considerable fortune and ancient family—advantages which an extensive capacity prevented him alike from undervaluing or over-rating. Some peculiar circumstances in his private history had rendered him to me an object of attention, of interest, and even of regard, which neither the reserve of his manners, nor occasional indications of an inquietude at times nearly approaching to alienation of mind, could extinguish.

I was yet young in life, which I had begun early; but my intimacy with him was of a recent date: we had been educated at the same schools and university; but his progress through these had preceded mine, and he had been deeply initiated into what is called the world, while I was yet in my noviciate. While thus engaged, I had heard much both of his past and present life; and although in these accounts there were many and irreconcileable contradictions, I could still gather from the whole that he was a being of no common order, and one who, whatever pains he might take to avoid remark, would still be remarkable. I had cultivated his acquaintance subsequently, and endeavoured to obtain his friendship, but this last appeared to be unattainable; whatever affections he might have possessed seemed now, some to have been extinguished, and others to be concentred: that his feelings were acute, I had sufficient opportunities of observing; for, although he could control, he could not altogether disguise them: still he had a power of giving to one passion the appearance of another in such a manner that it was difficult to define the nature of what was working within him; and the expressions of his features would vary so rapidly, though slightly, that it was useless to trace them to their sources. It was evident that he was a prey to some cureless disquiet; but whether it arose from ambition, love, remorse, grief, from one or all of these, or merely from a morbid temperament akin to disease, I could not discover: there were circumstances alleged, which might have justified the application to each of these causes; but, as I have before said, these were so contradictory and contradicted, that none could be fixed upon with accuracy. Where there is mystery, it is generally supposed that there must also be evil: I know not how this may be, but in him there certainly was the one, though I could not ascertain the extent of the other—and felt loth, as far as regarded himself, to believe in its existence. My advances were received with sufficient coldness; but I was young, and not easily discouraged, and at length succeeded in obtaining, to a certain degree, that common-place intercourse and moderate confidence of common and every day concerns, created and cemented by similarity of pursuit and frequency of meeting, which is called intimacy, or friendship, according to the ideas of him who uses those words to express them.

Darvell had already travelled extensively; and to him I had applied for information with regard to the conduct of my intended journey. It was my secret wish that he might be prevailed on to accompany me: it was also a probable hope, founded upon the shadowy restlessness which I had observed in him, and to which the animation which he appeared to feel on such subjects, and his apparent indifference to all by which he was more immediately surrounded, gave fresh strength. This wish I first hinted, and then expressed: his answer, though I had partly expected it, gave me all the pleasure of surprise—he consented; and, after the requisite arrangements, we commenced our voyages. After journeying through various countries of the south of Europe, our attention was turned towards the East, according to our original destination; and it was in my progress through those regions that the incident occurred upon which will turn what I may have to relate.

The constitution of Darvell, which must from his appearance have been in early life more than usually robust, had been for some time gradually giving way, without the intervention of any apparent disease: he had neither cough nor hectic, yet he became daily more enfeebled: his habits were temperate, and he neither declined nor complained of fatigue, yet he was evidently wasting away: he became more and more silent and sleepless, and at length so seriously altered, that my alarm grew proportionate to what I conceived to be his danger.

We had determined, on our arrival at Smyrna, on an excursion to the ruins of Ephesus and Sardis,[1] from which I endeavoured to dissuade him in his present state of indisposition—but in vain: there appeared to be an oppression on his mind, and a solemnity in his manner, which ill corresponded with his eagerness to proceed on what I regarded as a mere party of pleasure, little suited to a valetudinarian; but I opposed him no longer—and in a few days we set off together, accompanied only by a serrugee and a single janizary.[2]

We had passed halfway towards the remains of Ephesus, leaving behind us the more fertile environs of Smyrna, and were entering upon that wild and tenantless track through the marshes and defiles which lead to the few huts yet lingering over the broken columns of Diana—the roofless walls of expelled Christianity, and the still more recent but complete desolation of abandoned mosques—when the sudden and rapid illness of my companion obliged us to halt at a Turkish cemetery, the turbaned tombstones of which were the sole indication that human life had ever been a sojourner in this wilderness. The only caravansera[3] we had seen was left some hours behind us, not a vestige of a town or even cottage was within sight or hope, and this "city of the dead"[4] appeared to be the sole refuge for my unfortunate friend, who seemed on the verge of becoming the last of its inhabitants.

In this situation, I looked round for a place where he might most conveniently repose:—contrary to the usual aspect of Mahometan burial-grounds, the cypresses were in this few in number, and these thinly scattered over its extent: the tombstones were mostly fallen, and worn with age:—upon one of the most considerable of these, and beneath one of the most spreading trees, Darvell supported himself, in a half-reclining posture, with great difficulty. He asked for water. I had some doubts of our being able to find any, and prepared to go in search of it with hesitating despondency—but he desired me to remain; and turning to Suleiman, our janizary, who stood by us smoking with great tranquillity, he said, "Suleiman, verbana su," (i.e.

---

1 Greek cities in what is now Turkey; the temple of Diana at Ephesus was one of the seven wonders of the classical world.

2 A driver and an élite member of the Turkish army, serving as an armed guard, respectively.

3 "Inn" (Farsi).

4 A literal translation of *necropolis*, the Greek word for cemetery; cf. Byron, "On the Star of 'The Legion of Honour'" (1815) 37-38.

bring some water,) and went on describing the spot where it was to be found with great minuteness, at a small well for camels, a few hundred yards to the right: the janizary obeyed. I said to Darvell, "How did you know this?"—He replied, "From our situation; you must perceive that this place was once inhabited, and could not have been so without springs: I have also been here before."

"You have been here before!—How came you never to mention this to me? and what could you be doing in a place where no one would remain a moment longer than they could help it?"

To this question I received no answer. In the mean time Suleiman returned with the water, leaving the serrugee and the horses at the fountain. The quenching of his thirst had the appearance of reviving him for a moment; and I conceived hopes of his being able to proceed, or at least to return, and I urged the attempt. He was silent—and appeared to be collecting his spirits for an effort to speak. He began.

"This is the end of my journey, and of my life—I came here to die: but I have a request to make, a command—for such my last words must be—You will observe it?"

"Most certainly; but have better hopes."

"I have no hopes, nor wishes, but this—conceal my death from every human being."

"I hope there will be no occasion; that you will recover, and—"

"Peace!—it must be so: promise this."

"I do."

"Swear it, by all that"—He here dictated an oath of great solemnity.

"There is no occasion for this—I will observe your request; and to doubt me is—"

"It cannot be helped,—you must swear."

I took the oath: it appeared to relieve him. He removed a seal ring from his finger, on which were some Arabic characters, and presented it to me. He proceeded—

"On the ninth day of the month, at noon precisely (what month you please, but this must be the day), you must fling this ring into the salt springs which run into the Bay of Eleusis:[1] the day after, at the same hour, you must repair to the ruins of the temple of Ceres, and wait one hour."

"Why?"

"You will see."

"The ninth day of the month, you say?"

"The ninth."

---

1 The Bay of Eleusis, near Athens, is the site of the Eleusinian Mysteries in honour of the goddess Demeter and especially in honour of the return of her daughter, Persephone, from the underworld.

As I observed that the present was the ninth day of the month, his countenance changed, and he paused. As he sate, evidently becoming more feeble, a stork, with a snake in her beak, perched upon a tombstone near us; and, without devouring her prey, appeared to be stedfastly regarding us. I know not what impelled me to drive it away, but the attempt was useless; she made a few circles in the air, and returned exactly to the same spot. Darvell pointed to it, and smiled: he spoke—I know not whether to himself or to me—but the words were only, "'Tis well!"

"What is well? what do you mean?"

"No matter: you must bury me here this evening, and exactly where that bird is now perched. You know the rest of my injunctions."

He then proceeded to give me several directions as to the manner in which his death might be best concealed. After these were finished, he exclaimed, "You perceive that bird?"

"Certainly."

"And the serpent writhing in her beak?"

"Doubtless: there is nothing uncommon in it; it is her natural prey.[1] But it is odd that she does not devour it."

He smiled in a ghastly manner, and said, faintly, "It is not yet time!" As he spoke, the stork flew away. My eyes followed it for a moment, it could hardly be longer than ten might be counted. I felt Darvell's weight, as it were, increase upon my shoulder, and, turning to look upon his face, perceived that he was dead!

I was shocked with the sudden certainty which could not be mistaken—his countenance in a few minutes became nearly black. I should have attributed so rapid a change to poison, had I not been aware that he had no opportunity of receiving it unperceived. The day was declining, the body was rapidly altering, and nothing remained but to fulfil his request. With the aid of Suleiman's ataghan and my own sabre, we scooped a shallow grave upon the spot which Darvell had indicated: the earth easily gave way, having already received some Mahometan tenant. We dug as deeply as the time permitted us, and throwing the dry earth upon all that remained of the singular being so lately departed, we cut a few sods of greener turf from the less withered soil around us, and laid them upon his sepulchre.

Between astonishment and grief, I was tearless.

---

1 Cf. Pliny (c. 23-79 CE), *Natural History* 10.31.

Appendix G: John William Polidori, The Vampyre: A Tale (1819)

[John William Polidori (1795-1821) graduated from the University of Edinburgh medical school in 1815, when he was 19. In 1816, he became Lord Byron's personal physician and travelled with him through Europe until he and Byron quarrelled at the end of the summer. In a footnote to his Introduction of *Ernestus Berchtold* (Longman and Company, 1819), Polidori explains that he wrote "The Vampyre" at the "request of a lady" who, after hearing from Polidori of Byron's 1816 "Fragment" story, apparently would not believe a credible narrative could be constructed on such a foundation. Polidori took up the challenge, and left the lady the manuscript after working on it "in the course of three mornings." When published in the *New Monthly Magazine* on 1 April 1819, it was attributed to Lord Byron. Both men were keen to note the correct authorship. Polidori's Lord Strongmore is the archetype of the modern vampire. "The Vampyre" was very successful; six book texts were issued in London in 1819 alone, with the second issue's title page reading "a tale related by Lord Byron to Dr. Polidori"—Polidori's only credit for the story.]

IT happened in the midst of the dissipations attendant upon a London winter, that there appeared at the various parties of the leaders of the *ton*[1] a nobleman, more remarkable for his singularities, than for his rank. He apparently gazed upon the mirth around him, as if he could not participate therein. It seemed as if, the light laughter of the fair only attracted his attention, that he might by a look quell it, and throw fear into those breasts where thoughtlessness reigned. Those who felt this sensation of awe, could not explain whence it arose: some attributed it to the glance of that dead grey eye, which, fixing upon the object's face, seemed not to penetrate, and at one look to pierce through to the inward workings of the heart; but to throw upon the cheek a leaden ray that weighed upon the skin it could not pass. Some however thought that it was caused by their fearing the observation of one, who by his colourless cheek, which never gained a warmer tint from the blush of conscious shame or from any powerful emotion, appeared to be above human feelings and sympathies, the fashionable names for frailties and sins. His peculiarities caused him to be invited

---

1   The fashion, the vogue (French); by extension, people of fashion.

to every house; all wished to see him, and those who had been accustomed to violent excitement, and now felt the weight of *ennui*, were pleased at having something in their presence capable of engaging their attention. Nay more in spite of the deadly hue of his finely turned head, many of the female hunters after notoriety attempted to win his attentions, and gain, at least, some marks of what they might term affection. Lady Mercer,[1] who had been the mockery of every monster shewn in drawing-rooms since her marriage, threw herself in his way, and did all but put on the dress of a mountebank, to attract his notice:—but in vain:—when she stood before him, though his eyes were apparently fixed upon her's, still it seemed as if they were unperceived;—even her unappalled impudence was baffled, and she left the field. Yet though the common adultress could not influence even the guidance of his eyes, it was not that the sex was indifferent to him: but such was the caution with which he spoke to the virtuous wife and innocent daughter, that few knew he ever addressed himself to females. He had, however, the reputation of a winning tongue; and whether it was that this even overcame the dread of his singular character, or that they were moved by his apparent hatred of vice, he was as often among those females who adorn the sex by their domestic virtues, as among those who sully it by their vices.

About the same time, there came to London a young gentleman of the name of Aubrey: he was an orphan left with an only sister in the possession of great wealth, by parents who died whilst he was yet in childhood. Left also to himself by guardians, who thought it their duty merely to take care of his fortune, while they relinquished the more important charge of his mind to the care of mercenary and negligent subalterns, he cultivated more his imagination than his judgment. He had, hence, that high romantic feeling of honour and candour, which daily ruins so many milliners' apprentices. He believed all to sympathise with virtue, and thought that vice was thrown in by Providence as by authors in Romances merely for the picturesque effect of the scene: he thought that the misery of a cottage merely consisted in the

---

1 A caricature of Lady Caroline Lamb, who had once visited Byron disguised as a page, and who would later attend a masquerade dressed as Don Juan (Marchand 129, 321). Polidori borrowed the name "Ruthven" (the original name for his vampire) from Clarence de Ruthven, Lord Glenarvon, the villain of Lamb's novel *Glenarvon* (1816), an account of her affair with Byron. "Mercer" may be an equally insolent allusion to Margaret Mercer Elphinstone, who had been kind to Byron during the separation scandal. When he and his sister were snubbed at a party, she came up to him, "gave him a familiar nod, and said, 'You should have married *me*, and then this would not have happened to you!'" (Marchand 230-31).

vesting of clothes, which were as warm, perhaps warmer than the thin naked draperies of a drawing room, but which were more pleasing to the painter's eye by their irregular folds and various coloured patches. He thought, in fine, that the dreams of poets were the realities of life. He was handsome, frank, and rich: for these reasons, upon his entering into the gay circles, many mothers surrounded him, striving which should describe with least truth their languishing or romping favourites: many daughters at the same time, by their brightening countenances when he approached, and by their sparkling eyes, when he opened his lips, soon led him into false notions of his talents and his merit. Attached as he was to the romance of his solitary hours, he was startled at finding, that, except in the tallow and wax candles flickering, not from the presence of a ghost, but from a draught of air breaking through his golden leathered doors and felted floors, there was no foundation in real life for any of that congeries of pleasing horrors and descriptions contained in the volumes, which had formed the occupation of his midnight vigils. Finding, however, some compensation in his gratified vanity, he was about to relinquish his dreams, when the extraordinary being we have above described, crossed him in his career.

He watched him; the very impossibility of forming an idea of the character of a man entirely absorbed in himself, of one who gave few other signs of his observation of external objects, than the tacit assent to their existence, implied by the avoidance of their contact: at last allowed his imagination to picture some thing that flattered its propensity to extravagant ideas. He soon formed this person into the hero of a romance, and determined to observe the offspring of his fancy, rather than the individual before him. He became acquainted with him, paid him attentions, and so far advanced upon his notice, that his presence was always acknowledged. He gradually learnt that Lord Strongmore's affairs were embarrassed,[1] and soon found, from the notes of preparation in —— Street, that he was about to travel. Desirous of gaining some information respecting this singular character, who, till now, had only whetted his curiosity, he hinted to his guardians, that it was time for him to perform the grand tour, a tour which for many generations had been thought necessary to enable the

---

1 There really was a Lord Ruthven; Polidori may have changed the name to Strongmore in order to make the tale less libellous as well as less obviously Byronic and more his own. The new name has connotations of phallic potency and size. Byron's affairs were so embarrassed at the time of his leaving England in 1816 that he had had to sell his books; he had to leave London early on the morning of 23 April in order to avoid the bailiffs (Marchand 230, 233-34).

young to take some important steps in the career of vice, put themselves upon an equality with the aged, and not allow them to appear as if fallen from the skies, whenever scandalous intrigues are mentioned as the subjects of pleasantry or of praise, according to the degree of skill shewn in their conduct. They consented: and Aubrey immediately mentioning his intentions to Lord Strongmore, was surprised to receive from him a proposal that they should travel together. Flattered by such a mark of esteem from him, who, apparently, had nothing in common with other men, he gladly accepted the invitation, and in a few days they had passed the circling waters.

Hitherto, Aubrey had had no opportunity of studying Lord Strongmore's character, and now he found, that, though many more of his actions were exposed to his view, the results offered different conclusions from the apparent motives to his conduct. His companion was profuse in his liberality;—the idle, the vagabond, and the beggar, received from his hand more than enough to relieve their immediate wants. But Aubrey could not avoid remarking, that it was not upon the virtuous, reduced to indigence by the misfortunes attendant even upon virtue, that he bestowed his alms. These were sent from the door with hardly suppressed sneers; but when the profligate came to ask something, not to relieve his wants, but to allow him to wallow in his lust, or to sink him still deeper in his iniquity, he was sent away with rich charity. This was, however, attributed by him to the greater importunity of the vicious, which generally prevails over the retiring bashfulness of the virtuous indigent. There was one circumstance about the charity of his Lordship, which was however still more deeply impressed upon his mind: all those upon whom it was bestowed, inevitably found that there was a curse upon it, for they were all either led to the scaffold, or sunk to the lowest and the most abject misery. At Brussels and other towns through which they passed, Aubrey was surprized at the apparent eagerness, with which his companion sought for the centres of all fashionable vice; there he entered into all the spirit of the faro table.[1] He betted, and always gambled with success, except when the known sharper was his antagonist, and then he lost even more than he gained; but it was always with the same unchanging face, with which he generally watched the society around. It was not, however, so when he encountered the rash youthful novice, or the luckless father of a numerous family; then his very wish seemed

---

1 Byron himself was not a great gambler, but he would express enthusiasm for gambling in a journal entry of 1821-22 (*Byron's Letters and Journals* 9: 23). Faro is one of the oldest and simplest of card games. It is named after a picture of a pharaoh on a French deck of cards. It was a favourite of aristocrats in late-eighteenth- and early-nineteenth-century Europe.

fortune's law—his apparent abstractedness of mind was laid aside, and his eyes sparkled with vivid fire. In every town, he left the formerly affluent youth, torn from the circle he adorned, cursing, in the solitude of a dungeon, the fate that had drawn him within the reach of this fiend; whilst many a father sat frantic, amidst the speaking looks of mute hungry children, without a single florin of his late immense wealth, wherewith to buy even sufficient to satisfy their present craving. Yet he took no money from the gambling table; but immediately lost, to the ruiner of many, the last gilder he had just snatched from the convulsive grasp of the innocent. This might but be the result of a certain degree of knowledge, which was not, however, capable of combating the cunning of the more experienced. Aubrey often wished to represent this to his friend, and beg him to resign that charity and pleasure which proved the ruin of all, and did not tend to his own profit;—but he delayed it—for each day he hoped his friend would give him some opportunity of speaking frankly and openly to him; this, however, never occurred. Lord Strongmore in his carriage,[1] and amidst the various wild and rich scenes of nature, was always the same: his eye spoke less than his lip; and though Aubrey was near the object of his curiosity, he obtained no greater gratification from it than the constant excitement of vainly wishing to break that mystery, which to his exalted imagination began to assume the appearance of something supernatural.

They soon arrived at Rome, and Aubrey for a time lost sight of his companion; he left him in daily attendance upon the morning circle of an Italian countess, whilst he went in search of the memorials of another almost deserted city. Whilst he was thus engaged, letters arrived from England, which he opened with eager impatience; the first was from his sister, breathing nothing but affection; the others were from his guardians, these astonished him; if it had before entered into his imagination, that, there was an evil power resident in his companion, these seemed to give him almost sufficient reason for the belief. His guardians insisted upon his immediately leaving his friend, and urged, that such a character was to be dreaded, for the possession of irresistible powers of seduction, rendered his licentious habits too dangerous to society. It had been discovered, that his contempt for the adultress had not originated in hatred of her character; but that he had required, to enhance his gratification, that his victim, the partner of his guilt, should be hurled from the pinnacle of unsullied virtue, down to the lowest abyss of infamy and degradation: in fine, that all those

---

1 In 1816, despite his financial embarrassments, Byron travelled in an enormous and expensive replica of Napoleon's carriage (Marchand 232). He still had not paid for it when he died, eight years later.

females whom he had sought, apparently on account of their virtue, had, since his departure, thrown even the mask aside, and had not scrupled to expose the whole deformity of their vices to the public view.

Aubrey determined upon leaving one, whose character had not yet shown a single bright point on which to rest the eye. He resolved to invent some plausible pretext for abandoning him altogether, purposing, in the mean while, to watch him more closely, and to let no slight circumstances pass by unnoticed. He entered into the same circle, and soon perceived, that his Lordship was endeavouring to work upon the inexperience of the daughter of the lady whose house he chiefly frequented. In Italy, it is seldom that an unmarried female is met with in society; he was therefore obliged to carry on his plans in secret; but Aubrey's eye followed him in all his windings, and soon discovered that an assignation had been made, which would most likely end in the ruin of an innocent, though thoughtless girl. Losing no time, he entered the apartment of Lord Strongmore, and abruptly asked him his intentions with respect to the lady, informing him at the same time that he was aware of his being about to meet her that very night. Lord Strongmore answered, that his intentions were such as he supposed all would have upon such an occasion; and upon being pressed whether he intended to marry her, merely laughed. Aubrey retired; and, immediately writing a note, to say, that from that moment he must decline accompanying his Lordship in the remainder of their purposed tour, he ordered his servant to seek other apartments, and calling upon the mother of the lady, informed her of all he knew, not only with regard to her daughter, but also with regard to the character of his Lordship. The meeting was prevented. Lord Strongmore next day merely sent his servant to notify his complete assent to a separation;[1] but did not hint any suspicion of his plans having been foiled by Aubrey's interposition.

Having left Rome, Aubrey directed his steps towards Greece, and crossing the Peninsula, soon found himself at Athens. He there fixed his residence in the house of a Greek; and was soon occupied in tracing the faded records of ancient glory upon monuments that apparently, ashamed of chronicling the deeds of freemen only before slaves,[2] had hidden themselves beneath the sheltering soil or many coloured lichen. Under the same roof as himself, existed a being, so beautiful and delicate, that she might have formed the model for a

---

1 Possibly an allusion to Byron's recent separation.
2 The contrast between the ancient glory and the modern degradation of the Greeks was commonplace. Byron had exploited it both in *Childe Harold's Pilgrimage* (2.10, 74-76) and in *The Giaour* (103-41).

painter, wishing to portray on canvass the promised hope of the faithful in Mahomet's paradise,[1] save that her eyes spoke too much mind for any one to think she could belong to those beings who had no souls. As she danced upon the plain, or tripped along the mountain's side, one would have thought the gazelle a poor type of her beauties; for who would have exchanged her eye, apparently the eye of animated nature, for that sleepy luxurious look of the animal suited but to the taste of an epicure.[2] The light step of Ianthe[3] often accompanied Aubrey in his search after antiquities, and often would the unconscious girl, engaged in the pursuit of a Kashmere butterfly,[4] show the whole beauty of her form, floating as it were upon the wind, to the eager gaze of him, who forgot, in the contemplation of her sylph-like figure, the letters he had just decyphered upon an almost effaced tablet. Often would her tresses falling, as she flitted around, exhibit in the sun's ray such delicately brilliant and swiftly fading hues, as might well excuse the forgetfulness of the antiquary, who let escape from his mind the very object he had before thought of vital importance to the proper interpretation of a passage in Pausanias.[5] But why attempt to describe charms which all feel, but none can appreciate?—It was innocence, youth, and beauty, unaffected by crowded drawing-rooms and stifling balls. Whilst he drew those remains of which he wished to preserve a memorial for his future hours, she would stand by, and watch the magic effects of his pencil, in tracing the scenes of her native place; she would then describe to him the circling dance upon the open plain, would paint to him in all the glowing colours of youthful memory, the marriage pomp she remembered viewing in her infancy; and then, turning to subjects that had evidently made a greater impression upon her mind, would tell him all the supernatural tales of her nurse. Her earnestness and apparent belief of what she narrated, excited the interest even of Aubrey; and often as she told him the tale of the living vampyre, who had passed years amidst his friends, and

---

1 The houris: see Qur'an 44.51-59, 55.56.

2 Cf. Byron, *The Giaour* (473-92) and Byron's note to 490. As Byron points out, Islam (despite Western misconceptions) does not teach that women have no souls.

3 The first two cantos of *Childe Harold's Pilgrimage* are dedicated to "Ianthe," the eleven-year-old Lady Charlotte Harley, daughter of Byron's lover Lady Oxford. He describes her eye as "wild as the Gazelle's" (Ded. 28). The name means "Flower of the Narcissus" (*Complete Poetical Works* 2: 272-73).

4 Cf. *The Giaour* (388-99).

5 The author (fl. 143-76 CE) of *Description of Greece*, an encyclopedic work covering Greek history, topography, daily life, customs and rites, legends and folklore, and especially works of art, so that antiquarians used it as a guide to ruins.

dearest ties, forced every year, by feeding upon the life of a lovely female to prolong his existence for the ensuing months, his blood would run cold, whilst he attempted to laugh her out of such idle and horrible fantasies. But Ianthe cited to him the names of old men, who had at last detected one living among themselves, after several of their near relatives and children had been found marked with the stamp of the fiend's appetite. When she found him incredulous, she begged of him to believe her, for it had been remarked, that those who had dared to question their existence, always had some proof given, which obliged them, with grief and heartbreaking, to confess its truth. She detailed to him the traditional appearance of these monsters, and his horror was increased, upon hearing a pretty accurate description of Lord Strongmore. He, however, still persisted in persuading her, that there could be no truth in her fears, though at the same time he wondered at the many coincidences which had all tended to excite a belief in the supernatural power of Lord Strongmore.

Aubrey began to attach himself more and more to Ianthe; her innocence, so contrasted with all the affected virtues of the women amongst whom he had sought for his vision of romance, won his heart; and while he ridiculed the idea of a young man of English habits, marrying an uneducated Greek girl, still he found himself more and more attached to the almost fairy form before him. He would tear himself at times from her, and, forming a plan for some antiquarian research, he would depart, determined not to return until his object was attained; but he always found it impossible to fix his attention upon the ruins around him, whilst in his mind he retained an image that seemed alone the rightful possessor of his thoughts. Ianthe was unconscious of his love, and was ever the same frank infantile being he had first known. She always seemed to part from him with reluctance; but it was because she had no longer any one with whom she could visit her favourite haunts, to whom she could point out the beauties of the spots so dear to her infantile memory, whilst he was occupied in sketching or uncovering some fragment which had yet escaped the destructive hand of time. She had appealed to her parents on the subject of Vampyres, and they both, with several present, affirmed their existence, pale with horror at the very name. Soon after, Aubrey determined to proceed upon one of his excursions, which was to detain him for a few hours; when his hosts heard the name of the place, they all at once begged of him not to return at night, as he must necessarily pass through a wood, where no Greek would ever remain, after the day had closed, upon any consideration. They described it as the resort of the vampyres in their nocturnal orgies, and denounced the most heavy evils as impending upon him who dared to cross their path. Aubrey made light of their representations, and tried to laugh them out of the idea; but when he saw them shudder at his daring thus to mock a superior, infernal power, the very name of which apparently made their blood freeze, he was silent.

Next morning Aubrey set off upon his excursion unattended; he was surprised to observe the melancholy face of his host, and was concerned to find that his words, mocking the belief of these horrible fiends, had inspired them with such terror. When he was about to depart, Ianthe came to the side of his horse, and earnestly begged of him to return, ere night allowed the power of these beings to be put in action;—he promised. He was, however, so occupied in his research, that he did not perceive that day-light would soon end, and that in the horizon there was one of those specks which, in the warmer climates, so rapidly gather into a tremendous mass, and pour all their rage upon the devoted country.—He at last, however, mounted his horse, determined to make up by speed for his delay: but it was too late. Twilight, in these southern climates, is almost unknown; immediately the sun sets, night begins: and ere he had advanced far, the power of the storm was above—its echoing thunders had scarcely an interval of rest—its thick heavy rain forced its way through the canopying foliage, whilst the blue forked lightning seemed to fall and radiate at his very feet. Suddenly his horse took fright, and he was carried with dreadful rapidity through the entangled forest. The animal at last, through fatigue, fell, and he found, by the glare of lightning, that he was in the neighbourhood of a hovel which hardly lifted itself up from the masses of dead leaves and brushwood surrounding it. Dismounting, he approached, hoping to find some one to guide him to the town, or at least trusting to obtain shelter from the pelting of the storm. When near the door, the thunders, for a moment silent, allowed him to hear the dreadful shrieks of a woman mingling with the stifled, exultant mockery of a laugh, continued in one almost unbroken sound;—he was startled: but, roused by the thunder which again rolled over his head, he, with a sudden effort, forced open the door of the hut. He found himself in utter darkness: the sound, however, guided him. He was apparently unperceived; for, though he called, still the sounds continued, and no notice was taken of him. He found himself in contact with some one, whom he immediately seized; when a voice cried, "Again baffled!" to which a loud laugh succeeded; and he felt himself grappled by one whose strength seemed superhuman: determined to sell his life as dearly as he could, he struggled; but it was in vain: he was lifted from his feet and hurled with enormous force against the ground.—His enemy threw himself upon him, and kneeling upon his breast, had placed his hands upon his throat—when the glare of many torches penetrating through the hole that gave light in the day, disturbed him.—He instantly rose, leaving his prey, he rushed through the door, and in a moment the crashing of the branches, as he broke through the wood, was no longer heard. The storm was now still; and Aubrey, incapable of moving, was soon heard by those without. They entered; the light of their torches fell upon nothing but the mud walls, and the thatch loaded on every individual straw with heavy flakes of soot, though at this moment it was apparently untenanted. There was one spot slippery with blood but it was hardly visible on the black floor. No other trace was seen of human presence having disturbed its solitude for many years. At the desire of Aubrey they searched for her who had attracted him by her cries; he was again left in darkness; but what was his horror, when the light of the torches once more burst upon him, to perceive the airy form of his fair conductress brought in a lifeless corpse. He shut his eyes, hoping that it was but a vision arising from his disturbed imagination; but he again saw the same form, when he unclosed them, stretched by his side. There was no colour upon her cheek, not even upon her lip; yet there was a stillness about her face that seemed almost as attaching as the life that once dwelt there:—upon her neck and breast was blood, and upon her throat were the marks of teeth having opened the vein of the neck:—to this the men pointed, crying, simultaneously struck with horror, "A Vampyre! a Vampyre!"

A litter was quickly formed, and Aubrey was laid by the side of her who had lately been to him the object of so many bright and fairy visions, now fallen with the flower of life that had died within her. He knew not what his thoughts were—his mind was benumbed and seemed to shun reflection, and take refuge in vacancy—he held almost unconsciously in his hand a naked dagger of a particular construction, which had been found in the hut. They were soon met by different parties who had been engaged in the search of her whom a mother had missed. Their lamentable cries, as they approached the city, forewarned the parents of some dreadful catastrophe.—To describe their grief would be impossible; but when they ascertained the cause of their child's death, they looked at Aubrey, and pointed to the corpse. They were inconsolable; both died broken-hearted.

Aubrey being put to bed was seized with a most violent fever, and was often delirious; in these intervals he would call upon Lord Strongmore and upon Ianthe—by some unaccountable combination he seemed to beg of his former companion to spare the being he loved. At other times he would imprecate maledictions upon his head, and curse him as her destroyer. Lord Strongmore chanced at this time to arrive at Athens, and, from whatever motive, upon hearing of the state of Aubrey, immediately placed himself in the same house, and became his constant attendant. When the latter recovered from his delirium, he was horrified and startled at the sight of him whose image he had now combined with that of a Vampyre; but Lord Strongmore, by his kind words, implying almost repentance for the fault that had caused their separation, and still more by the attention, anxiety, and care which he showed, soon reconciled him to his presence. His lordship seemed quite changed; he no longer appeared that apathetiç being who had so astonished Aubrey; but as soon as his convalescence began to be rapid, he again gradually retired into the same state of mind, and Aubrey perceived no difference from the former man, except that at times he was surprised to meet his gaze fixed intently upon him, with a smile of malicious exultation playing upon his lips: he knew not why, but this smile haunted him. During the last stage of the invalid's recovery, Lord Strongmore was apparently engaged in watching the tideless waves raised by the cooling breeze, or in marking the progress of those orbs, circling, like our world, the moveless sun;—indeed, he appeared to wish to avoid the eyes of all.

Aubrey's mind, by this shock, was much weakened, and that elasticity of spirit which had once so distinguished him now seemed to have fled for ever. He was now as much a lover of solitude and silence as Lord Strongmore; but much as he wished for solitude, his mind could not find it in the neighbourhood of Athens; if he sought it amidst the ruins he had formerly frequented, Ianthe's form stood by his side—if he sought it in the woods, her light step would sound wandering amidst the underwood, in quest of the modest violet; and often she would suddenly turning round, show, to his wild imagination, her pale face and wounded throat, while a meek smile played upon her lips. He determined to fly scenes, every feature of which created such bitter associations in his mind. He proposed to Lord Strongmore, to whom he held himself bound by the tender care he had taken of him during his illness, that they should visit those parts of Greece neither had yet seen. They travelled in every direction, and sought every spot to which a recollection could be attached: but though they thus hastened from place to place, yet they seemed not to heed what they gazed upon. They heard much of robbers,[1] but they gradually began to slight these reports, which they imagined were only the invention of individuals, whose interest it was to excite the generosity of those, whom they defended from pretended dangers. In consequence of thus neglecting the advice of the inhabitants, they travelled on one occasion with only a few guards, more to serve as guides than as a defence. Upon entering, however, a narrow defile, at the bottom of which was the bed of a torrent, with large masses of rock brought down from the neighbouring precipices, they had reason to repent their negligence;

---

1 Byron had had a narrow escape from robbers on an excursion from Athens to Cape Colonna in December 1810 (*Byron's Letters and Journals* 2: 30-31).

for scarcely were the whole of the party engaged in the narrow pass, when they were startled by the echoed report of several guns, and by the whistling of bullets close to their heads. In an instant their guards had left them, and, placing themselves behind rocks, had begun to fire in the direction whence the report came. Lord Strongmore and Aubrey, imitating their example, retired for a moment behind the sheltering turn of the defile: but ashamed of being thus detained by a foe, who with insulting shouts bade them advance, and being exposed to unresisting slaughter, if any of the robbers should climb above and take them in the rear, they determined at once to rush forward in search of the enemy. Hardly had they lost the shelter of the rock, when Lord Strongmore received a shot in the shoulder, which brought him to the ground. Aubrey hastened to his assistance; and, no longer heeding the contest or his own peril, was soon surprised by seeing the robbers' faces around him—his guards having, upon Lord Strongmore's being wounded, immediately thrown up their arms and surrendered.

By promises of great reward, Aubrey soon induced them to convey his wounded friend to a neighbouring cabin; and having agreed upon a ransom, he was no more disturbed by their presence—they being content merely to guard the entrance until their comrade should return with the promised sum, for which he had an order. Lord Strongmore's strength rapidly decreased; in two days mortification ensued, and death seemed advancing with hasty steps. His conduct and appearance had not changed; he seemed as unconscious of pain as he had been of the objects about him: but towards the close of the last evening, his mind became apparently uneasy, and his eye often fixed upon Aubrey, who was induced to offer his assistance with more than usual earnestness—"Assist me! you may save me—you may do more than that—I mean not my life, I heed the death of my existence as little as that of the passing day; but you may save my honour, your friend's honour."—"How? tell me how? I would do any thing," replied Aubrey.—"I need but little—my life ebbs apace—I cannot explain the whole—but if you would conceal all you know of me, my honour were free from stain in the world's mouth—and if my death were unknown for some time in England— I—I—but life."—"It shall not be known."—"Swear!" cried the dying man, raising himself with exultant violence, "Swear by all your soul reveres, by all your nature dreads, swear that for a year and a day you will not impart your knowledge of my crimes or death to any living being, in any way, whatever may happen, or whatever you may see."—His eyes seemed bursting from their sockets: "I swear!" said Aubrey; he sunk laughing upon his pillow, and breathed no more.[1]

Aubrey retired to rest, but did not sleep; the many circumstances attending his acquaintance with this man arose upon his mind, and, he knew not why, when he remembered his oath a cold shivering came over him, as if from the presentiment of something horrible awaiting him. Rising early in the morning, he was about to enter the hovel, in which he had left the corpse, when a robber met him, and informed him that it was no longer there, having been conveyed by himself and comrades, upon his retiring, to the pinnacle of a neighbouring mount, according to a promise they had given his lordship, that it should be exposed to the first cold ray of the moon that rose after his death.[2] Aubrey was astonished, but taking several of the men, he determined to go and bury it upon the spot where it lay. When however he reached the summit he found no trace of the corpse, nor could he discover any remnant of the clothes, though the robbers assured him that they pointed out the identical rock on which they had laid the body. For a time his mind was bewildered in conjectures, but he at last returned, convinced that they had secretly buried his friend's remains for the sake of the dress in which he died.

Weary of a country in which he had met with such terrible misfortunes, and in which all apparently conspired to heighten that superstitious melancholy which had seized upon his mind, he resolved to leave it, and he soon arrived at Smyrna. While waiting for a vessel to convey him to Otranto,[3] or to Naples, he occupied himself in arranging those effects he had with him belonging to Lord Strongmore. Amongst other things there was a case containing several weapons of offence, more or less adapted to ensure the death of the victim. There were

---

1 The incident of the oath and death is the closest point of contact between Polidori's tale and Byron's fragment (Appendix F). Byron's oath, in turn, is based on the many similar oaths in *Fantasmagoriana*. Behind them all, perhaps, is the oath of silence in *Hamlet* (II.v.146-95). Polidori has heightened Byron's rhetoric; his oath, like Shakespeare's, is at once highly emotional and highly ritualized.

2 This simple technique of resuscitation replaces the elaborate ring ceremony in Byron's fragment. Polidori seems to have made up the idea that a dead vampire could be revived by moonlight. As a doctor, he was probably aware that it reversed the old Galenic notion that moonlight accelerated the decomposition of dead bodies (Ariès 360).

3 A port in southern Italy, the setting of *The Castle of Otranto* (1764), by Horace Walpole, the first Gothic novel.

several daggers and ataghans.[1] Whilst turning these over, and examining their curious forms, what was his surprise at finding a sheath apparently ornamented in the same style as the dagger discovered in the fatal hut—he shuddered—hastening to gain further proof, he found the weapon, and his horror may be imagined, when he discovered that it fitted, though peculiarly shaped, the sheath he held in his hand. His eyes seemed to need no further certainty—they seemed gazing to be bound to the dagger; yet still he wished not to believe his sight; but the particular form, the varying tints upon the haft and sheath were alike, and left no room for doubt; there were also drops of blood on each.

He left Smyrna, and on his way home, at Rome, he inquired concerning the lady he had attempted to snatch from Lord Strongmore's seductive arts. Her parents were in distress, their fortune ruined, and she had not been heard of since the departure of his lordship. Aubrey's mind became almost broken under so many repeated horrors; he was afraid that this lady had fallen a victim to the destroyer of Ianthe. He became morose and silent; and his only thought seemed to be how to urge the speed of the postilions, as if he were hastening to save the life of some one he held dear. He arrived at Calais; a breeze, which seemed obedient to his will, soon wafted him to the English shores. He hastened to the mansion of his fathers, and there, for a moment, he appeared to lose, in the embraces and caresses of his sister, all memory of the past. If she before, by her infantine caresses, had gained his affection, now that the woman began to appear, she was still more attaching as a companion.

Miss Aubrey had not that winning grace which gains the gaze and applause of the drawing-room assemblies. There was none of that ephemeral brilliancy which can only exist in the heated atmosphere of a crowded apartment. Her blue eye was never lit up by the levity of the mind beneath. There was a melancholy charm about it which did not seem to arise from misfortune, but from some feeling within, that appeared to indicate a soul conscious of a brighter realm. Her step was not that light footing, which strays where'er a butterfly or a colour may attract—it was sedate and pensive. When alone, her face was never brightened by the smile of joy; but when her brother breathed to her his affection, and would in her presence forget those griefs she knew destroyed his rest, who would have exchanged her smile for that of the voluptuary? It seemed as if those eyes,—that face were then playing in the light of their own native sphere. She was yet only eighteen, and had

---

1 In a note to *The Giaour* (355), Byron describes an ataghan as "a long dagger worn with pistols in the belt, in a metal scabbard, generally of silver; and, among the wealthier, gilt, or of gold" (*Complete Poetical Works* 3: 418).

not yet been presented to the world, her guardians having thought proper to delay her presentation at court until her brother's return from the continent, when he might be her protector. It was now, therefore, resolved that the next drawing-room,[1] which was fast approaching, should be the epoch of her entry into the "busy scene."[2] Aubrey would rather have remained in the mansion of his fathers, to feed upon the melancholy which overpowered him. He could not feel interest about the frivolities of fashionable strangers, when his mind had been so torn by the events he had witnessed; but he determined to sacrifice his own comfort to the protection of his sister. They therefore soon arrived in town, and prepared for the day, which had been announced as the one on which a drawing-room was to be held.

The crowd was excessive—a drawing-room had not been held for a long time, and all who were anxious to bask in the smile of royalty, hastened thither. Aubrey was there with his sister. While he was standing in a corner by himself, heedless of all around him, engaged in the recollection that the first time he had seen Lord Strongmore was in this very place—he felt himself suddenly seized by the arm, and a voice he recognized too well, sounded in his ear—"Remember your oath."[3] He had hardly courage to turn, fearful of seeing a spectre, that would blast him, when he perceived, at a little distance, the same figure which had attracted his notice on this spot upon his first entry into society. He gazed till his limbs almost refusing to bear their weight, he was obliged to take the arm of a friend, and forcing a passage through the crowd, to throw himself into his carriage, and be driven home. He paced the room with hurried steps, and fixed his hands upon his head, as if he were afraid his thoughts were bursting from his brain. Lord Strongmore again before him—circumstances started up in dreadful array—the dagger—his oath.—He roused himself, he could not believe it possible—the dead rise again!—He

---

1 "A levee held in a drawing room; a formal reception by a king, queen, or person of rank; that at which ladies are 'presented' at court" (*OED*).

2 This is not a very distinctive phrase—the quotation marks may mark it as a cliché rather than a quotation—but it does occur in the same context (a young woman's début in society after her brother's return from a journey) in Frances Sheridan's *Memoirs of Miss Sidney Bidulph* (1761): "It was just on his return to England that the busy scene of his sister's life opened" (9).

3 Another not-very-distinctive phrase, but Polidori may have remembered it from Sir Walter Scott's *Guy Mannering* (1815), which he and Byron had both read, and in which, as in his tale, there is a reference to an oath of silence (384). Polidori may also be thinking of a phrase from Lamb's *Glenarvon* (1816): "Lady Margaret reminded him of his vow; and a fearful silence ensued" (15; chap. 4).

thought his imagination had conjured up the image his mind was resting upon. It was impossible that it could be real—he determined, therefore, to go again into society; for though he attempted to ask concerning Lord Strongmore, the name hung upon his lips, and he could not succeed in gaining information. He went a few nights after with his sister to the assembly of a near relation. Leaving her under the protection of a matron, he retired into a recess, and there gave himself up to his own devouring thoughts. Perceiving, at last, that many were retiring, he roused himself, and entering another room, found his sister surrounded by several gentlemen, apparently in earnest conversation; he attempted to pass and get near her, when one, whom he requested to move, turned round, and revealed to him those features he most abhorred. He sprang forward, seized his sister's arm, and, with a hurried step, forced her towards the street: at the door he found himself impeded by the crowd of servants, who were waiting for their lords; and while he was engaged in passing them, he again heard that voice whisper close to him—"Remember your oath!"—He did not dare to turn, but, hurrying his sister, he soon reached home.

Aubrey became almost distracted. If before his mind had been absorbed by one subject, how much more completely was it engrossed now, that the certainty of the monster's living again pressed upon his thoughts. His sister's attentions were now unheeded, and it was in vain that she intreated him to explain to her what had caused his abrupt conduct. He only uttered a few words, and those terrified her. The more he thought, the more he was bewildered. His oath startled him;—was he then to allow this monster to roam, bearing ruin upon his breath, amidst all he held dear, and not avert its progress? His very sister might have been touched by him. But even if he were to break his oath, and disclose his suspicions, who would believe him? He thought of employing his own hand to free the world from such a wretch; but death, he remembered, had been already mocked. For days he remained in this state; shut up in his room, he saw no one, and eat[1] only when his sister came, who, her eyes streaming with tears, besought him, for her sake, to support nature. At last, no longer capable of bearing stillness and solitude, he left his house, roamed from street to street, anxious to fly that image which haunted him. His dress became neglected, and he wandered, as often exposed to the noon-day sun as to the mid-night damps. He was no longer to be recognized; at first he returned with the evening to his home; but at last he laid him down to rest wherever fatigue overtook him. His sister, anxious for his safety, employed people to follow him; but they were soon distanced by him, who fled from a pursuer swifter than any—

---

1 Then the standard past tense of the verb: "ate."

from thought. His conduct, however, suddenly changed. Struck with the idea that he left by his absence the whole of his friends, with a fiend amongst them, of whose presence they were unconscious, he determined to enter again into society, and watch him closely, anxious to forewarn, in spite of his oath, all whom Lord Strongmore should approach with intimacy. But when he entered into a room, his haggard and suspicious looks were so striking, his inward shudderings so visible, that his sister was at last obliged to beg of him to abstain from seeking, for her sake, a society, which affected him so strongly. When, however, remonstrance proved unavailing, the guardians thought proper to interpose, and, fearing that his mind was becoming alienated, they thought it high time to resume again that trust, which had been before imposed upon them by Aubrey's parents.

Desirous of saving him from the injuries and sufferings he had daily encountered in his wanderings, and of preventing him from exposing to the general eye those marks of what they considered folly, they engaged a physician to reside in the house, and take constant care of him. He hardly appeared to notice it, so completely was his mind absorbed by one terrible subject. His incoherence became at last so great, that he was confined to his chamber. There he would often lie for days, incapable of being roused. He had become emaciated, his eyes had attained a glassy lustre;—the only sign of affection and recollection remaining displayed itself upon the entry of his sister; then he would sometimes start, and, seizing her hands, with looks that severely afflicted her, he would desire her not to touch him. "Oh, do not touch him—if your love for me is aught, do not go near him!" When, however, she inquired to whom he referred, his only answer was, "True! true!" and again he sank into a state, whence not even she could rouse him. This lasted many months: gradually, however, as the year was passing, his incoherences became less frequent, and his mind threw off a portion of its gloom, whilst his guardians observed, that several times in the day he would count upon his fingers a definite number, and then smile.

The time had nearly elapsed, when, upon the last day of the year, one of his guardians entering his room, began to converse with his physician upon the melancholy circumstance of Aubrey's being in so awful a situation, when his sister was going next day to be married. Instantly Aubrey's attention was attracted; he asked anxiously to whom. Glad of this mark of returning intellect, of which they feared he had been deprived, they mentioned the name of the Earl of Marsden. Thinking this was a young Earl whom he had met with in society, Aubrey seemed pleased, and astonished them still more by expressing his intention to be present at the nuptials, and by desiring to see his sister. They answered not, but in a few minutes his sister was with him. He was apparently again capable of being affected by the influence of her lovely smile; for he pressed her to his breast, and kissed her cheek, wet with tears, flowing at the thought of her brother's being once more alive to the feelings of affection. He began to speak with all his wonted warmth, and to congratulate her upon her marriage with a person so distinguished for rank and every accomplishment; but he suddenly perceived a locket upon her breast; having opened it, what was his surprise at beholding the features of the monster who had so long influenced his life. He seized the portrait in a paroxysm of rage, and trampled it under foot. Upon her asking him, why he thus destroyed the resemblance of her future husband, he looked as if he did not understand her—then seizing her hands, and gazing on her with a frantic expression of countenance, he bade her swear that she would never wed this monster, for he—But he could not continue—it seemed as if that voice again bade him remember his oath—he turned suddenly round, thinking Lord Strongmore was near him but he saw no one. In the meantime the guardians and physician, who had heard the whole, and thought this was but a return of his disorder, entered, and forcing him from Miss Aubrey, desired her to leave him. He fell upon his knees to them, he implored, he begged of them to delay but for one day. They, attributing this to the insanity, they imagined had taken possession of his mind, endeavoured to pacify him, and retired.

Lord Strongmore had called the morning after the drawing-room, and had been refused with every one else. When he heard of Aubrey's ill health, he readily understood himself to be the cause of it; but, when he learned that he was deemed insane, his exultation and pleasure could hardly be concealed from those, among whom he had gained this information. He hastened to the house of his former companion, and, by constant attendance, and the pretence of great affection for her brother and interest in his fate, he gradually won the ear of Miss Aubrey. Who could resist his power? His tongue had dangers and toils to recount[1]—could speak of himself as of an individual having no sympathy with any being on the crowded earth, save with her, to whom he addressed himself;—could tell how, since he knew her, his existence had begun to seem worthy of preservation, if it were merely that he might listen to her soothing accents.—In fine, he knew so well how to use the serpent's art,[2] or such was the will of fate, that he gained her affections. The title of the elder branch falling at length

---

1 A reminiscence of Othello's courtship of Desdemona (I.iii.128-70), also recalled in *Glenarvon* (34; chap. 9).

2 Cf. Genesis 3.

to him, he obtained an important embassy, which served as an excuse (in spite of her brother's deranged state), for hastening the marriage, which was to take place the very day before his departure for the continent.

Aubrey, when he was left by the physician and his guardians, attempted to bribe the servants, but in vain. He asked for pen and paper; it was given him; he wrote a letter to his sister, conjuring her, as she valued her own happiness, her own honour, and the honour of those now in the grave, who once held her in their arms as their hope and the hope of their house, to delay but for a few hours that marriage, on which he denounced the most heavy curses. The servants promised they would deliver it; but giving it to the physician, he thought it better not to harass any more the mind of Miss Aubrey by, what he considered, the ravings of a maniac. Night passed on without rest to the busy inmates of the house; and Aubrey heard, with a horror that may more easily be conceived than described, the notes of busy preparation. Morning came, and the sound of carriages broke upon his ear. Aubrey grew almost frantic. The curiosity of the servants at last overcame their vigilance, they gradually stole away, leaving him in the custody of an helpless old woman. He seized the opportunity, with one bound was out of the room, and in a moment found himself in the apartment where all were nearly assembled. Lord Strongmore was the first to perceive him: he immediately approached, and, taking his arm by force, hurried him from the room, speechless with rage. When on the staircase, Lord Strongmore whispered in his ear—"Remember your oath, and know, if not my bride to day, your sister is dishonoured. Women are frail!"[1] So saying, he pushed him towards his attendants, who, roused by the old woman, had come in search of him. Aubrey could no longer support himself; his rage not finding vent, had broken a blood-vessel,[2] and he was conveyed to bed. This was not mentioned to his sister, who was not present when he entered, as the physician was afraid of agitating her. The marriage was solemnized, and the bride and bridegroom left London.

Aubrey's weakness increased; the effusion of blood produced symptoms of the near approach of death. He desired his sister's guardians might be called, and, when the midnight hour had struck, he related composedly the substance of what the reader has perused—and died immediately after.

---

1 In *Glenarvon*, Viviani/Glenarvon remarks that the heroine, Calantha, "is a woman, and as such, she must be frail" (69; chap. 21).

2 Haidée also dies of a broken blood-vessel in Byron, *Don Juan* 4.59.69 (1821).

The guardians hastened to protect Miss Aubrey; but when they arrived, it was too late. Lord Strongmore had disappeared, and Aubrey's sister had glutted the thirst of a VAMPYRE![1]

---

1 Strongmore's escape left room for a sequel, and in November 1819 Polidori reported to his sister: "I have just written to Longman to see if they would undertake to buy a second part of the *Vampyre* from me—as I must have something to engage my mind & I now find nothing to do" (Macdonald 173). Nothing came of the plan.

Appendix H: Substantive Variants

[The following collation lists the substantive variants between the 1818 version of *Frankenstein* and the later lifetime versions: the copy Shelley gave to her friend Mrs. Thomas in 1823, the second edition of 1823, and the third edition of 1831. The format is as follows: first we give the page and line numbers, and the reading, of the present edition of the 1818 text; then, after a right square bracket, the page and line numbers (where applicable) of M.K. Joseph's standard edition of the 1831 text; then the later reading; then, in brackets, an indication of which later version contains the variant. Passages more than six words long in the 1818 text have been abbreviated. Cuts to the 1818 text are indicated by the word *omitted*. Accidental variants are not listed. Original spelling errors are indicated by angled brackets. For a fuller listing of variants in the Thomas copy, including accidentals, see Rieger's and Crook's editions.]

47.5-8 Did I request ... PARADISE LOST.] *omitted* [2, 3]

48.1-8 TO / WILLIAM GODWIN, ... BY / THE AUTHOR.] *omitted* [2, 3]

50.17 completed.] 14.30 completed. [*Shelley adds a date.*] *Marlow, September*, 1817. [3]

51.21 for ever visible] constantly visible for more than half the year [T]

51.30 of eternal light?] ruled by different laws and in which numerous circumstances enforce a belief that the aspect of nature differs essentially from anything of which we have any experience. [T]

55.16 glory.] 20.3-4 glory: or rather, to word my phrase more characteristically, of advancement in his profession. [3]

55.26-27 He is, moreover, heroically generous.] I will relate to you an anecdote of his life, recounted to me by the parties themselves, which exemplifies the generosity, I had almost said the heroism of his nature. [T]

55.24-27 He is, indeed ... moreover, heroically generous.] 20.12-24 This circumstance, added to his well known integrity and dauntless courage, made me very desirous to engage him. A youth passed in solitude, my best years spent under your gentle and feminine fosterage, has so refined the groundwork of my character, that I cannot overcome an intense distaste to the usual brutality exercised on board ship: I have never believed it to be necessary; and when I heard of a mariner equally noted for his kindliness of heart, and the respect and obedience paid to him by his crew, I felt myself peculiarly fortunate in being able to secure his services. I heard of him first in rather a romantic manner, from a lady who owes to him the happiness of her life. This, briefly, is his story. [3]

56.7-8 the rope and the shroud] the ship and the crew [T]

56.6-9 has passed all ... not suppose that,] 21.7-12 is wholly uneducated: he is as silent as a Turk, and a kind of ignorant carelessness attends him, which, while it renders his conduct the more astonishing, detracts from the interest and sympathy which otherwise he would command.
    Yet do not suppose, [3]

56.23 snow";] snow";* [*Shelley adds a footnote*: *Coleridge's Antient Mariner.] [T]

56.24 albatross,] albatross,* [T]

56.24 safety.] 21.29-22.4 safety, or if I should come back to you as worn and woful as the 'Ancient Mariner?' You will smile at my allusion; but I will disclose a secret. I have often attributed my attachment to, my passionate enthusiasm for, the dangerous mysteries of the ocean, to that production of the most imaginative of modern poets. There is something at work in my soul, which I do not understand. I am practically industrious—painstaking; a workman to execute with perseverance and labour:—but besides this, there is a love for the marvellous, a belief in the marvellous, intertwined in all my projects, which hurries me out of the common pathways of men, even to the wild sea and unvisited regions I am about to explore.
    But to return to dearer considerations. [3]

56.28 Continue] 22.8 Continue for the present [3]

56.29-30 (though the chance is very doubtful)] 22.9 *omitted* [3]

57.9 my men are bold, and apparently firm] my crew are gallant fellows, & I am firm [T]

57.16 expected.] expected. The appearance of the sky is indiscribably beautiful; clear by day, and illuminated at night by the Aurora Borealis <ov> which spreads a roseate tinge over the heavens, & over the sea which reflects it's splendour. [T]

57.18 stiff gales, and the breaking] hard gales, and the carrying away [T]

57.18-19 the breaking of a mast] 23.1-2 the springing of a leak [3]

57.25-26 Remember me to ... Most affectionately yours,] 23.8-15 But success *shall* crown my endeavours. Wherefore not? Thus far I have gone, tracing a secure way over the pathless seas: the very stars themselves being witnesses and testimonies of my triumph. Why not still proceed over the untamed yet obedient element? What can stop the determined heart and resolved will of man?

My swelling heart involuntarily pours itself out thus. But I must finish. Heaven bless my beloved sister! [3]

57.32 recording it] recording it in writing [T]

58.8 plains] mountains & plains [T]

58.23-24 attention.] attention. Are we then near land, and is this unknown wast inhabited by giants, of which the being we saw is a specimen? Such an idea is contrary to all experience, but if what we saw was an optical delusion, it was the most perfect and wonderful recorded in the history of nature. [T]

60.26 the stranger seemed very eager] 26.32-33 a new spirit of life animated the decaying frame of the stranger. He manifested the greatest eagerness [3]

60.29 But] And [T]

60.29 But] 26.37 *omitted* [3]

61.10 speaks,] speaks, in his native language which is French, [T]

61.15-16 employments] 27.33 projects [3]

61.22 by gloom] by a gloom [T]

61.22-25 and then he ... never leaves him.] Which veils his countenance like deep night—he neither speaks or notices any thing around him, but sitting on a gun will gaze on the sea and I have sometimes observed his dark eyelash wet with a tear which falls <sinlently> silently in the deep. This unobtrusive sorrow excites in me the most painful interest, and he will at times reward my sympathy by throwing aside this veil of mortal woe, and then his ardent looks, his deep toned voice and powerful eloquence entrance me with delight. [T]

61.16-36 asked me many ... a possible acquisition.] 27.33-28.37 frequently conversed with me on mine, which I have communicated to him without disguise. He entered attentively into all my arguments in favour of my eventual success, and into every minute detail of the measures I had taken to secure it. I was easily led by the sympathy which he evinced, to use the language of my heart; to give utterance to the burning ardour of my soul; and to say, with all the fervour that warmed me, how gladly I would sacrifice my fortune, my existence, my every hope, to the furtherance of my enterprise. One man's life or death were but a small price to pay for the acquirement of the knowledge which I sought; for the dominion I should acquire and transmit over the elemental foes of our race. As I spoke, a dark gloom spread over my listener's countenance. At first I perceived that he tried to suppress his emotion; he placed his hands before his eyes; and my voice quivered and failed me, as I beheld tears trickle fast from between his fingers,—a groan burst from his heaving breast. I paused;—at length he spoke, in broken accents:—'Unhappy man! Do you share my madness? Have you drank also of the intoxicating draught? Hear me,—let me reveal my tale, and you will dash the cup from your lips!'

Such words, you may imagine, strongly excited my curiosity; but the paroxysm of grief that had seized the stranger overcame his weakened powers, and many hours of repose and tranquil conversation were necessary to restore his composure.

Having conquered the violence of his feelings, he appeared to despise himself for being the slave of passion; and quelling the dark tyranny of despair, he led me again to converse concerning myself personally. He asked me the history of my earlier years. The tale was quickly told: but it awakened various trains of reflection. I spoke of my desire of finding a friend—of my thirst for a more intimate sympathy with a fellow mind than had ever fallen to my lot; and expressed my conviction that a man could boast of little happiness, who did not enjoy this blessing.

'I agree with you,' replied the stranger; 'we are unfashioned creatures, but half made up, if one wiser, better, dearer than ourselves—such a friend ought to be—do not lend his aid to perfectionate our weak and faulty natures. [3]

62.12 Will you laugh] 29.17 Will you smile [3]

62.13-16 If you do ... for repeating them.] 29.18-29 You would not, if you saw him. You have been tutored and refined by books and retirement from the world, and you are, therefore, somewhat fastidious; but this only renders you the more fit to appreciate the extraordinary merits of this wonderful man. Sometimes I have endeavoured to discover what quality it is which he possesses, that elevates him so immeasurably above any other person I ever knew. I believe it to be an intuitive discernment; a quick but never-failing power of judgment; a penetration into the causes of things, unequalled for clearness and precision; add to this a facility of expression, and a voice whose varied intonations are soul-subduing music. [3]

62.17 August 19th,] 29.30 August 19. [3]

62.22 once] 29.33 at one time [3]

62.25 misfortunes] 30.3 disasters [3]

62.25-30 if you are ... do not doubt] 30.3-14 when I reflect that you are pursuing the same course, exposing yourself to the same dangers which have rendered me what I am, I imagine that you may deduce an apt moral from my tale; one that may direct you if you succeed in your undertaking, and console you in case of failure. Prepare to hear of occurrences which are usually deemed marvellous. Were we among the tamer scenes of nature, I might fear to encounter your unbelief, perhaps your ridicule; but many things will appear possible in these wild and mysterious regions, which would provoke the laughter of those unacquainted with the ever-varied powers of nature:—nor can I doubt but [3]

62.32 conceive] 30.17 imagine [3]

63.6 engaged] 30.34 imperatively occupied by my duties [3]

63.9 pleasure:] pleasure: [*Shelley adds comment*: impossible] [T]

63.11 day!] 31.3-9 day! Even now, as I commence my task, his full-toned voice swells in my ears; his lustrous eyes dwell on me with all their melancholy sweetness; I see his thin hand raised in animation, while the lineaments of his face are irradiated by the soul within. Strange and harrowing must be his story; frightful the storm which embraced the gallant vessel on its course, and wrecked it—thus! [3]

64.1-3 FRANKENSTEIN; / OR, / THE MODERN PROMETHEUS.] 31 *omitted* [3]

64.11-13 and it was ... down to posterity.] 31.17-19 a variety of circumstances had prevented his marrying early, nor was it until the decline of life that he became a husband and the father of a family [3]

64.26-27 grieved also for ... endeavour to persuade] 31.32-32.3 bitterly deplored the false pride which led his friend to a conduct so little worthy of the affection that united them. He lost no time in endeavouring to seek him out, with the hope of persuading [3]

65.21-22 When my father ... situation, that he] As my father's age encreased he became more attached to the quiet of a domestic life, and he gradually [T]

65.23 many of] *deleted* [T]

65.23 devoted himself] devoted himself with ardour [T]

66.7-8 signs even then] every sign [T]

67.5 I remember,] *deleted* [T]

67.12-27 No youth could ... on our memories] [*Shelley adds comment*: bad *and composes replacement*:] With what delight do I even now remember the details of our domestic circle, and the happy years of my childhood. Joy attended on my steps—and the ardent affection that attached me to my excellent parents, my beloved Elizabeth, and Henry, the brother of my soul, has given almost a religious and sacred feeling to the recollections of a period passed beneath their eyes, and in their society. [T]

65.21-67.33 When my father ... Clerval was absent.] 33.1-38.20 There was a considerable difference between the ages of my parents, but this circumstance seemed to unite them only closer in bonds of devoted affection. There was a sense of justice in my father's upright mind, which rendered it necessary that he should approve highly to love strongly. Perhaps during former years he had suffered from the late-discovered unworthiness of one beloved, and so was disposed to set a greater value on tried worth. There was a show of gratitude and worship in his attachment to my mother, differing wholly from the doating fondness of age, for it was inspired by reverence for her virtues, and a desire to be the means of, in some degree, recompensing her for the sorrows she had endured, but which gave inexpressible grace to his behaviour to her. Every thing was made to yield to her wishes and her convenience. He strove to shelter her, as a fair exotic is sheltered by the gardener, from every rougher wind, and to surround her with all that could tend to excite pleasurable emotion in her soft and benevolent mind. Her health, and even the tranquillity of her hitherto constant spirit, had been shaken by what she had gone through. During the two years that had elapsed previous to their marriage my father had gradually relinquished all his public functions; and immediately after their union they sought the pleasant climate of Italy, and the change of scene and interest attendant on a tour through that land of wonders, as a restorative for her weakened frame.

From Italy they visited Germany and France. I, their eldest child, was born at Naples, and as an infant accompanied them in their rambles. I remained for several years their only child. Much as they were attached to each other, they seemed to draw inexhaustible stores of affection from a very mine of love to bestow them upon me. My mother's tender caresses, and my father's smile of benevolent pleasure while regarding me, are my first recollections. I was their plaything and their idol, and something better—their child, the innocent and helpless creature bestowed on them by Heaven, whom to bring up to good, and whose future lot it was in their hands to direct to happiness or misery, according as they fulfilled their duties towards me. With this deep consciousness of what they owed towards the being to which they had given life, added to the active spirit of tenderness that animated both, it may be imagined that while during every hour of my infant life I received a lesson of patience, of charity, and of self-control, I was so guided by a silken cord, that all seemed but one train of enjoyment to me.

For a long time I was their only care. My mother had much desire to have a daughter, but I continued their single offspring. When I was about five years old, while making an excursion beyond the frontiers of Italy, they passed a week on the shores of the Lake of Como. Their benevolent disposition often made them enter the cottages of the poor. This, to my mother, was more than a duty; it was a necessity, a passion,—remembering what she had suffered, and how she had been relieved,—for her to act in her turn the guardian angel to the afflicted. During one of their walks a poor cot in the foldings of a vale attracted their notice, as being singularly disconsolate, while the number of half-clothed children gathered about it, spoke of penury in its worst shape. One day, when my father had gone by himself to Milan, my mother, accompanied by me, visited this abode. She found a peasant and his wife, hard working, bent down by care and labour, distributing a scanty meal to five hungry babes. Among these there was one which attracted my mother far above all the rest. She appeared of a different stock. The four others were dark-eyed, hardy little vagrants; this child was thin, and very fair. Her hair was the brightest living gold, and, despite the poverty of her clothing, seemed to set a crown of distinction on her head. Her brow was clear and ample, her blue eyes cloudless, and her lips and the moulding of her face so expressive of sensibility and sweetness, that none could behold her without looking on her as of a distinct species, a being heaven-sent, and bearing a celestial stamp in all her features.

The peasant woman, perceiving that my mother fixed eyes of wonder and admiration on this lovely girl, eagerly communicated her history. She was not her child, but the daughter of a Milanese nobleman. Her mother was a German, and had died on giving her birth. The infant had been placed with these good people to nurse: they were better off then. They had not been long married, and their eldest child was but just born. The father of their charge was one of those Italians nursed in the memory of the antique glory of Italy,—one among the *schiavi ognor frementi*, who exerted himself to obtain the liberty of his country. He became the victim of its weakness. Whether he had died, or still lingered in the dungeons of Austria, was not known. His property was confiscated, his child became an orphan and a beggar. She continued with her foster parents, and bloomed in their rude abode, fairer than a garden rose among dark-leaved brambles.

When my father returned from Milan, he found playing with me in the hall of our villa, a child fairer than pictured cherub—a creature who seemed to shed radiance from her looks, and whose form and motions were lighter than the chamois of the hills. The apparition was soon explained. With his permission my mother prevailed on her rustic guardians to yield their charge to her. They were fond of the sweet orphan. Her presence had seemed a blessing to them; but it would be unfair to her to keep her in poverty and want, when Providence afforded her such powerful protection. They consulted their village priest, and the result was, that Elizabeth Lavenza became the inmate of my parents' house—my more than sister— the beautiful and adored companion of all my occupations and my pleasures.

Every one loved Elizabeth. The passionate and almost reverential attachment with which all regarded her became, while I shared it, my pride and my delight. On the evening previous to her being brought to my home, my mother had said playfully,—'I have a pretty present for my Victor—to-morrow he shall have it.' And when, on the morrow, she presented Elizabeth to me as her promised gift, I, with childish seriousness, interpreted her words literally, and looked upon Elizabeth as mine—mine to protect, love, and cherish. All praises bestowed on her, I received as made to a possession of my own. We called each other familiarly by the name of cousin. No word, no expression could body forth the kind of relation in which she stood to me—my more than sister, since till death she was to be mine only.

CHAPTER II

We were brought up together; there was not quite a year difference in our ages. I need not say that we were strangers to any species of disunion or dispute. Harmony was the soul of our companionship, and the diversity and contrast that subsisted in our characters drew us nearer together. Elizabeth was of a calmer and more concentrated disposition; but, with all my ardour, I was capable of a more intense application, and was more deeply smitten with the thirst for knowledge. She busied herself with following the aerial creations of the poets; and in the majestic and wondrous scenes which surrounded our Swiss home—the sublime shapes of the mountains; the changes of the season; tempest and calm; the silence of winter, and the life and turbulence of our Alpine summers,—she found ample scope for admiration and delight. While my companion contemplated with a serious and satisfied spirit the magnificent appearances of things, I delighted in investigating their causes. The world was to me a secret which I desired to divine. Curiosity, earnest research to learn the hidden laws of nature, gladness akin to rapture, as they were unfolded to me, are among the earliest sensations I can remember.

On the birth of a second son, my junior by seven years, my parents gave up entirely their wandering life, and fixed themselves in their native country. We possessed a house in Geneva, and a *campagne* on Belrive, the eastern shore of the lake, at the distance of rather more than a league from the city. We resided principally in the latter, and the lives of my parents were passed in considerable seclusion. It was my temper to avoid a crowd, and to attach myself fervently to a few. I was indifferent, therefore, to my schoolfellows in general; but I united myself in the bonds of the closest friendship to one among them. Henry Clerval was the son of a merchant of Geneva. He was a boy of singular talent and fancy. He loved enterprise, hardship, and even danger, for its own sake. He was deeply read in books of chivalry and romance. He composed heroic songs, and began to write many a tale of enchantment and knightly adventure. He tried to make us act plays, and to enter into masquerades, in which the characters were drawn from the heroes of Roncesvalles, of the Round Table of King Arthur, and the chivalrous train who shed their blood to redeem the holy sepulchre from the hands of the infidels.

No human being could have passed a happier childhood than myself. My parents were possessed by the very spirit of kindness and indulgence. We felt that they were not the tyrants to rule our lot according to their caprice, but the agents and creators of all the many delights which we enjoyed. When I mingled with other families, I distinctly discerned how peculiarly fortunate my lot was, and gratitude assisted the development of filial love.

My temper was sometimes violent, and my passions vehement; but by some law in my temperature they were turned, not towards childish pursuits, but to an eager desire to learn, and not to learn all things indiscriminately. I confess that neither the structure of languages, nor the code of governments, nor the politics of various states, possessed attractions for me. It was the secrets of heaven and earth that I desired to learn; and whether it was the outward substance of things, or the inner spirit of nature and the mysterious soul of man that occupied me, still my enquiries were directed to the metaphysical, or, in its highest sense, the physical secrets of the world.

Meanwhile Clerval occupied himself, so to speak, with the moral relations of things. The busy stage of life, the virtues of heroes, and the actions of men, were his theme; and his hope and his dream was to become one among those whose names are recorded in story, as the gallant and adventurous benefactors of our species. The saintly soul of Elizabeth shone like a shrine-dedicated lamp in our peaceful home. Her sympathy was ours; her smile, her soft voice, the sweet glance of her celestial eyes, were ever there to bless and animate us. She was the living spirit of love to soften and attract: I might have become sullen in my study, rough through the ardour of my nature, but that she was there to subdue me to a semblance of her own gentleness. And Clerval—could aught ill entrench on the noble spirit of Clerval?—yet he might not have been so perfectly humane, so thoughtful in his generosity—so full of kindness and tenderness amidst his passion for adventurous exploit, had she not unfolded to him the real loveliness of beneficence, and made the doing good the end and aim of his soaring ambition. [3]
67.34 I feel pleasure] 38.21 I feel exquisite pleasure [3]

67.37 But,] 38.24 Besides, [3]

68.1 must not omit to] 38.25 also [3]

68.9 state] relate [T]

68.18-22 my father. I ... book, and said] my father who looking carelessly at the title-page of my book, said [T]

68.18-21 I cannot help ... they utterly neglect.] 39.6 *omitted* [3]

68.30-33 with my imagination ... from modern discoveries.] 39.17-18
have contented my imagination, warmed as it was, by returning
with greater ardour to my former studies. [3]

69.5-15 and although I ... by reality; and] 39.28-40.20 I have
described myself as always having been embued with a fervent
longing to penetrate the secrets of nature. In spite of the intense
labour and wonderful discoveries of modern philosophers, I always
came from my studies discontented and unsatisfied. Sir Isaac
Newton is said to have avowed that he felt like a child picking up
shells beside the great and unexplored ocean of truth. Those of his
successors in each branch of natural philosophy with whom I was
acquainted, appeared even to my boy's apprehensions, as tyros
engaged in the same pursuit.

The untaught peasant beheld the elements around him, and was
acquainted with their practical uses. The most learned philosopher
knew little more. He had partially unveiled the face of Nature, but
her immortal lineaments were still a wonder and a mystery. He
might dissect, anatomise, and give names; but, not to speak of a
final cause, causes in their secondary and tertiary grades were
utterly unknown to him. I had gazed upon the fortifications and
impediments that seemed to keep human beings from entering the
citadel of nature, and rashly and ignorantly I had repined.

But here were books, and here were men who had penetrated
deeper and knew more. I took their word for all that they averred,
and I became their disciple. It may appear strange that such should
arise in the eighteenth century; but while I followed the routine of
education in the schools of Geneva, I was, to a great degree, self
taught with regard to my favourite studies. My father was not scientific, and I was left to struggle with a child's blindness, added to
a student's thirst for knowledge. Under the guidance of my new
preceptors, [3]

69.16-17 the latter obtained my most] 40.22 the latter soon obtained
my [3]

69.27-70.2 The natural phaenomena ... in my mind.] 40.31-36 And
thus for a time I was occupied by exploded systems, mingling, like
an unadept, a thousand contradictory theories, and floundering
desperately in a very slough of multifarious knowledge, guided by

an ardent imagination and childish reasoning, till an accident again changed the current of my ideas. [3]

70.22 clouds.] clouds. [*Shelley adds comment*: you said your family was not <sientific>] [T]

70.16-71.24 The catastrophe of ... of each other.] 41.15-42.13 Before this I was not unacquainted with the more obvious laws of electricity. On this occasion a man of great research in natural philosophy was with us, and, excited by this catastrophe, he entered on the explanation of a theory which he had formed on the subject of electricity and galvanism, which was at once new and astonishing to me. All that he said threw greatly into the shade Cornelius Agrippa, Albertus Magnus, and Paracelsus, the lords of my imagination; but by some fatality the overthrow of these men disinclined me to pursue my accustomed studies. It seemed to me as if nothing would or could ever be known. All that had so long engaged my attention suddenly grew despicable. By one of those caprices of the mind, which we are perhaps most subject to in early youth, I at once gave up my former occupations; set down natural history and all its progeny as a deformed and abortive creation; and entertained the greatest disdain for a would-be science, which could never even step within the threshold of real knowledge. In this mood of mind I betook myself to the mathematics, and the branches of study appertaining to that science, as being built upon secure foundations, and so worthy of my consideration.

Thus strangely are our souls constructed, and by such slight ligaments are we bound to prosperity or ruin. When I look back, it seems to me as if this almost miraculous change of inclination and will was the immediate suggestion of the guardian angel of my life—the last effort made by the spirit of preservation to avert the storm that was even then hanging in the stars, and ready to envelope me. Her victory was announced by an unusual tranquillity and gladness of soul, which followed the relinquishing of my ancient and latterly tormenting studies. It was thus that I was to be taught to associate evil with their prosecution, happiness with their disregard.

It was a strong effort of the spirit of good; but it was ineffectual. Destiny was too potent, and her immutable laws had decreed my utter and terrible destruction. [3]

71 CHAPTER II.] 42 CHAPTER III [3]

72.1-2 but her illness ... she quickly recovered.] 42.24-25 her illness was severe, and she was in the greatest danger. [3]

72.2 During her confinement,] 42.25-26 During her illness, [3]

72.5-7 her favourite was ... infection was past.] 42.28-32 the life of her favourite was menaced, she could no longer control her anxiety. She attended her sick bed,—her watchful attentions triumphed over the malignity of the distemper,—Elizabeth was saved, but [3]

72.8 fatal.] 42.33 fatal to her preserver. [3]

72.9 very malignant,] 43.1-2 accompanied by the most alarming symptoms, [3]

72.10 her attendants] 43.2 her medical attendants [3]

72.11 admirable woman] amiable woman [T]

72.11 admirable woman] 43.4 best of women [3]

72.16 your younger cousins.] 43.9 my younger children. [3]

73.1 journey to] 43.37 departure for [3]

73.3-13 This period was ... forgetful of herself.] 44.2-16 It appeared to me sacrilege so soon to leave the repose, akin to death, of the house of mourning, and to rush into the thick of life. I was new to sorrow, but it did not the less alarm me. I was unwilling to quit the sight of those that remained to me; and, above all, I desired to see my sweet Elizabeth in some degree consoled.

She indeed veiled her grief, and strove to act the comforter to us all. She looked steadily on life, and assumed its duties with courage and zeal. She devoted herself to those whom she had been taught to call her uncle and cousins. Never was she so enchanting as at this time, when she recalled the sunshine of her smiles and spent them upon us. She forgot even her own regret in her endeavours to make us forget. [3]

73.20-23 Henry had a ... a cultivated understanding.] Henry loved poetry and his mind was filled with the imagery and sublime sentiments of the masters of that art. A poet himself, he turned with disgust from the details of ordinary life. His own <soul> mind was all the possession that he prized, beautiful & majestic thoughts the only wealth he coveted—daring as the eagle and as free, common laws could not be applied to him; and while you gazed on him you felt his soul's spark was more divine—more truly stolen from Apollo's sacred fire, than the glimmering ember that animates other men. [T]

73.14-29 I had taken ... have accompanied me.] 44.17-36 Clerval spent the last evening with us. He had endeavoured to persuade his father to permit him to accompany me, and to become my fellow student; but in vain. His father was a narrow-minded trader, and saw idleness and ruin in the aspirations and ambition of his son. Henry deeply felt the misfortune of being debarred from a liberal education. He said little; but when he spoke, I read in his kindling eye and in his animated glance a restrained but firm resolve, not to be chained to the miserable details of commerce.

We sat late. We could not tear ourselves away from each other, nor persuade ourselves to say the word 'Farewell!' It was said; and we retired under the pretence of seeking repose, each fancying that the other was deceived: but when at morning's dawn I descended to the carriage which was to convey me away, they were all there— my father again to bless me, Clerval to press my hand once more, my Elizabeth to renew her entreaties that I would write often, and to bestow the last feminine attentions on her playmate and friend. [3]

74.14-19 professors, and among ... upon those subjects.] 45.24-34 professors. Chance—or rather the evil influence, the Angel of Destruction, which asserted omnipotent sway over me from the moment I turned my reluctant steps from my father's door—led me first to M. Krempe, professor of natural philosophy. He was an uncouth man, but deeply embued in the secrets of his science. He asked me several questions concerning my progress in the different branches of science appertaining to natural philosophy. I replied carelessly; and, partly in contempt, mentioned the names of my alchymists as the principal authors I had studied. [3]

74.38 missed] 46.17 *omitted* [3]

74.39 for I] 46.18 for I have said that I [3]

74.40-42 had so strongly ... at his recommendation.] 46.20-21 reprobated; but I returned, not at all the more inclined to recur to these studies in any shape. [3]

74.43 and repulsive] 46.22 and a repulsive [3]

75.1 doctrine.] 46.24-32 pursuits. In rather a too philosophical and connected a strain, perhaps, I have given an account of the conclusions I had come to concerning them in my early years. As a child, I had not been content with the results promised by the modern professors of natural science. With a confusion of ideas only to be accounted for by my extreme youth, and my want of a guide on such matters, I had retrod the steps of knowledge along the paths of time, and exchanged the discoveries of recent enquirers for the dreams of forgotten alchymists. [3]

75.11 spent almost in solitude.] 47.5-7 of my residence at Ingolstadt, which were chiefly spent in becoming acquainted with the localities, and the principal residents in my new abode. [3]

76.4-5 I departed highly ... the same evening.] 48.6-24 Such were the professor's words—rather let me say such the words of fate, enounced to destroy me. As he went on, I felt as if my soul were grappling with a palpable enemy; one by one the various keys were touched which formed the mechanism of my being: chord after chord was sounded, and soon my mind was filled with one thought, one conception, one purpose. So much has been done, exclaimed the soul of Frankenstein,—more, far more, will I achieve: treading in the steps already marked, I will pioneer a new way, explore unknown powers, and unfold to the world the deepest mysteries of creation.

I closed not my eyes that night. My internal being was in a state of insurrection and turmoil; I felt that order would thence arise, but I had no power to produce it. By degrees, after the morning's dawn, sleep came. I awoke, and my yesternight's thoughts were as a dream. There only remained a resolution to return to my ancient studies, and to devote myself to a science for which I believed myself to possess a natural talent. On the same day, I paid M. Waldman a visit. [3]

76.8 kindness.] 48.28-30 kindness. I gave him pretty nearly the same account of my former pursuits as I had given to his fellow-professor. [3]

76.9 my little narration] 48.31 the little narration [3]

76.19-20 to his statement, ... without any presumption] to him with interest for he spoke without presumption [T]

76.22 and I, at the same time,] 49.7-11 I expressed myself in measured terms, with the modesty and deference due from a youth to his instructor, without letting escape (inexperience in life would have made me ashamed) any of the enthusiasm which stimulated my intended labours. I [3]

77.4 destiny.] destiny.* [*Shelley adds a footnote*: *If there were ever to be another edition of this book, I should re-write these two first chapters. The incidents are tame and ill arranged—the language sometimes childish.—They are unworthy of the rest of the <w book> narration.] [T]

77 CHAPTER III.] 50 CHAPTER IV [3]

77.18-24 It was, perhaps ... and resolution, now] 50.14-18 In a thousand ways he smoothed for me the path of knowledge, and made the most abstruse enquiries clear and facile to my apprehension. My application was at first fluctuating and uncertain; it gained strength as I proceeded, and soon [3]

77.27-28 I improved rapidly.] 50.22 my progress was rapid. [3]

78.21 Unless I had been animated] The event of these enquiries interested my understanding, I may say my imagination, until I was exalted to a kind of transport. And indeed unless I had been animated [T]

83.6-9 a disease that ... of my nerves.] my voice became broken, my trembling hands almost refused to accomplish their task; I became as timid as a love-sick girl, and alternate tremor and passionate ardour took the place of wholesome sensation and regulated ambition. [T]

83.6-10 a disease that ... away such symptoms;] 56.28-34 the fall of a leaf startled me, and I shunned my fellow-creatures as if I had been guilty of a crime. Sometimes I grew alarmed at the wreck I perceived that I had become; the energy of my purpose alone sustained me: my labours would soon end, and I believed that exercise and amusement would then drive away incipient disease; [3]

83 CHAPTER IV.] 57 CHAPTER V [3]

83.31 and straight black lips.] straight black lips. And the contortions that ever and anon convulsed & deformed his un-human features. [T]

85.11 wetted by the rain] 59.12 drenched by the rain [3]

86.6-8 it was not ... any thing except] 60.14-15 all necessary knowledge was not comprised in the noble art of [3]

87.30 the extent of my disorder] the violence of the attack [T]

88 CHAPTER V.] 63 CHAPTER VI [3]

88.35 *To* V. FRANKENSTEIN.] *deleted* [T]

89.4-5 and this makes ... your dear mother.] and this suspicion fills us with anguish. I perceive that your father <conceals> attempts to conceal his fears from me; but cheerfulness has flown from our little circle, only to be restored by a certain assuranance that there is no foundation for our anxiety. At one time [T]

89.6-7 My uncle was ... and could hardly] My uncle being almost persuaded that you were indeed dangerously ill, could hardly [T]

88.35-89.37 "To V. FRANKENSTEIN ... remember Justine Moritz?] 63.23-64.34 It was from my own Elizabeth:—

'My dearest Cousin,

'You have been ill, very ill, and even the constant letters of dear kind Henry are not sufficient to reassure me on your account. You are forbidden to write—to hold a pen; yet one word from you, dear Victor, is necessary to calm our apprehensions. For a long time I have thought that each post would bring this line, and my persuasions have restrained my uncle from undertaking a journey to Ingolstadt. I have prevented his encountering the inconveniences and perhaps dangers of so long a journey; yet how often have I regretted not being able to perform it myself! I figure to myself that the task of attending on your sick bed has devolved on some mercenary old nurse, who could never guess your wishes, nor minister to them with the care and affection of your poor cousin. Yet that is over now: Clerval writes that indeed you are getting better. I eagerly hope that you will confirm this intelligence soon in your own handwriting.

'Get well—and return to us. You will find a happy, cheerful home, and friends who love you dearly. Your father's health is vigorous, and he asks but to see you,—but to be assured that you are well; and not a care will ever cloud his benevolent countenance. How pleased you would be to remark the improvement of our Ernest! He is now sixteen, and full of activity and spirit. He is desirous to be a true Swiss, and to enter into foreign service; but we cannot part with him, at least until his elder brother return to us. My uncle is not pleased with the idea of a military career in a distant country; but Ernest never had your powers of application. He looks upon study as an odious fetter;—his time is spent in the open air, climbing the hills or rowing on the lake. I fear that he will become an idler, unless we yield the point, and permit him to enter on the profession which he has selected.

'Little alteration, except the growth of our dear children, has taken place since you left us. The blue lake, and snow-clad mountains, they never change;—and I think our placid home, and our contented hearts are regulated by the same immutable laws. My trifling occupations take up my time and amuse me, and I am rewarded for any exertions by seeing none but happy, kind faces around me. Since you left us, but one change has taken place in our little household. Do you remember on what occasion Justine Moritz entered our family? [3]

90.8 at her house] 65.4-5 at our house [3]

90.18-19 "After what I ... tale: for Justine] 65.16 'Justine, you may remember, [3]

91.40 good spirits] 67.8 better spirits [3]

91.40-92.2 yet I cannot ... my dearest cousin.] 67.8-13 but my anxiety returns upon me as I conclude. Write, dearest Victor,—one line—one word will be a blessing to us. Ten thousand thanks to Henry for his kindness, his affection, and his many letters: we are sincerely grateful. Adieu! my cousin; take care of yourself; and, I entreat you, write! [3]

92.4 "Geneva, March 18th, 17—."] "Geneva, March 18th, 17—."* [Shelley adds a footnote: *This letter ought to be re-written.] [T]

93.7 believed Cornelius Agrippa as firmly as the gospel] 68.28-29 believed in Cornelius Agrippa as firmly as in the gospel [3]

93.17-22 was no natural ... my own part,] 69.3-12 had never sympathised in my tastes for natural science; and his literary pursuits differed wholly from those which had occupied me. He came to the university with the design of making himself complete master of the oriental languages, as thus he should open a field for the plan of life he had marked out for himself. Resolved to pursue no inglorious career, he turned his eyes toward the East, as affording scope for his spirit of enterprise. The Persian, Arabic, and Sanscrit languages engaged his attention, and I was easily induced to enter on the same studies. [3]

93.26 orientalists.] 69.17-20 orientalists. I did not, like him, attempt a critical knowledge of their dialects, for I did not contemplate making any other use of them than temporary amusement. I read merely to understand their meaning, and they well repaid my labours. [3]

93.29 and garden] 69.24 and a garden [3]

94.21 loving and beloved] 70.25 loved and beloved [3]

95 CHAPTER VI.] 71 CHAPTER VII [3]

95.3 "*To* V. FRANKENSTEIN.] 71.12 *omitted* [T, 3]

95.10 gay welcome] 71.17 glad welcome [3]

95.13 an absent child?] 71.21 my long absent son? [3]

95.29 they had been playing together,] 72.6-7 he had been playing with him, [3]

96.9 my darling infant!'] 72.27 my darling child!" [3]

96.12 teazed] entreated [T]

96.12-13 a very valuable ... of your mother.] a miniature that she possessed of your mother. Which was set in jewels. [T]

97.6-9 raise my spirits ... his angel mother.] 73.32-74.3 say a few words of consolation; he could only express his heartfelt sympathy. 'Poor William!' said he, 'dear lovely child, he now sleeps with his angel mother! Who that had seen him bright and joyous in his young beauty, but must weep over his untimely loss! To die so miserably; to feel the murderer's grasp! How much more a murderer, that could destroy such radiant innocence! Poor little fellow! one only consolation have we; [3]

97.10 he does not ... the murderer's grasp;] 74.4-5 The pang is over, his sufferings are at an end for ever. [3]

97.12 a fit subject] 74.6-7 a subject [3]

97.12-17 the survivors are ... of his brother."] 74.7-8 we must reserve that for his miserable survivors.' [3]

98.24-25 half a league to the east of] 75.22-23 at the distance of half a league from [3]

98.25 The sky was serene; and,] The sky above was serene; [T]

98.34 increased.] increased. <but> And the clouds were gathering on the <ris> horison, mass rising above mass, while the lightning they emitted shewed their shapes and size. [T]

98.43 storm] 76.12 tempest [3]

100.17 Besides] And [T]

100.17 Besides,] 77.33 And then [3]

100.29 respectable parent] 78.6 venerable parent [3]

101.2-5 Our father looks ... is quite inconsolable."] the sense of Our misfortune is yet unalleviated; the silence of our father is uninterrupted, and there is something more distressing than tears in his unaltered sadness—while poor Elizabeth, seeking solitude and for ever weeping, already begins to feel the effects of incessant grief— for her colour is gone, and her eyes are hollow & lustreless [T]

101.8-9 But, tell me, ... my poor Elizabeth?"] You must assist me in acquiring sufficient calmness to console my father and support my poor Elizabeth" [T]

101.1-10 But we are ... "She indeed] 78.19-31 You come to us now to share a misery which nothing can alleviate; yet your presence will, I hope, revive our father, who seems sinking under his misfortune; and your persuasions will induce poor Elizabeth to cease her vain and tormenting self-accusations.—Poor William! he was our darling and our pride!'

Tears, unrestrained, fell from my brother's eyes; a sense of mortal agony crept over my frame. Before, I had only imagined the wretchedness of my desolated home; the reality came on me as a new, and a not less terrible, disaster. I tried to calm Ernest; I enquired more minutely concerning my father, and her I named my cousin.

'She most of all,' said Ernest, [3]

101.15 straw."] 79.1-2 straw. I saw him too; he was free last night!' [3]

101.16-17 but we were ... she was discovered.] 79.3-5 replied my brother, in accents of wonder, 'but to us the discovery we have made completes our misery. [3]

101.20-21 all at once become so extremely wicked?"] 79.9-10 suddenly become capable of so frightful, so appalling a crime?' [3]

101.32 and, after several days,] 79.21 for several days. During this interval, [3]

102.18-19 and, in this ... an evil result.] 80.16-21 My tale was not one to announce publicly; its astounding horror would be looked upon as madness by the vulgar. Did any one indeed exist, except I, the creator, who would believe, unless his senses convinced him, in the existence of the living monument of presumption and rash ignorance which I had let loose upon the world? [3]

102.20-29 made great alterations ... slight and graceful.] 80.22-26 altered her since I last beheld her; it had endowed her with loveliness surpassing the beauty of her childish years. There was the same candour, the same vivacity, but it was allied to an expression more full of sensibility and intellect. [3]

102.42 kind] 81.4 kind and generous [3]

103.3 "Sweet niece] 81.9 'Dearest niece [3]

103.4 judges] 81.10 laws [3]

103 CHAPTER VII.] 81 CHAPTER VIII [3]

103.34 quickly] instantly [T]

104.8 when one inquired] when some one inquired [T]

104.35 several hours] the greater part [T]

104.37 Unable to rest or sleep,] 83.22-25 Most of the night she spent here watching; towards morning she believed that she slept for a few minutes; some steps disturbed her, and she awoke. It was dawn, and [3]

104.38 early] 83.25 *omitted* [3]

105.15 would pledge] pledge [T]

106.3 Excellent Elizabeth!] 85.8 *omitted* [3]

106.3 was heard;] 85.8-9 followed Elizabeth's simple and powerful appeal; [3]

106.32 When I returned home,] 86.3-7 This was strange and unexpected intelligence; what could it mean? Had my eyes deceived me? and was I really as mad as the whole world would believe me to be, if I disclosed the object of my suspicions? I hastened to return home, and [3]

106.38 benevolence?] 86.14 goodness? [3]

107.3 ill-humour,] 86.17 guile, [3]

107.4 wish] 86.20 desire [3]

107.11 further] 86.26 farther [3]

107.19 me?"] 86.35-36 me, to condemn me as a murderer?' [3]

108.7 my] 87.27 *omitted* [3]

108.7-10 I will every ... I never can] 87.28-32 Do not fear. I will proclaim, I will prove your innocence. I will melt the stony hearts of your enemies by my tears and prayers. You shall not die!—You, my play-fellow, my companion, my sister, perish on the scaffold! No! no! I never could [3]

108.11-33 "Dear, sweet Elizabeth ... increase of misery."] 87.33-88.2 Justine shook her head mournfully. 'I do not fear to die,' she said; 'that pang is past. God raises my weakness, and gives me courage to endure the worst. I leave a sad and bitter world; and if you remember me, and think of me as of one unjustly condemned, I am resigned to the fate awaiting me. Learn from me, dear lady, to submit in patience to the will of Heaven!' [3]

108.37 the dreary boundary] 88.6 the awful boundary [3]

109.31-110.3 As we returned ... I then endured.] 89.5-33 And on the morrow Justine died. Elizabeth's heart-rending eloquence failed to move the judges from their settled conviction in the criminality of the saintly sufferer. My passionate and indignant appeals were lost upon them. And when I received their cold answers, and heard the harsh unfeeling reasoning of these men, my purposed avowal died away on my lips. Thus I might proclaim myself a madman, but not revoke the sentence passed upon my wretched victim. She perished on the scaffold as a murderess!

From the tortures of my own heart, I turned to contemplate the deep and voiceless grief of my Elizabeth. This also was my doing! And my father's woe, and the desolation of that late so smiling home—all was the work of my thrice-accursed hands! Ye weep, unhappy ones; but these are not your last tears! Again shall you raise the funeral wail, and the sound of your lamentations shall again and again be heard! Frankenstein, your son, your kinsman, your early, much-loved friend; he who would spend each vital drop of blood for your sakes—who has no thought nor sense of joy, except as it is mirrored also in your dear countenances—who would fill the air with blessings, and spend his life in serving you—he bids you weep—to shed countless tears; happy beyond his hopes, if thus inexorable fate be satisfied, and if the destruction pause before the peace of the grave have succeeded to your sad torments!

Thus spoke my prophetic soul, as, torn by remorse, horror, and despair, I beheld those I loved spend vain sorrow upon the graves of William and Justine, the first hapless victims to my unhallowed arts. [3]

110 END OF VOL. I.] 89 *omitted* [2, 3]

111 FRANKENSTEIN; / OR, THE / *MODERN PROMETHEUS.* / [VOL. II.]] 90 *omitted* [2, 3]

111 CHAPTER I.] CHAPTER VIII. [2]

111 CHAPTER I.] 90 CHAPTER IX [3]

111.24 had] 90.21-22 had perhaps never [3]

111.30-31 and endeavoured to ... to immoderate grief.] At first he suspected some latent cause for my affliction, but when I assured him that the late events were the causes of my dejection, he called to his aid philosophy and reason, while he endeavoured to restore me to a calmer state of mind. [T]

111.30-31 to reason with ... to immoderate grief.] 90.26-30 by arguments deduced from the feelings of his serene conscience and guiltless life, to inspire me with fortitude, and awaken in me the courage to dispel the dark cloud which brooded over me. [3]

112.3 bitterness] 91.7-8 bitterness, and terror its alarm [3]

113.3 anger] 92.15 abhorrence [3]

113.13-14 She had become ... of human life.] 92.26-28 The first of those sorrows which are sent to wean us from the earth, had visited her, and its dimming influence quenched her dearest smiles. [3]

113.22 Yet] 93.9 But [3]

113.43 cousin] 93.22 friend [3]

114.3-36 Be calm, my ... we ascended still] 93.22-94.32 Dear Victor, banish these dark passions. Remember the friends around you, who centre all their hopes in you. Have we lost the power of rendering you happy? Ah! while we love—while we are true to each other, here in this land of peace and beauty, your native country, we may reap every tranquil blessing,—what can disturb our peace?'

And could not such words from her whom I fondly prized before every other gift of fortune, suffice to chase away the fiend that lurked in my heart? Even as she spoke I drew near to her, as if in terror; lest at that very moment the destroyer had been near to rob me of her.

Thus not the tenderness of friendship, nor the beauty of earth, nor of heaven, could redeem my soul from woe: the very accents of love were ineffectual. I was encompassed by a cloud which no beneficial influence could penetrate. The wounded deer dragging its fainting limbs to some untrodden brake, there to gaze upon the arrow which had pierced it, and to die—was but a type of me.

Sometimes I could cope with the sullen despair that overwhelmed me: but sometimes the whirlwind passions of my soul drove me to seek, by bodily exercise and by change of place, some relief from my intolerable sensations. It was during an access of this kind that I suddenly left my home, and bending my steps towards the near Alpine valleys, sought in the magnificence, the eternity of such scenes, to forget myself and my ephemeral, because human, sorrows. My wanderings were directed towards the valley of Chamounix. I had visited it frequently during my boyhood. Six years had passed since then: I was a wreck—but nought had changed in those savage and enduring scenes.

I performed the first part of my journey on horseback. I afterwards hired a mule, as the more sure-footed, and least liable to receive injury on these rugged roads. The weather was fine: it was about the middle of the month of August, nearly two months after the death of Justine; that miserable epoch from which I dated all my woe. The weight upon my spirit was sensibly lightened as I plunged yet deeper in the ravine of Arve. The immense mountains and precipices that overhung me on every side—the sound of the river raging among the rocks, and the dashing of the waterfalls around, spoke of a power mighty as Omnipotence—and I ceased to fear, or to bend before any being less almighty than that which had created and ruled the elements, here displayed in their most terrific guise. Still, as I ascended [3]

115.1 We passed] 95.4 I passed [3]

115.2 us, and we began] 95.5 me, and I began [3]

115.3 we entered] 95.6 I entered [3]

115.5-6 we had just passed] 95.9 I had just passed [3]

115.7 we saw] 95.10 I saw [3]

115.8 we heard] 95.12 I heard [3]

115.13-26 During this journey ... I did not.] 95.17-31 A tingling long-lost sense of pleasure often came across me during this journey. Some turn in the road, some new object suddenly perceived and recognised, reminded me of days gone by, and were associated with the light-hearted gaiety of boyhood. The very winds whispered in soothing accents, and maternal nature bade me weep no more. Then again the kindly influence ceased to act—I found myself fettered again to grief, and indulging in all the misery of reflection. Then I spurred on my animal, striving so to forget the world, my fears, and, more than all, myself—or, in a more desperate fashion, I alighted, and threw myself on the grass, weighed down by horror and despair.

At length I arrived at the village of Chamounix. Exhaustion succeeded to the extreme fatigue both of body and of mind which I had endured. For a short space of time [3]

115.26 many hours] 95.32 *omitted* [3]

115.27 lightning] 95.32 lightnings [3]

115.28 ran below my window] 95.34-37 pursued its noisy way beneath. The same lulling sounds acted as a lullaby to my too keen sensations: when I placed my head upon my pillow, sleep crept over me; I felt it as it came, and blest the giver of oblivion. [3]

115 CHAPTER II.] CHAPTER IX. [2]

115 CHAPTER II.] 96 CHAPTER X [3]

115.30-32 The next day ... valley until evening.] 96.2-14 I spent the following day roaming through the valley. I stood beside the sources of the Arveiron, which take their rise in a glacier, that with slow pace is advancing down from the summit of the hills, to barricade the valley. The abrupt sides of vast mountains were before me; the icy wall of the glacier overhung me; a few shattered pines were scattered around; and the solemn silence of this glorious presence-chamber of imperial Nature was broken only by the brawling waves, or the fall of some vast fragment, the thunder sound of the avalanche, or the cracking, reverberated along the mountains, of the accumulated ice, which, through the silent working of immutable laws, was ever and anon rent and torn, as if it had been but a plaything in their hands. [3]

116.2-4 My father was ... not relapse again!"] The affectionate smile with which Elizabeth welcomed my altered mood excited me to greater exertion; and I felt as I spoke long forgotten sensations of pleasure arise in my mind. I knew that this state of being would only be temporary, that gloom and misery was near at hand, but this knowledge only acted as a stimulant, and <gave> added a tingling sensation of fear, while the blood danced along my veins—my eyes sparkled and my limbs even trembled beneath the influence of unaccustomed emotion. [T]

115.38-116.5 I returned in ... rain poured down] 96.19-29 I retired to rest at night; my slumbers, as it were, waited on and ministered to by the assemblance of grand shapes which I had contemplated during the day. They congregated round me; the unstained snowy mountain-top, the glittering pinnacle, the pine woods, and ragged bare ravine; the eagle, soaring amidst the clouds—they all gathered round me, and bade me be at peace.

Where had they fled when the next morning I awoke? All of soul-inspiriting fled with sleep, and dark melancholy clouded every thought. The rain was pouring [3]

116.6-13 I rose early ... to go alone] 96.30-97.1 so that I even saw not the faces of those mighty friends. Still I would penetrate their misty veil, and seek them in their cloudy retreats. What were rain and storm to me? My mule was brought to the door, and I resolved to ascend [3]

116.13 alone] 97.9 without a guide [3]

117.11 mutability!] mutability!* [*Shelley adds a footnote*: *Shelley's Poems.—"On Mutability."] [T]

118.5 anger and hatred] 99.7 rage and hatred [3]

119.30 bloody as they may be] 101.6 bloody as they are [2, 3]

119.36 remembrance] 101.12 remembrance,' I rejoined, [2, 3]

120 CHAPTER III.] CHAPTER X. [2]

120 CHAPTER III.] 102 CHAPTER XI [3]

121.29 trees.] 103.16 trees.* [*Shelley adds a footnote*: *The moon.] [2, 3]

124.3-4 Then overcome by ... and fell asleep.] After my meal I felt overcome by fatigue, and lying down among some straw, I fell asleep. [T]

124.18 the open country, and] the open country, Night came on as I wandered with wild agitation among the hedges and fields that surrounded me; I felt chill, and darkness, which ever filled me with dread, seemed to press with double weight upon my blinded organs. I looked around for shelter and [T]

124.35 pool] rivulet [T]

127.5 or the songs] 109.35 nor the songs [3]

127.7 letters.] letters. I continued however to watch the countenances of the Cottagers and the changes I perceived were at once the excitements and the aliments of a boundless curiosity. [T]

127 CHAPTER IV.] CHAPTER XI. [2]

127 CHAPTER IV.] 110 CHAPTER XII [3]

127.37 unhappy] sorrowful [T]

128.10-11 and they suffered ... very distressing degree.] They had appeared to me rich, because their possessions incomparably transcended mine, but I soon learnt, that many of these advantages were only <p> apparent, since their delicate frame made them subject to a thousand wants of the existence of which I was entirely ignorant. [T]

128.13 one cow, who] 111.13 one cow, which [3]

132.10 joy.] joy. / END OF VOL. I. [2]

132 CHAPTER V.] FRANKENSTEIN; / OR, / THE MODERN PROMETHEUS. / CHAPTER I. [2]

132 CHAPTER V.] 116 CHAPTER XIII [3]

132.13 from what I was] 116.3-4 from what I had been [2, 3]

132.22 him—I observed that] 116.13 him—that I observed [2, 3]

133.19 or herself understood] 117.15 nor herself understood [2, 3]

133.29 one sound] 117.26 some sound [2, 3]

134.27-28 treatment as I had] 118.33 treatment I had [2, 3]

134.29 entered.] entered. Nay if by moonlight I saw a human form, with a beating heart I squatted down amid the bushes fearful of discovery. And think you that it was with no bitterness of heart that I did this? It was in intercourse with man alone that I could hope for any pleasurable sensations and I was obliged to avoid it—Oh truly, I am grateful to thee my Creator for the gift of life, which was but pain, and to thy tender mercy which deserted me on life's threshold to suffer—all that man can inflict [T]

135.7 degeneration] 119.19 degenerating [2, 3]

135.33 acquisitions] 120.9 advantages [2, 3]

135.35 profit] 120.12 profits [3]

136.3 endowed] 120.15 endued [2, 3]

136.14 nor known or felt] 120.26 nor known nor felt [2, 3]

136.32 of the birth] 121.7 and the birth [3]

137 CHAPTER VI.] CHAPTER II. [2]

137 CHAPTER VI.] 122 CHAPTER XIV [3]

137.31 had] 122.27 had accidentally [2, 3]

138.32 father's] 123.23 father [2, 3]

138.34 father] 123.24 parent [2, 3]

139.9 the being immured] 124.7 being immured [2, 3]

139.10 puerile] 124.8 infantile [2, 3]

139.16 had quitted] 124.15 quitted his [2, 3]

140.8 greatly] 125.8 *omitted* [3]

140.30 impotence] 125.33 ruin [3]

140.36 when] 126.2 while [2, 3]

140.37 would have] 126.3 *omitted* [2, 3]

140.43 with him] 126.10 *omitted* [2, 3]

141.16 father's] 126.27 father [2, 3]

141.20 small] 126.31 *omitted* [3]

141.33 CHAPTER VII.] CHAPTER III. [2]

141.33 CHAPTER VII.] 127 CHAPTER XV [3]

142.35 unlike] 128.22 unlike to [2, 3]

143.34 created] 129.27 *omitted* [2; 3]

144.4 rose within me.] rose within me. while neither the feeling of remorse of self accusation mingled with my throes; although the contempt with I was treated also prevented any sublime defiance to have a place in my mind. [T]

144.19 ineffaceable] 130.16 indelible [2, 3]

144.20 Cursed] 130.18 "Accursed [3]

144.24 from its] 130.22 even from the [2, 3]

144.26 detested.'] 130.24 abhorred." [3]

145.2 wisdom] 131.3 sagacity [3]

145.21 or shared] 131.24 nor shared [3]

146.1 turned] 132.6 directed [3]

146.33 sunk] 133.5 sank [3]

147.14 Are these Germans] 133.30 Are they Germans [2, 3]

148.23 protectors.] protectors. They returned sooner than I expected and their inopportune appearance destroyed the fruits of so many months patience and expectation. My presence of mind deserted me at this crisis, I thought that [T]

149 CHAPTER VIII.] CHAPTER IV. [2]

149 CHAPTER VIII.] 135 CHAPTER XVI [3]

150.1 by degrees have] 137.2 by degrees to have [2, 3]

154.8 and, two months] 142.4 and, in two months [2, 3]

154.35 would punish] 142.33 will punish [2, 3]

155.1 impregnable] 143.6 invulnerable [3]

155.18 was seeking] 143.24 seeking [3]

155.19 when I perceived ... passing near me.] 143.25-26 I entered a barn which had appeared to me to be empty. A woman was sleeping on some straw; [3]

155.22 whose smiles] 143.30 whose joy-imparting smiles [3]

155.23 she shall not escape:] 143.30-144.4 And then I bent over her, and whispered "Awake, fairest, thy lover is near—he who would give his life but to obtain one look of affection from thine eyes: my beloved, awake!"

'The sleeper stirred; a thrill of terror ran through me. Should she indeed awake, and see me, and curse me, and denounce the murderer? Thus would she assuredly act, if her darkened eyes opened, and she beheld me. The thought was madness; it stirred the fiend within me—not I, but she shall suffer: the murder I have committed because I am for ever robbed of all that she could give me, she shall atone. The crime had its source in her: be hers the punishment! [3]

155.24-25 have learned how] 144.6 had learned now [3]

155.25 approached her unperceived] 144.6 bent over her [3]

155.26 dress.] 144.8 dress. She moved again, and I fled. [3]

156 CHAPTER IX.] CHAPTER V. [2]

156 CHAPTER IX.] 144 CHAPTER XVII [3]

156.9 refuse] 144.28 refuse to concede [2, 3]

156.36 you curse] 145.23-24 you shall curse [2, 3]

158.24-26 I thought I ... render me harmless.] 147.22-23 I must not be trifled with: and I demand an answer. [2, 3]

159.7 heaven,] 148.14 Heaven, and by the fire of love that burns my heart, [3]

159.36 siroc] sirocco [T]

159.38-160.20 but my presence ... degree of tranquillity.] 149.9-23 I took no rest, but returned immediately to Geneva. Even in my own heart I could give no expression to my sensations—they weighed on me with a mountain's weight, and their excess destroyed my agony beneath them. Thus I returned home, and entering the house, presented myself to the family. My haggard and wild appearance awoke intense alarm; but I answered no question, scarcely did I speak. I felt as if I were placed under a ban—as if I had no right to claim their sympathies—as if never more might I enjoy companionship with them. Yet even thus I loved them to adoration; and to save them, I resolved to dedicate myself to my most abhorred task. The prospect of such an occupation made every other circumstance of existence pass before me like a dream; and that thought only had to me the reality of life. [3]

160 END OF VOL. II.] 149 *omitted* [2, 3]

161 FRANKENSTEIN; / OR, THE / *MODERN PROMETHEUS.* / [VOL. III.]] 149 *omitted* [2, 3]

161.5 CHAPTER I.] CHAPTER VI. [2]

161.5 CHAPTER I.] 149 CHAPTER XVIII [3]

161.16-17 could not resolve ... returning tranquillity.] 150.3-5 shrunk from taking the first step in an undertaking whose immediate necessity began to appear less absolute to me. A change indeed had taken place in me: [3]

162.1 this exordium] 150.29 his exordium [3]

162.4 your cousin] 150.32 our dear Elizabeth [3]

162.13 your cousin] 151.5 Elizabeth [3]

162.39 cousin] 151.33 Elizabeth [3]

163.12-18 any variation was ... some accident might] 152.11-24 I had an insurmountable aversion to the idea of engaging myself in my loathsome task in my father's house, while in habits of familiar intercourse with those I loved. I knew that a thousand fearful accidents might occur, the slightest of which would disclose a tale to thrill all connected with me with horror. I was aware also that I should often lose all self-command, all capacity of hiding the harrowing sensations that would possess me during the progress of my unearthly occupation. I must absent myself from all I loved while thus employed. Once commenced, it would quickly be achieved, and I might be restored to my family in peace and happiness. My promise fulfilled, the monster would depart for ever. Or (so my fond fancy imaged) some accident might meanwhile [3]

163.22-164.4 the guise of ... restore my tranquillity.] 152.28-153.20 a guise which excited no suspicion, while I urged my desire with an earnestness that easily induced my father to comply. After so long a period of an absorbing melancholy, that resembled madness in its intensity and effects, he was glad to find that I was capable of taking pleasure in the idea of such a journey, and he hoped that change of scene and varied amusement would, before my return, have restored me entirely to myself.

The duration of my absence was left to my own choice; a few months, or at most a year, was the period contemplated. One paternal kind precaution he had taken to ensure my having a companion. Without previously communicating with me, he had, in concert with Elizabeth, arranged that Clerval should join me at Strasburgh. This interfered with the solitude I coveted for the prosecution of my task; yet at the commencement of my journey the presence of my friend could in no way be an impediment, and truly I rejoiced that thus I should be saved many hours of lonely, maddening reflection. Nay, Henry might stand between me and the intrusion of my foe. If I were alone, would he not at times force his abhorred presence on me, to remind me of my task, or to contemplate its progress?

To England, therefore, I was bound, and it was understood that my union with Elizabeth should take place immediately on my return. My father's age rendered him extremely averse to delay. For myself, there was one reward I promised myself from my detested toils—one consolation for my unparalleled sufferings; it was the prospect of that day when, enfranchised from my miserable slavery, I might claim Elizabeth, and forget the past in my union with her. [3]

164.19 August] 153.36 September [3]

164.19-25 departed, to pass ... be our feelings?"] 153.36-154.8 again quitted my native country. My journey had been my own suggestion, and Elizabeth, therefore, acquiesced: but she was filled with disquiet at the idea of my suffering, away from her, the inroads of misery and grief. It had been her care which provided me a companion in Clerval—and yet a man is blind to a thousand minute circumstances, which call forth a woman's sedulous attention. She longed to bid me hasten my return,—a thousand conflicting emotions rendered her mute, as she bade me a tearful silent farewell. [3]

164.30-31 for I resolved ... a free man.] 154.13 omitted [3]

165.8 to listen] 154.32 in listening [2, 3]

165.13 passed by] 154.37 passed [3]

165.27-28 depressed in mind] depressed by remor [T]

166.40 *Leigh Hunt's "Rimini."] 156.36 *omitted* [2, 3]

167 CHAPTER II.] CHAPTER VII. [2]

167 CHAPTER II.] 157 CHAPTER XIX [3]

168.19 amusement.] 158.21-27 amusement. He was also pursuing an object he had long had in view. His design was to visit India, in the belief that he had in his knowledge of its various languages, and in the views he had taken of its society, the means of materially assisting the progress of European colonisation and trade. In Britain only could he further the execution of his plan. [3]

168.21 dejected mien.] 158.29 dejected mind. [2, 3]

169.5 packed] 159.19 packed up [2, 3]

170.3 abhorrent] 160.21 intolerable [2, 3]

171.42 Coupar] Cupar [T]

173.17 sequel] 164.17 consummation [2, 3]

173 CHAPTER III.] CHAPTER VIII. [2]

173 CHAPTER III.] 165 CHAPTER XX [3]

175.34 deserts of Scotland] desert hills of Scotland [T]

176.3 weakness] 167.27 irresolution [2, 3]

176.5 resolution] 167.29 determination [2, 3]

177.39-43 nearly a year ... our future proceedings.] 169.36-170.8 he was wearing away his time fruitlessly where he was; that letters from the friends he had formed in London desired his return to complete the negotiation they had entered into for his Indian enterprise. He could not any longer delay his departure; but as his journey to London might be followed, even sooner than he now conjectured, by his longer voyage, he entreated me to bestow as much of my society on him as I could spare. He besought me, therefore, to leave my solitary isle, and to meet him at Perth, that we might proceed southwards together. [3]

178.4 pack] 170.12 pack up [2, 3]

179.17 little] 171.36 slenderly [2, 3]

179.27 and sunk] 172.10-11 all left behind, on whom the monster might satisfy his sanguinary and merciless passions. This idea plunged me [3]

179.40 eagerly] 172.32 carefully [2, 3]

180.10-11 very much surprised] 173.6 much surprised [3]

180.18 gruff] 173.14 hoarse [2, 3]

181 CHAPTER IV.] CHAPTER IX. [2]

181 CHAPTER IV.] 174 CHAPTER XXI [3]

181.27 fell all his length] 174.33 fell at his length [2, 3]

181.32 upon] 175.5 on [2, 3]

181.35 He] 175.9 It [2, 3]

181.36 five and twenty] twenty [T]

183.1-2 that faintly reminds ... recognition. The trial,] 176.24-25 The examination, [2, 3]

183.9-10 agonizing suffering] 176.33 agonies [2, 3]

184.9-10 but you will ... sessions come on.] 178.7 *omitted* [2, 3]

184.36 at] 178.35 with [2, 3]

184.37 when] 178.36 while [2, 3]

184.40-41 remain miserably pent ... in a world] 179.2-3 desire to remain in a world which to me was [2, 3]

185.29-30 "It was not ... examining your dress,] 180.1-2 'Immediately upon your being taken ill, all the papers that were on your person were brought me, and I examined them [3]

187.23 on the Orkney Islands] in the Orkney Islands [T]

187.28 allowed] 182.18 permitted [3]

188.12-24 I remember, as ... so much misery.] 183.8-24 Yet one duty remained to me, the recollection of which finally triumphed over my selfish despair. It was necessary that I should return without delay to Geneva, there to watch over the lives of those I so fondly loved; and to lie in wait for the murderer, that if any chance led me to the place of his concealment, or if he dared again to blast me by his presence, I might, with unfailing aim, put an end to the existence of the monstrous Image which I had endued with the mockery of a soul still more monstrous. My father still desired to delay our departure, fearful that I could not sustain the fatigues of a journey: for I was a shattered wreck,—the shadow of a human being. My strength was gone. I was a mere skeleton; and fever night and day preyed upon my wasted frame.

Still, as I urged our leaving Ireland with such inquietude and impatience, my father thought it best to yield. We took our passage on board a vessel bound for Havre-de-Grace, and sailed with a fair wind from the Irish shores. [3]

188.25 My father slept in the cabin; and] 183.25 *omitted* [3]

188.37 remembered shuddering at] 183.37-184.1 remembered, shuddering, [3]

188.39 during] 184.3 in [2, 3]

189.5 took a double dose] 184.11 swallowed double my usual quantity, [3]

189.12-13 and pointed to ... were now entering.] 184.18-23 the dashing waves were around: the cloudy sky above; the fiend was not here: a sense of security, a feeling that a truce was established between the present hour and the irresistible, disastrous future, imparted to me a kind of calm forgetfulness, of which the human mind is by its structure peculiarly susceptible. [3]

189 CHAPTER V.] CHAPTER X. [2]

189 CHAPTER V.] 184 CHAPTER XXII [3]

189.15-27 We had resolved ... he would not] 184.25-185.10 The voyage came to an end. We landed, and proceeded to Paris. I soon found that I had overtaxed my strength, and that I must repose before I could continue my journey. My father's care and attentions were indefatigable; but he did not know the origin of my sufferings, and sought erroneous methods to remedy the incurable ill. He wished me to seek amusement in society. I abhorred the face of man. Oh, not abhorred! they were my brethren, my fellow beings, and I felt attracted even to the most repulsive among them, as to creatures of an angelic nature and celestial mechanism. But I felt that I had no right to share their intercourse. I had unchained an enemy among them, whose joy it was to shed their blood, and to revel in their groans. How they would, each and all, abhor me, and hunt me from the world, did they know my unhallowed acts, and the crimes which had their source in me!

My father yielded at length to my desire to avoid society, and strove by various arguments to banish my [3]

189.29-30 prove to me the futility of pride.] inspire me with more philosophic sentiments. But his arguments drawn from general observation failed in reaching the core of my incurable disease. [T]

190.4 caused by] 185.24 the offspring of [2, 3]

190.8 feeling] 185.29 persuasion [3]

190.9 for ever chained my tongue,] 185.30-35 in itself would for ever have chained my tongue. But, besides, I could not bring myself to disclose a secret which would fill my hearer with consternation, and make fear and unnatural horror the inmates of his breast. I checked, therefore, my impatient thirst for sympathy, and was silent [3]

190.10 whole] 185.35 *omitted* [3]

190.11 secret.] 185.36-186.2 secret. Yet still words like those I have recorded, would burst uncontrollably from me. I could offer no explanation of them; but their truth in part relieved the burden of my mysterious woe. [3]

190.13 "What do you ... are you mad?] 186.4-5 'My dearest Victor, what infatuation is this? [3]

190.21-22 whole human race."] whole human race." What could induce me to talk thus incoherently of the dread<ful subject> that I dared not explain?—In truth, it was insanity, not of the under-standing but of the heart, which <produced a state of sickness> caused me always to think of one thing, of one sentiment, and <that> thus there would at times escape to my lips, as a half stifled <groan> sigh may, though else unseen & unheard, just move<s> the flame that surrounds the marty at the stake. But though he sigh, he will not recant, & though I more weak, gave vent to my pent up thoughts in words such as these, yet I shrunk unalterably from any thing that should reveal the existence of my enemy [T]

190.36 the sea of ice] Montanvert and the sea of ice [T]

190.37-39 We arrived at ... In this city,] 186.29 A few days before we left Paris on our way to Switzerland, [3]

191.1 "*To* VICTOR FRANKENSTEIN.] 186.31 *omitted* [3]

191.2 DEAREST] 186.31 dear [2, 3]

191.10 devoid] 187.3 void [2, 3]

191.19-20 and I have ... your affectionate cousin.] 187.12 and all my doubts satisfied. [3]

192.1 cousin] 187.36 friend [3]

192.8-9 interested] 188.8 disinterested [T, 3]

192.15 do not answer it] 188.15 do not answer [3]

192.29 if he was victorious] 188.30-31 if he were victorious [2, 3]

193.16-17 concentered] 189.25 centred [2, 3]

193.28 My cousin] 189.37 The sweet girl [3]

193.36 I thought on] 190.8 I thought of [2, 3]

193.39 or looked] 190.11 nor looked at any one [2, 3]

194.10 my cousin] 190.24 Elizabeth [3]

194.23 the lessons of my father] the views my father entertained [T]

194.40 I prepared] 191.18 I had prepared [3]

195.14-18 A house was ... at the schools.] 191.36-192.5 Through my father's exertions, a part of the inheritance of Elizabeth had been restored to her by the Austrian government. A small possession on the shores of Como belonged to her. It was agreed that, immediately after our union, we should proceed to Villa Lavenza, and spend our first days of happiness beside the beautiful lake near which it stood. [3]

195.22-23 gained a greater degree of tranquillity] gained I imagined a greater degree of security [T]

195.33-34 the following day] 192.22 on the following day [3]

195.35 observed] 192.24 recognised [2, 3]

195.38-40 pass the afternoon ... the next morning.] immediately depart for a small estate we possessed at Evian. [T]

195.38-41 pass the afternoon ... go by water.] 192.28-31 a commence our journey by water, sleeping that night at Evian, and continuing our voyage on the following day. The day was fair, the wind favourable, all smiled on our nuptial embarkation. [3]

196.10 I took the hand] <Why> Then gazing on the beloved face of Elizabeth on her graceful form and languid eyes, <of with> instead of feeling the exultation of a—lover—a husband—<in> a sudden gush of tears blinded my sight, & as I turned away to hide the invol-untary emotion fast drops fell in the wave below. Reason again awoke, and shaking off all unmanly—or more properly all natural thoughts of mischance, I smiled as I took the hand [T]

197.6-8 we walked for ... to the inn,] leaving the shore we sought the retreat of our house and garden. <but> Again as I entered the iron gates of the demesne, an <unres> unexplainable feeling bade me hold—yet Elizabeth unwarned, and fearless passed on, and I, again half ashamed—& for the first time dreading <less> lest any unholy sight should meet her sense, any shadow of the fiend, should cross her, <I> hastily walked on, and passing my arm round her prayed with a feeling of bitter tenderness, that she might never suffer ill. Thus we entered the <at> mansion—and still not speaking, for both our hearts were too full, we went to a balcony that overhung the lake [T]

197.22 relax the impending] 194.26 shrink from the [2, 3]

197.23 were extinguished] 194.27 was extinguished [2, 3]

197.25 at length she said,] 194.29-30 but there was something in my glance which communicated terror to her, and trembling she asked, [3]

197.28 dreadful] 195.2 fearful [3]

198.16 fainted.] 195.28 fell senseless on the ground. [3]

198.17-18 people of the inn] servants [T]

198.26 deathly] 196.2 deadly [2, 3]

198.39 shot] 196.18 fired [T, 3]

199.3 conjured] 196.24-25 conjured up [2, 3]

199.6 did not accompany them; I was exhausted:] 196.28-31 attempted to accompany them, and proceeded a short distance from the house; but my head whirled round, my steps were like those of a drunken man, I fell at last in a state of utter exhaustion; [3]

199.8 lay] 196.32-33 was carried back, and placed [3]

199.10-13 At length I ... a long time;] 196.36-197.3 After an interval, I arose, and, as if by instinct, crawled into the room where the corpse of my beloved lay. There were women weeping around—I hung over it, and joined my sad tears to theirs—all this time no distinct idea presented itself to my mind; [3]

199.13 reflecting] 197.4 reflecting confusedly [3]

200.8 niece] 198.9 Elizabeth [3]

200.14 an apoplectic fit was brought on,] 198.15-16 the springs of existence suddenly gave way: he was unable to rise from his bed, [3]

200.19-20 but awoke] 198.22 but I awoke [2, 3]

200.25 But liberty had been a] 198.28 Liberty, however, had been an [2, 3]

201.7 provisionally] 199.18 for an interval [2, 3]

201.15 detection] 199.28 seizure [3]

201.20 my auditor] 199.34 my own auditor [3]

202.2 and that, while] 200.21 and thus, while [2, 3]

202.3 endeavour to] 200.22 *omitted* [2, 3]

202 CHAPTER VII.] CHAPTER XII. [2]

202 CHAPTER VII.] 201 CHAPTER XXIV [3]

202.27 modelled] 201.11 moulded [2, 3]

203.6 around] 201.30 round [2, 3]

203.15 seen not] 202.6 not seen [2, 3]

203.23 and by the spirits] 202.15 and the spirits [2, 3]

203.24 I swear] 202.15 *omitted* [2, 3]

204.19 trace] 203.17 trace of him, [2, 3]

204.20 often] 203.17 *omitted* [2, 3]

204.32 I may not doubt] 203.30-31 I will not doubt [2, 3]

205.1 bringing] 204.4 I brought [2, 3]

205.38 omit] 205.7 give up [2, 3]

205.40 those] 205.8-9 my departed friends, [2, 3]

207.30 when] 207.12 *omitted* [2, 3]

207.31 carried] 207.13 conveyed [2, 3]

208.6 enemy] 207.36 foe [3]

208.33 still] 208.23 *omitted* [3]

208.38-39 Yet, do I dare ask you] 208.32 And do I dare to ask of you [2, 3]

209.1 live] survive [2]

209.1 live to make ... as I am.] 208.37-209.1 survive to add to the list of his dark crimes. [3]

209.11 congealed] 209.11 congeal [2, 3]

209.14 agony] 209.15 anguish [3]

209.34-35 Or to what do your questions tend?] 210.1 *omitted* [2, 3]

210.14 feelings] 210.17 spirit [2, 3]

210.19 real beings] 210.23 beings themselves [2, 3]

210.31 felt as if I were] 210.37 believed myself [2, 3]

210.40 feeling] 211.10 thought [2, 3]

211.34 invaded] 212.10 contemplated [2, 3]

212.12-15 We may survive ... good heart.

Yet] 212.31-34 Yet it is terrible to reflect that the lives of all these men are endangered through me. If we are lost, my mad schemes are the cause.

And [3]

212.18-19 failings of your heart-felt expectations are,] 213.2 failing of your heart-felt expectations is, [2, 3]

212.31 day's expectation] 213.16 day of expectation [2, 3]

213.15 desired] 213.34 demanded [2, 3]

213.19 demand] 214.1 requisition [2, 3]

213.24 desired] 214.7 insisted [2, 3]

213.40 surrounded] 214.25 surrounded it [3]

213.41 dangers] 214.25 *omitted* [2, 3]

213.43 name] 214.28 names [T, 2, 3]

214.11-12 might be] 215.3-4 may be [2, 3]

214.12 mutable,] 215.4 mutable, and [3]

214.22 further] 215.14 farther [3]

215.38 but] 216.27 *omitted* [2, 3]

216.8-9 my fellow-creatures] 217.9 the beings of my own species [2, 3]

217.37 may not answer] 219.14 cannot answer [2, 3]

217.42 looks upon] 219.19 eyes to [2, 3]

218.10 more] 219.31 *omitted* [2, 3]

218.14 ye] 219.35 you [3]

219.22 bringing forth] 221.15-16 unfolding [2, 3]

219.24 vice] 221.17 crime [3]

219.24 crime] 221.18 guilt [3]

219.26 call] 221.19 run [2, 3]

219.26 deeds] 221.20 sins [3]

219.27 he] 221.21 the same creature [2, 3]

219.31 quite alone] 221.26 alone [2, 3]

219.36 whilst] 221.31 while [2, 3]

220.15 they] 222.16 these hands [2, 3]

220.16 it] 222.17 that imagination [2, 3]

220.22 hither] 222.25 thither [3]

220.35 chirping] 223.3 warbling [2, 3]

221.5 hast] 223.12 hadst [2, 3]

221.5 yet] 223.12 *omitted* [2, 3]

221.5-6 desirest not my ... my own misery.] 223.13-14 wouldst not desire against me a vengeance greater than that which I feel. [2, 3]

221.7 may not cease] 223.16 will not cease [2, 3]

Appendix I: Introduction to Shelley's 1831 Edition

[Mary Shelley substantially revised the novel for its 1831 appearance as volume No. 9 in Colburn and Bentley's Standard Novels series. With Percy dead almost ten years, Mary had worked hard to establish herself as a respectable member of London society, despite the sensationalism of her youthful adventures, and this effort is evident in some of the textual changes, and most especially, in her introduction. After 1831, Mary did no further work on *Frankenstein*.]

THE Publishers of the Standard Novels,[1] in selecting 'Frankenstein' for one of their series, expressed a wish that I should furnish them with some account of the origin of the story. I am the more willing to comply, because I shall thus give a general answer to the question, so very frequently asked me—'How I, then a young girl, came to think of, and to dilate upon, so very hideous an idea?' It is true that I am very averse to bringing myself forward in print; but as my account will only appear as an appendage to a former production, and as it will be confined to such topics as have connection with my authorship alone, I can scarcely accuse myself of a personal intrusion.

It is not singular that, as the daughter of two persons of distinguished literary celebrity, I should very early in life have thought of writing. As a child I scribbled; and my favourite pastime, during the hours given me for recreation, was to 'write stories.' Still I had a dearer pleasure than this, which was the formation of castles in the air—the indulging in waking dreams—the following up trains of thought, which had for their subject the formation of a succession of imaginary incidents. My dreams were at once more fantastic and agreeable than my writings. In the latter I was a close imitator—rather doing as others had done, than putting down the suggestions of my own mind. What I wrote was intended at least for one other eye—my childhood's companion and friend; but my dreams were all my own; I accounted for them to nobody; they were my refuge when annoyed—my dearest pleasure when free.

I lived principally in the country as a girl, and passed a considerable time in Scotland. I made occasional visits to the more picturesque parts; but my habitual residence was on the blank and dreary northern shores of the Tay, near Dundee. Blank and dreary on retrospection

---

1 Henry Colburn and Richard Bentley published the 1831 version of *Frankenstein* as No. 9 in their inexpensive series of "Standard Novels."

I call them; they were not so to me then. They were the eyry of freedom, and the pleasant region where unheeded I could commune with the creatures of my fancy. I wrote then—but in a most common-place style. It was beneath the trees of the grounds belonging to our house, or on the bleak sides of the woodless mountains near, that my true compositions, the airy flights of my imagination, were born and fostered. I did not make myself the heroine of my tales. Life appeared to me too common-place an affair as regarded myself. I could not figure to myself that romantic woes or wonderful events would ever be my lot; but I was not confined to my own identity, and I could people the hours with creations far more interesting to me at that age, than my own sensations.

After this my life became busier, and reality stood in place of fiction. My husband, however, was, from the first, very anxious that I should prove myself worthy of my parentage, and enrol myself on the page of fame. He was for ever inciting me to obtain literary reputation, which even on my own part I cared for then, though since I have become infinitely indifferent to it. At this time he desired that I should write, not so much with the idea that I could produce any thing worthy of notice, but that he might himself judge how far I possessed the promise of better things hereafter. Still I did nothing. Travelling, and the cares of a family, occupied my time; and study, in the way of reading, or improving my ideas in communication with his far more cultivated mind, was all of literary employment that engaged my attention.

In the summer of 1816, we visited Switzerland, and became the neighbours of Lord Byron. At first we spent our pleasant hours on the lake, or wandering on its shores; and Lord Byron, who was writing the third canto of Childe Harold, was the only one among us who put his thoughts upon paper. These, as he brought them successively to us, clothed in all the light and harmony of poetry, seemed to stamp as divine the glories of heaven and earth, whose influences we partook with him.

But it proved a wet, ungenial summer, and incessant rain often confined us for days to the house. Some volumes of ghost stories, translated from the German into French, fell into our hands. There was the History of the Inconstant Lover, who, when he thought to clasp the bride to whom he had pledged his vows, found himself in the arms of the pale ghost of her whom he had deserted. There was the tale of the sinful founder of his race, whose miserable doom it was to bestow the kiss of death on all the younger sons of his fated house, just when they reached the age of promise. His gigantic, shadowy form, clothed like the ghost in Hamlet, in complete armour, but with the beaver up, was seen at midnight, by the moon's fitful beams, to advance slowly along the gloomy avenue. The shape was lost beneath the shadow of the castle walls; but soon a gate swung back, a step was heard, the door of the chamber opened, and he advanced to the couch of the blooming youths, cradled in healthy sleep. Eternal sorrow sat upon his face as he bent down and kissed the forehead of the boys, who from that hour withered like flowers snapt upon the stalk. I have not seen these stories since then; but their incidents are as fresh in my mind as if I had read them yesterday.

'We will each write a ghost story,' said Lord Byron; and his proposition was acceded to. There were four of us. The noble author began a tale, a fragment of which he printed at the end of his poem of Mazeppa.[1] Shelley, more apt to embody ideas and sentiments in the radiance of brilliant imagery, and in the music of the most melodious verse that adorns our language, than to invent the machinery of a story, commenced one founded on the experiences of his early life. Poor Polidori had some terrible idea about a skull-headed lady, who was so punished for peeping through a key-hole—what to see I forget—something very shocking and wrong of course; but when she was reduced to a worse condition than the renowned Tom of Coventry,[2] he did not know what to do with her, and was obliged to despatch her to the tomb of the Capulets, the only place for which she was fitted.[3] The illustrious poets also, annoyed by the platitude of prose, speedily relinquished their uncongenial task.

I busied myself *to think of a story*,—a story to rival those which had excited us to this task. One which would speak to the mysterious fears of our nature, and awaken thrilling horror—one to make the reader dread to look round, to curdle the blood, and quicken the beatings of the heart. If I did not accomplish these things, my ghost story would be unworthy of its name. I thought and pondered—vainly. I felt that blank incapability of invention which is the greatest misery of authorship, when dull Nothing replies to our anxious invocations. *Have you thought of a story?* I was asked each morning, and each morning I was forced to reply with a mortifying negative.

Every thing must have a beginning, to speak in Sanchean phrase;[4] and that beginning must be linked to something that went before. The Hindoos give the world an elephant to support it, but they make the

---

1 Byron, *Mazeppa, a Poem* (1819) 59-69.

2 Who was struck blind for spying on Lady Godiva.

3 Capulet is Juliet's family name, in Shakespeare's *Romeo and Juliet*, and the tragedy ends in her family tomb. Polidori's *Ernestus Berchtold* does contain an incident corresponding vaguely to this anecdote, but the resemblance is slight.

4 In Cervantes's *Don Quixote*, which Shelley read in 1816, Sancho declares: "in this matter of government everything depends upon the beginning" (II.xxxiii).

elephant stand upon a tortoise.[1] Invention, it must be humbly admitted, does not consist in creating out of void, but out of chaos; the materials must, in the first place, be afforded: it can give form to dark, shapeless substances, but cannot bring into being the substance itself. In all matters of discovery and invention, even of those that appertain to the imagination, we are continually reminded of the story of Columbus and his egg.[2] Invention consists in the capacity of seizing on the capabilities of a subject, and in the power of moulding and fashioning ideas suggested to it.

Many and long were the conversations between Lord Byron and Shelley, to which I was a devout but nearly silent listener. During one of these, various philosophical doctrines were discussed, and among others the nature of the principle of life, and whether there was any probability of its ever being discovered and communicated. They talked of the experiments of Dr. Darwin, (I speak not of what the Doctor really did, or said that he did, but, as more to my purpose, of what was then spoken of as having been done by him,) who preserved a piece of vermicelli in a glass case, till by some extraordinary means it began to move with voluntary motion.[3] Not thus, after all, would life be given. Perhaps a corpse would be re-animated; galvanism had given token of such things: perhaps the component parts of a creature might be manufactured, brought together, and endued with vital warmth.

Night waned upon this talk, and even the witching hour had gone by, before we retired to rest. When I placed my head on my pillow, I did not sleep, nor could I be said to think. My imagination, unbidden, possessed and guided me, gifting the successive images that arose in my mind with a vividness far beyond the usual bounds of reverie. I saw—with shut eyes, but acute mental vision,—I saw the pale student of unhallowed arts kneeling beside the thing he had put together. I saw the hideous phantasm of a man stretched out, and then, on the working of some powerful engine, show signs of life, and stir with an uneasy, half vital motion. Frightful must it be; for supremely frightful would be the effect of any human endeavour to mock the stupendous

---

1 Cf. Shaftesbury, *Characteristicks* (2nd rev. ed. 1715) II.202; and Wollstonecraft, *Vindication* 226; V.iv.

2 In this famous story, also found in Washington Irving's *Christopher Columbus* (1828), the navigator, provoked by the suggestion that someone else might have discovered the Americas, challenged the company to stand an egg on its end. "Everyone attempted it, but in vain; whereupon he struck it upon the table so as to break the end, and left it standing on the broken part; illustrating in this simple manner, that when he had once shown the way to the New World, nothing was easier than to follow it" (V.vii).

3 Cf. Darwin, *The Temple of Nature* Additional Note I, 1-3 (Appendix B.1.d).

mechanism of the Creator of the world. His success would terrify the artist; he would rush away from his odious handywork, horror-stricken. He would hope that, left to itself, the slight spark of life which he had communicated would fade; that this thing, which had received such imperfect animation, would subside into dead matter; and he might sleep in the belief that the silence of the grave would quench for ever the transient existence of the hideous corpse which he had looked upon as the cradle of life. He sleeps; but he is awakened; he opens his eyes; behold the horrid thing stands at his bedside, opening his curtains, and looking on him with yellow, watery, but speculative eyes.

I opened mine in terror. The idea so possessed my mind, that a thrill of fear ran through me, and I wished to exchange the ghastly image of my fancy for the realities around. I see them still; the very room, the dark parquet, the closed shutters, with the moonlight struggling through, and the sense I had that the glassy lake and white high Alps were beyond. I could not so easily get rid of my hideous phantom; still it haunted me. I must try to think of something else. I recurred to my ghost story,—my tiresome unlucky ghost story! O! if I could only contrive one which would frighten my reader as I myself had been frightened that night!

Swift as light and as cheering was the idea that broke in upon me.[1] 'I have found it! What terrified me will terrify others; and I need only describe the spectre which had haunted my midnight pillow.' On the morrow I announced that I had *thought of a story*. I began that day with the words, *It was on a dreary night of November*, making only a transcript of the grim terrors of my waking dream.

At first I thought but of a few pages—of a short tale; but Shelley urged me to develope the idea at greater length. I certainly did not owe the suggestion of one incident, nor scarcely of one train of feeling, to my husband, and yet but for his incitement, it would never have taken the form in which it was presented to the world. From this declaration I must except the preface. As far as I can recollect, it was entirely written by him.

And now, once again, I bid my hideous progeny go forth and prosper. I have an affection for it, for it was the offspring of happy days, when death and grief were but words, which found no true echo in my heart. Its several pages speak of many a walk, many a drive, and many a conversation, when I was not alone; and my companion was one who, in this world, I shall never see more. But this is for myself; my readers have nothing to do with these associations.

I will add but one word as to the alterations I have made. They are principally those of style. I have changed no portion of the story, nor

---

1 Cf. Wollstonecraft, *Vindication* 244-45; VI (Appendix A.2.f).

introduced any new ideas or circumstances. I have mended the language where it was so bald as to interfere with the interest of the narrative; and these changes occur almost exclusively in the beginning of the first volume. Throughout they are entirely confined to such parts as are mere adjuncts to the story, leaving the core and substance of it untouched.

M.W.S.

London, October 15, 1831

Works Cited/Recommended Reading

Adams, Stephen. Rev. of Robinson 2008, in *The Daily Telegraph*, 24 August 2008.

Aldini, John. *An Account of the Late Improvements in Galvanism, with a Series of Curious and Interesting Experiments Performed before the Commissioners of the French National Institute, and Repeated Lately in the Anatomical Theatres of London. To Which Is Added, an Appendix, Containing the Author's Experiments on the Body of a Malefactor Executed at Newgate. &c. &c.* London: Cuthell and Martin and J. Murray, 1803.

Ariès, Philippe. *The Hour of Our Death.* Trans. Helen Weaver. 1981. Rpt. New York: Vintage Books, 1982.

Baldick, Chris. *In Frankenstein's Shadow: Myth, Monstrosity, and Nineteenth-Century Writing.* Oxford: Clarendon Press, 1987.

Bewell, Alan. "An Issue of Monstrous Desire: *Frankenstein* and Obstetrics." *Yale Journal of Criticism* 2 (1988-89): 105-28.

Brooks, Peter. "Godlike Science/Unhallowed Arts: Language, Nature, and Monstrosity." Levine and Knoepflmacher 205-20.

Burwick, Roswitha. "Goethe's *Werther* and Mary Shelley's *Frankenstein*." *The Wordsworth Circle* 24.1 (1993): 47-52.

Butler, Marilyn, ed. and introd. *Frankenstein; or, The Modern Prometheus.* By Mary Wollstonecraft Shelley. London: William Pickering, 1993. ix-li.

Byron, George Gordon. *Byron's Letters and Journals.* Ed. Leslie A. Marchand. 12 vols. London: John Murray, 1973-82.

———. *Complete Poetical Works.* Ed. Jerome J. McGann. 7 vols. Oxford: Clarendon P, 1980-91.

Cameron, Kenneth N. "A Major Source of *The Revolt of Islam*." *PMLA* 56 (1941): 175-206.

Cox, Jeffrey N., ed. and introd. *Seven Gothic Dramas 1789-1825.* Athens: Ohio State UP, 1992.

Croker, John Wilson. Rev. of *Frankenstein*, by Mary Shelley. *Quarterly Review* 18 (1817-18): 379-85.

Crook, Nora. "Did Mary Shelley Write *Frankenstein*? Or Did Percy Shelley Spoil It?" In Tatsuo Tokoo *et al.* (eds.), *A Milestone of Shelleyan Scholarly Pursuits in Japan: Essays Commemorating the 15th Anniversary of the Founding of Japan Shelley Studies Centre.* Tokyo: Eihosha, 2007. 3-18.

———, ed. *Frankenstein; or, The Modern Prometheus.* Introd. Betty T. Bennett. The Novels and Selected Works of Mary Shelley, vol. 1. London: William Pickering, 1996.

Crouch, Laura E. "Davy's *A Discourse, Introductory to A Course of Lectures on Chemistry*: A Possible Scientific Source of *Frankenstein*." *Keats-Shelley Journal* 27 (1978): 35-44.

Darwin, Erasmus. *The Botanic Garden; A Poem, in Two Parts. Part I. containing The Economy of Vegetation. Part II. The Loves of the Plants. With Philosophical Notes.* London: J. Johnson, 1791.

———. *The Temple of Nature; or, The Origin of Society: A Poem. With Philosophical Notes.* London: J. Johnson, 1803.

Davy, Humphry. *A Discourse, Introductory to A Course of Lectures on Chemistry, Delivered in the Theatre of the Royal Institution on the 21st of January, 1802.* London: Sold at the House of the Royal Institution, 1802.

Dawson, John. "'Pater Absconditus': Delving into Werther's Neuroses." *AUMLA* 68(1987): 251-60.

Fleck, P.D. "Mary Shelley's Notes to Shelley's Poems and *Frankenstein*." *Studies in Romanticism* 6 (1966-67): 226-54.

Florescu, Radu, with Alan Barbour and Matei Cazacu. *In Search of Frankenstein.* Boston: New York Graphic Society, 1975.

Gilbert, Sandra M., and Susan Gubar. *The Madwoman in the Attic: The Woman Writer and the Nineteenth-Century Literary Imagination.* New Haven: Yale UP, 1979.

Godwin, William. *Enquiry Concerning Political Justice and Its Influence on Morals and Happiness.* 3rd ed. 1798. Ed. F.E.L. Priestley. 2 vols. Toronto: U of Toronto P, 1946.

———. *Memoirs of the Author of "The Rights of Woman." A Short Residence in Sweden and Memoirs of the Author of "The Rights of Woman."* By Mary Wollstonecraft and William Godwin. Ed. Richard Holmes. Harmondsworth: Penguin, 1987. 201-77.

———. *St. Leon.* Ed. Pamela Clemit. Oxford: Oxford UP, 1994.

———. *Things as They Are; or, The Adventures of Caleb Williams.* Ed. David McCracken. Oxford: Oxford UP, 1982.

Goethe, Johann Wolfgang von. *The Sorrows of Werter.* [Trans. Daniel Malthus.] New ed. London: J. Dodsley, 1789.

Hatlen, Burton. "Milton, Mary Shelley, and Patriarchy." *Bucknell Review* 28.2 (1983): 19-47.

Hazlitt, William. *The Spirit of the Age: or Contemporary Portraits.* 1825. Garden City, NY: Doubleday, n.d.

Hindle, Maurice, ed. and introd. *Frankenstein; or, The Modern Prometheus.* By Mary Wollstonecraft Shelley. Harmondsworth: Penguin, 1992.

Hitchcock, Susan Tyler. *Frankenstein: A Cultural History.* New York: Norton, 2007.

Homans, Margaret. *Bearing the Word: Language and Female Experience in Nineteenth-Century Women's Writing.* Chicago: U of Chicago P, 1986.

Howard, Jennifer. "The Birth of Frankenstein," rev. of Robinson 2008, in *The Chronicle of Higher Education Review*, 7 November 2008.

Jacobus, Mary. "Is There a Woman in This Text?" *New Literary History* 14 (1982-83): 117-41.

Johnson, Barbara. "My Monster/My Self." *Diacritics* 12 (1982): 2-10.

Jones, Steven. Rev. of Robinson 1996, in *Romantic Circles Reviews*, 1 January 1998. http://www.rc.umd.edu/reviews-blog/?p=308

Joseph, M.K., ed. and introd. *Frankenstein; or, The Modern Prometheus*. By Mary Wollstonecraft Shelley. Oxford: Oxford UP, 1969.

Keats, John. *The Letters of John Keats, 1814-1821*. Ed. Hyder Edward Rollins. 2 vols. Cambridge, MA: Harvard UP, 1958.

King, Lester S. *The Philosophy of Medicine: The Early Eighteenth Century*. Cambridge, MA: Harvard UP, 1978.

Lamb, Lady Caroline. *Glenarvon*. 1816. Ed. Frances Wilson. London: Everyman, 1995.

Lauritsen, John. *The Man Who Wrote Frankenstein*. Provincetown, MA: Pagan Press, 2007.

———. Letter, *The Chronicle of Higher Education*, 5 December 2008.

Levine, George, and U.C. Knoepflmacher, eds. *The Endurance of Frankenstein: Essays on Mary Shelley's Novel*. Berkeley: U of California P, 1979.

Macdonald, D.L. *Poor Polidori: A Critical Biography of the Author* of *The Vampyre*. Toronto: U of Toronto P, 1991.

Marchand, Leslie A. *Byron: A Portrait*. New York: Knopf, 1970.

McWhir, Anne. "Teaching the Monster to Read: Mary Shelley, Education and *Frankenstein*." *The Educational Legacy of Romanticism*. Ed. John Willinsky. Waterloo: Wilfrid Laurier UP/Calgary Institute for the Humanities, 1990.

Mellor, Anne K. *Mary Shelley: Her Life, Her Fiction, Her Monsters*. New York: Routledge, 1988.

Milton, John. *The Complete Poetry of John Milton*. Ed. John T. Shawcross. Rev. ed. Garden City, NY: Anchor Books, 1971.

Moers, Ellen. "Female Gothic." Levine and Knoepflmacher 77-87.

Murray, E.B. "Changes in the 1823 Edition of *Frankenstein*." *The Library* 6.3 (1981): 320-27.

———. "Shelley's Contribution to Mary's *Frankenstein*." *Keats-Shelley Memorial Bulletin* 29 (1978): 50-68.

Peake, Richard Brinsley. *Presumption; or, The Fate of Frankenstein* (1823). Cox 385-425.

Plutarch. *Plutarch's Lives*. Trans. John Dryden et al. Rev. Arthur Hugh Clough. 3 vols. Philadelphia: John D. Morris, n.d.

Polidori, John William. *The Diary of Dr. John William Polidori, 1816,*

Relating to Byron, Shelley, etc. Ed. William Michael Rossetti. London: Elkin Mathews, 1911.

———. *The Vampyre and Ernestus Berchtold; or, The Modern Oedipus.* Ed. D.L. Macdonald and Kathleen Scherf. Peterborough: Broadview, 2008.

Pollin, Burton R. "Philosophical and Literary Sources of *Frankenstein.*" *Comparative Literature* 17 (1965): 97-108.

Poovey, Mary. *The Proper Lady and the Woman Writer: Ideology as Style in the Works of Mary Wollstonecraft, Mary Shelley, and Jane Austen.* Chicago: U of Chicago P, 1984.

Pratt, Lynda. "Who Wrote the Original *Frankenstein?*" Rev. of Robinson 2008, in *The Times Literary Supplement*, 29 October 2008.

Punter, David. *The Literature of Terror: A History of Gothic Fictions from 1765 to the Present Day.* London: Longmans, 1980.

Rev. of *Frankenstein*, by Mary Shelley. *The Edinburgh Magazine, and Literary Miscellany* 2 (1818): 249-53.

Rev. of *Frankenstein*, by Mary Shelley. *Gentleman's Magazine* 88.1 (1818): 334-35.

Rieger, James, ed. and introd. *Frankenstein; or, The Modern Prometheus.* By Mary Wollstonecraft Shelley. 1974. Chicago: U of Chicago P, 1982. xi-xxxvii.

Robinson, Charles. "Editing and Contextualizing *The Frankenstein Notebooks*," *Keats-Shelley Journal* 46 (1997): 36-44.

———, ed. *Frankenstein; or, The Modern Prometheus. The Original Two-Volume Novel of 1816-1817 from the Bodleian Library Manuscript, by Mary Wollstonecraft Shelley (with Percy Shelley).* Oxford: Bodleian Library, 2008.

———. "Texts in Search of an Editor: Reflections on *The Frankenstein Notebooks* and on Editorial Authority," in Alexander Pettit (ed.), *Textual Studies and the Common Reader: Essays on Editing Novels and Novelists.* Athens, GA: U of Georgia P, 2000. 91-110.

———. *The Frankenstein Notebooks: A Facsimile Edition of Mary Shelley's Manuscript Novel, 1816-17 (with alterations in the hand of Percy Bysshe Shelley)*.... 2 vols. New York: Garland, 1996.

St Clair, William. *The Godwins and the Shelleys: The Biography of a Family.* London: Faber, 1989.

Scott, Walter. "Remarks on Frankenstein, or the Modern Prometheus; a Novel." *Blackwood's Edinburgh Magazine* 2 (1818): 613-20.

———. *Guy Mannering; or, The Astrologer.* London: Dent, 1906.

Sharrock, Roger. "The Chemist and the Poet: Sir Humphry Davy and the Preface to *Lyrical Ballads.*" *Notes and Records of the Royal Society of London* 17 (1962): 57-76.

Shelley, Mary Wollstonecraft. *History of a Six Weeks' Tour.* London: T. Hookham, 1817.

————. *The Journals of Mary Shelley, 1814-1844*. Ed. Paula R. Feldman and Diana Scott-Kilvert. 2 vols. Oxford: Clarendon P, 1987.

————. *The Letters of Mary Wollstonecraft Shelley*. Ed. Betty T. Bennett. 3 vols. Baltimore: Johns Hopkins UP, 1980-88.

Shelley, Percy Bysshe. *The Letters of Percy Bysshe Shelley*. Ed. Frederick L. Jones. 2 vols. Oxford: Clarendon P, 1964.

————. "On 'Frankenstein.'" *The Works of Percy Bysshe Shelley in Verse and Prose Now First Brought Together with Many Pieces not Before Published*. Ed. Harry Buxton Forman. 8 vols. London: Reeves and Turner, 1880. 7: 9-14.

Sheridan, Frances. *Memoirs of Miss Sidney Bidulph, Extracted from Her Own Journal, and Now First Published*. Intro. Sue Townsend. Mothers of the Novel. London: Pandora, 1987.

Small, Christopher. *Ariel like a Harpy: Shelley, Mary and* Frankenstein. London: Victor Gollancz, 1972.

Thomas, Louisa. "Their Love is Alive." Rev. of Robinson 2008, in *Newsweek*, 4 September 2009.

Utterson, Sarah Elizabeth Brown, trans. *Tales of the Dead*. Ed. Terry Hale. London: The Gothic Society, 1992.

Vasbinder, Samuel Holmes. *Scientific Attitudes in Mary Shelley's* Frankenstein. Ann Arbor: UMI Research P, 1984.

Veeder, William. *Mary Shelley &* Frankenstein: *The Fate of Androgyny*. Chicago: U of Chicago P, 1986.

Volney, Constantin François de Chasseboeuf, comte de. *The Ruins, or, Meditation on the Revolutions of Empires: and The Law of Nature*. Trans. Joel Barlow and the author. New York: Truth Seeker Company, 1950.

Wetzels, Walter D. "Aspects of Natural Science in German Romanticism." *Studies in Romanticism* 10 (1971): 44-59.

Wolf, Leonard, ed. and introd. *The Annotated Frankenstein*. New York: Clarkson N. Potter, 1977.

Wollstonecraft, Mary. *Mary and the Wrongs of Woman*. Ed. Gary Kelly. Oxford: Oxford UP, 1976.

————. *Posthumous Works of the Author of A Vindication of the Rights of Woman*. Ed. William Godwin. 4 vols. London: Joseph Johnson, 1798. Rpt. New York: Garland, 1974.

————. *A Vindication of the Rights of Men and A Vindication of the Rights of Woman*. Ed. D.L. Macdonald and Kathleen Scherf. Peterborough: Broadview P, 1997.

Wordsworth, William. *The Poetical Works of Wordsworth*. Ed. Thomas Hutchinson. New ed. rev. Ernest de Selincourt. London: Oxford UP, 1936.

Zonana, Joyce. "'They Will Prove the Truth of My Tale': Safie's Letters as the Feminist Core of Mary Shelley's *Frankenstein*." *Journal of Narrative Technique* 21 (1991): 170-84.